MURDER ON
WASHINGTON SQUARE

Victoria Thompson

BERKLEY PRIME CRIME, NEW YORK

THE BERKLEY PUBLISHING GROUP
Published by the Penguin Group
Penguin Group (USA) Inc.
375 Hudson Street, New York, New York 10014, USA
Penguin Group (Canada), 90 Eglinton Avenue East, Suite 700, Toronto, Ontario M4P 2Y3, Canada
(a division of Pearson Penguin Canada Inc.)
Penguin Books Ltd., 80 Strand, London WC2R 0RL, England
Penguin Group Ireland, 25 St. Stephen's Green, Dublin 2, Ireland (a division of Penguin Books Ltd.)
Penguin Group (Australia), 250 Camberwell Road, Camberwell, Victoria 3124, Australia
(a division of Pearson Australia Group Pty. Ltd.)
Penguin Books India Pvt. Ltd., 11 Community Centre, Panchsheel Park, New Delhi—110 017, India
Penguin Group (NZ), 67 Apollo Drive, Rosedale, North Shore 0632, New Zealand
(a division of Pearson New Zealand Ltd.)
Penguin Books (South Africa) (Pty.) Ltd., 24 Sturdee Avenue, Rosebank, Johannesburg 2196, South Africa

Penguin Books Ltd., Registered Offices: 80 Strand, London WC2R 0RL, England

This is a work of fiction. Names, characters, places, and incidents either are the product of the author's imagination or are used fictitiously, and any resemblance to actual persons, living or dead, business establishments, events, or locales is entirely coincidental. The publisher does not have any control over and does not assume any responsibility for author or third-party websites or their content.

MURDER ON WASHINGTON SQUARE

A Berkley Prime Crime Book / published by arrangement with the author

PRINTING HISTORY
Berkley Prime Crime mass-market edition / April 2002

Copyright © 2002 by Victoria Thompson.
Except from *Savage Run* copyright © 2002 by C. J. Box.
The Edgar® name is a registered service mark of the Mystery Writers of America, Inc.
Cover art by Karen Chandler.

ISBN: 978-0-425-18430-1

BERKLEY® PRIME CRIME
Berkley Prime Crime Books are published by The Berkley Publishing Group,
a division of Penguin Group (USA) Inc.,
375 Hudson Street, New York, New York 10014.
The name BERKLEY PRIME CRIME and the BERKLEY PRIME CRIME design are trademarks belonging to Penguin Group (USA) Inc.

PRINTED IN THE UNITED STATES OF AMERICA

17 16 15 14 13 12 11 10 9

Praise for national bestselling author
VICTORIA THOMPSON

and her Edgar® Award–nominated
Gaslight Mystery series . . .

"Fascinating . . . Sarah and Frank are appealing characters . . . Thompson vividly recreates the gas-lit world of old New York."
— *Publishers Weekly*

"A series which will appeal to Anne Perry fans."
— *Mystery Scene*

MURDER ON ASTOR PLACE
*Nominated for the Best First Mystery Award
by* Romantic Times *magazine*

"Victoria Thompson is off to a blazing start with Sarah Brandt and Frank Malloy in *Murder on Astor Place*. I do hope she's starting at the beginning of the alphabet. Don't miss her first tantalizing mystery."
— Catherine Coulter, *New York Times* bestselling author

"A marvelous debut mystery with compelling characters, a fascinating setting, and a stunning resolution. It's the best mystery I've read in ages."
— Jill Churchill, author of *The Merchant of Menace*

"Spellbinding. A bravura performance that will leave you impatient for the next installment." — *Romantic Times*

continued on the next page . . .

MURDER ON ST. MARK'S PLACE

Nominated for the Edgar® Award

"Lovers of history, mystery and romance won't be disappointed. Exciting . . . will hold the reader in thrall."

—*Romantic Times*

"As Victoria Thompson colorfully demonstrates in her latest Gaslight Mystery, New York City at the beginning of the twentieth century is a dangerous place for its melting pot immigrants . . .[She] weaves a fine mystery for readers who enjoy solving a difficult puzzler."   —Harriet Klausner

MURDER ON GRAMERCY PARK

"The inclusions of genuine facts make this novel much more superior to most of those found in the subgenre . . . The lead protagonists are a winning combination."

—Harriet Klausner

"Gripping—satisfying in its twists and turns under the gaslight"   —*KLIATT*

To my beautiful daughter Ellen and her new husband Dave.
May all your dreams come true.

I

SARAH OPENED THE DOOR TO FIND A RAGGED LITTLE BOY on her front stoop. He was fidgeting from one grubby bare foot to the other, either impatient or nervous. He clutched a folded piece of paper to his sunken chest and glared up at her suspiciously.

"You Mrs. Brandt?" he demanded.

"Yes, I am," she replied, eyeing him cautiously. He might be young in years, but she knew he was as dangerous as a serpent. Obviously, he was a street Arab, one of the hundreds of homeless children who lived on the streets, doing whatever was necessary to stay alive. What on earth did he want and how did he know her name?

"Here," he said, thrusting the paper at her.

She took it gingerly, still watching him with one eye while she unfolded it. Someone needing her services as a midwife must have hired the boy to fetch her. Usually a family member or a neighbor came to tell her a woman's time had come, but perhaps they'd had no one to send.

"Dear Mrs. Brandt," the note read in a careful, masculine hand. "I find myself in need of some professional advice from you on behalf of a lady of my acquaintance. However, this is a matter of some delicacy, and I would prefer that my mother not be made aware of it. Would you be so kind as to meet me this evening at five o'clock in Washington Square near the hanging tree?" The note was signed, "Your obedient servant, Nelson Ellsworth."

Nelson lived next door to her with his elderly mother. Mrs. Ellsworth had become one of Sarah's dearest friends, in spite of the difference in their ages. She hardly knew Nelson, however, since he was so seldom at home. According to Mrs. Ellsworth, he spent long hours working at the bank. He hoped to become a vice president soon.

"You gotta answer," the boy informed her, still dancing from one dirty foot to the other. His clothes were filthy, too, and his body was skeletally thin. Every instinct demanded that she take him inside and give him a hot meal and clean clothes and a warm bed. She'd be a fool to do so, though. Once in her house, he'd probably steal everything of value and vanish.

"Please tell the gentleman that I said yes," she told the boy.

"No, you gotta write it! He won't pay if you don't write it, and he promised me a nickel!" he cried, his small body fairly quivering with urgency.

She should have known Nelson would be careful. He wasn't one to take chances, even with five cents. The boy could simply throw the paper away and return whatever message he wanted to if Nelson hadn't required a written reply.

"Just a moment." Sarah carefully closed the door, resisting the urge to lock it. She couldn't bring herself to insult the boy that much, no matter how little she trusted him.

Her front room had been converted into a medical office when her physician husband had conducted his practice there. Since his death, Sarah used it to see the patients who were able to come to her. She went to her desk and found a pencil.

"I would be happy to meet with you, unless I am on a call," she wrote and signed her name. Babies arrived when they wished, and Sarah could never make a firm appointment with anyone.

She folded the paper again as she made her way back to the front door. This whole thing was very puzzling. There was only one reason someone would require her professional opinion, and Nelson Ellsworth was not only a male but a bachelor, too. In fact, according to his mother, he did not even have any lady friends. Which meant that his mother probably didn't know him nearly as well as she thought!

The boy still stood on the porch, looking even more unhappy than he had before. She held out the paper, and he snatched it from her fingers. In that instant, their eyes met, and Sarah saw him for the child that he was. He couldn't have been more than seven or eight, and she wondered what evil things he had been forced to do to stay alive this long. Her heart ached with a longing she refused to identify.

"If you ever need help . . ." she began, ignoring all common sense. But her effort was wasted. The boy was gone, running down the street as fast as his skinny legs could carry him, off to find Nelson Ellsworth and earn his nickel.

Sarah sighed. It was just as well. What had she been thinking to invite a child like that to visit her? She smiled at the thought of what her friend Detective Sergeant Frank Malloy would have to say about her sentimental feelings for a street urchin. He would be horrified and wouldn't hesitate to let her know it. When she might have an opportunity to share those feelings, however, she couldn't imagine. She hadn't seen Malloy for several weeks, not since he'd taken his son Brian home from the hospital.

Brian had been born with a club foot, but a surgeon Sarah knew had operated on him to correct it. The cast might even be off by now. Sarah decided she might actually be brazen enough to pay the child a visit, just to see how he was doing. She'd have to be careful not to go when Malloy might be home, of course. She wouldn't want him or Malloy's mother to think she was using his child as an excuse to see him. Especially Malloy's mother, who hated the sight of her. Besides, she knew if she visited Brian, Malloy would feel obligated to come by and thank her later.

Washington Square was quiet that evening as Sarah made her way through the Greenwich Village streets toward it. The nurses with their baby buggies were gone, the old men playing chess and checkers and the respectable ladies taking the air had all retired to their homes for supper. Soon night would fall, and the Square would fill again, but with an entirely different class of people. In the darkness, prostitutes would ply their trade, and pickpockets and other thieves would gather to prey on the customers the women would attract. This time was the twilight of the Square, between the respectable and the dissolute, when a gentleman and a lady could meet without attracting too much attention.

As always when she was here, Sarah's gaze instinctively found the house where she had been raised. It sat on the east side of the Square, perched like a middle-aged woman who still bore signs of her previous beauty but who was beginning to show the inevitable effects of age. Sarah knew the place had become a boardinghouse after her parents sold it. The Deckers had moved uptown to escape the rising tide of immigrants whose lodgings were encroaching the Square on the south side. But it would always be her home, and she felt a twinge of sadness for happy times now gone forever.

Nelson Ellsworth sat stiffly on a bench near the giant elm tree that was said to have been used as a hanging tree in the early part of the century. Beyond him, across the expanse of green grass, the large fountain sparkled in the fading sunlight. Put there to provide water for thirsty horses, it also provided an oasis of beauty amid the harsh brick and mortar of the city. Sarah's bedroom window had looked out on the fountain, and she'd spent many hours as a young girl watching it.

Nelson rose as soon as he saw Sarah. He wore a tailored

suit that was still neat even after a day of work, and his shirt and tie were immaculate. Still a young man, he was already beginning to stoop from hours spent over a ledger, and his face was pale from too little sun. Like the boy who had brought her the note, he seemed anxious, but he was too well mannered to bounce from one foot to the other or to rush to meet her. Yet even from yards away, she could sense his tension.

"Mrs. Brandt," he said when she was close enough that he didn't have to shout. "How good of you to come."

"I must admit I was intrigued by your note," she said, giving him her hand when she reached him.

"I'm sure you were more than intrigued," he said, his face fixed in a smile that did not reach his eyes. He took out his handkerchief and dusted the bench for her to sit. "I'm sorry I had to ask you to keep this meeting a secret from my mother," he said when they were settled.

"Your mother doesn't have to know everything I do, Mr. Ellsworth," Sarah told him with a smile.

"I'm sure she would disagree with that sentiment," Nelson said, returning her smile ruefully. Mrs. Ellsworth considered it her duty to learn the intimate details of everyone else's lives, and she devoted herself to the task.

"Now you must tell me what delicate matter has driven you to seek advice from a midwife," Sarah said encouragingly.

His smile vanished instantly. "This is most embarrassing," he said. "And please believe that I would not have involved you in this matter if I had any other resources, but—"

"Please don't apologize," Sarah said, hoping to relieve some of his social agonies. "I'm flattered that you felt you could safely confide in me. But I can't help you if you don't tell me the situation—and believe me, you needn't stand on ceremony."

Some of the stiffness went out of him, and he rubbed his forehead, as if it ached. "All right, although I'm not certain exactly where to begin."

"This involves a young lady, I gather?"

Nelson nodded miserably.

"Then tell me how you met her."

He drew his breath and let it out in a long sigh of resignation. "She came into the bank one day. She was so very frightened and obviously desperate. She wanted to make a loan, and she asked for the manager. He wasn't in, so the clerk sent her to me. We don't make loans to young women with no means of support," he told Sarah, as if he were offering an excuse.

"No one would expect you to," Sarah assured him. "But I'm sure you don't make loans to young women under any circumstances."

This was so obvious, it didn't merit a response. "Her mother was ill and needed medical care," he continued, "but they hardly had enough to live on. She was hoping to borrow some money from the bank, but I had to disappoint her. She was very upset. She was afraid her mother was going to die."

"That *would* be upsetting," Sarah agreed, still wondering how this encounter led to Nelson needing the services of a midwife.

"The bank couldn't lend her the money, of course, but I . . . Well, I couldn't just turn her away, could I? There's no telling what a young woman will do if she feels desperate enough. She even hinted that she . . . that she might have to . . . to . . ."

"To compromise her virtue?" Sarah supplied helpfully.

"Yes, yes," Nelson agreed gratefully. "She was so innocent and sweet, I couldn't bear the thought of her degrading herself. She only needed a hundred dollars, so I . . ." His voice trailed off, and he looked away in embarrassment.

Sarah's imagination conjured several possible things Nelson could have done, but she doubted he was capable of any of them, although the fact that he needed her services proved she was at least partially mistaken in his character. "You didn't take money from the bank, did you?" she asked, offering the only criminal possibility she could think of.

"Oh, no!" Nelson cried, horrified at the thought. "Nothing like that! I . . . I loaned her the money myself from my own funds."

Although he had said she "only" needed a hundred dollars, that was still a lot of money. More than three months' wages for a laborer. "You were very generous, especially when she probably had no hope of being able to repay you." Unless, of course, she became Nelson's mistress. Perhaps that would explain why Mrs. Ellsworth thought Nelson had been working such late hours.

"I had no illusions she would repay me, Mrs. Brandt. I was giving her the money out of Christian charity." Nelson's pale blue eyes were tortured, and his smooth banker's hands made a pleading gesture as he silently begged for her understanding.

Sarah was still not certain what he wanted from her, but she was sure it wasn't her absolution. "That was very noble of you," she offered.

He recoiled as if stung. *"Noble!"* he scoffed. "I assure you, I was far from noble!"

"Are you saying you took advantage of her?" Sarah asked, still unable to believe him capable of such a thing.

"No, not . . . not then, at least. In fact, I never expected to see her again. As I said, I did not believe her capable of repaying the loan, so what other reason would she have for returning except to humiliate herself? Then one evening a week or so later, she was waiting for me on the street when I came out of the bank. She was even more distraught than before. Her mother had died, you see and . . ."

"And she needed more money," Sarah guessed.

"Oh, no, that's not why she came," Nelson insisted. "She just wanted to tell me that she couldn't pay the rent in her rooming house anymore, and she was being evicted, so she wouldn't be able to repay my loan for a while. She didn't know where to tell me to find her, since she didn't know where she would be living and . . ."

"And you gave her more money." This time Sarah wasn't guessing.

"She didn't ask for it," Nelson assured her. "She didn't

even want to take it, but she was penniless. I couldn't just let her be thrown out into the streets, could I? You know what happens to girls like that when they don't have any money and no one to take care of them."

Sarah knew only too well. "How much did you give her this time?"

"Not much. Just enough to pay her rent and keep her for a month. She was going to find a job, so she could support herself."

This would be highly unlikely. Jobs for young women paid so poorly that the girls could hardly afford to give their own families a pittance for their board, much less provide their own independent accommodations. And a girl who'd lived a sheltered life in a respectable home wouldn't last a day in one of the sweatshops. "I don't suppose she was able to find a suitable position," Sarah said.

"I had no idea it was so difficult for young women to earn a living!" Nelson said, outraged. "Poor Anna looked everywhere. I called on her several times to make sure she was all right, but she was becoming more and more disheartened. I offered to pay her expenses for another month, but that only distressed her more. I . . . I . . . ." His pale face flushed, and he could no longer meet her eye.

"Am I to assume you gave her more than comfort?" Sarah asked as discreetly as she could.

"I have no excuse," Nelson said, covering his face with both hands. "What I did was despicable. To take advantage of someone so helpless and unprotected . . ."

Sarah would reserve judgment until she'd heard the entire story. "There's no use flogging yourself over it now. I'm going to assume that your indiscretion has resulted in this Anna being with child. Am I correct?"

"That's what she believes," Nelson confirmed bleakly. "I have offered to marry her. It is the least I can do, but . . ."

Sarah thought she saw the problem. "I'm sure you want to do the right thing, but marriage is a huge commitment, particularly with someone you hardly know. If there was no child after all, then it wouldn't be necessary."

"I'm not trying to escape my responsibilities, Mrs. Brandt," Nelson quickly assured her. "I would feel obligated to marry Anna even if there is no child. I dishonored her, after all. But she . . . she refuses to consider it!"

This was not what Sarah had expected to hear. "Why won't she marry you?" she asked in amazement.

"She said she doesn't want to disgrace me. You see, she assumed from the beginning that I was married, because of my responsible position at the bank and everything. She was shocked to learn I wasn't, but even then, she said everyone would know why I'd married her, and I would be pitied and tied to a woman who would be of no assistance to me in my ambitions. I won't deny those things are important to me, Mrs. Brandt, but I can't—"

"What does she want from you, then?" Sarah asked, tired of his justifications and trying to make sense of the whole thing.

He looked ashamed to have to say the words aloud. "She wants a sum of money so she can go away somewhere and raise the child by herself."

At last Sarah was beginning to understand. "How much did she want?"

"A . . . a thousand dollars should be sufficient." He would not look her in the eye. "Invested properly, it could bring—"

"Do you even *have* a thousand dollars?" Sarah asked in amazement.

"No, but—"

"And where does she propose you get it?"

This time the color staining his face was more than embarrassment. "She doesn't know a lot about business, Mrs. Brandt, and she believes I am very successful. I work in a bank, you see, and many people believe bankers own the money in their institutions. I'm sure she has no idea that I couldn't simply write a check for that amount."

Sarah no longer believed this Anna was the innocent Nelson thought her. Anna's refusal to marry him made no sense at all for a respectable girl, and Sarah was growing more concerned for Nelson every moment. "You still haven't told me why you invited me to meet you," she reminded him.

"Oh, I'm sorry! I thought it would be clear. I was hoping . . . that is, if you would be so kind, could you speak with Anna? She may not even be . . . uh . . . I mean, if there is no child, if that is the case, she would be under no obligation to marry me. But if she is, then . . . Well, I would certainly take care of her and the child, but I couldn't possibly send her away."

He looked so distressed that Sarah had an urge to hug him. Or slap him. How could he have gotten himself into such a predicament? She tried to imagine what his mother would say to all this. Mrs. Ellsworth had confided in Sarah many times that she wished her son would marry and have a family. She dearly wanted grandchildren to spoil before she died. Would she mind that the first of them had been conceived in such a shameful way? And what about this Anna herself? What kind of person was she to have gotten herself into such a predicament? She might be truly innocent as Nelson believed, but Sarah seriously doubted it. Most women in her position would be pathetically grateful for an offer of marriage, and many would even plead for it. Some women had been known to marry men who had raped them just to preserve their good name. In fact, men less honorable than Nelson sometimes used rape to force otherwise unwilling women to marry them. This knowledge made Sarah doubly skeptical of Anna's protests.

Although she wasn't certain how much assistance she could offer to either of them, she couldn't refuse Nelson's request. She owed it to his mother. "Where can I find Anna to speak with her?" she asked with resignation.

"Oh, Mrs. Brandt, I shall be forever in your debt!" Nelson exclaimed.

"Don't thank me until I've actually done something," she warned, knowing full well that settling this matter might take far more than her own intervention. "Where is she?"

"Her rooming house is only a block away. I can take you there right now."

"Is she expecting you?"

Nelson flushed again. "Yes, I . . . that is, I often stop on my way home from work to see how she's doing."

Sarah refrained from complimenting him on his solicitousness. His visits to Anna were probably amply rewarded. "Let's not keep her waiting then," Sarah said, rising from the bench.

They walked toward the south side of the Square, where the dwellings were still small and wooden. The contrast between them and the mansions sitting on the north side was stark, clearly illustrating how the Square seemed to serve as a dividing line of sorts between rich and poor. Some of these smaller buildings dated back a hundred years, including the shack said to have sheltered Daniel Megie, the hangman who had used the famous hanging tree at the Northwest corner of the Square. Behind these buildings the streets stretched away toward the tip of Manhattan Island. Houses that had formerly been family homes were now boarding houses and tenements and brothels. Sarah reserved her comments and even her speculations until Nelson stopped before one of the smaller homes on Thompson Street.

"This is where she lives," Nelson said. "She's been fortunate to have such understanding landlords."

"I thought you were paying her rent," Sarah said, thinking they didn't have to be understanding so much as broadminded to accept such an arrangement.

"I am," Nelson said sheepishly, "but they could have still thrown her out and found a more reliable tenant, one who didn't have to depend on . . . on the charity of others."

"Charity" was an interesting description of Nelson's assistance. The landlords could also have thrown her out for immoral behavior. Sarah had to assume that Nelson's assignations with this Anna had taken place here, since he couldn't have taken her to his own home, and renting a hotel room for such activities was probably much too daring and scandalous for Nelson even to consider. If that was the case, the landlords were broadminded indeed. Or else they were less than respectable themselves.

Sarah preceded Nelson up the steps of the stoop and allowed him to ring the bell. In a few moments a slender woman laced very tightly into a very fashionable gown of blue and silver plaid opened the front door. Her first reaction was a slight frown when she saw Sarah and didn't recognize her. Then she noticed Nelson, and the frown become a worried scowl.

"Mr. Ellsworth, what a surprise," she said, glancing uneasily at Sarah and back to Nelson again. "What brings you here this lovely evening?"

"Mrs. Walcott, this is Mrs. Brandt, a friend of mine whom I've brought to meet Miss Blake. We were hoping she would be available," Nelson explained.

Mrs. Walcott hardly looked reassured. "A friend, you say? I'm sure I can't imagine why you've brought her here to meet Miss Blake." Mrs. Walcott was taking Sarah's measure and apparently trying to figure out her relationship to Nelson. Sarah offered her no assistance and merely smiled sweetly. "I'm afraid Miss Blake really isn't up to meeting anyone right now, though. She isn't feeling well."

Sarah thought it was very presumptuous of the landlady to make this decision for Miss Blake, but it was Nelson who replied. "Then all the more reason for her to see us. Mrs. Brandt is a trained nurse."

Now Mrs. Walcott really was at a loss. If Anna Blake was ill, how could she turn away a nurse who might help her? But plainly, she was loath to admit Sarah to the house under any circumstances. "I . . . I'll have to ask Miss Blake if she . . . Well, I can't make decisions for her, now can I?" she concluded somewhat belatedly, satisfied that she had struck the proper note between concern and caution.

"We'll be happy to wait inside while you consult with her," Sarah said, still smiling sweetly but moving determinedly forward across the doorsill and forcing Mrs. Walcott to make way or be trampled.

Her eyes widened in surprise, but she stepped back and allowed them to enter without making a fuss. Once inside, Sarah noted that Mrs. Walcott was a woman of at least thirty years whose hair was still a rich brown color and styled rather elaborately for a woman who kept a boarding house. A style like that usually required the assistance of a lady's maid and several hours of preparation, neither of which someone of Mrs. Walcott's situation in life was likely to have. Then it dawned on her: the landlady was wearing a wig. It was, Sarah had to concede, a clever compromise for a woman vain enough to want to look her best but who had neither the time nor the resources to accomplish it naturally.

Sarah and Nelson paused in the foyer, waiting for instructions, and Mrs. Walcott straightened, or rather stiffened, to her full height. Sarah noticed the woman was several inches taller than she'd realized, as tall as Nelson Ellsworth, in fact, yet still very feminine in spite of her modest curves. "Please, have a seat in the parlor," she said, gesturing gracefully toward the doorway to their right. Sarah admired the lace mitts she wore. Another affectation assumed to suggest wealth, she guessed. Surely she didn't wear lace like that all the time. It could hardly survive the labors of normal life. "I'll see if Miss Blake can receive you."

She turned and started up the stairs, her back ramrod straight and her stiff skirts rustling discreetly. Even Sarah had to admit she made an impressive picture.

Left to themselves, Nelson motioned for Sarah to enter the parlor. He was familiar with the place—too familiar, Sarah knew. She entered the modestly furnished room and looked around, seeking some clue as to the true character of the occupants of this house. Mrs. Walcott had taken great pains to be as simple yet elegant as she could in her decor as well as in her dress. This could have been a parlor in any middle-class family home. A pair of shepherd girl figurines adorned the mantelpiece along with some silverplated candlesticks and a few other knickknacks. The piecrust table beside the sofa held an painted glass lamp and several more inexpensive ornaments, all sitting on a lace doily. Crocheted antimacassars protected the back and arms of the sofa and chairs. The entire effect was fussy but not overly so. In short, just the impression every respectable family wanted to give.

"Do you think she'll see me?" Sarah asked when she'd learned all she could from the room itself.

Nelson had already begun to pace. "I don't know. I can't imagine why she's ill. She was perfectly fine yesterday," he said with a worried frown.

Sarah could imagine many reasons why she might be ill, particularly if she were truly with child, but she said, "Perhaps the landlady was just making a polite excuse for her, in case she didn't want to meet your *friend*."

Nelson looked up in surprise. "I should have phrased that differently, shouldn't I?" he asked with some concern. "I mean, we *are* friends, at least I hope we are, but that might have sounded—"

"It sounded perfectly fine," Sarah assured him, "and it was perfectly correct. I'm just suggesting that perhaps Anna would like to know more about me before we meet. Or rather, before she decides if she wants us to meet."

This prospect worried Nelson even more, but Sarah was weary of reassuring him. She took a seat on the wine-colored horsehair sofa to wait while he continued to pace restlessly. After a few moments, the front door opened, and a young woman came into the house. Dressed for the street in a navy blue serge suit and a lovely little hat that Sarah couldn't help admiring, she had raven black hair and porcelain skin, a classic Irish lass. Not traditionally beautiful or even particularly pretty, she nevertheless was appealing with her youth and blooming health. She seemed surprised to see someone in the parlor and stepped into the doorway, peering at them curiously,

"Oh, hello, Mr. Ellsworth," she said, her face not quite smiling as she stared beyond him at Sarah.

"Hello, Miss Porter," he replied with the ease of familiarity. "How are you today?"

"Very well, thank you," she said, still looking at Sarah expectantly.

Nelson reluctantly obliged her by introducing them. Sarah found she was still his "friend," and Miss Porter, she learned, was another boarder. She seemed just as suspicious of Sarah as the landlady had been.

"Mrs. Walcott said that Miss Blake isn't feeling well," Nelson said, a question in his tone.

"She was fine when I went out this morning," Miss Porter reported reassuringly, "so I'm sure it isn't anything serious."

Before Nelson could reply, they heard the sound of footsteps on the stairs. Miss Porter looked back over her shoulder and said, "Here she is now."

Nelson hurried out into the foyer, brushing unceremoniously past Miss Porter, who gave Sarah one last curious look before nodding her head, murmuring how nice it was to have met her and politely withdrawing.

"Anna," Sarah heard Nelson saying, "Mrs. Walcott said you were ill. Are you sure you're well enough to receive us?"

Sarah didn't catch the softly spoken reply, and then the mysterious Anna appeared in the doorway, clutching Nelson's arm as if for support.

Well, Sarah couldn't help thinking. Now she understood a lot. Anna Blake was a disturbing mixture of innocence and alluring sensuality. Dressed in a simple gingham gown, with her light brown hair tied back from her face with a ribbon and falling to her shoulders, she gave the impression of pure innocence. Yet the gingham dress clung faithfully, if modestly, to very womanly curves, and the face framed by the girlish curls wore a full-lipped, pouty frown guaranteed to stir more than protective feelings in the male breast.

Sarah rose from the sofa, feeling the need to meet Anna Blake on her own level. She tried a small smile to reassure the girl. It had exactly the opposite effect.

She turned on Nelson, her cheeks flaming. "What have I done to be humiliated like this, Mr. Ellsworth?" Without giving him a chance to reply, she turned back to Sarah. "I know why you've come here, but you're wasting your time. I have no intention of forcing Mr. Ellsworth into marriage when someone else has a prior claim to his affections."

For a moment Sarah had no idea what she was talking about, and from Nelson's expression, he didn't either. But then the meaning of her words sank in. "Do you think that Mr. Ellsworth and I are . . . are . . ." Sarah searched for the proper word. *"Betrothed?"*

From the way her expression tightened and her lovely brown eyes filled with tears, Sarah knew she was correct.

"Let me assure you that we are *not* engaged," Sarah said quickly, but again her assurance had exactly the opposite effect she'd intended.

This time Anna Blake's face crumbled in despair. "Oh, Mr. Ellsworth, you swore to me that you were a free man, and now you bring your *wife* here to shame me!" She pulled a handkerchief from her sleeve and began to weep piteously into it, her round shoulders shaking with the force of her sobs.

"Anna, please," Nelson begged, wanting to take her in his arms but aware of the impropriety of it with Sarah watching. "I told you the truth! Mrs. Brandt isn't my wife or my fiancée either! Don't cry, please. There's no reason to cry. Mrs. Brandt is only a friend of mine, and she came here to help you."

Sarah thought that might be stretching the truth a bit, but she said, "Mr. Ellsworth is correct. He asked me to meet you because I'm a midwife, and he thought that I could—"

"A *midwife!*" she fairly shrieked, raising her face from her handkerchief and glaring at him in outrage. "Have you no concern for what's left of my good name? Why don't you drag me to the village square and have me branded a harlot?"

"Anna, please, I didn't mean—"

"Miss Blake!" Sarah said loudly and firmly in the voice she used to calm hysterical relatives who were upsetting her laboring patients. Both Anna and Nelson looked up at her in surprise, silenced for the moment. Sarah took advantage by saying, "I don't have the time or the patience to

argue with you, Miss Blake. Mr. Ellsworth is my neighbor, and he asked me to visit you because he was concerned for your welfare. He thought perhaps you might have mistaken your condition because of your innocence and inexperience. If that is the case, I can reassure you and there will be no need for you to distress yourself further for no reason. If you are indeed with child, then I can advise you how best to care for yourself."

Anna Blake stared at her for a long moment. Sarah thought she was using the time to comprehend what she had said, but Anna surprised her yet again.

This time her expression was horror when she turned back to Nelson. "You brought this woman here to . . . to *murder* our child! What kind of a monster are you? If you lack the honor to provide for us, then at least have the decency to let your child live! I'd beg in the streets before I'd kill it! How can you have ever thought less of me?"

"Oh, for heaven's sake," Sarah said in disgust as Nelson sputtered and stammered, trying to reassure her. "I'm a *midwife,* not an abortionist, Miss Blake," she said loudly enough to be heard over the wailing and the blandishments, but neither of them seemed inclined to listen. Sarah gave up. "Mr. Ellsworth, this is plainly a waste of time. If Miss Blake wishes to consult with me, you may bring her to my office. Meanwhile, I'll leave you alone to sort this out between yourselves."

"Mrs. Brandt, I'm so sorry," Nelson began, but he could go no further because Anna was weeping again, sobbing as if her heart would break.

As she stepped into the foyer, Sarah noticed that Mrs. Walcott was lurking in the shadows, just out of sight, listening to everything that was being said. She stared back at Sarah unrepentantly when caught in the act, and Sarah, more than disgusted with all the inhabitants of this house, let herself out.

She paused on the stoop to take a deep breath of the crisp autumn air to clear her head. Nelson Ellsworth had gotten himself involved in a real-life melodrama. The only thing lacking was a villain with a handlebar moustache tying poor Anna Blake to the railroad tracks. Furious with herself for being drawn into the mess, she was almost back at Washington Square before she started remembering details of the scene she had just witnessed that she'd been too busy to register before.

Anna Blake appeared to be the innocent young girl Nelson believed her to be, but Sarah thought back to the moment when their eyes had first met. Anna hadn't cringed or even seemed the least bit embarrassed, in spite of her protests to the contrary. In fact, she'd seemed almost defiant or . . . Sarah shook her head, certain she must have been mistaken. But no, she recalled clearly the odd impression she'd had that Anna Blake was actually *glad* to see Sarah, or at least relieved.

Why she should have been, Sarah had no idea. After all, if Sarah did have a prior claim to Nelson's affections, as she'd so quaintly phrased it, she should have been as humiliated as she'd claimed to be. In fact, she'd been determined to make Sarah her rival, in spite of all the protests she and Nelson had made. And for all her weeping and protestations, Sarah couldn't help recalling that Anna's delicate face hadn't grown the least bit blotchy, nor had her eyes gotten red or her little, turned-up nose started running.

Well, it was all beyond her, but since it also wasn't her problem to solve, she mentally washed her hands of the whole situation. If Anna Blake decided to see her as a patient, she'd deal with her. If not, she'd keep her promise not to mention the situation to Nelson's mother and let him sort it out himself.

2

THE NEXT MORNING, SARAH LEFT THE HOUSE TO FIND Nelson Ellsworth's mother out sweeping her front porch. This wasn't particularly surprising, since Mrs. Ellsworth had made sweeping her front porch her life's work, the better to know everything going on in the neighborhood first-hand. For once, Sarah knew a secret her next-door neighbor didn't, but she would honor her pledge to keep it.

"Good morning, Mrs. Brandt," Mrs. Ellsworth called when she saw Sarah. "Are you off to deliver a baby?"

"No, I'm off to visit Mr. Malloy's son," she replied, knowing this would capture Mrs. Ellsworth's complete attention.

"How is the sweet little thing doing? Do they know if the surgery was successful yet?" Mrs. Ellsworth asked in concern. She was particularly fond of Detective Sergeant Frank Malloy, although Malloy wasn't the type of man old ladies were typically fond of. She even seemed to think that Malloy and Sarah would make a good match. Mrs. Ellsworth was probably the only person in New York who believed an Irish Cop and a Knickerbocker Debutante could live happily ever after, but Sarah humored her romantic notions.

"Mr. Malloy hasn't seen fit to keep me informed of Brian's progress, so I'm going to see for myself," Sarah said.

"Good for you!" Mrs. Ellsworth said approvingly. "Please tell Mr. Malloy I send my best wishes for the boy."

"I doubt I'll be seeing Mr. Malloy," Sarah said. "I'm sure he's working at this time of day."

Mrs. Ellsworth's wrinkles slid into a frown. "You're going to visit Mr. Malloy's *mother* then?"

"I'm going to visit his *son*," Sarah corrected her with a smile, "but I'm afraid his mother will most certainly be there, too."

Mrs. Ellsworth shook her head. Sarah had told her that Mrs. Malloy didn't approve of her son's acquaintance with Sarah. For some reason, the old woman thought Sarah had set her cap for Frank Malloy, and she disapproved even more than Mrs. Ellsworth approved of such a match. "You must take something along with you for good luck, then," she said, searching in the pocket of her skirt for what she might have available in the way of good luck charms.

"I won't need luck," Sarah scolded her. "I'm just going for a visit."

"That woman might give you the evil eye or something," Mrs. Ellsworth warned. The old woman was a firm believer in things like the evil eye and good luck charms. "You can't be too careful. Here, take this." She came down her porch steps and pressed a shiny new penny into Sarah's hand.

Sarah couldn't help herself. "This will protect me from the evil eye?" she asked skeptically.

"Pennies are notoriously lucky," Mrs. Ellsworth assured her. "I'd give you a rabbit's foot, but I don't seem to have one with me. The only other thing I have is a nutmeg," she said, pulling it out of her pocket to prove it. "Nutmegs are also very lucky, but only in protecting you from rheumatism and boils, which won't be of much use to you with Mrs. Malloy, now will it? But if you'd prefer a rabbit's foot, I'm sure I can find one in the house if you don't mind waiting . . ."

"Oh, no, don't go to any trouble," Sarah said, biting back a smile. "I'm sure the penny will do very nicely. Thank you very much."

Sarah waved good-bye and was walking away when Mrs. Ellsworth stopped her again.

"Oh, Mrs. Brandt, I almost forgot. Did you have a visitor last night? Late, I mean. Someone who knocked on your door?" For some reason, Mrs. Ellsworth looked a little anxious.

"If I did, I slept through it," Sarah replied, a little worried herself. She would hate to have missed a call to deliver a baby. "Why, did you hear someone knocking?"

Mrs. Ellsworth frowned, absently fingering her nutmeg, as if for comfort. "Yes, but . . . Well, I'm sure it's nothing. Just an old woman's fancies. I didn't mean to keep you. Give Mr. Malloy's son a kiss for me."

"I will," she promised and walked away shaking her head. Hearing knocking was probably some kind of omen. Mrs. Ellsworth was always seeing omens in everything. Sarah hoped it didn't portend something evil. Even though Sarah knew it meant nothing, poor Mrs. Ellsworth would worry herself sick over it.

Frank Malloy's flat was in the Seventeenth Ward, where the Irish and the German immigrants had settled in adjoining neighborhoods and had now begun to mix. The streets were noisy from the roar of the Second Avenue Elevated Railroad, the clatter of horses and wagons on the cobblestones, the cries of the drivers and the street vendors and ragmen, the squeals of children playing in the gutters, and the shouts of women calling warnings to them and gossip to each other. Sarah absorbed the clamor into her very pores, drawing life from it. This was the city she loved, not the tidy orderliness of the neighborhood where her wealthy parents lived uptown.

On such a lovely day, she had expected to find Mrs. Malloy outside with the other women who had gathered on the stoop to visit and gossip and escape the confines of their small, dingy flats. But the old woman wasn't there, nor was Brian. Sarah suspected Mrs. Malloy's habit had been to keep him inside, hidden away. For the first three years of his life, she had believed him to be a simple-minded cripple. Now she knew he was deaf, and his club foot had been surgically repaired, or at least it had been operated on. Of course, Mrs. Malloy would consider his deafness equally as shameful as being feebleminded, so Sarah shouldn't be surprised he was still being hidden away.

Although Sarah had never met any of the neighbors, they obviously knew who she was and greeted her with knowing smiles.

"You'll be looking for the Malloys, now won't you?" one of the women asked with a grin that revealed several missing molars. "Francis isn't home, though. He works for a living, he does."

Sarah managed not to look embarrassed or annoyed. "Is *Mrs.* Malloy at home?" she asked pointedly.

"She usually is," another woman said sourly. Her pinched expression revealed either a dislike for Mrs. Malloy or for the entire world in general. "Keeps that boy locked up so nobody'll know what's wrong with him. As if we don't all know just the same."

Sarah bit her tongue to keep from replying. "Thank you," she said, making her way past them up the front stairs and into the tenement building.

The front door stood open to allow both light and air into the passageway and up the stairs. In the winter and at night, when the door was closed, the area would be pitch dark except for what little light might escape beneath the doors to the various flats. The hallway smelled like cabbage, but it probably always did, from years of people cooking cabbage here. The floors were relatively clean, though, evidence that the tenants took pride in their home, no matter how they might struggle otherwise.

On the second floor, Sarah found the correct door and knocked. In a few moments, it opened a crack and one suspicious eye peered out.

"Good morning, Mrs. Malloy," Sarah said with determined cheerfulness. "Mr. Malloy told me I might find you and Brian home today," she lied. "I'd like to see how Brian's doing since the surgery, and I've brought him a small gift."

Now she was at the woman's mercy. She only hoped that her mention of Malloy's name had served as a warning that her son would not be pleased if she turned Sarah away. Of course, he knew nothing of this visit, and when he found out, he might well be angry that she'd come, but Sarah would deal with that later.

"The boy has enough toys," the old woman said. "We don't need no charity from the likes of you."

"I know Brian has plenty of toys," Sarah said, keeping her tone pleasant. "But I saw this, and I couldn't resist. I wanted to see how his foot is doing, so I used that as an excuse to bring him something."

The eye kept peering at her, and for a moment Sarah was afraid Mrs. Malloy was going to slam the door in her face. But then Sarah heard a scuffling sound, and the door jerked open far enough for her to see Brian had crawled over to see for himself who had come to call. At the sight of Sarah, he started jumping up and down on his knees and reaching out for her.

She hoped Mrs. Malloy couldn't disappoint him, not even to spite Sarah, and she was right. Grudgingly, the woman opened the door wide enough for her to enter. Sarah reached down and picked the boy up, settling him on her hip so his cast was in front of her and she could examine it.

"Oh, my, you're getting so big," she exclaimed, smiling into his face.

He returned her smile, his sky blue eyes glittering with happiness. He was, she had to admit, one of the most beautiful children she had ever seen. She thought of Malloy's dark, scowling features and realized Brian must take after his deceased mother.

"Soon you'll be too big for me to lift," she told him.

"He can't hear you, you know," Mrs. Malloy said, closing the door behind her. "You're wasting your breath."

Sarah ignored her and carried Brian over to the sofa. She sat down and settled him on her lap.

"Can I look at your foot?" she asked, pointing to the cast, and he obligingly held it up for her, beaming with pride. He might not understand the words, but he had no trouble discerning what she wanted. Unfortunately, seeing the cast told her nothing, since nothing was visible except the tips of his tiny toes. "Does he have much pain?" she asked the old woman.

"He cried a lot with it at first," Mrs. Malloy admitted grudgingly after a moment's hesitation. She didn't want to tell Sarah a thing, but she also must be anxious for a professional opinion on the boy's progress. Anxious enough that she'd even seek it from Sarah. "Francis said that was normal, but he kept trying to kick the thing off his leg. Must've thought that was what was making it hurt."

"It's hard when you can't explain things to him," Sarah said. "You can't even tell him it's going to make his foot better."

"How do we know that it will?" Mrs. Malloy asked, the fear in her voice unmistakable.

"The doctor couldn't promise a miracle, but he did think Brian would be able to walk when his foot has healed," Sarah assured her. "He might have to wear a special shoe, but that's a small thing when it means he'll be able to walk."

"Doctors," Mrs. Malloy grunted. "What do they know?" She walked over and sat down on the chair opposite, still scowling at Sarah with disapproval.

Sarah had no answer for that. The truth was that doctors knew very little about many things, and medicine was as much intuition and guesswork and luck as it was skill and knowledge. Still, her friend, Dr. David Newton, had performed many such operations on feet even more deformed than Brian's. If anyone could repair Brian's foot, he had done it.

Sarah turned her attention back to Brian. "Look what I brought you," she said, speaking to the boy even though she knew he had no idea what she was saying. She reached into her purse and pulled out a small wooden trolley car with wheels that really turned.

His face lit up, and he snatched the toy out of Sarah's hand, simultaneously sliding off her lap so he could try out his new toy. His cast clunked on the bare wood floor, but he hardly noticed. Apparently, he wasn't feeling much pain anymore. Sarah watched him pushing the car across the floor, trying out the wheels. Seeing his happiness and energy, she felt a familiar ache deep inside of her.

She and her husband Tom had wanted children. Sarah had wanted a house full of them, but they had never been blessed. Then Tom had died and with him all hope that she would ever hold a child of her own. She wasn't old, of course, and if she remarried, there was still a chance . . . but she wasn't planning to remarry. What man could take Tom's place? So she would spend the rest of her life delivering other women's babies instead. That wouldn't fill the empty ache in her heart, but it would help.

"Is Francis coming home?" Mrs. Malloy asked out of the blue.

Sarah wasn't sure how to answer that. "I suppose he will. I really have no idea."

"You ain't planning to meet him here?" She seemed surprised.

"No, I told you, I just wanted to see Brian."

Mrs. Malloy sniffed. "I guess you see enough of Francis other places."

Now Sarah understood the purpose of the questions. "Actually, I haven't seen him since the day of Brian's operation," she assured the old woman.

"Then when did he ask you to come by and check on the boy?" Mrs. Malloy asked triumphantly.

Oops, she'd been caught in a lie, but Sarah wasn't going to squirm. "At the hospital. He asked me to stop by whenever I had a chance," Sarah lied again. "I would have been here sooner, but I've been very busy with my work."

"Your *work*," the old woman scoffed. "A woman should be home caring for her own babies, not out at all hours with someone else's."

Her careless words had touched a raw nerve, but Sarah only winced inwardly. "Do you know when the cast will come off?" she asked to change the subject.

Mrs. Malloy glanced down at Brian, as if she'd almost forgotten he was there. He was terribly quiet, and Sarah saw to her surprise that he'd taken a toy horse and attached it to the front of the trolley with some string. The horse was now pulling the trolley, just the way horses pulled the ones that hadn't been electrified yet in the streets outside. Once again she marveled at how clever he was. If only he could speak and understand. If only he weren't deaf.

"It'll come off in a couple more weeks, Francis says," Mrs. Malloy replied to her question about Brian's cast. "Then we'll know if all this cutting did the poor boy any good."

She didn't sound like she was holding out any hope. That would be her way of protecting herself, of course. Don't hope for anything good, and you'll never be disappointed. Or don't give the Devil a chance to crush your hopes. Or don't tempt the fates. Whatever her reason, she'd never be optimistic about anything, least of all a loved one.

Sarah decided not to offer encouragement that the old woman didn't want. Instead she slid off her chair and knelt on the floor so Brian could better show her his handiwork.

Sarah was just beginning to think about what to have for lunch the next day when someone began pounding on her back door. Hardly anyone except Mrs. Ellsworth ever came to her back door, which opened into the small yard behind her row house, and her neighbor wouldn't be pounding like that unless something was terribly wrong. Sarah hurried to see who was there and opened the door to a distraught Mrs. Ellsworth.

"Oh, Mrs. Brandt, thank heaven you're home!" she cried, flinging herself into Sarah's arms. Her face was pale, and she was trembling.

"What is it?" Sarah asked in alarm. "Has someone attacked you?"

"Oh, no, I—"

"Is someone in your house? Should I get help?"

"No, I—"

"Here, sit down, you're all wet," Sarah said, forcing her into one of the kitchen chairs. It had been raining off and on all morning, and Mrs. Ellsworth had crossed over from her own yard without even an umbrella. Or a cloak, for that matter. And she still wore her house dress and apron. Something *was* terribly wrong. "Is it Nelson? Is he sick?"

"No, it's—"

"Are *you* sick then?"

"*No!*" she almost shouted. "And if you'll be still for a minute, I'll tell you what *did* happen!"

Chastened, Sarah pulled a towel from the peg by the sink and handed it to her before taking another of the kitchen chairs. "Go ahead."

"A man came to my door just now. Says he's a reporter."

"A newspaper reporter?" Now Sarah was confused. Why would a newspaper reporter have come to Mrs. Ellsworth's door? Being a very fount of neighborhood gossip would hardly make her a good source for news. "What did he want?"

"He wants to know about Nelson. He said Nelson has been arrested!"

"*Arrested!* Whatever for?"

"For . . . for murder!" Mrs. Ellsworth's voice shook on the word.

"There must be some mistake," Sarah exclaimed, picturing meek and mild Nelson Ellsworth in her mind. Murder was a crime of passion, and Nelson didn't have a passionate bone in his body. And then she remembered Nelson's secret liaison with Anna Blake and realized she was wrong. Nelson did have at least a spark of passion. "Who . . . whom is he supposed to have killed?" she asked, afraid she already knew.

"Some woman. They found her in the Square, Washington Square, this morning. They said Nelson was her lover! Can you imagine? How could anyone make such a terrible mistake?"

Sarah wasn't about to answer that question. "Where is the reporter now?"

"Still standing on my doorstep, I imagine, unless he went on his way. I slammed the door in his face and came right over here."

"Stay right where you are," Sarah said, patting Mrs. Ellsworth's frail hand reassuringly. "I'll see what I can find out from him."

She hurried through her house, out to the office. When she opened the front door, she saw the rain had let up to a light drizzle. Indeed, a man was standing on the Ellsworths' front stoop. He'd turned up his collar and pulled his hat low over his eyes to protect himself from the rain, so Sarah couldn't tell very much about him from here.

"Sir!" she called to get his attention.

He'd been looking up, as if considering how he might scale the wall and gain entrance to the Ellsworth house through one of the windows above. He turned to Sarah.

"Are you the reporter?" she asked.

"Yes, ma'am," he said. "Do you know Nelson Ellsworth? I'd like to ask you a few questions—"

"I'd like to ask *you* a few questions, too," Sarah said. "Could you come over here?"

He hurried down the porch steps and through the drizzle to Sarah's door. "I'm Webster Prescott with *The World*," he said, naming one of the several newspapers published in the city. He showed her a dog-eared card identifying him as a reporter.

"Please come in, Mr. Prescott," she said, admitting him to the house and closing the door behind them.

Now she could see that he was very young, hardly more than twenty. Tall and gangly under his cheap, damp suit, he didn't seem quite sure what to do with his hands and feet.

He looked around curiously. "What is this, some kind of doctor's office?"

Sarah didn't feel obligated to explain. "I'm a midwife," she said.

He removed his hat, being careful not to let it drip too much on Sarah's floor. She took it from him gingerly and hung it by the door. His hair was light brown and a little curly around the edges, giving him an even greater illusion of youth. If he'd been a police officer, Malloy would have called him a "Goo Goo." She wondered what baby newspaper reporters were called.

"Please come in and tell me what this is all about," she said, ushering him to the desk where she interviewed patients. She motioned for him to take a seat in the visitor's chair while she sat behind the desk.

He'd pulled a small notebook and pencil from his inside pocket. "How long have you known Nelson Ellsworth?" he asked, poised to scribble her reply in his notebook and looking up at her expectantly with his pale blue eyes.

"I think you need to answer a few questions for me first," she said. "What's this about a murder?"

He registered surprise, then glanced around as if to make sure they were alone. "How did you know about the murder?"

"That hardly matters. Who was murdered?"

Mr. Prescott consulted his notebook. "A woman named Anna Blake," he said, and Sarah was hard pressed not to groan aloud. This was just what she had feared. "They found her stabbed to death in Washington Square Park this morning, early. Right under the hanging tree. You know where I mean?"

Sarah felt a cold chill. She knew only too well. She'd just been there two days ago with Nelson Ellsworth. "If she was killed in the Square at night, anyone could have done it," Sarah pointed out. "A woman alone after dark could have been the victim of a robber or worse. Have you thought of that?"

Mr. Prescott shrugged one bony shoulder. "It ain't my job to decide that. The police arrested this Nelson Ellsworth. Looks like she was his mistress or something. She probably wanted money or threatened to cause him trouble, so he killed her. Happens all the time."

Sarah doubted it happened *all* the time, but before she

could reply, Mrs. Ellsworth came rushing into the room. "That's a lie!" she cried. "My son didn't even know this woman!"

She looked wild, and her face was scarlet. Sarah feared she might have apoplexy. "Please, sit down," she urged her, jumping up and forcing Mrs. Ellsworth down into the chair she'd just vacated.

"Nelson would never have a mistress, and he would certainly never kill anyone!" she said to Sarah. Her tone was pleading, her eyes begging Sarah to reassure her.

Sarah only wished she could. "Don't work yourself up into a state. We'll get to the bottom of this. I'll find Malloy, and he'll sort everything out."

Mrs. Ellsworth brightened at this prospect, and she turned to the reporter triumphantly. "Detective Sergeant Frank Malloy is a good friend of ours, and he won't be very pleased that you've come here bothering us!"

Prescott sat up straighter, his eyes widening. "Malloy?" he repeated, then looked at Sarah. "Of course, you're a midwife! Then you must be Mrs. Brandt. I should've known."

"How did you know my name?" Sarah demanded.

"Everybody in the press shacks knows who you are," he said, referring to the rooms across the street from Police Headquarters where reporters rented space and waited for a news story to break. "Is it true they locked you up in a cell when you went to Headquarters to see Malloy?"

"No, it most certainly is *not* true!" Sarah snapped. She *had* been locked into an interrogation room, but that was only for her protection. She saw no need to explain that to Mr. Prescott, however. "You said they'd arrested Mr. Ellsworth. Do you know where they're holding him?"

"They took him to Headquarters, him being such a respectable citizen. Seems like the Commissioners want to keep an eye on the case and make sure everything's done right and proper. I'll tell you what, if you give me some information about Ellsworth, I'll write him up real nice. He'll need public opinion on his side if he don't want to meet up with Old Sparky."

Mrs. Ellsworth made a strangled sound in her throat. Old Sparky was the nickname that had been given to New York's new electric chair.

"Mr. Prescott," Sarah said quickly, "we have nothing to say to you, and I'm going to have to ask you to leave now. You're upsetting Mrs. Ellsworth."

"You think she's upset now, just wait until her boy's tried for murder," Prescott said reasonably. "I'm telling you, you'll need my help. I don't need much. Just tell me what he was like as a kid and where he went to school and—"

"Mr. Prescott," Sarah said in a tone she'd learned from Malloy. "If you aren't out of here in ten seconds, I'm going to go out on my front porch and start screaming that you're attacking me. Then you can find out firsthand what it's like to be questioned by the police."

Prescott jumped to his feet, looking aggrieved. "There's no call for you to be like that. I'm just trying to do my job."

"Then do it somewhere else. Your ten seconds are already half gone."

Giving Sarah a murderous scowl, he made for the front door, almost forgetting to grab his hat on the way out. He left the door hanging open, so Sarah hurried to close it, turning the lock with a decisive click.

"Oh, Mrs. Brandt, whatever shall we do?" Mrs. Ellsworth wailed.

"We'll find Malloy. He'll take care of this," Sarah said with more confidence than she felt. If the police had Nelson in custody, they could have already beaten a confession out of him, guilty or not. Even Malloy might not be able to help then. Their only hope was that Prescott had been right about the Commissioners wanting to be careful with this case because Nelson was a respectable citizen.

The city had already dealt with one scandalous murder trial recently in which a young Italian woman had stabbed her lover to death when he refused to marry her. Thousands of newspapers had been sold over the misfortunes of Maria Barberi, and the press would pounce like hungry jackals on another case with the same potential for salacious reports.

"I'm going to go straight to Police Headquarters," she told Mrs. Ellsworth.

"I'll go with you!" the old woman exclaimed, jumping to her feet.

"I don't think that's wise. There'll be dozens of reporters swarming around, and if they found out who you are . . . No, I want you to go home and lock yourself in. Don't open the door to anyone you don't know. If Mr. Prescott found you so quickly, others will, too. I'll be back just as soon as I can, but don't worry if it takes a long time. I might not even be able to find Malloy for a while if he's out on a case."

"Oh, thank you, Mrs. Brandt," the old woman said, taking Sarah's hands in hers. "I don't know what I would have done without you!"

"Don't thank me yet," Sarah said, wondering what on earth she would tell her friend if her son really had killed Anna Blake.

Just as Sarah had suspected, Mulberry Street was swarming with reporters jostling for a good spot from which to view the comings and goings at Police Headquarters. The cab Sarah had taken over had to let her off a block away. Fortunately, the morning rain was over, and the sun was trying halfheartedly to break through the clouds. Sarah had still brought her umbrella, though, and she gave thought to using it to force her way through to the building.

Fortunately, saying "Excuse me!" several times very loudly, and shoving a few times in a very unladylike manner, got her almost to the narrow stairs that led up to the arched doorway of the four-story building.

"Let the lady through, you vultures!" a voice called from above her, and she looked up to see the imposing figure of Tom, the doorman to Police Headquarters.

The reporters looked around in surprise to see a female in their midst, and Sarah took advantage of their momentary distraction to squeeze through and make her way up the steps to the front door, which Tom obligingly opened for her.

"'Morning, Mrs. Brandt," he said, tipping his derby hat.

"Thank you very much, Tom," she said as she slipped past him into the receiving area of Police Headquarters.

The desk sergeant looked up, and when he saw Sarah, his normal scowl slid one notch lower in disapproval. "You'll be wanting Malloy, I expect," he said, "Or have you come for Commissioner Roosevelt this time?" he added sarcastically.

Police Commissioner Theodore Roosevelt was an old family friend, and he kept an office upstairs. Sarah had visited him here when she'd needed his help in the past. She smiled sweetly. "I'd be happy to see either one of them. Whoever is available."

"Mr. Roosevelt ain't in right now," he told her a little too smugly. "But I'll see if I can scare up Malloy for you. Would you be wanting to wait?"

She could see from the gleam in his eye that he remembered the time he'd sent her to wait in the depths of the basement, but she had the upper hand now. "I'll be upstairs. I'm sure Miss Kelly can find a place for me to sit where I won't be in anyone's way." Minnie Kelly was the first female secretary in the history of the New York City Police Department, just one of Roosevelt's innovations and a constant source of aggravation to the old guard. "No need to escort me," she added, knowing full well he'd had no intention of doing so. "I know my way."

Minnie Gertrude Kelly was a small, comely girl with raven black hair which she wore in a severe chignon so as not to appear too flashy. She looked up from her typewriter and greeted Sarah with a friendly smile.

"I'm sorry, but Commissioner Roosevelt isn't in today, Mrs. Brandt," she said.

"I know, but I needed a place to wait while someone tries to find Frank Malloy for me," she explained.

Minnie understood completely. She knew all about

Sarah's adventures in the bowels of the building and invited her to have a seat.

"Do you know anything about the murder this morning? The woman who was killed in Washington Square?" Sarah asked.

"Yes, I heard. What a terrible thing. At first everyone assumed she was a . . . a lady of the evening, but then someone recognized her. They said she was a respectable woman from a good family. She lived in a rooming house nearby. But they've already arrested the man who did it, I heard."

"I know," Sarah said. "He's my next-door neighbor."

"How awful!" Minnie exclaimed. "Do you have any idea why he did such a terrible thing?"

"That's why I'm here," Sarah said. "I don't think he did it at all, and I'm afraid he might be persuaded to confess anyway."

Minnie nodded her understanding. "Would you like for me to telephone Mr. Roosevelt? He might be able to help."

"I think that would be a very good idea."

Unfortunately, Teddy wasn't at home either, but Minnie left him a message on Sarah's behalf, and Sarah settled in to wait. She was just beginning to think that perhaps she should demand to see Nelson herself when she heard familiar footsteps in the hallway. In another moment, Frank Malloy's burly figure appeared. He wore a suit that needed to be pressed, and he needed a shave. His bloodshot eyes told her he hadn't gotten much sleep the night before.

As usual, he didn't look at all happy to see her, but she wasn't going to let that distract her. "Malloy, have you heard about Nelson Ellsworth?" she asked, jumping to her feet.

"Of course I heard about him," Malloy said, his dark eyes almost black as he glared at her. "He started telling everybody in sight that he's a friend of mine as soon as they took him into custody."

"He didn't kill that woman, Malloy. You know that, don't you?"

"What makes you so sure?" Malloy was in one of his disagreeable moods. He hardly ever had any other kind.

"Because I know him. He couldn't even strike a woman, much less kill one."

"People do strange things, Mrs. Brandt. You of all people should know that."

He was referring, of course, to the people they had encountered on the murder cases they had solved together.

"I know that Nelson Ellsworth would not commit murder. And I have to try to save him from being accused of it, for his mother's sake, if nothing else. She did save my life, you know."

He frowned, trying to give her one of his blackest looks, but she wasn't fooled. In exasperation, he turned to Minnie Kelly. "Miss Kelly, has Mr. Roosevelt started hiring female police detectives?"

Minnie bit back a smile. "No, sir, I don't believe he has."

"I just wanted to be sure," he said, "because from the way Mrs. Brandt was talking, I thought he might've put her on the force."

"Malloy," Sarah said through gritted teeth, "you know as well as I do that most detectives would just give Nelson the third degree until he confessed so they could wrap this case up nice and neatly. Nobody wants a lot of bad publicity about a respectable young woman getting killed on a public square within sight of people's homes, and they won't get any if they lock the killer up the same day. But what if Nelson didn't do it? That means an innocent man will be punished, and the real killer will go free!"

He sighed in disgust. "I'm so glad you explained that, because I never would've figured it out by myself."

"You don't have to be sarcastic," she snapped. "I know you understand what needs to be done, but I had to come down to make sure you knew he'd been arrested before it was too late to help him."

"And then I suppose you were going to go home and go back to delivering babies again," he said wearily.

"No, then I was going to give you some important information about the case."

Malloy rubbed the bridge of his nose as if his head was hurting him. "I was afraid you were going to say that. Well, I guess there's only one way to get you out of here. Do you think you could escort Nelson Ellsworth safely home?"

Sarah gaped at him. "Home? Are they going to let him go?"

"For now. And I'm coming with you. Mr. Ellsworth has a lot of questions to answer, and from the look of things, so do you."

"You know I'll do anything I can to help you, Malloy," Sarah said with as much gratitude as she could muster.

"Yeah," he said grimly. "That's what I'm afraid of."

3

MAKING THEIR ESCAPE FROM POLICE HEADQUARTERS was far easier than getting in had been for Sarah. Malloy brought Nelson up from the basement where he'd been held since being picked up from his job at the bank. He looked a little worse for wear, but at least he didn't seem to be bloody or bruised. Malloy led them both to a back door that opened into an alley. Cabs wouldn't normally be cruising in this neighborhood looking for potential customers, and they couldn't risk drawing attention to themselves at any rate, so they started out on foot.

Walking as quickly as Sarah's skirts would allow, they made their way over to Broadway, where they were soon lost in the crowds of people heading home for their evening meals.

Only then did Sarah begin to feel safe.

"How are you?" she asked Nelson when they had reached the corner of Fourth Street and turned toward Washington Square. Now that she had a chance to look at him more closely, she could see that he looked terrible. His face was pale and his tie was askew. He had a streak of dirt on the sleeve of his suit coat, and his eyes were haunted.

"Anna is dead," he said, as if that were his only concern.

"I know, Nelson," she said kindly, realizing that he was in no condition to discuss this on a public street. She glanced at Malloy, who frowned and shook his head slightly, warning her against saying more.

None of them spoke again until they'd reached the northeast corner of the Square, where the hanging tree stood. Nelson's steps slowed, and he stopped completely when they came abreast of the tree.

"They said they found her there," he said, gazing at the ground at the foot of the tree. There was no indication someone had died on the spot only a few hours ago. "But what was she doing here in the middle of the night?"

Sarah looked at Malloy, expecting to see some sign that he recognized this wasn't the reaction of a guilty man. Instead, she saw that his expression was closed, betraying none of his own opinions.

"Come on, Ellsworth," he said. "We need to get you off the street before some of those reporters catch up with us."

Nelson acted as if he didn't even hear Malloy, so Sarah took his arm. "Nelson, your mother will be worried about you. Come along, now."

Reluctantly, he allowed Sarah to urge him on his way again. They were now well within a neighborhood where they could have found a cab, but Sarah realized they'd be home sooner if they kept walking. In a cab they would be captives of the traffic that clogged every intersection and often moved at a snail's pace. Besides, she thought the exercise was probably good for Nelson. If he sat down for a moment, he might fall apart.

They were almost to Bank Street when Sarah remembered Webster Prescott. "A reporter came to Nelson's house," she told Malloy. "That's how I found out about the murder. There might be more waiting there by now."

Malloy nodded. "We'd better go down the alley then. We can go into your house. They won't expect to find him there."

Sarah led the two men into her small rear garden. The

flowers were all dead now, but the remaining greenery gave an air of sanctuary to the place. Sarah glanced over the fence to the Ellsworths' house, hoping Mrs. Ellsworth might be looking out and see them, but all the curtains were tightly drawn. The trio made their way up to her back door. Once inside, she helped Malloy seat Nelson at her kitchen table, then hurried to the front room of the house to peek out at the street. Just as she'd suspected, several men stood on the sidewalk in front of the Ellsworth house, waiting and talking among themselves. At least Mrs. Ellsworth had managed to hold them at bay while Sarah was gone. The poor woman must be nearly frantic by now.

She turned to find Malloy had followed her. "I've got to go over and tell Mrs. Ellsworth that Nelson is here and safe."

"You can't go over there. Those reporters will eat you alive."

Sarah couldn't help but smile at the image. "I managed to get through a whole crowd of them on Mulberry Street," she reminded him.

"They didn't know who you were."

"Well, I've got to tell Mrs. Ellsworth everything is all right, and I don't want to go sneaking around the back. If those reporters see me, they'll surround the place, and we'll never get Nelson out of here. Don't worry, I have a plan."

Malloy made a noise that sounded suspiciously like a groan.

Frank gave a brief thought to tying Sarah Brandt up. That was probably the only way to keep her from causing trouble. On the other hand, the prospect of having her accosted by a bunch of rabid reporters was enormously entertaining. Of course, there weren't many reporters out there, only five or six. They'd probably get the worst of it, and Frank certainly had no love for the boys from Newspaper Row. Maybe he *should* let her go.

Mrs. Brandt was pulling a lethal-looking pin from her hat and then removed the hat itself. She set it on the desk and hurried back to the kitchen. Frank followed more slowly, and by the time he got there, she'd taken off her jacket and was tying on an apron. At least she'd come to her senses.

"Can you fix something to eat? Ellsworth hasn't had anything all day, and I don't want him fainting on me," he said.

She gave him one of her looks. "I'll take care of it when I get back. Meanwhile"—she reached into the cupboard and pulled out what looked like a bottle of whiskey—"give him a shot of this."

It *was* whiskey, he realized as he took the bottle from her, and by the time that registered, she'd grabbed a teacup and was heading back to the front room. "Where are you going?"

"To borrow a cup of sugar from my next-door neighbor," she called back over her shoulder.

She was out the front door before he could stop her, and when he peeked out the front window, he saw her acting very surprised and indignant at the reporters who instantly converged on her with their questions. It took her only a minute to break away from them and make it up to Mrs. Ellsworth's front door. In another moment, she was inside. Frank shook his head in admiration. Of course, she'd have to get back again, and that might not be so easy.

Still holding the bottle of whiskey, Frank returned to the kitchen, where he found Nelson Ellsworth still sitting exactly where he'd left him. He'd better start paying attention to his prisoner. If Ellsworth decided to escape while Frank was busy dealing with Sarah Brandt, he'd never hear the end of it. Taking Mrs. Brandt's advice, he grabbed a glass off the shelf and poured Ellsworth two fingers' worth.

"Here," he said, thrusting it into Ellsworth's hand. "Drink it down. You'll feel better."

Ellsworth looked at the glass as if he'd never seen one before. "I don't drink spirits," he said faintly.

"This is the perfect time to start."

Ellsworth proved him wrong. He obediently, if gingerly, took a swig of the amber liquid and immediately began to choke. Frank saved him from spilling the rest of the liquor down the front of his suit and pounded him on the back until he stopped coughing.

When he'd caught his breath, he looked up accusingly with red-rimmed eyes.

"See, I told you you'd feel better," Frank said unrepentantly and sat down at the table across from him. "All right, Ellsworth, tell me about Anna Blake."

Nelson reached up and rubbed his eyes with his thumb and forefinger. "I can't believe she's dead," he said hoarsely.

"Believe it. Now talk to me. How did you meet her?"

He looked like he was going to start crying. "I can't—"

"Yes, you can, because I'm the only hope you've got, Nelson. I promised Broughan that if he let me take you home, I'd find out who really killed the girl," he said, naming the detective who'd been assigned to solve Anna Blake's murder. "If you don't help me, then I'll have to turn you back over to him, and you don't want that. See, Broughan is a lazy drunk, and he'd rather lock up an innocent man than find the guilty one if it means he's going to have to exert himself. You're real easy to catch, and I don't think he'd be able to resist the temptation. If you don't help me, I can't help you. Now start talking."

Ellsworth had gone chalk white, but he reached for the glass of whiskey and took another swallow. This time he didn't choke, although it was a near thing. "All right," he said, clearing his throat. "I met her when she came into the bank . . ."

Sarah's plan to get into the Ellsworth house was perfect, she realized, unless Webster Prescott was one of the reporters. He'd know she wasn't just an innocent neighbor coming over to borrow a cup of sugar. Fortunately, he wasn't among the men who surrounded her the instant she started next door.

"Hey, miss—"

"Who are you?"

"Where are you going?"

"Do you know Nelson Ellsworth?"

The questions came simultaneously, so Sarah didn't have to feign confusion. "Who are you, and what are you doing here?" she demanded with an outrage that wasn't the least feigned.

A chorus of voices answered her, naming the *Sun*, the *Commercial Advertiser*, the *Evening Post*, the *Mail and Express*, the *Daily Graphic*, the *Herald*, the *Examiner*, and even the *Times*, virtually all of the newspapers being published in the city. If one of them was, like Webster Prescott, from the *World*, she didn't hear.

"I only read the *News*," she said haughtily, naming the penny scandal sheet that circulated mainly in the tenements, and tried to force her way past them.

She got a few steps farther when someone called, "Nelson Ellsworth killed a woman last night. What do you have to say about that?"

Sarah gave him her most withering glare. "I say that's preposterous! Now get out of my way before I start screaming. I assure you there are many people on this street who will immediately come to my rescue."

She didn't know if it was her tone or her threat that moved them, but they let her pass, although they kept close, hovering at the foot of the porch steps. Sarah pounded on the front door and called, "Mrs. Ellsworth, it's Sarah! Let me in!"

The door opened almost instantly, telling Sarah that her neighbor had witnessed her approach. By the time she had slipped inside and Mrs. Ellsworth had slammed the door shut, the reporters were on the porch, screaming their questions. The old woman drove home the bolt an instant before they started pounding on the door.

Mrs. Ellsworth looked as if she were ready to collapse, and Sarah took her arm and led her through the house to the kitchen in the rear, as far from the front door as they could get. The pounding lasted only another minute or two before the reporters gave up and went back to their vigil.

They probably thought they'd lie in wait for Sarah to come out again. She'd worry about that later.

"Nelson?" Mrs. Ellsworth asked weakly when Sarah had seated her at her kitchen table.

"He's sitting at my kitchen table at this very moment. Malloy is with him."

She covered her face with both hands. "Thank God! I've been so frightened. I should have known Mr. Malloy would help us, though. He'll straighten everything out." Then she dropped her hands and turned her moist gaze to Sarah. "Why didn't you bring him here, though?"

"Because of the reporters," Sarah said. "We came in the back door so they wouldn't see us. We'll bring him over when it gets dark," she added rashly. She'd have to get Malloy to agree to that first, but what other choice did he have? The two men could hardly stay at her house all night. Of course, Malloy might also decide to lock Nelson up again.

"How could this have happened?" Mrs. Ellsworth was saying. "Nelson doesn't even know this woman—what was her name?"

"Anna Blake," Sarah supplied, "and I'm afraid he *did* know her, very well, in fact."

"That's impossible! He never said a thing to me!" she insisted. "I know all of Nelson's friends."

"I don't know why he didn't introduce her to you," Sarah said, although she had a very good idea. "But I met her."

"You? Why?" Mrs. Ellsworth was obviously over-whelmed by all of this and now she was also offended by what Sarah was telling her.

"You'll have to discuss that with Nelson. He asked for my . . . discretion."

"He didn't want me to know about her?" The old woman was incredulous. "What kind of a woman was she?"

"The kind who gets murdered in Washington Square in the middle of the night," Sarah said baldly.

"Oh, my poor Nelson!" she wailed. "What has he done?"

Sarah wished she could answer "nothing," but instead she took the old woman in her arms and offered what comfort she could.

"So when Anna told me about . . . about the child . . . I . . . I . . ."

Frank signed impatiently. Nelson was making the whole sordid story even worse with his delicacy. He wasn't sure why Nelson should care about protecting Anna Blake's good name now that she was dead, but he supposed that's what a gentleman might do.

"What did you do?" he prompted with more patience than he felt.

"I . . . You aren't going to like this part," he warned nervously.

Frank hadn't liked any of it so far. Ellsworth had pretty much given him more than enough reason to suspect him of murdering Anna Blake. Broughan would've had him locked in a cell down at The Tombs by now. "Tell me anyway," he said, not bothering to sound patient.

"I . . . Well, naturally, when Anna told me there might be a child, I . . . I went to Mrs. Brandt."

"You *what*?" Frank nearly shouted.

Ellsworth flinched. "She's a midwife," he reminded Frank unnecessarily. "I thought . . . Well, Anna was an innocent girl. How could she be sure? I don't know much about these things, but I do know . . . I mean, I've heard my friends talk. The ones who are married. Sometimes a woman thinks . . . but then she finds out she's wrong. I would've married her either way, of course," he added hastily, "but she was so frightened. And she had this idea that she wasn't good enough for me, or at least that's what she said. I know, it doesn't make any sense," he said to Frank's skepticism, "but I thought maybe she just couldn't stand the thought of being married to a man like me. I'm not very exciting or romantic. Not at all the sort of man a young woman would be interested in."

Frank was hardly listening to his protests because something suddenly didn't make any sense at all. "She didn't want to marry you? Even after you'd seduced her?"

A pained expression twisted his face. "I can't blame her, of course, and as much as I would have gladly taken her as my wife, I didn't want to force her. If she married me and then found out there wasn't a . . . a necessity for it, well, she'd hate me, don't you think? How could I live with myself?"

"So you told Mrs. Brandt your problem. What did she do?" Frank prodded, hoping that if he heard more, the story would start to make sense again.

"She accompanied me to Anna's rooming house. I thought perhaps she could . . . well, make sure of Anna's condition."

Ellsworth was right. Frank really didn't like this part. "And did she?"

"She didn't have a chance. Anna was terribly upset when I introduced her. She thought . . ."

"She thought what?" Frank was very much afraid he was going to have to get rough with Ellsworth after all, just to hurry things along.

"I know this will sound ridiculous to you, but Anna thought that Mrs. Brandt and I were . . . romantically involved."

Frank did think it sounded ridiculous. "Why would she think that?"

"I told you, she's very innocent," Nelson said, unconsciously using the present tense. "She couldn't imagine any other reason why another woman would have accompanied me there. And nothing I said would reassure her, so Mrs. Brandt didn't get to speak with her at all."

"If this woman didn't marry you, what was she going to do?" Frank asked, wondering if Sarah Brandt had been as suspicious of this story as Frank was becoming.

"She . . . well, you understand her parents were dead. Her mother had just passed away, of course, and she had no one to turn to."

Which was a very good reason to marry someone like

Nelson, who had a steady job and a comfortable income. And an even better reason to trick him into marriage with an imaginary pregnancy, if necessary. "She had *you* to turn to," Frank reminded him.

"She was an honorable woman, Mr. Malloy," Nelson said defensively. "She felt unworthy, after what had happened between us. She was even too embarrassed to meet my mother. She just wanted to go away where no one knew her."

"So she and the baby could starve to death?" Frank suggested curiously.

A scarlet flush flooded Nelson's face. "I would have helped her financially, of course. In fact, that's all she wanted of me. I told you she was honorable."

Or crazy, Frank thought. Why take money to raise an illegitimate child alone when you could be married? What was wrong with the woman? Could she possibly have been so stupid? He'd have to find out more about this Anna Blake. Maybe when he had, he'd be able to make sense of this. Meanwhile, he'd break one of his cardinal rules and have a taste of Sarah Brandt's whiskey. After this, he'd earned it.

He and Nelson sat in silence for what seemed a long time until they heard a commotion at the front door.

"Stay here," Frank warned. "We don't want anyone to see you."

He got to the front room just as Sarah Brandt slammed the door behind her. The shadows of the clamoring reporters danced on the other side of the frosted glass window, and their voices were muffled shouts. "They found out who I am," she said accusingly.

"That was pretty easy to do, considering they know you live next door," Frank replied.

"No," she said in disgust, "I don't mean they found out I'm Nelson's neighbor. They found out I'm *your* 'lady friend.'"

"My what?" he asked with a frown, but she was already stomping past him on her way back to the kitchen, leaving him no choice but to follow.

"How are you doing?" she asked Ellsworth in a gentle tone she had never used with Frank.

"I'm fine," he said, although he was obviously far from fine. "How is my mother taking all of this? She isn't strong, you know. The shock must have been awful."

"Now that she knows you aren't locked in jail, she's doing much better. I promised her you'd come home after it gets dark and no one can see you." She looked up at Frank, daring him to contradict her.

"I don't see any reason why he can't go home tonight," he said mildly, "so long as he gives me his word he won't try to run away."

"Run away?" Ellsworth echoed indignantly. "I don't have anything to run away from!"

Frank could have given him a long list of things he should run away from, but he said, "Are you hungry, Ellsworth? Because I sure am."

Mrs. Brandt gave him an impatient look, but she turned away and began rummaging around for something edible.

"I don't think I could eat anything," Ellsworth said, "but a cup of tea would be very nice."

"You should try to eat," Frank said, not entirely unselfishly. If Ellsworth didn't want anything, she might not fix anything. "You'll need your strength."

"Malloy is right," she said, surprising Frank. He thought this might be the first time she'd admitted he'd been right about anything. "And I think we could all use some tea."

Soon the kitchen was uncomfortably warm, in spite of the evening chill that had settled over the city. Frank stayed there, though. He was enjoying the comfortable domesticity of the scene. For once he needed no excuse to watch Sarah Brandt to his heart's content.

He liked the way the lamplight shone on her golden hair and the way she moved, so confidently yet so feminine. She really was a fine figure of a woman. She would fill a man's arms quite nicely. Or his bed. The thought caused him a pain that was part longing for what could never be and part grief for what he could never have again. The loss of his wife Kathleen was a wound that would never completely heal, but lately when he dreamed he was loving a woman, she wasn't Kathleen. Instead, she had golden hair and Sarah Brandt's face. It was a dream that could never come true, but since no one ever need know about it, he figured it was harmless enough. And no one ever *would* know, least of all Sarah Brandt.

She turned and set a teapot on the table, then fetched two cups. She poured Ellsworth's for him and even put some milk into it. "Do you need some sugar?" she asked in that gentle tone again.

"A spoonful, please," he replied, and she stirred that in, too. Then she went back to her cooking.

Frank cleared his throat expectantly. She glanced over her shoulder at him. "The next time you're falsely accused of murder, I'll pour your tea, too," she said with that smirk that made him want to shake her. Or at least lay his hands on her.

He didn't really want any tea, but he took some anyway. Pouring it was a distraction of sorts. In a few more minutes, she served their supper, which was potatoes fried with onions and eggs. She put some on a plate for Ellsworth, even though he protested that he couldn't eat a thing, and then passed the serving plates to Frank.

While Ellsworth picked at his food, Mrs. Brandt said very casually, "Can you think of anyone who might have wanted Anna out of the way?"

Ellsworth looked up in surprise. "Certainly not! She didn't have any enemies. She hardly even know anyone in the city."

"An old friend then, someone who knew her before she came to the city. Do you know where she was from?" she prodded.

Nelson considered a moment. "I think . . . She may have been from the Hudson Valley, but I can't recall the name of a town. Perhaps she never actually told me the name."

"If her mother was sick, why did they come to the city in the first place?" Frank asked between mouthfuls. Mrs.

Brandt wasn't as good a cook as his mother, but right now, that didn't really matter.

"Her father had died and left them penniless," Ellsworth explained. "Anna's mother wasn't sick at first, and they both thought they might find work in the city. But of course, the work they found only paid a pittance, and then her mother got sick . . . Poor thing, Anna was at her wit's end when I met her."

"She was very lucky to find someone like you, Nelson," Sarah Brandt said sweetly. "Someone who was willing to help her without expecting anything in return."

Even in the dim light of the gas jets, Frank could see that Ellsworth's face had gone scarlet, because they all knew he'd eventually gotten something in return, expected or not. "I didn't force her," he said. "You must believe that!"

"Of course we believe that," she assured him. "Did Anna have any other friends in the city? Perhaps she'd met someone when she came here."

"I . . . I got the impression she was quite alone," Ellsworth said. "Besides, she might have been killed . . ." He had to stop and fight back a rush of emotion. "By a stranger," he finished. "At that time of night, in a public square . . ."

"But why would she have been out so late, alone?" she asked, still sweet and gentle. Frank was beginning to admire her technique. "Can you think of any reason?"

"No, I can't," Ellsworth wailed. "I've asked myself the same thing a hundred times. She would've known it wasn't safe. At that time of night, the Square is filled with all sorts of dangerous people."

"But if she was from a small town, maybe she *didn't* know that," she offered. "Is it possible she just decided to go for a walk? Could she have been that naive?"

Ellsworth's shoulders sagged with despair, and he covered his face with his hands. "I don't know."

But all this conjecture had given Frank an idea. "Do you think she would have gone out to meet *you*?"

Ellsworth looked up. "But I never would've asked her to meet me someplace after dark!" he objected.

"She might not have known that, though. Suppose someone sent her a message and said it was from you. Would she have gone out to meet you?"

"I don't know. She might have," he conceded.

Frank checked the serving bowl and kept the last scoop of potatoes from going to waste.

"Do you think someone lured her out that night to kill her?" Mrs. Brandt asked him while he was refilling his plate.

Frank shrugged one shoulder. "It's possible. I'm just trying to figure out how it might've happened. We know she was out there and someone killed her. If it wasn't Nelson here—"

"And it wasn't!" Ellsworth cried.

"Then it had to be someone else. Was it a stranger? If so, why was she there in the first place, where she was easy prey? Prostitutes work in the Square after dark. Why would she risk being mistaken for one by some drunken customer?"

"Which means she must have had a good reason for being there," Mrs. Brandt guessed. She was getting much too good at this sort of thing. "And that could only mean she was expecting to meet someone. Someone important to her." She turned to Ellsworth. "If you were her only friend in the city, she must have thought she was meeting you."

"But why wouldn't he have just come to the house, the way he always did?" Frank asked. "Or at least wait until morning to meet her? Why would he ask her to do something dangerous?"

"Please, I can't . . ." Ellsworth begged, dropping his head into his hands again. "I can't think anymore. Isn't it dark enough for me to go home yet?"

Frank sighed. He wouldn't mind being rid of Ellsworth. He wouldn't get any more from him tonight. "I'll check to see if the reporters are still there."

A quick trip to the front room told him that only two of the more persistent reporters remained, and they were standing across the street under the gaslight which had recently been lit, not paying much attention to the house.

"I think you could make it now if you're quiet," he told Ellsworth when he got back to the kitchen.

"Malloy will go with you," Mrs. Brandt said, without bothering to consult him. He shot her an irritated look, but she didn't pay any attention. "Try to get a good night's sleep."

"And don't try to go to work in the morning," Frank warned him.

"But Mr. Dennis will be expecting me!" Ellsworth protested. "If I don't go, I could lose my job."

"If the bank fills up with reporters who write stories that say a killer works there, you'll *definitely* lose your job," Frank pointed out.

"It's just for a few days, until we find the real killer," Mrs. Brandt added reassuringly. "I'm sure Mr. Dennis will understand when he hears what happened."

Frank wanted to challenge her on the "we," but he refrained. He preferred getting Ellsworth home as quickly as possible. Arguing with Sarah Brandt could wait a few more minutes.

Ellsworth looked like he might pass out, but Frank got him to his feet and helped him out the back door. Mrs. Brandt's garden was pitch dark. Even though the street out front was lighted, not a beam of it could penetrate the row of houses in between. The two men made their way carefully down her walk and opened the back gate. Frank winced when it squeaked, but he waited a moment, and when the noise didn't seem to have aroused any alarm, he led Ellsworth into the alley and around to his own yard.

Frank knocked lightly on the back door, and in a moment, the curtain in the window beside it moved and a shadowed face peered out. A second later, they heard a cry of recognition, and the back door flew open.

"Quiet!" Frank warned, before the old woman started screaming at the sight of her son. "Get him inside and turn out the lights and don't either of you go outside until you hear from me. Do you understand?"

"I can't thank you enough, Mr. Malloy," Ellsworth stammered.

"Thank me later. Now get inside before someone hears us." He shoved Ellsworth into the house and pulled the door shut. In another minute he was back at Sarah Brandt's back door.

He wasn't surprised to see her waiting there, watching to make sure everything went all right. He'd been planning to bid her good night, but she stepped aside for him to enter, which he was more than happy to do.

"What's going to happen now?" she asked when he was inside again.

"I guess I'll have to find out if there was anyone else who might've wanted to kill Anna Blake. Otherwise, Nelson is in a lot of trouble."

"He didn't do it. You know that, don't you, Malloy?"

"I don't think it's very likely," he admitted, "but that might not be enough to keep him from frying."

She winced. "Then we have to find out who really killed her. Are you investigating the case?"

"No, Broughan has it."

"Oh." Her expression fell. She knew Broughan. He'd helped Frank out one time on a case she'd been involved with. "He won't be much help, will he?"

"He won't be *any* help. I had to promise I'd get Ellsworth to confess before he'd let me take him home."

"Oh, dear."

"Yes, oh dear," Frank agreed. Then he remembered one more thing he needed to deal with before he left. "Were you just teasing me before or do you really know something about this case that I need to know?"

"Oh, I'd almost forgotten. Sit down, and I'll tell you about my meeting with Anna Blake."

Frank pushed the dirty dishes away and sat back down at the table. "I'd been meaning to ask you about that," he said in a tone that should have warned her he was angry, but she didn't seem to notice. Or else she didn't care.

"Nelson sent me a note and asked me to meet him at Washington Square."

"Wait, stop right there," Frank said. "He sent you a note? Why didn't he just come to your front door if he wanted to talk to you?"

"Because his mother would have wanted to know why he was talking to me. You know she doesn't miss a thing that happens on this street. So I met him at the Square on Monday afternoon."

"Where in the Square?" Frank asked, thinking this sounded too familiar.

She hesitated. "By the hanging tree," she finally admitted.

"Right where this Anna died."

"So it appears."

"That's interesting. Go on."

"We met, and he told me about Anna and how she thought she was expecting a baby. He thought maybe I could help her."

Frank frowned. "Did he want you to do something to the baby? To get rid of it?"

"Oh, no! I think perhaps he was hoping she wasn't expecting at all. That would have solved all his problems. But if she was, he wanted me to offer her assistance and reassure her, I think. Maybe even convince her to marry Nelson."

"Now that's the part I don't understand. Why would a woman in her position *not* want to marry the man who'd ruined her?"

"I didn't understand that either," she said, "until I met Anna. You see, she wasn't at all what I was expecting."

"What were you expecting?"

"I thought she'd be young and innocent and frightened out of her wits. Instead, she wasn't nearly as young as Nelson seemed to think. She tried hard to look young. Her clothes and her hair and her manner were designed to make her appear so, but I could see she was way past the blush of youth. She was a very good actress, but her eyes gave her away. They weren't innocent at all."

"But Ellsworth was fooled."

"Oh, yes, completely. And when Nelson introduced me,

she became hysterical. At first she insisted on believing that I was Nelson's fiancée who had come to denounce her. He finally convinced her I was a midwife, and then she started accusing him of bringing me there to kill her baby! Can you imagine? She wouldn't listen to anything he said, so finally, I left him there to comfort her and went home."

"You'd think she'd be happy to find out you weren't Nelson's fiancée," Frank said.

"Yes, you would, but she actually seemed disappointed. It was as if she *wanted* me to stand in the way of their love."

"If she didn't want to marry Nelson, what *did* she want?"

"She wanted money. A thousand dollars, so she could go away and not bother Nelson again."

"Where on earth would Nelson get a thousand dollars?" Frank had been saving for years to amass enough money to pay the $14,000 bribe necessary to get promoted to Captain, and he knew how difficult it was to come by an extra $1,000. That was a goodly portion of Nelson's annual salary, and no one paid him rewards for doing his job well, the way they did Frank.

"I don't think he could have gotten that much money without a great deal of sacrifice," she said, "but that doesn't matter now."

"Oh, it matters a great deal, Mrs. Brandt," he contradicted her. "Because if she was blackmailing him and he couldn't pay, he had a perfect motive for murder."

4

Frank walked slowly from Washington Square to Anna Blake's boardinghouse on Thompson Street, ignoring the brisk morning chill that warned of winter's coming. He was trying to get a feel for the neighborhood and judge how long it might have taken Anna to walk from her rooming house to the Square where she died. He looked carefully around, seeing what she would have passed on her way and who might have had an opportunity to see her. The people who might have seen her or her killer weren't here now. They'd crawled back into their hidey-holes until the sun set again.

The first thing he usually did when investigating a crime was to ask the neighbors what they saw and heard and if they knew any gossip that might help identify the guilty party. In this case, the people who might have seen Anna Blake or her killer that night weren't the kind who'd feel any civic duty to aid the police. In fact, they'd evade him or lie if they had to, just to keep from getting involved with the police. So coming back here to question the nighttime denizens of the Square was a waste of time.

The house where Anna Blake had lived looked no different from the others on the street. Formerly a family home, it had long since been converted into cheap lodging for those who couldn't afford a flat of their own but who earned enough to keep a decent roof over their head. Less fortunate folks would find refuge in flop houses where they could get a bed for a nickel a night or space on the floor for a few pennies. No decent woman would go into a flop house, though, and only the lowest of prostitutes frequented them. So Frank knew a lot about Anna Blake just from seeing where she lived.

Although she'd been unable to find suitable employment, she'd managed to find the three to five dollars a week she would need for room and board here, or else they would have thrown her out of the house. Frank already knew Nelson Ellsworth had been paying her rent, but she'd lived in this house before he came along to rescue her. This meant she'd had some source of income before Nelson. Supposedly, she and her mother had been penniless and unable to find work. Then the mother needed an operation, for which Nelson loaned Anna money. Had she been living on that loan? And what had happened to the mother? Buried in a pauper's grave? Or had she ever existed at all? Interesting questions. Perhaps Anna's landlady could shed some light on them.

But the person who answered the door wasn't the landlady or even a lady at all. The man was of medium height, thin but with a slight paunch underneath a stylish waistcoat. A short, neat beard covered the lower half of his face. He wore a well-fitted suit, as if he had just been going out.

"Another policeman," he said with disgust. People always seemed to know Frank was a cop.

"Detective Sergeant Frank Malloy," Frank said by way of introduction. "And who would you be?"

"Oliver Walcott," he replied with a long-suffering sigh. "And I've already told the police everything I know about poor Anna."

"Then it'll all be fresh in your mind," Frank said pleasantly, forcing his way past Walcott into the front hallway. The place was well furnished and cleaner than most such houses.

"I was just going out," Walcott protested.

"I won't keep you long." Frank wandered into the parlor, glancing around and taking in every detail.

Left with no choice, Walcott followed but pointedly did not offer Frank a seat. He took one anyway, on the sofa.

"You're the landlord, I take it," Frank said.

"My wife and I, yes," Walcott said.

"Is your wife in?"

"No, she's shopping, I believe. I don't know when she'll be back. Mrs. Walcott can spend the entire day shopping if she sets her mind to it."

"Then I'll come back later and talk to *her*," Frank said. "Now why don't you tell me everything *you* know about Anna Blake?"

Walcott surrendered with bad grace, seating himself on a chair opposite Frank, but perching on the edge, as if only planning to stay there a few moments. "Anna only lived here a few months. Three or four, I believe, although I can't be sure. My wife could tell you exactly."

"How long did her mother live here with her before she died?" Frank asked casually.

Walcott's forehead creased into a frown. "Her mother?" he echoed uncertainly. "I don't . . . her mother never lived here at all. She's dead, or so I was led to believe."

"Do you know how long ago she died?"

Walcott considered a moment. "I'm sure I don't know exactly, but I gathered she'd been gone for a long while. Anna was all alone in the world and had been for some time."

No dying mother. No operation. This explained a lot about Anna Blake. "Was she employed?"

"I . . . not that I know of. Really, Detective, you should be talking to my wife. I didn't know Anna very well."

"She lived in your house," Frank reminded him.

"Yes, but *I* hardly ever do," Walcott replied.

"What do you mean by that?"

"I mean that I travel extensively."

"For your business?" Frank guessed.

"No, I . . . that is, I simply like to travel, and do so at every opportunity."

"What business are you in?" Frank prodded.

Again Walcott hesitated, but Frank thought he seemed slightly embarrassed. "I . . . I don't have a business. You see, Mrs. Walcott's family left her a small inheritance. Not a lot, but enough that with our income from our lodgers, I do not have to be employed. She likes staying home and taking care of our guests—I believe they substitute for the children we never had—and I am free to come and go as I please."

"How many boarders do you have?"

"Sometimes we have three, but two usually . . . I mean, Anna was one of them. Catherine Porter is the other, at the moment. Now, I suppose, we only have one."

"Then you had an empty room, but I didn't see a sign advertising it," Frank noted.

"Oh, we don't put out a sign. We prefer to obtain our lodgers by recommendation. We set high standards, you see."

"About their ability to pay, I guess."

Walcott seemed surprised. "Yes, I suppose . . . Well, of course, we don't take anyone who wouldn't be able to support themselves, but we want respectable young ladies, too. If you put out a sign, you never know who might come along."

"It's my understanding that Anna Blake didn't have a job. How did she convince you she could pay the rent?" Frank inquired.

"Well, uh, that is . . . You'd really have to ask Mrs. Walcott about that. She handles all the arrangements. I don't involve myself in such matters."

Frank was becoming annoyed with Walcott, but he didn't let it show. "Tell me what happened the night Anna died."

Now it was Walcott's turn to be annoyed, and he didn't bother to hide it. "I don't know what happened. I wasn't here that night."

"Where were you? Traveling?" He managed to make his skepticism known.

"Yes, I was in Philadelphia."

"Can you prove it?" Frank asked mildly.

Walcott's face had grown red. "If necessary," he replied tightly.

"So you would have no idea why Anna went out that night?"

"None at all."

"Was she in the habit of going out alone at night?"

"We keep a decent house here, Detective. Any young ladies in the habit of going out at night would be asked to leave."

"I guess that means you wouldn't allow them gentleman callers, either."

"In the parlor, where they could be chaperoned," Walcott snapped.

"Then can you explain how Anna Black got herself with child?"

"What?" Walcott looked genuinely shocked.

"Anna Blake claimed she was with child, and from what I've been given to understand, she got that way right here in your house."

"I can't imagine who gave you an idea like that, but it's completely false. Such a thing could never happen here."

"How can you be sure? You said yourself that you don't spend much time at home."

Walcott was insulted now. "My wife would never let such a thing happen either. She's very careful. She has her own reputation to protect, after all."

"Maybe she didn't know about it," Frank suggested, but Walcott wasn't going to be placated.

"Are you finished with me?" he asked, rising from his chair. "As I told you, I have an appointment and—" The sound of someone knocking on the front door interrupted him, and he signed in exasperation. "I hope that isn't one of those reporters. There were about a dozen of them outside this morning when we woke up. I thought they were going to break down the door. Poor Catherine, our other lodger, was nearly hysterical with fright."

"How did you get rid of them?" Frank asked curiously.

"I told them the name of the bank where Nelson Ellsworth is employed," he said, and Frank nearly groaned aloud. So much for protecting Nelson's employer from the onslaught of the press.

Frank saw a maid come from the rear of the house to answer the door, and then he did groan aloud because the person she admitted was Sarah Brandt.

"Malloy," she said when she saw him through the open parlor door, smiling too smugly for Frank's taste.

He rose to his feet, but he didn't return her greeting as she brazenly came into the room without waiting for an invitation. She waited a moment for him to make introductions, and when he didn't, she offered Walcott her hand.

"I'm Sarah Brandt, a friend of Anna Blake's."

Even Frank was impressed with her audacity. Walcott was simply confused.

"I'm sorry, Miss Brandt, but Anna . . . Something terrible has happened and—"

"It's Mrs. Brandt, and I know what happened to poor, dear Anna," she told him. "I've come to see if there is anything I can do to help. I'm sure Mrs. Walcott must be very upset, and I thought I might be of some assistance to her. Is she receiving visitors?"

"She's out shopping," Frank informed her.

Mrs. Brandt raised her fine eyebrows to express her surprise at such a thing

"I'll be sure to tell her you called," Mr. Walcott assured her hastily.

"The other lodger is pretty upset," Frank offered. "Maybe she'd appreciate a visit."

Mrs. Brandt's eyebrows rose higher, probably to express her shock that Frank had asked for her assistance, but she was gracious enough not to betray any other reaction.

"Are you a friend of Miss Porter's, too?" Walcott asked her suspiciously.

Frank never got to hear what bold-faced lie Sarah

Brandt might have told because just then someone else started pounding insistently on the front door.

"Reporters," Walcott muttered furiously, and this time he didn't wait for the maid to answer.

Striding purposefully back out into the foyer, he opened the door, prepared to do battle with a member of the Fourth Estate. Instead, a very distraught middle-aged man pushed his way into the house. "Where is she?" he demanded.

Walcott seemed genuinely alarmed. "This isn't an opportune time, Mr. Giddings," he said, hurrying over and closing the door to the parlor in Frank's face. But if he'd thought the act would give him privacy, he was mistaken.

"Don't try to stop me," Giddings shouted, his voice clearly audible through the door. "I have to see her. Where is she?"

"She isn't here," Walcott said anxiously. "You must leave. The police—"

"Don't threaten me with the police! Do you think I give a damn about them? I've got to see her. *Anna!*" he cried. "Anna, come down here!"

Walcott said something Frank couldn't understand, and then he heard the sounds of a scuffle. In another moment, footsteps pounded up the stairs, and Giddings was calling for Anna again.

Frank exchanged a questioning glance with Mrs. Brandt.

"I think you should be the one to deal with him," she said generously. "I'll see if I can find out anything from the maid."

It galled Frank, but he said, "See if that other girl lodger is still here. Maybe she knows something, too."

Frank opened the parlor door and found Walcott staring helplessly up the stairs, as if unable to decide upon a course of action. Giddings was throwing open doors on the second floor and calling Anna's name.

Frank shouldered Walcott out of the way and started climbing the stairs. By the time he'd reached the top, Giddings was standing in the open doorway of one of the rooms, staring stupidly into it. Hearing Frank's approach, he turned accusingly.

"Where is she?" he demanded. Then he realized Frank wasn't Walcott. "Who are you?"

"Detective Sergeant Frank Malloy with the New York City Police," he said. His tone wasn't particularly menacing, but it didn't have to be. Those words were enough to strike fear into a normally law-abiding citizen who had been causing a disturbance.

Giddings stiffened. "I've done nothing wrong," he insisted.

"Besides forcing your way into someone's home?" Frank inquired mildly.

"I was just—"

"Who are you looking for?" Frank asked sharply.

"I . . . Really, it isn't important." Giddings was starting to sweat in spite of the coolness of the day. He was probably remembering stories he'd heard about the police and how they treated people they arrested, innocent or not. Frank supposed he owed the press a debt of gratitude for their sensational stories if they put the fear of God into people like this Giddings.

"Were you looking for Anna Blake?" Frank asked.

"I . . . Yes, I was concerned about her. I haven't seen her for several days and—"

"What is your relationship to her?"

Giddings needed a moment to think about that. "We're . . . that is . . . She's my fiancée," he finally decided. He sounded oddly defensive.

Frank did not betray his surprise. "Then I suppose you haven't seen the morning papers."

"What does that have to do with anything?" Giddings asked impatiently.

"Because if you had, then you'd know . . . Well, I'm sorry to have to tell you, but Anna Blake was murdered the night before last."

Frank watched his face carefully. He'd interrogated enough people that he knew a genuine reaction from a phony one, and the emotions played across Giddings's face in exactly the right order. First shock, then disbelief.

"There must be some mistake," he insisted, his mind unable to grasp such a horrible truth. "She was . . . She couldn't be . . ."

"I assure you, there is no mistake. Anna Blake is dead."

For a moment, Giddings couldn't seem to get his breath. He reached out blindly for the doorframe and grabbed it for support. "How? When?" he asked faintly, the blood draining from his face as he slowly accepted what Frank had told him.

"Maybe you should sit down first," Frank suggested. He glanced down the stairs and saw Walcott waiting, listening intently to every word. "Is this Anna's room?" he asked Giddings, nodding toward the doorway where he stood.

The man nodded. Frank found it interesting he knew this fact if he'd never visited Anna's room, as Walcott had insisted. He took Giddings's arm and led him inside, closing the door behind him. Walcott would have to come upstairs and put his ear to the panel if he wanted to eavesdrop.

There was a chair in the corner of the sparsely furnished room, by the window, and Frank deposited Giddings into it. Then he perched on the edge of Anna's carelessly made bed and waited. Human nature being what it was, he knew Giddings would break the silence very soon.

Frank took the time to study Giddings. His clothes were good quality. He was a man accustomed to dressing well, although his suit was a bit wrinkled, and his linen far from fresh. He'd been wearing it more than one day, which was probably unusual for a man of his obvious position in life. His hat was on crooked, and he hadn't thought to remove it, a gesture that would have come naturally to him under other circumstances. He was well-fed but haggard, with dark circles under his eyes and a tightness around his mouth. A man of comfortable circumstances who found himself dealing with a crisis he couldn't resolve.

Then, to Frank's surprise, Giddings reached into his

coat pocket and pulled out a silver flask. With practiced ease, he removed the top and took a healthy swallow. He didn't offer to share before placing the flask safely back into his pocket.

"How did she die?" he asked when he'd given the whiskey a moment to work.

"Someone stabbed her. It happened in Washington Square."

He started in surprise. "Who did it?"

"We don't know yet."

"But if someone stabbed her in a public place like that, someone must have seen who did it!"

"It happened at night. No one found her until morning." He let that sink in, and then he said, "Do you know why she was out alone at that hour?"

"Of course not!"

"She wasn't going to meet you, then?"

"I'd never expect a female to go out alone at night to meet me," he insisted, affronted. "That wouldn't be safe. I always called on Anna here at the house."

"You said you were engaged," Frank reminded him. "When were you planning to get married?"

Giddings blanched again, proving Frank's theory that this had been a lie. "I . . . We . . . we hadn't yet set a date," he hedged.

"Is that because you're already married, Mr. Giddings?" Frank inquired.

Now Giddings was frightened. "I can't imagine why that's any of your business," he tried.

"When a woman is murdered, everything about her is my business. Now tell me how you met Anna Blake and what your relationship with her really was."

Giddings rubbed a hand across his forehead. When his fingers bumped the brim of his hat, he quickly reached up and removed it, looking at it in amazement, as if he'd never seen it before.

"How did you meet her, Mr. Giddings?" he prodded.

"I'm an attorney," he said, losing what little of Frank's respect he still had. "Miss Blake came to me with a legal problem. She . . . something to do with a will. She was supposed to have received a legacy when her mother died, but an uncle had produced a more recent will which left everything to him. Anna insisted the second will had been forged, and she needed some legal advice."

Anna Blake, Frank realized, had been a woman with a lively imagination. "Let me guess, she couldn't pay your fee."

"Of course not! She was penniless," Giddings said defensively. "Her mother had died and her uncle had stolen her inheritance. She had sold all of her possessions to keep herself while she tried to find work, but you know how difficult it would be for a young woman of good family to find a suitable position. She couldn't earn enough to keep a roof over her head. By the time she came to me, she was desperate. The only choice open to her was to . . . to sell herself. I couldn't allow that to happen! What decent man could?"

"So as a decent man, you took her as your mistress instead," Frank said.

Somehow, Giddings managed to work up some outrage. The color rose in his face and he started sputtering in protest, but his bluster soon evaporated under Frank's unrelenting glare.

"You took her as your mistress," Frank repeated.

"No, it didn't happen like that!"

"How did it happen?"

Giddings had nearly ruined his well-made hat in his agitation, but Frank resisted the urge to take it from him. Instead, he sat still and waited. As he expected, Giddings came up with words to fill the silence.

"At first I just gave her some money. To keep her from the streets, you understand. I felt it was my Christian duty."

Anna Blake had inspired Christian duty in many men, apparently. Frank nodded encouragingly.

"She was very grateful," Giddings continued more confidently. "She promised she would repay me when she found work, but even when she found a place to take her on, they turned her out after only a few days. She didn't know how to operate mechanical equipment, and the other girls treated her badly because she was so obviously better than they. The experience completely broke her spirit."

"So you gave her some more money," Frank said. "And eventually you became lovers."

"No man had ever been kind to her before," Giddings explained anxiously. "She fell in love with me! I was all she had in the world. How could a man resist such a temptation?"

"How indeed," Frank agreed solemnly. "I expect any decent man would've done the same in your position."

Giddings had the grace to flush and look ashamed. Frank enjoyed his humiliation for a moment before returning to the business at hand.

"Did she ask you to divorce your wife and marry her?" he asked.

"My wife would never consent to a divorce. The scandal . . ."

"Your wife wouldn't *have* to consent, and we both know it, Giddings," Frank said brutally. "*You* didn't want a divorce because the scandal would hurt your business."

"I have a son to think of," Giddings tried. "I couldn't ruin his life."

"So you paid her off," Frank guessed.

"Her demands were small at first. She had simple needs, she said. But then . . ."

"Then she found out she was with child," Frank supplied.

Giddings looked up in genuine terror. "I couldn't allow my family to find out! Or my partners! Our clients wouldn't tolerate immoral behavior from a member of the firm."

"So you paid her to keep silent."

"But it was never enough! She kept wanting more and more. She thought I was rich, but I'm not. I earn a comfortable living, but I have a family to support and a home and servants and—"

"Where did you get the extra money, then?" Frank asked.

He rubbed his forehead again. Thinking about all of this was obviously painful for him. "I did nothing illegal," he said after a moment.

"Would other people agree with that?" Frank asked mildly.

Giddings pressed his lips together until they turned white, refusing to reply.

"Well, then, suppose you tell me what law firm employs you so I can find out if they agree that you didn't do anything illegal."

"They'll tell you nothing," he insisted. "Attorneys know they don't have to tell the police anything."

This was true, much to the frustration of the police, but Frank figured he'd try anyway. If they were angry enough at Giddings, they might just enjoy betraying him. Or maybe someone at the firm enjoyed good old-fashioned gossip.

"Where were you night before last?" Frank asked.

Giddings refused to meet Frank's eye. "At home in bed, I'm sure."

"You can prove that?"

"I don't have to prove it!"

"You do if I decide to charge you with Anna Blake's murder," Frank said. "Now do you have any witnesses that you were home all night?"

"My . . . my wife," he admitted reluctantly.

"Then I'm sure she'll be glad to vouch for you."

From the expression on Giddings's face, Frank could see that he wasn't sure his wife would do any such thing. If she were angry enough, she might even lie to implicate him. Of course, if she was as afraid of scandal as Frank figured she was, she'd probably lie to *protect* him, no matter how much she hated him for betraying her. And there was always the issue of financial security to consider. If Giddings went to prison or was executed, who would support his wife? Many women would resign themselves to living with an unfaithful murderer if the alternative was starvation.

"Is it really necessary for you to talk to my wife?" Giddings asked.

"I could wait a few days to see if we find the killer . . . assuming, of course, that it isn't you."

"I would appreciate such a consideration," Giddings said with surprising meekness for an attorney.

"Do you have a card? So I can get in touch with you," Frank asked. A printed card would have Giddings's true address on it, so he wouldn't have to take the man's word. He didn't want to lose him now that he'd had the good fortune to find him.

Giddings fished around absently in his coat pocket and produced an engraved business card for Smythe, Masterson and Judd, Attorneys at Law. Impressive-sounding name, but Frank didn't recognize it, which meant they probably didn't involve themselves in criminal prosecutions.

"May I go now?" Giddings asked.

"Are you going to tell your wife that your mistress is dead?" Frank asked. "I'm sure she'll be very relieved."

Giddings refused to reply. He had a little pride left.

But Frank had no more patience. "Get out of here," he said, and Giddings fled.

Sarah waited until Malloy had safely led Mr. Giddings into the bedroom and closed the door before emerging from the parlor. She thought perhaps Mr. Walcott had forgotten about her in all the excitement. Indeed, he looked surprised when she said, "Do you mind if I use your convenience?"

He needed a moment to place her and another to register her request. At least he didn't seem overly embarrassed by it. "I . . . of course not. It's . . ." He gestured vaguely toward the back of the house.

Sarah thanked him and breathed a silent sigh of relief that the house apparently didn't have an indoor convenience, since she only needed an excuse to go wandering around the rear of the house alone. She made her way quickly down the hallway to the kitchen, where she had expected to find the maid. Instead she found Catherine Porter. She was sitting at the kitchen table drinking a cup of tea. At the sight of Sarah, she frowned.

"Are you looking for something?" she asked.

Before Sarah could answer, the maid came slamming in the back door. "I'm telling you, I ain't going back into that cellar until Mr. Walcott does something about that smell! It's a dead rat, I'm that sure," she was saying, and then she saw Sarah and caught herself up short. "Something I can do for you, miss?"

Sarah smiled at her good fortune at finding both of them together. "I was going to ask if you could help me find Miss Porter," she said. "Do you mind if I sit down with you for a few minutes?" she asked Catherine.

"Oh, no, miss," the maid answered for her, to Catherine's obvious annoyance. "Could I get you some tea?" She was young and apparently inexperienced. Sarah could probably get her to talk easily. Catherine Porter, on the other hand, already looked suspicious.

"I would love some tea," Sarah said, undaunted, taking a seat at the table.

Catherine Porter looked at her through weary, red-rimmed eyes. Her face was drawn and dark circles had formed beneath her eyes. She'd pulled her thick, dark hair carelessly back with a tattered ribbon. Her dress was old and faded, one she would have saved for wearing around the house. She fingered the worn collar self-consciously when she saw Sarah looking at it.

"You're that woman who came with Mr. Ellsworth the other day," Catherine said as the maid poured Sarah's tea. "Are you his wife?"

Sarah realized that, like Anna Blake, Catherine Porter was also older than her usual manner of dress would indicate. Certainly old enough to be feeling the urgency to marry before her looks faded along with her chances of catching a suitable husband. If that was actually her goal.

"Oh, no, I'm not his wife," Sarah said. "He's a neighbor of mine, and he'd asked me to meet Miss Blake."

"I guess his wife's too upset to even think about coming around here," Catherine said.

"She would be, if she existed, but Mr. Ellsworth isn't married," Sarah said, a little confused.

"He's not?" Catherine seemed genuinely surprised, and then grew even more suspicious. "Did he send you here? What do you want from me? I don't know anything about Anna."

"Mr. Ellsworth didn't send me," Sarah reassured her. "I just came to express my condolences," she lied. "What a terrible tragedy."

Catherine's lips tightened, but she didn't reply.

"Oh, it was that," the maid offered, setting the teacup down in front of Sarah. She remained standing, probably thinking it too familiar to sit down with Sarah there. "We was just a minute ago saying how awful it was. Miss Blake was so pretty. The gentlemen all liked her, that's certain."

"Gentlemen?" Sarah asked, surprised that Anna's suitors had apparently been numerous. "Did Miss Blake have other gentlemen callers besides Mr. Ellsworth and that fellow who came in just now?"

"She—"

"Hush, Mary," Catherine snapped, cutting the girl off. Then to Sarah, "She's just a foolish girl. Don't know what she's saying."

"I do, too," Mary protested, but fell silent when Catherine glared at her in warning.

"The thing that puzzles me the most," Sarah continued, wishing now that she'd caught the talkative maid alone. She'd have to come back another time, "is why she was in the Square so late at night. Was she accustomed to going out alone like that?"

"Of course not," Catherine said defensively. They all knew only a prostitute would have been in the Square alone after dark.

"Then do you know what made her go out that night?"

"No, we don't know anything," Catherine insisted.

"Mary only works days, so she wasn't here, and I was asleep. First thing I knew about it is when the police came in the morning to tell us she was dead."

"The patrolman recognized her," Mary supplied. "He come to tell the Walcotts."

"How did the patrolman happen to know her?" Sarah asked.

"He knows all the girls," Catherine said quickly, before the maid could answer. "Fancies himself a ladies' man. He's forever bothering us."

Sarah made a mental note to have Malloy check this out. Maybe Anna Blake had come to the notice of the police in a less ordinary way. "It's fortunate he knew her. Her body might have gone unclaimed otherwise."

"Oh, Mrs. Walcott would've been looking for her if she didn't come home," Mary said. "She wasn't one to let her boarders go disappearing without a trace. All her clothes was here, too, so we'd know she didn't just run away, wouldn't we?"

Catherine gave the maid an impatient glance. Plainly, she was afraid the girl was going to say something she didn't want Sarah to hear. For her part, Sarah was determined to find out what that might be.

"How long did you know Miss Blake?" Sarah asked Catherine.

Catherine considered her answer before giving it. "A few months."

"You met her when she moved in here, then?" Sarah guessed.

"No, when *I* did. She was already here."

"I thought she hadn't lived here long herself."

"She was here when I came," Catherine said, not really answering the implied question.

"Didn't you two know each other before?" Mary asked and was silenced by another dark look from Catherine.

Yes, Sarah really would have to come back when the maid was alone. "I certainly hope this tragedy won't frighten *your* friends away, Miss Porter," Sarah tried.

As she had hoped, this got a rise out of her. "What do you mean by that?"

Sarah shrugged. "I simply meant that people who normally call here might be concerned about the notoriety. The newspapers haven't been kind to poor Mr. Ellsworth. Few people would want to risk being associated with a scandal like this."

"Oh, Miss Porter's gentlemen would never—" Mary began, but Catherine cut her off with a murderous glare. How interesting. Miss Porter had numerous callers, too.

"They've put Mr. Ellsworth in jail now," Catherine said. "We won't be hearing anything more about it."

"Oh, Mr. Ellsworth wasn't arrested," Sarah corrected her. "He was allowed to go home last night. The police don't believe he's guilty." This wasn't exactly a lie. Malloy, at least, didn't think he was guilty.

"Why wouldn't they?" Catherine asked in dismay. "Who else could've done it?"

"Anyone," Sarah pointed out. "At that time of night, she might have been murdered just for the few coins in her purse."

"But she didn't even have her purse with her," Mary supplied helpfully. "It's still up in her room."

"Mary," Catherine snapped. "Don't you have work to do upstairs?"

"I ain't going up there until that policeman leaves," Mary said. "I don't want him putting me in jail!"

"Oh, Mary, at least *act* like you've got good sense!" Catherine said in exasperation.

"I can't be nothing else but what I am," Mary replied huffily. "I ain't no stage actress like you."

Furious, Catherine made as if to rise from her chair, and Sarah didn't want to see where that might lead. "Are you an actress?" she asked quickly, drawing Catherine's attention from the poor maid. "Would I have seen you in anything?"

As Sarah had hoped, she sank back down into her chair. "I did a little musical theater," she admitted reluctantly, still glaring at Mary, daring her to say another word. "But that was a long time ago."

When she was truly the young girl she pretended to be, Sarah thought, but she said, "How exciting. I always thought it would be fun to be in the theater."

"It isn't," Catherine said. Sarah thought she detected bitterness in the words.

She wanted to pursue this topic, but footsteps in the hallway distracted them, and then Mr. Walcott appeared in the doorway.

"Mrs. Brandt," he said, taking in the scene with disapproval. "I was afraid you'd gotten lost."

"Not at all. I was just telling Miss Porter how sorry I am about her friend."

Mr. Walcott exchanged a glance with Catherine, but Sarah couldn't decipher the silent message that passed between them. "That detective was asking after you, Mrs. Brandt," he said. "I believe he wanted to escort you home."

Sarah knew perfectly well Malloy had no such intention, but they did need to compare notes. She would have liked to stay and question the women some more, but she'd have to come back when they weren't together if she hoped to get any more information.

"Thank you for the tea," Sarah said to Mary, then turned to Catherine. "Please let me know if I can do anything for you." She pulled out her card and laid it on the table. Catherine Porter didn't even glance at it. She was too busy watching Mr. Walcott.

"After you, Mrs. Brandt," Walcott said, with a flourish that was an oddly effeminate gesture. The eyes that glared at her were hardly effeminate, though. She'd seen that expression before and knew better than to waste her time resisting. Mr. Walcott wanted her out of his house, and he wasn't going to be distracted from his purpose. She preceded him down the hallway.

At least she had a little new information for Malloy. She only hoped it would help them find Anna Blake's real killer.

5

"THE MAID ONLY WORKS IN THE DAY, AND CATHERINE claims she was asleep when Anna left the house. She doesn't have any idea what made her do it," Sarah reported as she and Malloy walked back toward Washington Square. "Oh, and she must have left in a hurry because she didn't take her purse with her. What did you learn from that fellow, what's his name?"

"Giddings." He reached into his pocket and pulled out a business card. "Gilbert Giddings."

"He's an attorney?" she asked, shamelessly peering at the card.

Malloy stuffed it back into his pocket and pretended to be annoyed. "So he says," Malloy said.

"And he was also one of Anna Blake's gentlemen friends," she said when he offered nothing else.

"One of many, apparently," Malloy allowed.

"Was he giving her money, too?"

"Yes."

Sarah gave him an impatient look. "Malloy, you are the most insufferable . . . Do I have to give you the third degree to get information out of you?"

This ridiculous threat brought a small grin to Malloy's

face, but he said, "There's nothing much to tell. Anna Blake told him some cock-and-bull story about how an uncle cheated her out of her inheritance—"

"But her mother was destitute when she died," Sarah protested.

"Not according to Giddings."

"That's a different story than the one she told Nelson."

"She needed a different story because she needed a different reason to go to an attorney than to a banker," he pointed out. "Giddings took pity on her, gave her some money, and the next thing you know, she's in a family way and needing more money than he can afford to give her."

"Didn't he offer to marry her?"

Malloy gave her a pitying look. "He's already married."

"Oh," Sarah said, then remembered something. "Catherine Porter thought Nelson was married. She seemed very surprised to find out he wasn't. Wouldn't you think if a man was calling on a woman, you'd *expect* him to be single, not the other way around?"

"Unless you were planning to blackmail him."

"Blackmail?" Sarah echoed in amazement.

"Yes, blackmail. That's what Anna Blake was doing to Giddings, and what she was probably trying to do to Nelson, but it wasn't going to work. Nelson wanted to marry her, not pay her off for her silence, the way Giddings was."

"If that's what she wanted to do, then why did she choose a bachelor like Nelson?"

Malloy shrugged. "Maybe she thought he was married. Catherine Porter apparently did."

Sarah tried to make sense of it. "I guess we can ask Nelson."

"We certainly can't ask Anna Blake," Malloy pointed out blandly.

Sarah ignored this provocation. "What did Mr. Walcott have to contribute?"

"Not much. He was out of town when Anna Blake was killed. Says he spends very little time at the house. He's too busy spending his wife's inheritance to bother with the comings and goings of her boarders."

This didn't make sense either. "If she has an inheritance, why do they take in boarders?"

"It wasn't much, I gathered. Not enough to support them and pay for Walcott's travels, at least. And he claims his wife likes cooking and cleaning for other people."

Sarah made a rude noise at such a preposterous notion. "I'll be interested to hear her side of that story. Where was she today?"

"Shopping, he said. I'll go back another time and talk to her. What's she like?"

Sarah considered. "Well groomed and nosy."

Malloy raised his eyebrows at this assessment. "Your powers of observation amaze me, Mrs. Brandt. How would you describe Mr. Walcott?"

"Vain and selfish."

"Why vain?" he asked curiously. Malloy had already given her the reasons to think him selfish.

"Did you see how carefully his hair was arranged? And how meticulous his clothes were? He spends a lot of time making sure he looks his best. He wants others to think as well of him as he thinks of himself."

"Considering how much time you spent with him, that's very impressive," Malloy allowed.

"Oh, stop with the blarney, Malloy. You're turning my head. And speaking of blarney, did you see the newspapers this morning?" she asked, outraged anew at the thought of them.

"I try to avoid reading the newspapers as much as I can," he said.

"They said the most horrible things about poor Nelson! As far as they're concerned, he's another Jack the Ripper, slashing innocent women to death in the dark of night," she said in disgust.

"What did you expect? They're trying to sell papers, not get the facts right."

"But they're *newspapers*! Don't they have an obligation to tell the truth? Mr. Pulitzer has devoted himself to uncovering scandal and corruption in society," she said, naming the publisher of the *World*. "His paper is always crusading for one cause or another. Why would he allow his reporters to make up lies about innocent people?"

"That's something you'll have to ask Mr. Pulitzer," Malloy said with a tolerant grin. "The fact is that newspapers will publish anything if they think it will make people buy papers. Look at that Italian woman who killed her lover, for instance."

The story had sold millions of papers through her trial after she slashed her lover's throat because he refused to marry her. "The press certainly wasn't very kind to Miss Barberi," she recalled, remembering the salacious details they had published about her.

"That isn't even her name," Malloy said.

"What do you mean?"

"I mean her real name is Barbella. Somebody got it wrong in the beginning, and the rest of them picked it up. I asked a reporter once why they didn't correct the mistake, and he said that Barberi sounded like barbarian, so it made better copy."

"That's horrible!" Sarah exclaimed.

"I'm not arguing with you. I'm just telling you what goes on. Let me guess what they said about Nelson. They said he's an evil seducer who ruined an innocent young woman, got her with child, and then killed her so he didn't have to support them."

Sarah sighed. "One even suggested he'd killed her just because he got tired of her and wanted to find a new victim for his evil lusts."

"Very imaginative. At this rate, the police are going to have to arrest him just so the public feels safe from a monster."

Sarah groaned. "What are we going to do?"

"*We* are not going to do anything. *You* are going home to make sure Nelson and his mother stay safely in their house while *I* go back to Thompson Street and try to figure out who really killed Anna Blake before Bill Broughan decides to close this case by locking up Nelson Ellsworth."

They'd reached Washington Square and stopped on the sidewalk at the southwest corner.

"What are we going to do about the newspapers?" Sarah asked.

Malloy looked pained. "Didn't you hear what I just said? *You* do not have to do anything at all except worry about the Ellsworths."

"Malloy, you know you need my help in this! I can get more information out of Catherine Porter and the maid. I just need to catch them when Walcott isn't around."

"Do you honestly think anyone will ever let you back in that house again?"

He might be right about that, so Sarah decided not to argue. "Then I can talk to the newspapers and try to get them to print the truth."

"How are you going to explain your interest in Nelson Ellsworth's welfare?"

"We're neighbors!"

"You're a woman, and he's a man. You are no relation to him. You will be drawing the unpleasant attention of the press to yourself by trying to convince people he is innocent of killing a woman he seduced. Why would you do such a thing unless you were also his mistress?"

"No one will think that!" Sarah insisted without much conviction.

"Your mother would."

Sarah glared at him, furious because he was right. Her mother would be very upset, but it wouldn't be the first time Sarah had disappointed her. "I long ago stopped trying to please my mother."

"Then protect yourself for your own sake. Believe me, you don't want to know what the press will say about you if you become Nelson's champion. Making a scandal of Felix Decker's daughter would sell a lot of newspapers."

Sarah's family was one of the oldest in the city, descendants of the original Dutch settlers, nicknamed the Knickerbockers. Their socially prominent position made them perfect targets, too. Sarah had already caused them enough heartache by marrying beneath her social station and forsaking their way of life. Plastering their name all over the scandal sheets would be unforgivable.

"I hate it when you're right, Malloy."

"And I'm always amazed when you admit I am," he countered. "Now go home. I've got work to do. I need to get this murder solved fast because I've still got my own work to do, too. Don't forget, I'm not even assigned to this case, and if anyone finds out I'm doing Broughan's job for him, I'll be the laughingstock of the department."

"I suppose you want me to tell you how grateful I am that you're helping poor Nelson," she said with a smirk.

"I do, but I don't expect you will," he replied with a smirk of his own. "Good day, Mrs. Brandt."

He tipped his hat and walked away, leaving Sarah shaking her head.

Frank strolled back to Thompson Street. The weather was turning colder. Soon the leaves would fall and winter would come with a vengeance. Tuesday evening had been a bit warmer than today but still chilly. Why had Anna Blake gone out that night? Surely not for a pleasant evening stroll. And why hadn't she taken her purse? Had she been in a hurry?

He'd check to see if Mrs. Walcott was home yet so he could question her, and then he'd try the neighbors. He should search Anna's room, too. Maybe someone had sent her a note asking her to meet him that night. That would be too convenient, but it was certainly worth a try. He wasn't going to get very far at all until he found out why she'd left the house in the first place.

The maid at the Walcott house told him Mrs. Walcott hadn't come back yet and Mr. Walcott had gone out, too. She wouldn't admit him to the house without their permission, certainly not to search the dead woman's room. He could have forced his way in, but he decided to wait until the landlady could escort him. No use in alienating the Walcotts before he had all the information they could give him.

As he left the Walcotts' he noticed a curtain on the front window of the house next door moving. Someone was watching him, which meant someone was very curi-

ous about the goings-on at the neighbors' house. If that
person was as nosy as Mrs. Ellsworth was about her neighbors, he could learn a lot about the Walcotts and their
boarders.

The woman who opened the door had snow white hair
and a round pleasant face. Her faded blue eyes glittered
with delight at the sight of her visitor, and she clapped her
hands together as she peered up at Frank.

"Are you from the police?" she asked breathlessly.

"Yes, ma'am, I am," he said, removing his bowler hat
and holding it in front of him respectfully. "Detective
Sergeant Frank Malloy. Would you mind if I asked you a
few questions about your neighbors, Mrs. . . . ?"

"It's Miss. Miss Edna Stone. Oh, my, no, I wouldn't
mind at all. I'm not sure I can help you in any way. I have
no idea who killed that girl, you know. How could I? They
said in the newspaper that she died in the Square. What a
horrible thing."

Frank nodded solemnly. "I was hoping you might have
seen something that night. Maybe something you didn't
even realize was important at the time. Could I come in
and speak with you about it?"

"Oh, gracious me, of course you may. Excuse the mess.
I've been so upset about that poor girl's death, I haven't
had a chance to tidy up."

She escorted him into a parlor that was so spotlessly
clean, even his mother couldn't have found fault with it.
He wondered what on earth she could do to tidy it up.

"Please sit down, Mr. Detective Sergeant. Would you
like some coffee?"

Frank allowed that he would. If she gave him coffee,
she'd settle in for a nice long visit. He really doubted she'd
seen anything the night Anna Blake had died, but he was
sure she could tell him a lot of gossip about her and the
others in the house. He made himself comfortable and
looked around the room while he waited. Miss Stone had
doilies everywhere and almost as many knickknacks as his
mother, but he didn't see a speck of dust on anything. No

photographs, either. Miss Stone might very well be alone in the world.

The old woman returned a few minutes later with two cups of coffee and a plate of cookies on a gleaming silver tray.

"You didn't have to go to so much trouble," he protested.

"No trouble at all," she assured him, settling into her own chair and handing him one of the cups. "These cookies are probably stale. There's no one here to eat them but me."

The cookies were fresh and delicious. Frank ate two and complimented her on them before he asked his first question. "How long have you lived here, Miss Stone?"

"I've lived here all my life, Mr. Detective Sergeant. I was born in this house."

Which meant she'd inherited it from her family, along with enough money to keep herself modestly even though she'd never married. How fortunate for her. Few women were so lucky.

"How long have the Walcotts lived next door?"

"Not quite a year now, I expect. They bought the place from Mr. Knight. His wife had died, and he was tired of living there all alone. At least that's what Mrs. Walcott told me. Mr. Knight never even mentioned he was selling. Didn't even say good-bye, either. Just up and left. Moved uptown, she said, into one of those fancy apartment buildings. I knew him forty years, and he didn't say one word to me. Of course, he got funny after his wife died. Never was very sociable, and when she was gone, he just stayed inside most of the time. Didn't even work in his garden anymore. Widowers get like that sometimes."

"What do you know about the Walcotts?"

Miss Stone considered the question. "I'm trying to remember if she told me where they came from. Can't say I recall, but they were thrilled with the house. Mr. Knight sold them most of his furniture, too, since he didn't need it in his new place. Seems like she said her family left her a legacy or some such thing. That's how they could buy the house."

"When did they start taking in boarders?"

"Almost right away. Her husband couldn't work, you know. Had some sort of nervous condition. So they needed the money."

Frank almost smiled at the description of Mr. Walcott as nervous. "I thought she had a legacy."

"She didn't say, but it couldn't have been much. Not enough to keep them, at least. She said she enjoyed having company in the house. They'd never been blessed with children, and she liked having other people around. Her husband liked to travel, so the boarders were company for her, as well as income."

So far this story agreed mostly with the one Walcott had told him. "I understand that the two women who were living there lately had only been there a few months. Who lived there before?"

Miss Stone frowned as she tried to remember. "I don't know all their names. One had red hair, I remember, and I'd swear it wasn't natural. You know how you can just tell," she added conspiratorially. "The way she carried herself, well, she didn't seem quite respectable either, if you know what I mean. In my day, a young woman didn't flaunt herself like that. But she didn't stay long. Probably, the Walcotts agreed with me and turned her out. There was another one, Blevins or Cummings her name was. Something like that. Real pretty girl. She was there longer, but they told me she got married. I'm not surprised, as many men as came to call on her, she probably had her pick."

"Do a lot of men come to the house?" Frank asked.

Miss Stone looked insulted. "It's not that kind of a house, Mr. Detective Sergeant. I know the difference."

"I didn't mean to say it was. I just understood that the two women living there now also had several suitors each. I was wondering if you'd noticed that."

A little mollified, she said, "I'm not one for minding my neighbors' business, you understand, but I couldn't help noticing that each girl seemed to have two or three different gentlemen who called on her. I don't know how they kept them straight."

"Or how they kept them from encountering each other," Frank observed.

Miss Stone smiled her agreement. "The girls didn't step out with their gentlemen, either, the way girls do nowadays. I don't think it's right, you understand. A young woman should never be alone in the company of a young man unless they're engaged, and even then . . . But I suppose I'm hopelessly old-fashioned. Girls today, they do heaven knows what. Except these girls didn't. The men would go inside to call on the girls, and then they'd leave alone. They never even took the girls for walks in the park or anything like that. They were very respectable."

Frank could think of another explanation. If the men in question were married, they couldn't take a chance of being seen in a public place. Liaisons like the ones Frank knew took place there—liaisons that resulted in pregnancy—also couldn't happen in a public place.

"Did you ever speak with any of the boarders?" Frank asked.

"I don't believe I did. Young women like that, they don't have time for an old lady like me."

"What about their gentleman friends?"

"Oh, gracious, no! They were always in too much of a hurry. Pulling their hats down over their eyes so they could pretend they didn't see me and didn't need to speak."

Frank nodded his understanding. He suspected the men were actually trying to avoid being recognized, but he didn't bother to explain that to Miss Stone. "Did you notice anything unusual the night Anna Blake was killed?"

She offered Frank the cookie plate while she tried to remember. He took two more.

"Of course, I didn't know she was going to be murdered," Miss Stone explained, "so I wasn't paying particular attention, you understand."

Frank nodded again as he chewed on a cookie.

"This probably has nothing at all to do with that poor girl's death."

Frank kept nodding and chewing.

"I have a difficult time sleeping. That happens when you get older. I was in bed, so I don't know what time it might have been, although I know it was late, but I thought I heard someone opening the cellar door."

"At the Walcott house?"

"I can't be perfectly sure. I didn't get up to look. Why should I? Only a busybody would be that curious. And the houses are so close together, it could have been the neighbor on the other side, for all I know. You see, I told you it probably didn't have anything to do with the murder."

Frank had to agree. Anna Blake wasn't murdered in anyone's cellar. "It does prove you're observant and have a good memory," Frank said to placate her. "Did you notice anything earlier in the evening? Do you remember which gentlemen came to call?"

"I don't want you to think I just sit by my window watching who comes and goes next door," Miss Stone said, a little offended.

Frank gave her his charming smile, the one that used to work on his mother when he was a boy. "I know that a lady living alone likes to know who comes and goes in the neighborhood. You can't be too careful, you know. I'm sure if you saw anything suspicious, you'd report it immediately."

Miss Stone allowed herself to be placated again. "Of course I would. Except I didn't see anything suspicious that night. I did see a gentleman come to call earlier in the evening, but I'm not even sure which one it was. They're very careful about turning their faces away, you understand, and I never imagined it would be important to keep track of them."

"Do you have any idea when he left?"

"I'm sorry to say I don't. Why would that . . . ? Oh, I see, if the girl had left with him, he might be the killer."

Miss Stone was proving to be quite a detective herself. Too bad she wasn't quite as nosy as Mrs. Ellsworth. He bet Mrs. Ellsworth could've told him the eye color and religious affiliation of each and every one of the Walcotts' gentlemen callers.

"Have I been any help at all?" she asked anxiously.

"It's hard to tell," Frank lied. "Sometimes the smallest detail is the one that solves the case. Like I said, you may have seen something important without realizing it. If you think of anything else, please send for me." He gave her his card, thanked her for the refreshments, and took his leave.

Frank glanced at the Walcott house as he left Miss Stone's. All seemed quiet, and he considered trying again to talk with Mrs. Walcott. Then he decided he'd have a better chance of seeing Giddings at his place of business at this time of day, something he could do without breaking his promise not to tell Giddings's wife what had happened. Frank wanted to find out if he was the one who'd called on Anna the night she died. He'd stop by the Walcotts' early tomorrow to catch the landlady before she had a chance to leave the house. Maybe she could at least explain why someone had opened her cellar door late that night.

Sarah arrived home to discover several reporters on the sidewalk in front of the Ellsworths' house. Poor Mrs. Ellsworth, the most exciting thing to happen on this street in her lifetime, and she already knew all about it. More, in fact, than she wanted to know.

Sarah debated the wisdom of trying to get past the reporters to the Ellsworths' front door, but she decided to try to sneak in the back instead. Unfortunately, she still had to deal with them. As soon as they recognized her, they converged on her, plying her with shouted questions and offering her bribes to get them in to see the Ellsworths.

"Mr. Ellsworth had nothing to do with Anna Blake's murder," she tried shouting above the din.

"How do you know?" one of them asked. "Was he with you that night?"

"Why are you trying to protect him?" another called.

Malloy was right, she thought in disgust. There was no way to convince these jackals of the truth. They were only interested in uncovering a scandal—or inventing one. She shoved her way through them and up her front steps and into her house, slamming the door behind her.

Once inside, she went to the window to see what they would do. Deprived of their latest prey, they returned to their vigil at the Ellsworths' front stoop, waiting for a new victim. Poor Mrs. Ellsworth, held prisoner in her own home. Nelson, at least, had gotten himself into this mess with his poor judgment, but his mother had done nothing at all. Sarah wondered if they had enough food or if they needed anything. At least their captivity meant they hadn't been able to get out to buy a newspaper and had been spared that outrage.

Sarah went to her own pantry and found a few potatoes, half a loaf of stale bread, and a bag of beans. She'd shop for them tomorrow, if Malloy still hadn't solved the case by then. In the meantime, at least they wouldn't starve. Throwing the food items into a market basket, Sarah went to her back door and checked to make sure no reporters had taken up a vigil in the alley. Finding the way clear, she hurried next door and banged on the door.

Mrs. Ellsworth peered out before letting her in. "Oh, Mrs. Brandt, thank heaven you're here! I'm half insane with worrying. Has Mr. Malloy found the killer yet?"

"Not yet," she said, "but I'm sure it won't be much longer." Malloy wouldn't thank her for the lie, but it was all she had to offer. "Where's Nelson?"

"Up in his room. I think he's a little embarrassed about everything that happened, and he's also mourning that poor girl. He really cared for her. And when he saw what they wrote about him in the newspaper . . ." Her voice broke.

"How did you see a newspaper?" Sarah asked in dismay.

"Mr. Holsinger across the street brought one over this morning, before the reporters got here."

"How thoughtful of him," Sarah said sarcastically.

"Oh, he wasn't being kind," Mrs. Ellsworth assured her. "He was furious that Nelson had brought a scandal into the neighborhood. He wanted to know what we were going to do about it."

"What did he have in mind?" Sarah asked in astonishment.

"Heaven knows," Mrs. Ellsworth said with a sigh, sinking down into one of the kitchen chairs. She looked as if she hadn't slept much the night before, and Sarah wanted to check her pulse and her heartbeat to make sure she wasn't truly ill. Perhaps she'd bring her medical bag when she came the next time.

Sarah set her market basket on the table. "I didn't know if you had any food in the house, but I knew you couldn't go shopping, so I brought over what I had."

"That's kind of you, but neither of us feels very hungry, I'm afraid."

"You can't stop eating. You'll make yourself sick. How are you feeling?"

Mrs. Ellsworth looked up at Sarah through bloodshot eyes. "Frightened," she said. "What if Mr. Malloy can't find the real killer, and they arrest Nelson? He could be executed!"

"Don't think that way! Malloy will find the killer, and if he doesn't, I will. Nelson will never go to jail," she promised rashly.

Mrs. Ellsworth smiled sadly. "You are such a good friend, Mrs. Brandt."

Sarah returned her smile. "As I recall, you've been a good friend to me, too. Now let's peel these potatoes and see if we can't get some hot food into the two of you."

Mrs. Ellsworth found a knife, and Sarah took it from her and began to peel. "Which newspaper did Mr. Holsinger bring you?" she asked after a moment.

"The World," she said with a frown of distaste. "I wonder if it was written by that rude young man who told us Nelson had been arrested."

"It seems likely," Sarah said, remembering him only too well.

"He looked like such a nice young man, but . . . Can

you tell me, Mrs. Brandt, are the things he said about Nelson true?"

"I'm sure very little of it was true," Sarah hedged.

"But was that poor girl with child, like the paper said? Nelson won't talk about it at all. I think he's trying to protect me, but the truth can't be any worse than what I'm imagining."

"She'd told Nelson she was with child," Sarah said, deciding that telling the truth was really the only way to protect her friend. "He thought perhaps she might be mistaken, so he asked me to visit her to make sure."

"What a cad!" she exclaimed in outrage. "I'd never expect my own son to behave so unchivalrously! To seduce an innocent girl was bad enough. He should have offered to marry her at once!"

"He did," Sarah assured her. "But for some reason, she didn't want to marry him."

This shocked Mrs. Ellsworth as much as it had Sarah. "Why on earth not?"

"According to Nelson, she didn't think she was good enough for him or something. At least that's what she said. Nelson is a modest man, and he was afraid she just couldn't stand the idea of being married to him."

"That's ridiculous! Nelson is a fine catch, and a girl in her position would marry a hunchbacked imbecile, in any case, just to give her child a name."

Sarah could only agree. "I don't pretend to understand any of this. I'm just repeating what I was told. Nelson thought that if there wasn't a child, Anna wouldn't be forced into a marriage she didn't want."

"So he asked you to make sure," Mrs. Ellsworth guessed. "And did you?"

"No. Miss Blake wouldn't even speak with me. And the next day she was murdered."

"No wonder they think Nelson did it," the old woman sighed. "A man who didn't want to be forced into marriage kills his paramour in a fit of rage."

"Nelson would never have a fit of rage," Sarah reminded her.

"Oh, Mrs. Brandt," she cried, burying her head in her hands. "What are we going to do?"

Sarah only wished she had an answer. "Malloy will find the killer," she tried again.

"But if he doesn't, Nelson will go on trial, and the newspapers have already convicted him. Remember what happened to that Italian girl? The one who killed her lover? She only did what any woman would have done in her position, and the newspapers made her out to be the devil incarnate!"

"Not every woman in her position would have slashed the man's throat in a public place," Sarah reminded her.

"But don't you agree she was justified? He'd seduced her and then refused to marry her and called her names in front of all those people and then said he was sailing back to Italy to leave her in disgrace. But when the newspapers got through with her, she was a wicked vixen who'd killed an upstanding gentleman for no reason at all. And that's what they're doing to Nelson!"

"But don't forget, they're giving that girl a new trial, and this time the newspapers are telling the truth about what happened." Indeed, they'd painted the victim as black this time as they'd painted Maria Barberi the first time.

"Only because some rich woman championed that girl's cause and got her a new trial. Unless someone champions Nelson, he's going to die." Mrs. Ellsworth's wrinkled face crumbled in grief and then she was sobbing into her hands.

Sarah took the woman into her arms and offered what comfort she could, but even as she patted the bowed shoulders, she knew she had to do more. She had to do what Mrs. Ellsworth had said and what Malloy had warned her against, because if she didn't try to save Nelson Ellsworth, he very likely *would* be executed. And how would she comfort his mother then?

Frank found the law firm of Smythe, Masterson and Judd in a building uptown identified only with a small brass plate. Apparently, people who needed the services of these gentlemen knew what they did and where to find them, so they didn't need to advertise.

Inside, the offices were furnished richly, in dark masculine colors with none of the feminine frills so common in private homes. Paintings of men hunting adorned the walls above overstuffed chairs, and the place smelled of expensive cigars.

The clerk seemed a little alarmed when Frank walked in. Like most people, he recognized Frank immediately as a policeman, even though he wore an ordinary suit of clothes and should have been indistinguishable from thousands of other men in the city. People always knew, though, and Frank had long since given up trying to fool anyone. He usually found that actually worked to his advantage.

"May I help you?" the young man asked.

"I'd like to see Gilbert Giddings," he said, offering no other explanation. He didn't want to say anything that might get Giddings in trouble later if he'd had nothing to do with Anna Blake's death. He didn't want to get himself into any trouble either. Antagonizing an attorney unnecessarily made about as much sense as poking a bear in the eye with a stick.

The mention of Giddings's name, however, only seemed to alarm the clerk more. "Please wait . . . uh, have a seat and I'll . . . I'll be right back," he stammered as he hurried off into the rear offices.

Frank hardly had time to sit down before the clerk was back. He seemed a bit calmer, and he escorted Frank down a hallway to a large office at the far end. Frank was extremely impressed that Giddings commanded such magnificent accommodations until he realized the man behind the desk was not Gilbert Giddings.

The clerk made his escape without introducing him.

"I was looking for Giddings," Frank said.

"I know. Wilbur told me," the man behind the desk said. He was an older man with just the slightest bit of white fuzz left on his round head. He didn't stand, probably because it was an effort to wrestle his equally round body up out of the oversized chair in which he sat. Or else because he didn't think Frank was worth the effort. He also didn't invite Frank to sit. "I'm Albert Smythe, the senior partner here. Perhaps I can help you instead."

"I'm Detective Sergeant Frank Malloy with the New York City Police," Frank replied, "and only Giddings can help me."

"Then you have wasted your time coming here, Mr. Malloy. Mr. Giddings is no longer employed here."

6

Frank DIGESTED THIS INFORMATION. GIDDINGS HAD given no indication of this earlier today. He had, however, offered his business card without protest, probably because he knew Frank wouldn't find him here. "That's interesting," Frank said, betraying no reaction. "I don't suppose you know where he is now employed."

"I do not believe he is employed anywhere," Mr. Smythe said.

And if he was, Smythe wouldn't have told a policeman, Frank thought, but he said, "I need to speak with him on official business. Even though he no longer works for you, maybe you could help me locate him."

"I am not in the habit of assisting the police," he said without the slightest compunction.

"That's a shame," Frank replied, not offended in the least. "You see, I need to speak to Giddings about the murder of a young woman who may have been carrying his child. If he's arrested for the crime, I might be annoyed enough by your lack of cooperation to make sure the newspapers mention the name of your law firm as his employer."

Smythe's bloodless lips tightened and a slight flush rose

on his flabby, white neck, but he betrayed no other outward sign of his true emotions. "You are an expert negotiator," he allowed grudgingly. "You should have been an attorney."

Frank couldn't help a small grin. "My mother wanted me to have a respectable profession." Since police work was considered completely disreputable by people like Smythe, Frank wouldn't have been surprised to be summarily thrown out.

But Smythe merely nodded his acknowledgment of the barb. "Wilbur will help you find Giddings's address."

He must have given some sort of silent signal, because at that moment the clerk knocked and came into the office, a questioning look on his young face.

"Please provide this gentleman with Mr. Giddings's home address, Wilbur. Good day to you, sir," he said, dismissing Frank.

"I'll remember your assistance," Frank promised.

"I'll be happier if you forget you ever heard my name," Smythe said and went back to reading the papers on his large, shiny desk.

Wilbur escorted Frank back to the front office and bid him be seated while he found the information Frank wanted. A few moments later, the boy handed him a sheet of expensive, watermarked paper bearing the neatly printed address of a house in the genteel neighborhood near Gramercy Park.

Frank carefully folded the paper and put it in his pocket, taking his time as Wilbur continued to wait apprehensively. Maybe he was afraid Frank would arrest him or something. He felt like shouting "Boo!" just to see the fellow jump, but somehow resisted the urge.

Out on the street, Frank checked his watch and found that he still had time to stop by the Giddings home before going to his own flat for supper. Giddings's house was on his way home anyway.

Most nights he worked too late to see his son before the boy went to sleep. For too long, he'd used his job as an excuse to completely avoid the anguish that seeing Brian caused him. Not only was the boy's existence a constant reminder of the mother who had died giving him life, but his pitiful condition was a painful affront, proving how helpless Frank was at the hands of fate.

Sarah Brandt and her meddling had changed all that. Everyone else had branded Brian a feeble-minded cripple, but she saw what no one had ever noticed. She'd shamed Frank into taking the boy to see a surgeon who had operated on his club foot, with a promise Brian would be able to walk when he was finished. Then she had seen the intelligence glimmering in Brian's bright blue eyes when no one else had bothered to look for it, and she had realized that his mind was fine, except for being locked inside of a body that couldn't hear. Soon Frank would make a choice about what kind of training he was going to get for the boy, but he'd decided to wait until his foot was healed before making any more changes in Brian's young life.

Of course, he might have just been using that as an excuse. If the truth were told, it wasn't the boy he was so worried about upsetting. His mother was difficult in the best of times, and now she was frightened. She wanted what was right for Brian, of course, but she didn't agree with Frank about what that might be, especially if it meant Frank didn't need her to care for the child any longer. Nothing he said made much difference, so arguing with her was frustrating and annoying. But he'd tolerate her tonight for the boy's sake. In some ways it was a blessing Brian couldn't hear.

Frank took the Third Avenue Elevated Train downtown and got off at Twenty-Third Street. He couldn't help noticing how different this area was from the neighborhood where he lived, just a few blocks south. The city was like that, changing character almost from street to street, the comfortable middle-class living cheek-by-jowl with the desperately poor and the obscenely rich. As bad as things were in the city, with people being killed every day for a few coins and homeless children starving or freezing in every nook and cranny, he wondered that it wasn't worse.

If the poor ever decided to rise up, their sheer numbers would overpower those who considered themselves the powerful ones in the city.

If that ever did happen, which side would Frank be on? he wondered as he found the Giddings home in the middle of a row of neatly kept homes. Unlike similar homes located below Washington Square, such as the one where Anna Blake had lived, all these houses still held only single families. No boardinghouses or brothels here. Giddings had done quite well for himself at Smythe, Masterson and Judd. Until recently, that is.

Frank climbed the front steps, noticing they hadn't been swept in a day or two. Giddings's servants were poorly disciplined. Frank made a loud clatter with the brass knocker and waited. Although he'd made enough noise to rouse the dead, no one responded the first time or even the second time he pounded the metal against the shiny plate. Finally, he saw one of the front curtains move as someone looked out, and he gave the knocker another determined try, hoping to convince whoever was inside that he wasn't leaving until someone answered the door.

At last the door opened a crack, just enough for someone to peer out.

"Who are you and what do you want?" a woman asked.

If this was a maid, she was poorly trained. "I'm Detective Sergeant Frank Malloy from the New York City Police, and I'm here to see Gilbert Giddings."

His tone told her he would force his way inside if necessary, and the door opened a bit farther. Now he could see the woman, and she wasn't a maid. Her clothes were simple, a white shirtwaist and black skirt, which meant she could have been the housekeeper, except Frank knew she wasn't. She held herself too stiffly, and her manner was too polished, too commanding, for her to have been a servant.

"Come inside before my neighbors hear you," she said sharply and stepped aside to admit him.

The moment he entered the house, he knew something wasn't right. It had a cold, empty feeling. A glance around told him why—it really was empty, or very nearly. The entry had no furniture or carpet, and when he glanced into the front parlor, he saw that it, too, had been cleared. It wasn't the newness of a house recently inhabited, either. He could see where carpets had lain on the floors and bright places on the wallpaper where pictures had once hung.

"Mr. Giddings isn't here," she said.

Frank turned his attention back to the woman. "Are you Mrs. Giddings?" he guessed.

She seemed reluctant to reply, but finally, she nodded once. She might have been an attractive woman if her face hadn't been so bloodless and pinched. Plainly, she was under a great strain and had summoned every ounce of her courage and strength to bear up under it.

"When do you expect him back?" Frank asked.

Her hands were gripping each other so tightly in front of her that the knuckles were white. "I don't . . . Do you mind . . . ?" She took a fortifying breath. "Could you tell me why you wish to see him?"

The question had cost her a great deal of effort, and Frank didn't like the feeling of pity that stirred in his chest. Pity was an emotion that could get him in trouble if he let it blind him to the truth. Still, he had no intention of telling her his real reason for wanting to find her husband. He'd promised Giddings not to say anything to ruin him for at least a few days. He'd broken that promise with Smythe only because Smythe obviously knew about Giddings's faults and the old attorney had no intention of making the news public. Mrs. Giddings would be hurt by the knowledge, however, so until it was absolutely necessary for her to know, he was determined to keep it from her.

"It's a private matter," he told her. "Nothing to concern you. I just need some information from him."

He saw the muscles in her jaw work, as if she were clenching it to help maintain her composure. Now that his eyes had adjusted to the dim interior light, he could see that her dark hair, which was pulled severely back from her face and knotted at her neck, had streaks of silver running through it. Her eyes were shadowed from lack of sleep, and tension practically radiated from her. "Did Mr. Smythe send you?" she asked.

"He gave me your address," Frank admitted.

He'd thought the reply harmless enough, but Mrs. Giddings cried out. The sound was short and sharp, as if someone had struck her, and she instantly covered her mouth with one hand. "He said he wouldn't prosecute!" she said when she'd regained a little of her composure. "He said if Gilbert resigned quietly, he wouldn't press charges! Surely he hasn't changed his mind. He only cares about his good name. He must know Gilbert would never say a thing!" She looked as if she might faint.

"Maybe you should call your maid or something," Frank suggested, knowing he didn't want to deal with a fainting woman.

"I don't have a maid!" she said, her voice almost strangled with bitterness. "I've let all the servants go. Can't you see? Why do you think I answered my own door? And we paid the money back. We had to sell almost everything we owned, but we paid back every penny. What more does he want from us?"

"What money is that?" Frank asked.

"The money Gilbert st—" she began, but caught herself. "You don't know about the money?" she asked, her eyes narrowing suspiciously. "I thought you said you're from the police."

"I am," Frank said, his mind racing for a way to ease her suspicions and keep her talking at the same time, "but Mr. Smythe didn't give me any details."

She took a step backward. "Why did you want to see Gilbert, then?"

"I told you, I need to ask him some questions."

"About what?"

"It's a private matter," Frank repeated.

She wasn't going to tell him a thing, he knew. She was probably going to order him out, too, but the sound of a door closing in the back of the house distracted her.

"Mother, where are you?" a male voice called.

She turned to Frank, nearly desperate now. "Get out of

here," she said in an urgent whisper. "Go before he sees you."

But it was too late. A tall young man came into the hall-way from the door behind the stairs, and he stopped when he saw Frank. "Who are you?" he asked with a frown.

His clothes were shabby and dirty, and he wore sturdy work boots. Giddings the Lawyer's son was doing manual labor. Giddings had been fired from his job, his family had sold everything of value that they owned to pay Smythe a debt, and his young son was struggling to help. This was not a happy home.

"He's no one," Mrs. Giddings replied for Frank. "He was just leaving."

"If you're a bill collector, you can talk to me," the boy said, striding belligerently up to Frank. He was still gangly with youth, probably no more than sixteen, but in spite of his ragged appearance, he had a dignity about him. He was like his mother in that. Determined to protect her, he lifted his hairless chin and glared at Frank. "You don't have any right to come here. We've told you we'll pay you as soon as we've sold the house."

"I'm not a bill collector," Frank said. He couldn't help admiring the way the boy had assumed his manhood and all the responsibilities that went with it.

"Who are you, then?" he asked, looking him up and down with contempt.

"Harold, don't get involved in this," his mother begged. "Go to your room. I'll take care of it."

"You've taken care of enough," Harold said stubbornly. "What do you want?" he asked Frank again.

"I came to see your father. If you'll just tell me where to find him—"

"He's probably at some bar," the boy said, his lip curl-ing with distaste. "He'll be there until they throw him out and he doesn't have any choice but to come home. But at least he won't be with that woman anymore," he said to his mother, laying a comforting arm across her shoulders. "I can promise you that."

"What woman are you talking about?" Frank asked,

wondering how the boy knew Anna Blake would no longer be receiving visitors.

"Stop it, Harold," Mrs. Giddings said, this time in a tone that brooked no argument. "This man is from the police. Mr. Smythe sent him."

"The police," the boy echoed in alarm, all his bravado evaporating. "What do you want with my father?"

"What do you think he wants?" his mother asked, no longer bothering to hide her bitterness. "Smythe wasn't satisfied with getting the money back. Now he's going to put your father in prison." A lesser woman would have broken under this weight, but Mrs. Giddings hung on to her composure with the last vestiges of her strength, determined not to humiliate herself in front of a stranger.

"I'm not going to arrest him," Frank tried in an attempt to ease her anguish, but the boy wasn't listening.

"It's that woman," Harold said, his voice shrill with rage. "She did this. She made him steal that money, and now he's going to shame us by going to prison. I'm going to kill him!" he cried and would have made for the front door if Frank hadn't grabbed him.

He put up a struggle, but he was no match for Frank's superior size and strength, and his mother's pleas. By the time Frank had subdued him, he was sobbing with fury and shame.

"Where can I take him?" he asked Mrs. Giddings, as he held the boy up on his feet. She led them down the hallway to the back parlor.

This room had also been scavenged for salable items, but a few pieces of furniture remained, among them a well-worn sofa. Frank sat the boy down on it. He slumped over, head in his hands, still weeping.

His mother sat down beside him, holding him to her and offering what comfort she could.

"Your husband stole money from his employer to pay off his mistress," Frank said. He wasn't asking a question.

Mrs. Giddings looked up from consoling her son, her eyes dark with hatred. "You already knew that."

Frank wasn't going to contradict her. Besides, he now

knew that Giddings had stolen money to pay off Anna
Blake and ruined himself and his family in the process,
which meant Giddings had more reason to want Anna
Blake dead than Nelson Ellsworth did.

"How long did your husband know this young
woman?" Frank asked.

"I have no idea," Mrs. Giddings said, patting her son's
back as he continued to weep out his grief on her shoulder.
"Don't you have any decency? And what does any of this
matter? Leave us alone!"

Frank could have told her how it mattered, but he still
wanted to spare her unnecessary anguish. If Giddings
wasn't the killer . . . He also wanted to ask the boy some
questions, but he figured this wasn't the time to get a
straight answer out of him. Better to wait and catch him
alone, without his mother to protect him. It wouldn't take
much at all to frighten the boy into telling everything he
knew.

"Which bar does your husband usually go to?"

"He doesn't consult me," Mrs. Giddings told him, still
stubbornly clinging to her pride. "I'm afraid we can't help
you."

Or wouldn't, at least. Frank figured she wasn't going to
make it easy for him to put her husband in jail, if that's
what he intended, no matter how angry she might be at
him.

"Just tell your husband I called," Frank said, and
showed himself out.

So Giddings's family knew all about his affair with
Anna Blake. And Frank knew some interesting information about Giddings. He was desperate indeed if he'd
stolen from his own law firm to pay her off. Unlike Nelson, he had a family and a reputation to protect from the
scandal she could cause him, so he'd been ripe for blackmail. Frank was beginning to regret never having met
Anna Blake in life. She must have been an interesting
woman to have inspired such foolish devotion.

• • •

"I knew something terrible was going to happen," Mrs. Ellsworth confided to Sarah as they cleaned up the kitchen after their meager supper. "Remember I asked if you'd heard knocking the other night?"

"Yes," Sarah said, not really certain. She didn't make an effort to remember all of Mrs. Ellsworth's superstitions.

"I heard it three nights in a row. That means someone is going to die. I knew it was going to happen, and I was so afraid it would be someone I knew," she said sadly as she took the dishes off the tray she'd taken up to Nelson earlier.

He hadn't come down, and he'd barely touched the food on the tray. Sarah hoped it wasn't only grief for such an undeserving woman that had him so upset.

"The things you worry about never happen," Sarah said, quoting her mother. "It's the things you never imagine that hurt you the worst."

"That's the truth," Mrs. Ellsworth said with a sigh and looked up, as if she might be able to see her son if she did. "I just wish he could go to work. If he had something to take his mind off all of this, but . . ."

"But the reporters would never give him a moment's peace," Sarah said.

"I'm so afraid he's going to lose his job," the old woman said. "The people at the bank are only concerned about the good name of the bank. No one wants to leave their money in a place run by scoundrels and . . . and murderers." She shuddered.

"Nelson isn't a murderer," Sarah reminded her.

"What difference does it make? The newspapers say he is, and so people believe that. Next I expect the neighbors to come and tell me we have to move because we're giving the place a bad name."

"That isn't going to happen. Malloy and I are going to find who really did this so all our lives can get back to normal again. But first I'm going to track down that reporter Webster Prescott and make him write the truth about Nelson."

Mrs. Ellsworth's eyes lit up with hope. "Can you do that?"

"I'm certainly going to try. And if I have to, I'll go to the bank and ask them to give Nelson the benefit of the doubt until we can get this thing settled."

"Oh, Mrs. Brandt, I couldn't ask you to do that!" she protested.

"You didn't ask me; I volunteered. Besides, I'm sure my father knows the bank's owner personally. He'll be happy to put in a good word for Nelson," she promised rashly. Her father certainly wouldn't be happy to do any such thing, but Sarah felt certain she could prevail upon him to do it anyway.

"What on earth would we do without you?" Mrs. Ellsworth asked, taking Sarah's hand in both of hers.

Frank wearily climbed the stairs to his flat. The sounds of family arguments and babies crying echoed faintly in the stairwell. He reached the door and knocked, not bothering to find his key. His mother opened the door without asking who it was.

"Ma, I've told you it's not safe—"

"I saw you coming," she said, waving away his protests. "Or rather the boy did. He watches for you every night."

Frank felt a twinge of guilt, but he forgot it the instant Brian managed to crawl around her to reach him. His little face was so full of joy at seeing his father, Frank felt guilty again, this time because he knew he wasn't worthy of such adoration. That didn't stop him from picking the boy up and hugging him fiercely. Brian hugged him back, his thin arms clinging with amazing strength around Frank's neck.

Brian's red-gold curls were silken against Frank's cheek, and he smelled sweet and clean and innocent when Frank buried his face in the soft curve of his neck. The only thing missing was Brian crying, "Papa! Papa!" the way other boys his age would have. Of course, other boys his age would have run, not crawled, to greet their fathers, but soon that should change as well.

"How's he doing?" he asked his mother as he carried Brian over to the sofa and sat down, setting the boy on his lap. He inspected the cast, which was growing dirtier every day.

"He don't cry so much or try to get it off," she reported, disapproval thick in her voice just the same. "I don't think it hurts him much anymore. Or maybe he's just used to it."

"How'll you keep up when Brian starts running around the place?" Frank asked, only half in jest. "It won't be long now."

She crossed herself, as if to ward off a curse. "It ain't good to wish for too much," she reminded him. "You'll just be disappointed."

Brian was showing Frank the cast, trying with gestures to convince him to take it off. "In good time, son," he said, even though Brian couldn't hear him. "Then you'll be able to walk."

His mother made a rude noise. "I'll get your supper."

"Are you going with me when I take Brian to get the cast off?" Frank asked.

She just gave him one of her looks and retreated into the kitchen.

The next morning Frank decided to begin his day with a visit to the morgue. It was Saturday, but he was sure to find someone around, and he wanted to learn all he could about how Anna Blake had died. Chances were slim he'd discover anything that would help him identify her killer, but it was worth a chance. Besides, he now had two men who could possibly have been the father of her child. Maybe if the coroner could tell him how far along she was, he could figure out which one really was. He wasn't sure what that would tell him, but the more information he had, the better off he'd be.

The entire morgue smelled of death, even the offices, and Frank steeled himself against the grimness of the place. The gray walls and barren corridors seemed to stretch for miles and echo with the sound of his footsteps. He found the coroner in his shabby little office, writing a report. Dr. Haynes looked up, his eyes weary behind his glasses.

"Which one is yours?" he asked, not bothering with a greeting. In a place like this, social amenities were meaningless.

"Anna Blake, stabbed in Washington Square," he added, in case the name meant nothing.

Dr. Haynes shuffled through some papers on his desk and found the one he was looking for. He peered closely at it for a moment. "I thought that one was Brougham's."

"I'm helping him," Frank said without blinking.

Haynes stared at him in amazement but made no comment on this astonishing bit of news. "What do you want to know, besides that somebody stabbed her and she's dead?"

"Do you know what she was stabbed with?"

"A knife," Haynes said just to be aggravating.

"You're better than that," Frank chided, trying to stir what might remain of the man's pride. "Big, small, butcher knife, stiletto, or what?"

"Bigger than a stiletto. She wasn't killed by the Black Hand," he said, referring to the Italian secret society famous for using the thin-bladed knife. "Smaller than a butcher knife. The blade was no longer than six inches. Probably just an ordinary kitchen knife, in fact. They didn't find it, whatever it was."

"If it was lying around, someone would've taken it. That's a pretty desperate bunch in the Square after dark. What else can you tell me about her?"

Haynes studied the report another moment, his forehead wrinkled in thought. Frank imagined him picturing the dead woman in his mind, trying to recall what she looked like. But maybe he was just being fanciful.

"She didn't get stabbed where she was found," he said after a moment.

"What makes you think that?" No one had even suggested such a thing until now.

"The way she bled. She'd bunched up her shawl and held it against the wound for a while, to keep it from bleeding, I guess. You could see where it was wrinkled and the one end was soaked with blood. But blood seeped down the whole front of her skirt anyway. That means she was on her feet for a while before she got too weak. I don't think somebody who got stabbed would just stand still in the middle of the Square on a dark night if they could stand at all, so she was probably trying to get herself some help."

"Why didn't she just call out?" Frank wondered aloud.

"Who there would help her?" Haynes replied.

"You're right. She'd be a fool to let that bunch know she was wounded. They'd fall on her like vultures, taking whatever she had and leaving her to die. She must've been trying to get back home, where she's be safe."

"Did she live close by?"

"Just a couple blocks from the Square. How far could she have gone with a wound like that?"

"Not far. You could check for blood stains on the ground. She probably left some along the way."

Frank shook his head. "It rained that morning. Even still, after three days, I doubt there'd be any trace left. The Square is a busy place."

Haynes nodded. "But if she was walking, maybe somebody saw her."

"In the dark? And if they did, how will I find them?" Frank replied in disgust. "Decent people would've been locked in their houses, and the others wouldn't tell a cop anything." He sighed. "What else can you tell me about her?"

"What else do you need to know?"

"How far along was she?"

"How far along?" Haynes echoed in confusion.

"She was expecting a child. How far along was she?"

"She wasn't expecting a child."

Frank stared at him in amazement. "Are you sure?"

"Sure as I can be. I saw her insides, you know. Not only that, she was using a sponge."

"Where would she be wearing a sponge?" he asked in confusion.

Haynes grinned and shook his head. "I forget you Catholic boys don't believe in those things."

"What things?"

"Things that keep a woman from getting pregnant."

"How would a sponge do that?"

Haynes's grinned widened. "A woman puts it up inside of her. Keeps the man's . . . uh, seed from getting in to make a baby. From what I saw, this one had seen some recent use, too."

Frank sank down in the dingy metal chair in front of Haynes's desk. This was very interesting information. "Can I see that report for myself, Doc?"

"Help yourself, if you can read my chicken scratching." Haynes handed the paper to him.

This changed everything, Frank realized as he painstakingly deciphered the crabbed handwriting. Anna Blake wasn't what she'd seemed at all, and Frank had a good idea he'd uncover some even more unsavory facts now that he knew the truth about her. He also had a feeling he might find a lot more people who wanted her dead besides poor Nelson.

But the biggest problem he had now was how he was going to tell Sarah Brandt about the sponge.

Sarah looked up at the imposing building on Park Row that housed the *World*. Mr. Joseph Pulitzer had spared no expense in making his building the most ostentatious on the street where all the major newspapers in the city had their offices. Standing twenty-six stories, it had been the tallest building in the world when it was built a few short years ago, and it still towered over most of the city. The title of tallest building hadn't stood very long before someone built a taller one in Chicago, but the building's dome was covered with copper that glittered like gold in the morning sunlight. Surely that would distinguish it for a longer time. Outside on the sidewalk, a lighted globe, seventeen feet in diameter, showed the points of the compass. People loved a spectacle, and Pulitzer gave it to them with his building and with his newspapers.

Sarah had to thread her way through the jumble of pushcart vendors displaying their fruits and vegetables to the hoards of people walking across the Brooklyn Bridge in both directions. The entrance to the bridge was nearby, and between the crowds of workers coming and going on the bridge and those employed in the newspaper offices, the vendors did a brisk business.

Inside, Sarah could feel the rumble of the giant presses that churned out the morning and evening editions of the *World*. The sensation made the building feel as if it were alive and trembling. Everywhere people, mostly men, were coming and going in a great hurry, either off to find news or coming in to write it. She'd thought that Saturday morning would be a good time to catch Webster Prescott in, but now she was afraid she'd been mistaken. Did reporters ever go to their offices? She realized she was woefully ignorant of the habits of newspapermen. For all she knew, he spent all his time standing on the sidewalk outside the homes of those unfortunate enough to have made themselves newsworthy.

Sarah made her way to the elevators, checked the building directory, and gave the correct floor number to the operator when the car arrived. A few moments later, the operator opened the doors on an enormous room that covered the entire floor of the building. Sarah stepped off the elevator with a confidence she didn't feel, and the elevator doors slammed shut behind her.

The room was lined with row after row of desks, broken only by the columns that supported the ceiling. Tall windows on all four sides let in the sunlight and revealed a breathtaking view of the city in every direction. No one else seemed aware of the view, however. About a third of the desks were occupied by men writing furiously or typing on typewriters. Others, most of whom were hardly old enough to be called men, were hurrying here and there, carrying sheaves of papers, depositing them on desks and picking up more.

One of these boys glanced at her curiously as he passed,

and she stopped him. "Excuse me, but could you tell me where Webster Prescott would be?"

"Pres? Sure," the boy said, scanning the room. "His desk's over there and . . . looks like he's sitting at it, too. Can you see him?"

"Yes," Sarah said, peering in the direction he indicated. "Thank you."

She made her way through the noisy room, drawing more curious stares which she ignored. This far above the presses, she could no longer feel the vibrations of them, but the clatter of typewriters and the rumble of men's voices were equally loud and disturbing. She tried to imagine sitting in a room like this all day and cringed at the thought. But then, the reporters would be out a lot, getting their stories, so perhaps it wasn't as bad as it might seem.

She stopped in front of Prescott's desk. He was engrossed in the story he was writing, but when her shadow fell across it, he looked up. She saw the recognition register on his face and the frown as he tried to dredge up a name to go with her face.

"Sarah Brandt," she supplied.

"Nelson Ellsworth's neighbor," he added happily. He obviously thought her presence meant something good for him, a scoop perhaps. "Please, sit down, Mrs. Brandt. Let me find you a chair."

He borrowed one from a neighboring desk where no one was sitting and pulled it up for her. "What brings you here this fine morning?" he asked pleasantly when she was settled and he'd taken his own seat.

"I've come to ask you a favor," she said.

His smile evaporated. He'd be wanting *her* to do a favor for *him*. "I'll be happy to help if I can," he said, although she could see he was only being polite so as not to alienate a potential source of news.

"I want you to print the truth about Nelson Ellsworth."

Now she had his attention again. "What truth do you want me to tell?" He reached blindly for the notebook that lay open on his desk and pulled a pencil from over his ear.

"First of all, Nelson didn't kill that woman."

This wasn't what he wanted to hear. "But the evidence—"

"—is misleading. It seems that Mr. Ellsworth wasn't the only man with whom Miss Blake was involved."

"She had another lover?" he asked, brightening again.

"Yes, and this one is married."

He began to scribble notes in his book. "What's his name?"

"I don't know," she lied. "But he's certainly an even likelier candidate than Nelson, and unless the newspapers stop blackening Nelson's name, he might well be convicted of the killing anyway, even though he wouldn't hurt a fly. Nelson was genuinely in love with Anna Blake and wanted to marry her. She's the one who refused. She wanted him to give her money instead."

Prescott's young face creased into a frown. "That's very strange."

"I thought so. No honest woman would prefer money to respectability. Nelson Ellsworth is an innocent victim in this. I think Anna Blake deliberately chose him, thinking he would be easy to fool. I'm not exactly sure what her plan was, but she wasn't interested in snagging an eligible husband. She could have had one in Nelson, and she refused him."

"Even though she was . . . well, in a family way?"

"So it appears. I came down here to tell you that there's a better story here than the one all the newspapers have been telling about Nelson, and it also happens to be the true one. You could make quite a name for yourself if you're the first one to discover it, Mr. Prescott."

His eyes were sparkling with anticipation, but he hadn't forgotten his instincts. "Why are you going to all this trouble to protect Ellsworth, Mrs. Brandt?"

Malloy had warned her about the danger of doing this, but she'd hoped Prescott was too naive or inexperienced to think of it. She'd been wrong about that, but she still might be able to convince him of her good intentions. "Because his mother once saved my life, and I owe her a debt of gratitude. Nelson is her only son, and I can't stand by and see him ruined and maybe even executed, especially when I know he's innocent."

Prescott wasn't as easily dissuaded. "How can you be so sure? Can you give him an alibi for that night?" he asked with a suggestive grin.

"No, I cannot," she replied, refusing to be ruffled. "An innocent man doesn't need an alibi."

Prescott shook his head sadly. "Oh, Mrs. Brandt, an innocent man needs an alibi most of all."

7

Saturday morning was probably a good time to catch her mother alone, Sarah thought. She'd made two promises to Mrs. Ellsworth, and seeing Webster Prescott was just the first. She'd also agreed to convince the bank not to fire Nelson. For that she'd need more than the gumption that had taken her into the *World*. For that she'd need Felix Decker. Since the best way to influence her father was through her mother, that's where Sarah headed next.

As she rode the Sixth Avenue Elevated uptown, she wondered whether she'd made the right decision in going to Prescott. He'd seemed enthusiastic about her story and had promised to investigate. Of course, that might mean he'd come up with something even more outlandish than the reports of Nelson being a killer. It might even mean involving herself in this scandal. That was, however, a chance she'd been willing to take. If her good name was completely ruined in this cause and decent women no longer hired her to deliver their babies, she could always throw herself on her father's mercy. He'd be only too glad to take her back into his home—and his control—once again, she thought grimly.

But she wouldn't borrow trouble, as Mrs. Ellsworth would have advised her. She had to hope Malloy was making progress in finding Anna's real killer. Meanwhile, she'd do what she could to make sure this terrible situation wasn't any worse for Nelson than it already had been and that he had a job to return to when he could safely leave his house again.

Her parents lived on Fifty-Seventh Street, not far from the Plaza Hotel and Marble Row on Fifth Avenue, home to the more ostentatious of the wealthy. The Deckers' town house appeared modest on the outside, which suited them. They had always been modest about their wealth.

The maid seemed surprised to see her, since few members of society were stirring at this hour, but she admitted her and escorted her to the back parlor, which was the comfortable room the family used. In a few minutes, the maid came back, alone.

"Your mother asked me to take you up to her room, since she isn't dressed yet," the girl said.

Sarah smiled. Her mother must be appalled that Sarah was not only dressed but out and about so early on a Saturday, although by most people's standards, it wasn't early at all. She followed the maid up the stairs and down the corridor. Her mother's voice bid her enter when the girl knocked.

Elizabeth Decker looked like a girl herself, draped in a silk dressing gown and half reclining on her settee. Her golden hair lay loose on her shoulders, and in the dimly lit room, the silver strands weren't visible. Neither were the fine lines that the years had etched on her lovely face, and the smile of greeting she gave Sarah banished any lingering illusion of age.

"Sarah, how delightful to see you!" she said, reaching up to return Sarah's kiss of greeting.

Her mother's cheek was soft beneath her lips, and Sarah felt a rush of fond memories at the touch. Memories of happier days, long before she and her sister had grown old enough to see the world the way it really was and to rebel against the lives they had been bred to assume.

"What urgent business has brought you out at this un-fashionable hour?" her mother asked, bringing her back to the present.

"What makes you think I have urgent business?" Sarah asked, seating herself on the slipper chair beside her mother. The room was decorated in shades of rose, with elaborately carved cherry wood furnishings. The color, Sarah realized, was very flattering to a woman of a certain age, especially when the morning light was filtered through it.

"I don't want to sound accusing, but it seems the only time you come to visit me is when you need my assistance in one of your wild escapades," she chided.

"Oh, Mother, I—"

"I'm not complaining, mind you," her mother said, rais-ing her hand to stop Sarah's protest. "I suppose I should be glad you live such an interesting life. Otherwise, I might never see you at all. Now, what is it you want me to do?"

"Actually, it's father's help I need this time," Sarah ad-mitted.

Her mother sighed in feigned disgust. "So you're only using me to influence your father," she complained. "I might have known it would come to this. Really, Sarah, I'd think you'd learned your lesson. The last time you asked for our help, it ended very badly."

Sarah winced, remembering just how badly. "No one is going to end up dead this time, I promise."

"I should hope not! Mrs. Schyler won't even speak to me anymore."

"Oh, Mother, you never liked her anyway. She's a terri-ble woman."

"Yes, but you might alienate someone I do like if I'm not careful. Who is it you want to meet this time?"

"I'm not sure," Sarah admitted.

"Not sure? Then how do you think your father can help?"

Sarah sighed. She'd have to tell her mother the whole story. "Well, you see, there's been a murder . . ."

"Oh, Sarah, how do you manage to get involved in

these things?" her mother cried in dismay. "I'm almost twice as old as you, and I've never even *known* anyone who was murdered!"

"I didn't know this person either," Sarah defended herself. "Not well, at least."

Her mother put a hand to her forehead and shook her head sadly.

"My neighbor has been accused of killing her, you see and—"

"Oh, dear, stop right there. Let me ring for some tea. I can see this is going to be a long story, and I, for one, need fortification. Pull the bell, will you, dear?"

An hour later, Sarah and her mother were finishing up their tea and the last of the delicious pastries the cook had sent up with it, just as Sarah finished her story.

"I promised Mrs. Ellsworth I'd help Nelson keep his job at the bank, but I know there's nothing I can do. If I walked in there and asked to see the president of the bank, they might let me in to see him, but he'd probably laugh right in my face or worse. It seems that when a woman takes an interest in helping a man, people always assume there is some romantic attachment between them. That's not only annoying, but it also causes people to misinterpret the woman's motives in trying to help."

"You don't have to instruct me in the ways of the world, Sarah. I understood them long before you were born. At least you have the good sense not to involve yourself in this. You could do this poor man more harm than good if you did. Can you imagine what the newspapers would say if they found out who your father is?"

Sarah simply nodded, knowing anything she said on the subject would upset her mother. She only hoped she never had to explain just how Webster Prescott had come to name her as Nelson Ellsworth's paramour in *The World*.

"You were right to come to us," her mother was saying. "I'm sure your father can speak to the president of this bank, whoever he is. Of course, if your friend is arrested for murder, I'm not sure even your father's influence would save the man's job."

"My friend Mr. Malloy is working on the case. I'm sure he'll find the real killer very soon," Sarah said to reassure her.

Her mother looked far from reassured, however. "Are you still seeing that policeman, Sarah?"

"I was never *seeing* him, Mother," Sarah said. "We are friends, nothing more."

"An unmarried female can never be just friends with an unmarried man, not in the eyes of the world. You must know that yourself. Do you have any idea how easily such a relationship can be misconstrued?"

"Of course I do," she insisted. "And believe me, there is nothing between us that could even be misconstrued."

"I hope not. You know we didn't approve of your marriage to Dr. Brandt. Not that we had anything against him, of course. He was a fine man. But you gave up everything for him, Sarah."

"I didn't give up anything I ever regretted losing," Sarah said, ignoring the flash of pain the mention of her late husband caused.

Another kind of pain flashed in her mother's eyes, but she chose not to dwell on it. "Even though we didn't want to see you so reduced in circumstances, at least Dr. Brandt was a respectable man with an honest profession. But a policeman, Sarah? They're worse than the criminals they deal with!"

Her mother was right; policemen were corrupt. Malloy was as honest as he could be, under the circumstances, but even that wouldn't meet her mother's standards. "You're worrying for no reason, Mother. I have no intention of marrying Mr. Malloy, and he has no intention of marrying me."

"I don't see how he could have," she said. "He's Irish, isn't he? They aren't allowed to marry outside their faith."

By "Irish," she meant "Catholic," and being Irish Catholic was a far greater sin in Elizabeth Decker's eyes than being a dishonest policeman. Sarah wanted to chasten her for such prejudice, but she knew it would be a waste of breath and would only distract her from her real purpose in being here. "As I said, we aren't going to marry, so it can't possibly matter," she said wearily.

Only then did she see the depth of concern in her mother's blue eyes. "There are more things than that to worry about, dear. Be careful, Sarah. I know you're lonely, and this man knows it, too. He'll try to prey on that loneliness. Don't let him deceive you, darling. Don't be a fool."

So that's what her mother was really concerned about! Sarah should have been angry at her lack of faith, but the thought of Malloy as a sly seducer of lonely widows was so ludicrous, she could only laugh. And when she thought of Malloy's mother and how she'd probably given him exactly the same warning about Sarah, she laughed harder.

Her mother stared at her incredulously. "Sarah?"

"Oh, mother, if you only knew . . . Believe me, you don't need to worry about Malloy, not for one moment. My virtue and reputation are safe. In fact, they couldn't be safer."

Her mother frowned in confusion, but she didn't press the matter. Sarah had either alarmed her or reassured her, but whichever it was, she was willing to let the subject drop.

"Is Father home today?" Sarah asked when she had composed herself.

"I believe he is. Let's find out, shall we?"

She and her mother discussed society gossip, avoiding personal topics by unspoken consent, while they waited for a servant to summon her father. A few minutes later, he knocked on the door connecting their bedrooms, and her mother bid him enter.

"Sarah, you're out early," he said, coming over to kiss her forehead. He wore a dressing gown and a collarless shirt. Plainly, he'd had no plans this morning. He turned to his wife. "Good morning, my dear. You're looking lovely." He also kissed her on the forehead.

Sarah realized she'd never seen her parents embrace. They would think displays of affection unseemly, of course, but still, she liked to think they did at least sometimes display affection, however privately. Why this thought should occur to her at this particular moment in her life, however, she had no idea.

Her father seated himself on the slipper chair that matched hers. "To what mischance do we owe the honor of your visit this morning?" he asked her with a hint of a smile.

"Father, I don't only visit you when I need help," she reminded him.

"No, but you rarely call at dawn on Saturday morning, either," he replied. "This must be urgent indeed."

"Someone has been murdered," her mother informed him with disapproval.

"Dare I ask who? Not someone we know, I hope."

"Not his time," her mother said. "A female of questionable morals, it would appear."

"Then why do you care?" her father asked Sarah, even more disapproving than her mother.

"Because my neighbor has been accused of the crime," Sarah said. "He's innocent, but the newspapers have already pronounced him guilty, and they're saying terrible things about him. Untrue things, and he's probably going to lose his job if someone doesn't do something."

Her father frowned. "Is this that Ellsworth fellow I read about in the papers? They said he seduced some poor woman and killed her when she demanded that he make her an honest woman."

"None of it is true," Sarah said, and briefly gave him the facts as she knew them. "I believe we are going to find the real killer soon, but meanwhile the reporters have been hounding Nelson's employers, and I'm afraid they're going to let him go, innocent or not."

"Who is this 'we' you mentioned?" her father asked.

"What?" Sarah asked in confusion.

"You said 'we' are going to find the killer. What did you mean? You aren't involved with that policeman again, are you?"

Sarah sighed wearily. "Mother already warned me not to let him seduce me, Father. I promise you, you have

nothing to worry about on that score. I only meant that Mr.
Malloy is working to find the killer, and I am working to
help the Ellsworths in whatever way I can. This is why I've
come to you," she quickly continued, before her parents
could press the issue. "If Nelson loses his position at the
bank under these circumstances, he'll never get another
one. He is the sole support of his elderly mother, who also
happens to be a dear friend of mine. Someone needs to
speak with his employer and convince him not to dismiss
him, so I thought I would try to repay the many kindnesses
Mrs. Ellsworth has done for me through the years by saving her son's job, if I could."

Her parents exchanged a glance, and some unspoken
communication passed between them without either of
them so much as batting an eye. Her father turned back to
her, his expression resigned. "What is it you think I can
do?"

Sarah managed not to let her feeling of triumph show. It
would be unseemly to gloat. "Obviously, I can't go into the
bank and beg them not to dismiss Nelson."

"Not without making herself a scandal," her mother
added.

"I was hoping you might have some influence with
someone there who could—"

"Which bank is it?" he asked.

Sarah gave him the name.

He considered for a moment, then turned to his wife.
"Young Dennis is in charge there," he told her.

"Richard?" she said, her expression brightening.

"Yes, his father thought he should have some practical
experience."

"You know him, then?" Sarah asked.

"Very well. His father and I were partners in a business
venture a few years ago."

"Oh, Father, that's wonderful! Would you be willing to
approach him? I wouldn't ask you if it wasn't so important,
but poor Mrs. Ellsworth is so frightened—"

"Of course, of course," he said, dismissing Mrs.
Ellsworth's fears with a wave of his hand. "I don't think it

would be fair for me to approach him on this subject, however. He would certainly feel an obligation to do me this favor, although he might wonder about my motives. Ellsworth is a stranger to me, after all. And if things go badly for Ellsworth, poor Dennis would believe I'd taken advantage of our friendship to get him into an awkward situation. Even worse, he'd be right."

Before Sarah could even register disappointment, her mother said, "But Sarah could argue his case, couldn't she? I mean, if you were to arrange for them to meet. You could summon him here on a business matter, then introduce him to Sarah. He'd realize you were just doing a favor for your daughter, indulging her in this whim even though you didn't really approve, but he'd still feel obligated to help because of his father's association with you."

"Yes," Sarah agreed eagerly. "And if, heaven forbid, things do go badly for Nelson, you can simply apologize for indulging your foolish daughter and dragging him into it."

"He'll forgive you that, surely," her mother said. "Men always understand when another man is imposed upon by a woman."

Her father frowned. "Why do I feel I'm being imposed upon right now?"

"Because you are, dear," her mother said with a sweet smile.

Sarah had just gotten back from delivering supper to the Ellsworths when someone knocked on her door. She smiled when she saw a familiar silhouette reflected through the frosted glass of the front door.

"Malloy," she said in greeting as she opened the door, but her welcoming smile froze on her face when she saw his expression.

"I guess you haven't seen the evening papers," he said, holding up a copy of the *World*.

"No, I—" she began, but he brushed past her, not really interested in her reply. "Is it about Nelson?" she asked as she glanced out onto the street before closing the door. At least the reporters appeared to have gone for the day. Malloy probably wouldn't have come to her front door if they hadn't.

"Was this your idea?" he asked, thrusting the paper at her.

She stared at the headline: WANTON WOMAN DRIVES LOVER TO MURDER.

Skimming the article, she wanted to groan aloud. Webster Prescott had completely misunderstood her plea for help.

"He calls Anna Blake everything but a prostitute," Malloy said. "Where did he get that idea? Every other paper still has her as an innocent victim."

"I just told him Nelson didn't kill her," Sarah insisted. "I asked him to help me save him from being executed!"

"He just might," Malloy said sourly, "if he can get the other papers to turn on Anna Blake, too." He pulled off his bowler hat and hung it on her coat rack without waiting for an invitation to stay.

"But according to this, he's still guilty of murder," Sarah argued. "How can that help him?"

"Because Anna Blake is no longer innocent. She's a harlot who seduced and blackmailed him and then threatened to kill his child unless he paid her. A woman like that deserves whatever she gets, and a lot of men would think she deserves to be murdered."

"That's ridiculous!" Sarah exclaimed.

"Is it? Have you forgotten what people said when Charity Girls were being murdered?"

A few months ago, she and Malloy had solved the murders of several girls who were so desperately poor that they sometimes traded their favors for a few trinkets. Because they went to dance halls and associated with young men, their deaths were ignored. As far as most people were concerned, they'd gotten what they deserved for their loose behavior.

"Men kill their wives and their mistresses all the time," Malloy reminded her. "How many of them ever go to prison, much less hang, for it? That's because their lawyers convince the jury the women were shrews or wantons or whatever, and the men on the jury start thinking how often they've wanted to commit murder in their own homes with far less provocation. If the woman was immoral, she deserved to die, so how can they convict this poor fellow? So they let him go."

Sarah did groan aloud this time. He was right, of course. Far too many women had been falsely vilified in death so that their killers could escape punishment. "I don't care what Anna Blake did, she didn't deserve to die!" Sarah insisted. "And even if she did, Nelson wasn't the one who killed her!"

"What did you offer this reporter to change his story?" Malloy said, his eyes fairly crackling with rage.

"What are you suggesting?" she countered, stung by his implication.

Malloy sighed in exasperation. "You must have promised him something. Reporters are like dogs. They never let go of a bone unless they see a bigger one."

"I simply told him the truth, that Anna Blake had other lovers, so Nelson wasn't necessarily the father of her child, and that she'd refused Nelson's offer of marriage in favor of blackmail."

"That's all?" Plainly he didn't believe it.

"That's *all*," she confirmed. "What other proof did I need that Anna Blake wasn't an honest woman when she refused an offer of marriage to give her child a name?"

"There was no child," Malloy said.

Sarah gaped at him. "What do you mean, no child?"

"Just that. Anna Blake wasn't expecting a child. Do you have any coffee?" He headed off toward her kitchen without waiting for a reply.

She followed in his wake, looking at the story again, trying to find even a hint that Prescott had believed her that Nelson was innocent. She found none.

Malloy sat down at her kitchen table without being invited and waited for her to serve him. She lifted the pot and judged there was enough for one cup in it. It had been sitting for quite a while, but she figured Malloy wouldn't care. She poured it into a cup and set it before him. "Do you want something to eat?"

He waved off her offer. "I'm on my way home."

"How is Brian doing?" she asked, instantly picturing his sweet face.

Malloy shrugged. "He doesn't like the cast, but it doesn't seem to be hurting him much anymore."

Sarah smiled. "He'll be so excited when he finds out he can walk."

Malloy nodded, apparently too superstitious to talk about it.

She decided to let the matter drop for now and sat down in front of him. "All right, what did you mean Anna Blake wasn't with child?" she asked him again.

"The coroner said she wasn't, and he looked pretty close. Besides, she was wearing a . . . a thing." He got very interested in his coffee and wouldn't meet her eye.

"What kind of thing?" she pressed.

He made a vague gesture with his hand, still not meeting her eye. "To keep her from . . ." He waved his hand again.

"From *what*?" she asked in exasperation.

"So she wouldn't get with child in the first place," he said impatiently.

Sarah let this information sink in. "What was she using? A sponge?" she asked in amazement.

Was Malloy blushing? "Yeah, that's . . . that's what the coroner said," he mumbled, still looking intently at his coffee.

Sarah bit back a smile. For someone who spent his life investigating the worst aspect of the human condition, he was awfully prudish. "She lied to Nelson about the baby, then."

"She lied to Giddings, too."

"Was she blackmailing him as well?"

"A lot more successfully than she was Nelson, from the looks of it. He lost his job when he got caught stealing from the law firm where he worked."

"Oh, dear. Do you know what this means? She probably would have tried to get Nelson to steal from the bank, too."

"Why would he? He didn't have a reputation or a family to protect."

He had a good point. "It just doesn't make any sense for her to have been trying to blackmail Nelson, does it?"

"A lot of this doesn't make any sense. I need to talk to her landlady and that other woman who lives there. I'm sure they know more than they're telling, and from what the old woman next door said, that other woman might be doing the same thing Anna was, only with different men."

"How would a neighbor know that?" Sarah asked.

Malloy gave her a pitying look. "Doesn't Mrs. Ellsworth know everything you do?"

"She doesn't know *everything* I do. She knows you call on me, but if I was seducing you and trying to blackmail you, she couldn't know that unless one of us told her," she pointed out.

He gave her one of his looks. "All right, the old woman didn't know about *everything*, but she did see several different men coming and going at the house, more than Anna could have accommodated by herself. They never stepped out with the women, either."

"If they were married, they couldn't risk being seen," Sarah guessed.

"That's what I thought."

"And if several men were calling on each of the women, the landlords had to know about it," Sarah said.

"Especially if they were entertaining the men in their rooms," Malloy pointed out.

"I thought you were going to see Mrs. Walcott today to find out about this."

"She wasn't home. Nobody was home when I called there this morning, and then I got a case of my own to work on. This isn't my case, remember, and I've got to at least pretend I'm doing my own work. Otherwise, they might get a little annoyed with me down at Mulberry Street."

"If it would help, I could call on her tomorrow with you," Sarah offered. "A Sunday afternoon call would be just the thing."

"Just the thing for what?" he asked with another of his looks.

"Just the thing to get her talking about her tenants."

"If she's running what amounts to a bawdy house, she's not likely to confide it in you," he pointed out.

"She's even less likely to confide it in you," Sarah pointed out right back. "And have you searched Anna's room yet? There might be a diary or some letters or something else. And the maid probably knows a lot, too. She just wouldn't say anything in front of that other woman, Catherine Porter. I'm sure I could get Catherine to talk, too, if I just had the chance."

"Are you going to ask them to line up and take their turns answering your questions?" Malloy asked sarcastically.

He was right, of course. She couldn't just show up on their doorstep and question them, one by one. Only Malloy could do that. "At least let me search her room. You know I'm good at that!"

She could see he was remembering the first time they'd met, when she'd found a vital clue for him while searching a murder victim's room.

"What excuse will you use for turning up on their doorstep?" he asked, downing the last of his coffee.

"I'll be coming as your assistant," she countered.

This drew the blackest look yet, but she merely smiled serenely.

"Mrs. Brandt," he said sternly, "you do not work for the police department, and you are not my assistant. You have no right to be investigating a murder at all. Besides, they already know you're a midwife."

"You know perfectly well you could bring a trained monkey along with you to question people and no one would dare challenge you. The police do whatever they want. If you say I can search the entire house and ask people whatever I want, then I can. What time should I meet you there?"

Someone started pounding at her door, a frantic sound she knew only too well.

"Sounds like someone wants to see you," Malloy observed.

"It's a baby. They always knock like that when it's a baby."

"Go ahead, then. I'll let myself out the back. I need to talk to Nelson Ellsworth again. There's something about this whole thing that smells bad, and maybe he can help me understand it."

"You aren't leaving until you tell me what time you'll be at the boardinghouse tomorrow," she warned when he got up and started for the back door.

His grin told her she didn't stand much chance of stopping him, even if he didn't tell her anything, but he said, "I'll probably be there around one o'clock, if you're finished with your duties by then."

Sarah smiled with satisfaction and went to answer the anxious summons.

Frank stood where Mrs. Ellsworth could see him through her back window in the fading sunlight. The door opened only a few seconds after he'd knocked, and Mrs. Ellsworth greeted him as if he were the Prodigal Son.

"Oh, Mr. Malloy, how good of you to come. I dropped a knife this afternoon, so I knew a gentleman would be calling. I hoped it was you, and not another of those awful reporters. Do you have any word? Have you found the killer yet?" she asked as he came into her kitchen. Now that he had a good look at her, he realized this ordeal was taking a toll. Her eyes were shadowed from lack of sleep, and her whole body seemed to have shrunken, as if she were drawing up into herself under the weight of this terrible burden.

"Not yet, I'm afraid," he told her, wishing he had better news. "But I have a few questions that Nelson might be able to answer."

"I'm sure he'll be happy to," she said. "He's been so upset. He hardly eats, and I have to beg him to come out of his room."

"Maybe he'd make an exception for me," Frank suggested.

"I'll be sure he does," the old woman promised. "Please, come in and have a seat in the parlor. I'll fetch him down."

Mrs. Ellsworth's parlor looked exactly as Frank would have imagined it. Immaculately clean and cluttered with figurines and ornaments and crocheted doilies, it had the look of a room kept for "good," and rarely used. Over the mantle hung a portrait of a man Frank assumed must be the elder Mr. Ellsworth. The painting made him look dyspeptic.

Frank seated himself on the horsehair sofa to wait.

A few minutes later, he heard footsteps on the stairs. Mrs. Ellsworth came down first to tell him Nelson would be following, and he did in another moment, moving as if he were the older of the two. If Mrs. Ellsworth looked tired, Nelson looked positively ill. He hadn't shaved in days, his hair had been carelessly combed, and his clothes were rumpled, like he'd been sleeping in them. His face was the worst, though. Haggard and pale, he stared at Frank with the hopelessness of a condemned man.

"If you'll excuse us, Mrs. Ellsworth," Frank said, rising to usher her out of the room. Plainly she didn't want to leave.

"Can I get you anything? Are you hungry?" she asked anxiously, looking for an excuse to return.

"No, we won't need anything," Frank assured her, closing the parlor door practically in her face. He hoped she wouldn't listen outside the door. She wouldn't want to hear the answers to the questions Frank had to ask.

Nelson had seated himself in one of the chairs and was staring up at him with resignation. "You're here to arrest me, aren't you?" he said.

"Not yet," Frank replied cheerfully. "We're still working on the case, and some questions have come up that I'm hoping you can answer."

"Questions about what?"

"About you and Anna Blake. When was the last time you were with her?"

"I saw her Monday evening, the night I went there with Mrs. Brandt. I stayed for a while after Mrs. Brandt left, but Anna was so upset, I finally left."

"You didn't see her the next night, the night she was killed?" Frank asked.

Nelson shook his head. "No, she told me not to come back, that she never wanted to see me again."

"So you weren't ever going to see her again?" Frank asked incredulously.

"Oh, no, she said that often, whenever she was upset. I would give her a day or two to calm down, then call on her again. She never seemed to remember that she'd told me not to come back, you see. This time I planned to give her several days, and then . . ."

His voice broke and he covered his eyes with his hand. Frank stared at him in pity, but he had no time for such indulgences. He needed Nelson to accept the truth about the dead woman. The sooner he did, the sooner he'd be a help in solving her murder.

"Nelson, this is very important. When was the last time you . . . uh . . . screwed Anna Blake?"

Nelson's eyes widened in shock. Plainly, no one had ever asked him such a thing. "Really, Mr. Malloy, that's hardly—" he began in outrage, but Frank didn't have the patience for his finer feelings.

"You've already told me you did it. How else could she have convinced you that you'd gotten her in a family way? Now just tell me when was the last time?"

"I . . . I don't really remember exactly," he hedged. "I mean, there was just the one time and—"

"Just one time?" Frank echoed in surprise.

Nelson flushed. "What kind of am man do you think I am? I couldn't take advantage of her like that!"

"You did it once, why not again?" Frank countered reasonably.

Nelson grew even redder, if that was possible. "The first time it was . . . Well, it was a mistake, a terrible mistake. I'll never forgive myself, but I wasn't myself at all, you see, and—"

"Who were you, if you weren't yourself?" Frank asked a little sarcastically.

Nelson had a the grace to look chagrinned. "It was the wine," he admitted reluctantly.

"What wine?"

"The wine that . . . Anna wasn't feeling well, and . . ." He gestured helplessly.

"Why don't you start at the beginning and tell me how it happened," Frank suggested.

"It's so ungentlemanly," Nelson protested.

"Seducing her was ungentlemanly," Frank countered. "Telling me how it happened might save your neck."

Nelson winced, but he couldn't argue with such logic. "I came to call on her, just the way I had been for several weeks. I was concerned about her, you see. She didn't have a friend in the world, and I didn't want her to end up on the street the way so many other girls do."

"Of course not," Frank said encouragingly. "And of course you had to give her money."

"It was just a loan," he insisted. "She was going to pay me back. She didn't want to take charity."

"That's very commendable, " Frank said, the irony lost on Nelson.

"One evening I stopped by on my way home from the bank, just to say hello, you understand. But Mrs. Walcott told me Anna was ill. She seemed very upset. She thought Anna might be going into a decline. Having lost her mother and no longer being able to provide for herself, Mrs. Walcott thought Anna might simply die to avoid what she considered a worse fate."

"Was she really sick?" Frank asked when he hesitated, lost in his memories.

"She seemed to be. Although it was highly improper,

and Mrs. Walcott assured me she never allowed gentleman callers above stairs, she asked me to go to Anna's room to see if I could help in some way. That's how concerned she was."

This was starting to make a lot of sense to Frank. Seducing a woman wasn't as easy as people made it sound. Women were usually trussed up in so many layers of corsets and clothing that just getting to them was half-a-day's work. Even rape required a lot of determination to dig through all those petticoats. But if Anna were ill, she'd be in her nightclothes, simplifying the process considerably.

"So you went to her room," Frank prodded.

"Yes, she was very ill indeed. I wanted to call a doctor immediately, but she begged me not to. She said she felt much better just having me there and knowing I cared about her. Mrs. Walcott had sent up a bottle of wine, thinking that might make Anna feel better. She didn't want to drink it. Her mother had been a temperance worker, you see, so I took some myself, just to encourage her. I don't know how much I drank before I finally convinced her to try some, but it must have been too much. By the time I realized I wasn't myself, it was too late."

"Are you telling me you turned into a raging beast?" Frank asked skeptically.

"Certainly not!" Nelson cried, but his outrage evaporated instantly. "At least I didn't realize I did. Later, Anna told me . . . Well, I started to feel a little unsteady, and Anna tried to help me to my feet so I could go back downstairs. The last thing I remember, my arms were around her and . . ."

"You don't remember what happened?" Frank asked in amazement.

"If I'd been in my right mind, it never *would* have happened!" he insisted. "When I came to myself again, Anna was curled up on the bed beside me, weeping piteously. I knew what I'd done, even before she told me I'd ruined her."

"What did you do then?"

"What do you think I did? I asked her to become my wife. I'm not a cad!"

"And what did she say?" Frank asked, not bothering to express his opinion on Nelson's honor.

"She . . . Well, she was naturally upset. I don't think she realized the implications. She just told me to go away and never see her again. She was terribly ashamed and wanted to forget this had ever happened. She made me swear I would never tell, and of course I never would have."

"So you just left?"

"I didn't have much choice. I couldn't stay there with her, even if she'd wanted me to. Mrs. Walcott would have thought that strange indeed."

"Indeed," Frank murmured.

"I resolved to come back the next day and make my offer again, when Anna was more composed and had had time to realize her situation. But when I did return, she wouldn't see me. She wouldn't see me for several weeks, and then . . ."

"Then you got an urgent message," Frank guessed.

"How did you know?"

"Just a lucky guess," Frank said wearily. "Nelson, there was no baby."

"What do you mean?"

"I mean, Anna Blake wasn't with child."

He frowned in confusion. "But she was so sure."

"The coroner assures me she wasn't, and what's more, she knew it. She was actually taking precautions not to be."

Now Nelson was really confused. "What kind of precautions?"

Frank didn't feel as embarrassed as he had with Sarah Brandt, but he still didn't have the proper words for this. "If a woman doesn't want to have a child, she can put a sponge inside of her to protect her from it. She was wearing one when she died. And Nelson . . . ?"

Nelson didn't want to hear the rest of this. "Yes?" he asked with great reluctance.

"She'd been with another man not long before she died."

Nelson closed his eyes as the full knowledge of his betrayal washed over him. "It wasn't me," he whispered.

"Then we've got to find out who it was."

8

SARAH GOT HOME EARLY THAT MORNING AFTER DELIVER-
ing a baby girl, so she had time for a brief nap before meeting Malloy at the Walcott house. Her nap was cut even
shorter when someone knocked on her door. Fearing another delivery would keep her from visiting Mrs. Walcott,
she was relieved to find one of her parents' servants with a
message from her mother, inviting her to supper that night
to meet Mr. Richard Dennis. Her father had kept his
promise!

She was still a little groggy when she left her house, but
the combination of her appointment this evening, the
prospect of learning more about Anna Blake, and the brisk
fall air quickly revived her. She took an umbrella with her
because it looked as if a storm was brewing.

By habit she glanced over at the Ellsworth house, expecting to see Mrs. Ellsworth coming out onto her porch,
broom in hand, to inquire into her business and warn her
about some omen or offer her a good luck charm. But the
shades were all pulled tight and the front door remained
tightly closed against intruders. She wondered if Malloy
had told Nelson about the story in *The World* that branded
him a perfectly justified killer instead of a wanton one.

Nelson probably wouldn't appreciate the difference. She would have to be very convincing with Mr. Dennis if she hoped to save Nelson's job at the bank. With any luck at all, she'd be able to influence him before he'd had a chance to act on the story.

Washington Square was busy on this cloudy Sabbath afternoon. Families dressed in their Sunday best hurried to their destinations, trying to beat the gathering storm. No one had time to remember a woman had died right here less than a week ago. Sarah hurried past the hanging tree, trying not to look at the place where Anna Blake had lain and trying not to think of the irony that she died beneath a tree of death.

Thompson Street was quieter than the Square, although people were rushing about here, too, on their way to or from Sunday visits. She saw no sign of Malloy when she arrived at the Walcott house, but then she hadn't heard the city clocks striking the hour yet either. Slowing her step, she looked around, wondering what she should do. Standing on the pavement in front of the house would be a little too obvious and would certainly attract attention, and besides, it might start raining at any moment. Her presence also might warn Mrs. Walcott that trouble was on the way and allow her to make her escape out the back door. She didn't have time to form a plan, however, because the front door of the Walcott house opened, and Catherine Porter looked out.

"Mrs. Brandt?" she called.

Sarah looked up in surprise. "Yes?"

"That police detective is here. He told me to watch for you."

So much for needing a plan. Sarah made her way up the front steps with as much dignity as she could manage, considering she was furious with Malloy for not waiting for her. He'd probably been there for an hour and was finished with his questioning. He'd let Sarah examine the dead woman's room and then they'd leave. She wanted to wring his neck.

Catherine closed the door, not quite meeting Sarah's

eye, as if she knew Sarah wanted to ask her about things she didn't want to discuss. "They're in the parlor," she said, gesturing to the closed doors. "He said to go on in when you got here."

Sarah would have preferred to be announced, but with a sigh of resignation, she slid open the pocket doors and found Malloy and Mrs. Walcott sociably drinking tea and chatting about the weather.

Malloy's expression changed at the sight of her. Although it couldn't exactly be called a smile, he did look somewhat pleased to see her. Mrs. Walcott, however, seemed less so. They both set down their cups and rose to their feet.

"Mrs. Brandt, isn't it?" Mrs. Walcott said with a practiced smile. "How nice of you to come." Once again, she was dressed in fashionable good taste, her artificial hair perfectly styled.

"I see Mr. Malloy told you to expect me," Sarah said, nodding to her hostess and giving Malloy a glare.

"As I explained, Mrs. Brandt has agreed to give me the benefit of her medical knowledge to assist me in this investigation," Malloy said with a straight face. "I'm told there are some delicate matters about this case that a female could address more easily."

Mrs. Walcott frowned. "I'm sure I don't know what you mean, Mr. Malloy. Please sit down, Mrs. Brandt. Would you like some tea?"

Sarah allowed that she would, and she took a seat beside Malloy on the sofa. While Mrs. Walcott served her, she tried to catch Malloy's eye so she could let him know just how unhappy she was with him, but he refused to cooperate.

"I'm very sorry about Miss Blake's death," she said finally.

"She was a lovely girl," Mrs. Walcott said, handing Sarah a fragile China cup and saucer.

"How long had she lived here?" Sarah asked.

"Oh, four or five months, I believe. Time passes so quickly, doesn't it?" Mrs. Walcott had a sweet, well-modulated voice. She could have passed herself off as a society matron in the right venue. Today she wore black, probably for mourning. She had a cameo brooch pinned at her throat, and black lace mitts on her hands once again. At least she looked the part of lady of the manor.

Sarah glanced at Malloy again, waiting for a cue. Had he already finished questioning her? "Have you been here long, Mr. Malloy?" she asked.

"Just a few minutes," he replied smugly, recognizing her annoyance and enjoying it. "I was waiting for your arrival. Mrs. Walcott, I'd like you to tell me exactly what happened the night Anna Blake died."

Mrs. Walcott's cup rattled in the saucer, and she quickly set it down. "Forgive me," she said, folding her hands tightly in her lap and lowering her head for a moment to regain her composure. "It's still very difficult to discuss this."

"I'm sure it is," Malloy agreed sympathetically, "but if we hope to find out who killed her, we have to know where she went and who she saw."

"Of course, although I don't believe I'll be much help to you."

"Just tell us what you know," Sarah said.

Mrs. Walcott nodded, took a deep breath, and began. "Anna had seemed distressed about something. Even more distressed than she had been ever since she discovered that . . . Well, I think you know her situation."

"I know what she said her situation was," Malloy corrected her. "She'd told two different men that they'd gotten her with child, if that's what you're talking about."

Mrs. Walcott registered her surprise, but she continued resolutely. "I'm sure I don't know any more than that some man had taken advantage of her and she was distraught, as anyone would be. I had begun to worry that she might harm herself. Many young women in her position do, you know."

"So she was unusually upset that night," Malloy prodded.

"All day, in fact. She hardly left her room."

"Did she have any callers?" Malloy asked.

Mrs. Walcott considered for a moment. "I'm sure this had nothing to do with her death, but . . ."

"Someone came to see her?"

"Yes, a . . . a young man," she admitted with apparent reluctance.

"Who was he?"

"I don't know. He didn't give his name, and she didn't reveal it. He wasn't here long, and Anna left the house shortly after he did."

"Did he go upstairs with her?"

Mrs. Walcott looked shocked. "Certainly not! I run a respectable house here."

Sarah knew Malloy could have disputed that, but instead he asked, "Was she happy to see this young man?"

"Not particularly. And while I didn't listen at the door or anything like that, I couldn't help but hear that their voices were raised at one point."

"They were arguing?"

"That was my assumption," Mrs. Walcott said primly.

"Where did Anna go when she left the house?"

"I'm not sure. She didn't confide in me, but I did gather she was meeting someone."

"Any idea who it was?"

Mrs. Walcott shook her head gently. Sarah observed that she took care not to disturb her elaborately coiffed wig. "I can't imagine she was meeting a woman," she said reluctantly. "She didn't know any other females that I'm aware of, and a woman would probably not be out herself in the evening like that."

"What time did she leave?"

"I didn't pay attention to the exact time," she said apologetically. "I had no idea it would be important."

"How long was it after the young man left?"

"Not long," she said, wrinkling her forehead as she tried to recall. "Not more than half an hour, I'd guess, although I can't be perfectly sure."

"Was it dark out when she left?"

"Certainly not. I never would have permitted her to go out after dark."

"How was she dressed?" Sarah asked, earning a frown from Malloy for interrupting.

Mrs. Walcott looked surprised at the question. "I don't think I noticed."

"If you saw the clothes in her room, could you tell which ones are missing?" Sarah asked.

Mrs. Walcott considered. "Probably."

"What difference does it make what she was wearing?" Malloy asked irritably.

Sarah ignored him. "Could we go up to her room to look?"

Mrs. Walcott looked to Malloy for his approval, irritating Sarah in turn, but she supposed he *was* in charge. He nodded grudgingly, and they all rose. Mrs. Walcott led the way out into the hall and up the stairs.

Malloy grabbed Sarah's arm, holding her back. "What difference does it make what she was wearing?" he asked in a whisper. "We could ask the coroner that."

"Isn't this a better way to get into her room than asking permission to search it?" she asked sweetly.

All she got in reply was a grunt, but he released her arm and allowed her to follow the landlady.

Upstairs, Mrs. Walcott was waiting for them outside the closed door, as if reluctant to enter without them. "I haven't disturbed anything in here. It . . . it didn't seem right. I'd be happy to send her things to her family, but I don't believe she had any."

She pushed open the door to the room and stepped aside for Sarah to enter. Malloy stood in the open doorway with Mrs. Walcott, watching her.

The room looked like thousands of others just like it all over the city. The furniture was cheap and worn. A metal bedstead dominated the small space. It had been carelessly made, the coverlet lying crooked. Some clothes hung on pegs along one wall. A dresser stood nearby, and a wash-stand occupied the opposite corner. A small, battered trunk sat at the foot of the bed.

Sarah began by examining the garments hanging on the pegs.

"Did you know that Nelson Ellsworth was paying Anna's rent?" Malloy asked the landlady while they watched Sarah.

"Good heavens, no!" She sounded thoroughly shocked.

"How did you think she managed, since she didn't have a job?" he asked curiously.

"She had an inheritance," Mrs. Walcott said. "At least, that's what she gave me to believe. Mr. Ellsworth was managing it for her. He worked at a bank, I believe. That's why he'd taken an interest in her."

"And what about Mr. Giddings?" Malloy asked.

"What about him?"

"He was giving her money, too. Who did you think *he* was, her rich uncle?"

Mrs. Walcott took offense at his tone. "He was her attorney," she sniffed indignantly. "They had matters of business to discuss about her mother's estate."

Mrs. Walcott was either stupid or lying, Sarah thought as she took a mental inventory of Anna Blake's wardrobe. Sarah saw the girlish gingham dress Anna had been wearing the one time they had met and another that was apparently her "good" dress, the one she would have saved for special occasions. She also had a black bombazine skirt and matching jacket, which would have done for almost any occasion. A fringed paisley shawl hung on one of the hooks, and Sarah fingered it, impressed by its quality. Probably a gift from a besotted admirer, she thought. Beside it hung a fancy hat, probably the one she saved for "good," and another, less ornate one, for everyday wear. What hat would she have been wearing when she went out? It seemed unlikely she'd own more than two.

The dresser drawers held extra pairs of undergarments and stockings, two waists, and a nightdress. A comb and brush lay on the dresser, and a glass bowl held extra hairpins. Oddly enough, the bottom drawer of the dresser held a case of some kind. Sarah glanced at Mrs. Walcott to see how closely she was being watched and if the other woman would offer some objection to her examining it.

Mrs. Walcott frowned when Sarah drew the case out of the drawer, but she didn't object when she opened it. To her surprise, Sarah discovered it contained a wide variety of face paint, far more than a respectable woman would ever need to own. Anna Blake had a more interesting background than she had led anyone to believe. She glanced at Malloy to make sure he'd seen the contents of the case before closing it and returning it to its proper place.

Lastly, she opened the trunk. As she had suspected, this contained Anna's winter clothing. A heavy wool cape and a rabbit fur muff lay on top. Beneath them were several woolen skirts and some jackets, a flannel petticoat, and a knitted scarf, nothing very intriguing.

Sarah caught Malloy's eye again. "Would you like to look around?"

He did, of course, and he was less discreet. Without asking for leave, he took the corner of the mattress and lifted it up to peer underneath. Then he picked up the pillows and pulled back the covers. He pulled out the drawers again and felt beneath them, in case something had been stuck to the bottoms. With calm efficiency, he searched all remaining crannies of the room and found nothing.

Except for the face paint, the room contained not one hint that Anna Blake was anything other than she had appeared to be. And of course, there were no letters or diaries giving more insight into her background or helpfully naming her killer.

Sarah turned to Mrs. Walcott. "Can you tell what she was wearing that night?"

The landlady looked at the clothing again. "She had a brown dress, I think. Yes, I believe that's what she was wearing. At least, that's all I can tell is missing."

Something had been bothering Sarah about Anna's wardrobe. Now she realized what it was, but she said nothing. Her theory could wait until she and Malloy were alone.

"What did this young man look like?" Malloy asked

Mrs. Walcott. "The one who called on Anna the night she died."

"Very ordinary. Tall and thin, the way boys are before they mature."

"How was he dressed?"

"He looked like a laborer. His clothes were coarse and dirty, although his manners were good. He was very polite to me, although he was impatient to see Anna."

"Was he polite to Anna?" Malloy inquired.

Mrs. Walcott looked away. "I hate to speak ill of the dead, but . . ."

"Anna wasn't polite to him?" Malloy guessed.

"She was angry with him for some reason, from the instant she saw him. As I said, they argued, and he left rather quickly after that, slamming the door behind him. And then, as I said, Anna left also." She seemed to realize something suddenly. "Oh, dear, do you suppose . . . ?"

"Suppose what?" Malloy asked with interest.

"That young man, he could have waited for her or seen her leaving. He could have followed her and started quarreling with her again," she said, shaking her head. "I never should have let her leave the house that night." With a graceful gesture, she pulled a lace-trimmed handkerchief from her sleeve and dabbed at her eyes, even though Sarah saw no visible tears.

Malloy ushered Sarah out of Anna's room, and Mrs. Walcott closed the door behind them.

"Is there any other way I can assist you?" Mrs. Walcott asked as they made their way down the stairs.

Malloy waited until they had reached the front hallway before replying. "I can't think of anything . . . Oh, wait, there *was* something. One of your neighbors said she heard your cellar door opening late that night. Could you explain that?"

Mrs. Walcott blinked in surprise and looked a bit nonplussed. "Yes, I can, although it's a bit embarrassing. And it can't have anything at all to do with Anna's death. You see, my maid has been complaining about an odor in the cellar. She thought some small animal had died down there, although we couldn't find anything. I opened the cellar door in an attempt to air it out."

"In the middle of the night?" Malloy asked skeptically.

"It wasn't the middle of the night," she said, waving such a thought away with her handkerchief. "I did wait until full dark, though. Leaving one's cellar door open in the daylight is simply inviting someone to sneak in and steal something. I didn't think anyone would see that it was open in the dark, though."

Malloy nodded. "Did the odor go away?"

"No, but I asked my husband to spread some lime, and that helped. I'm afraid the poor dead creature is in one of the walls. We're just going to have to wait for nature to take its course, I suppose."

Sarah and Malloy took their leave, although Sarah was loath to go out. The sky looked even more threatening than before, and the wind was picking up. She hoped she could get home before the storm broke. And how would she get to her parents' house tonight without getting soaked? She didn't want to look like a drowned rat when she was trying to convince Mr. Dennis not to dismiss Nelson Ellsworth from the bank. But of course, she had no choice about going out. Mrs. Walcott certainly wasn't going to invite her to stay.

As soon as they were safely away from the house, Sarah let Malloy know how displeased she was. "How long were you questioning her before I arrived?"

He gave her a measuring look, although she could see the amused glimmer in his dark eyes. "I'd only just gotten there myself. Do you think I'd presume to do my job without your assistance, Mrs. Brandt?"

She decided not to press the issue, since they both knew she had no right to assist him at all. "Did you see that case of face paint in Anna's room?"

"Yes. What would she have done with something like that?"

"Painted her face, obviously," Sarah said, "although she wasn't painted when I saw her, at least not noticeably. I doubt someone who was would have appealed to Nelson,

in any case. Anna's allure was her apparent youthful innocence and helplessness. Only a prostitute would need that
kind of paint for her face."

"Do you think she was a prostitute before she met Nelson?"

Sarah considered. "If she was, she must have been a
high-class one. She had a gentility about her that you don't
see in street walkers."

"High-class whores don't paint their faces like the street
walkers do, either," Malloy informed her, "for the same
reason Anna Blake didn't."

"I bow to your more extensive experience in such matters," Sarah couldn't resist saying. "But then why would
she need so much paint? It had obviously been used a lot,
so she must have needed it at some time in her life."

"What other kind of women paint their faces?" Malloy
asked, thinking aloud.

The answer was so obvious, Sarah felt foolish. "Actresses!"

"Stage actresses," Malloy agreed. "Could she have been
an actress?"

"Of course, it makes perfect sense!" Sarah cried in triumph. "And I'd forgotten, Catherine Porter was an actress,
too. The maid mentioned it, and she admitted it. Anna—
and probably Catherine, too—was pretending to be an innocent girl, telling Nelson and Giddings outrageous lies
but making them believe her stories. She was so convincing, they never doubted her for a moment, either!"

"To the point where Giddings was willing to jeopardize
everything he had to take care of her."

"Exactly! That's how she could be so convincing. In
fact, I remember thinking the first time I met her that Nelson had gotten himself into a melodrama."

"Actresses aren't generally known for their strict moral
standards, either," Malloy remarked.

"So they wouldn't mind the necessary seduction,"
Sarah said, deciding she'd better get hold of her hat before
it blew right off her head.

"Or the lying," Malloy said, holding on to his own hat.

"And in Nelson's case, at least, I don't think the seduction even happened."

"What?"

Malloy gave her a sideways glance. "There was only one . . . uh, incident. Nelson was overcome by drink at the time, and he doesn't actually remember what happened."

"If he was overcome with drink, nothing *could* have happened," Sarah pointed out indignantly.

Malloy frowned in disapproval. She supposed he didn't think she should know such an obviously masculine secret. "Our Mr. Ellsworth doesn't seem to be aware of that."

"If he doesn't remember, then what makes him think he did anything?" Sarah demanded.

"Miss Blake told him all about it. Tearfully."

Sarah groaned. "How could he be so stupid?"

"I'm afraid that's a mystery I don't have any hope of solving, so I'm going to content myself with just trying to figure out who killed her."

"If she was an actress, at least we can find out some more about her. Someone will know her at the theaters. We could ask around."

"Why?" Malloy asked with another frown.

"She might have had enemies before she ever met Nelson," Sarah suggested hopefully. "There might be dozens of people she knew before who wanted her dead."

Malloy gave her a pitying look.

"But it's not very likely, is it?" Sarah admitted.

Malloy shrugged. "There's always a chance. But I think Giddings is a better chance. He had very good reason to want Anna Blake dead."

"Except he didn't act like a killer that day he came to the house looking for her. He was genuinely distraught when he found out she was dead."

"Or maybe he's as good an actor as Anna Blake. He wasn't home when I went to his house, so I didn't get a chance to question him any more. I'll try again tomorrow, and if he's not home, I'll find him this time."

Sarah remembered something else. "Who do you think the young man was who visited Anna that night?"

"I think it was Giddings's son, Harold. He knew about Anna, and he wasn't happy about her. His family lost everything because of her. When Giddings got caught stealing from his law firm, he had to sell everything he owned to repay the debt, including their furniture."

Sarah winced. "How humiliating. His wife must be devastated."

"She's hiding it pretty well, trying to keep up a good front for the boy, I guess. But she's got to hate Anna Blake, too."

"Oh, my, do you think *Mrs.* Giddings could be the killer?" Sarah asked with genuine interest.

"Women commit murder, too," he reminded her.

She knew that only too well. "Did Mrs. Giddings strike you as a murderess?"

"Not really, but you can never tell about that kind of woman. They're good at hiding their real feelings."

Sarah could have given him a thousand examples of women of *all* kinds who were good at that, but she didn't bother. "Mrs. Giddings probably wouldn't have been out in the evening alone, though," Sarah said, "and certainly not in Washington Square."

"Anna wasn't killed in the Square."

"What do you mean? That's where she was found," Sarah reminded him.

"The coroner also told me that she walked a ways after she was stabbed. He could tell by the way she'd bled on her dress. She was stabbed somewhere else and was probably trying to get back home to get help when she collapsed in the Square."

"So she could have been stabbed anywhere," Sarah said, trying to figure out what this might mean. "Even someplace where she might have met Mrs. Giddings."

"Or her son," Malloy said.

Washington Square was just across the street, but they had to wait for a break in the steady stream of carriages and wagons to give them an opportunity to cross. The wind had started to stir up clouds of dust and dirt, and Sarah began to think this might not be an ordinary storm. While they stood there, squinting their eyes against the gritty wind, they heard someone calling Malloy's name.

Malloy muttered something under his breath that might have been a curse when he turned and saw who was running toward them. "Even God took a day of rest, Prescott," he grumbled when the gangly reporter reached them.

"I went to the boarding house where Miss Blake lived, and they said you'd just been there," Webster Prescott said. He was breathless from running, and his fair face had pinkened from the exertion. He looked like a very tall child who had been chasing his hoop in the street. "Good afternoon, Mrs. Brandt," he added with a gesture that might have been a tip of his straw hat if he hadn't been struggling to hold it on his head. "How nice to see you again."

Sarah could see the speculation in his eyes, but she wasn't about to confirm or deny anything about her relationship with Malloy, especially when she had no idea in what direction he might be speculating. "It's nice to see you, too, Mr. Prescott. I've been wanting to have a word with you about that story you wrote about Mr. Ellsworth," she added grimly.

He didn't seem to sense her anger. "My editor was very pleased with it, too. We sold out of last night's edition, and I ran a longer piece this morning. Now I need some more information, and I thought I might get it from Miss Blake's landlady."

"But she sent you packing," Malloy guessed.

Prescott wouldn't admit such a thing. "She said you had just questioned her and warned her against speaking to the press." He managed to appear offended.

"And you thought you'd get some information out of me?" Malloy asked incredulously.

Prescott smiled guilelessly. "No, but I thought Mrs. Brandt might be willing to share some with me."

"I certainly am not!" Sarah informed him. "I told you Nelson Ellsworth was *innocent*, and you twisted everything I said to make him sound guiltier than ever!"

"But after what I revealed about Anna Blake, he'll never be convicted," Prescott argued. "Most of the other papers have also started reporting that Anna Blake was a seductress who tried to ruin Ellsworth. By the time he goes to trial, there won't be a man in the city who'd judge him guilty."

"But he shouldn't go to trial at all!" Sarah fairly shouted. "He didn't kill her!"

Prescott opened his mouth, no doubt intending to say something even more infuriating, but Malloy interrupted him.

"Anna Blake was not expecting a child," he said.

"She wasn't? How do you know?" Prescott asked in amazement.

"The coroner told me, and he should know. She was only pretending to be distraught about her condition, but that was pretty easy for her, because she also happened to be an actress."

Sarah wanted to slap him. Why was he telling this traitorous reporter anything at all, much less information they'd gathered with such difficulty?

"An actress?" Prescott repeated, pulling a notebook out of his pocket. He snatched the pencil from behind his ear and had to remove his hat and tuck it under his arm because he no longer had a free hand with which to hold it while he wrote. "Where did she perform?"

"I don't know. That's up to you to find out, but it shouldn't be too hard. You probably have a lot of friends in the theater."

"Was Anna Blake her stage name?" Prescott asked, scribbling furiously in his notebook.

"That's something else you'll have to find out on your own."

"How did you discover that she was an actress?" Prescott asked.

"I'm a detective," Malloy reminded him with only a trace of irony. "Finding things out is my job."

"What else do you know about her that you're not telling?" Prescott asked, including Sarah in the inquiry.

She almost told him what she thought of his cheekiness,

but Malloy grabbed her elbow in a bruising grip to silence her.

"I know I'm going to start telling any other reporters who ask me everything I just told you, so if you want to scoop them, you'd better get busy."

Prescott's pink face split into a triumphant grin. "Thanks, Malloy. Mrs. Brandt," he added with another quick tip of his hat as he placed it back on his head, and he vanished into the crowd of people leaning against the wind while they waited to cross the street.

"Why did you tell him about Anna being an actress?" Sarah demanded, now almost as angry with Malloy as she was with Prescott.

"To get rid of him. We don't want him following us around. He might tip off the real killer once we start getting closer. And if he and the rest of the press are nosing around the theaters, they won't be bothering the Ellsworths."

"But what if Anna's killer is someone she knew at the theater?" Sarah asked indignantly.

"Then maybe he'll get frightened and make a mistake, and I'll catch him. But chances are it was somebody from Anna's present life who killed her. She was living very dangerously, after all. When you start ruining men's lives, you make people desperate. One of those people got desperate enough to kill her."

Suddenly, there was a break in the traffic, and Malloy fairly dragged her across the street, somehow managing to dodge the piles of horse droppings that had accumulated since the street cleaners had finished their duties early that morning. When they had arrived safely on the other side, in the Square, they paused for breath, turning their backs to the wind, and Malloy released her arm. Sarah rubbed her elbow and glared at him, but he wasn't paying attention.

"Someday somebody's going to figure out a way to control that mess," Malloy said, frowning back at the sweating, swearing drivers and their rigs that had once again closed ranks behind them.

"Are you going to see Giddings now?" she asked.

He gave her one of his looks. "Even God got a day off," he repeated.

She felt a pang of guilt. "I'm sorry. You're right, you should take some time and spend it with Brian. How much longer until he gets the cast off?"

"Week after next."

She could see the worry deep in his dark eyes. "He'll be fine," she assured him. "I'll go with you to the doctor's if you'd like. And if I don't have a delivery," she added.

He looked uncomfortable with her offer. She supposed he wanted her to go with him but didn't want to admit it. "Are you going home now?" he asked instead.

"For a while. I'm having supper with my parents this evening."

He glanced up at the threatening sky. "Better leave early if you want to get there. And remind Nelson not to leave the house yet. I'll be over to see him after I've talked to Giddings."

They parted company, and Sarah again walked past the spot where Anna Blake had died. But not where she had been attacked, she reminded herself. That had happened somewhere else. She couldn't help thinking that if she could discover where, she'd also know who the killer was.

The rain started long before Sarah was ready to go up-town, and when she had an opportunity to check the newspaper, she discovered that the storm was actually a hurricane that had moved up the coast. The winds were howling, but Sarah's mother had sent word that their carriage would come to fetch her and that she should come prepared to stay the night if necessary. Plainly, her mother wasn't going to let a mere act of God cheat her out of her daughter's company!

Sarah dressed carefully for the evening. She didn't care about trying to impress Mr. Dennis, but she didn't want to embarrass her mother. Elizabeth Decker placed great importance on appearances, and for all Sarah knew, so did Richard Dennis. The suit she'd bought this past summer at

Lord and Taylor wasn't the height of fashion, but at least it was presentable.

When she was satisfied that she wouldn't shame the Decker family name, Sarah wrapped herself in a cape to ward off the rain that had begun and stole over to the Ellsworths' house for a brief word with Mrs. Ellsworth.

"What are you doing out in this weather?" the old woman scolded Sarah when she opened her back door to admit her. "And I can see you have an engagement! Is it with Mr. Malloy?"

Sarah couldn't help smiling at the thought. "No, I'm going to visit my parents this evening." She decided not to mention the purpose of that visit so they wouldn't be disappointed if she wasn't successful in saving Nelson's job. "I just wanted to let you know that Mr. Malloy is still working hard on the case. He asked me to remind Nelson not to leave the house, and to tell you he'd be stopping by as soon as he spoke to one of the suspects tomorrow."

"Oh, dear, I've had a tingling in my left eye all day today. That's not a good sign, you know. The right eye means good fortune, but the left eye . . . Well, I don't know how much more bad news I can bear."

She looked as if she might weep, and Sarah wanted to offer at least some sort of comfort. Unfortunately, she didn't have any to offer, and if Mrs. Ellsworth knew what Webster Prescott had written about Nelson lately, more than her eye would be twitching. "Just stay out of sight. You know Mr. Malloy will take care of everything," she promised rashly. "It won't be much longer."

Mrs. Ellsworth let her go without any protests, which worried Sarah more than anything else. Ordinarily, the old woman liked nothing better than company, Sarah's in particular. She only hoped that when she returned home again, she'd be able to assure the Ellsworths that Nelson's job was secure. It wouldn't solve all their problems, but it would remove at least one worry.

Sarah's mother greeted her with concern. "I had no idea the storm would get so bad," she said when Sarah entered.

The maid had taken her cloak, although she was hardly wet, having spent so little time out in the rain. "I hope you're planning to stay the night."

"I'll have to. I couldn't bear to make your driver and horses go out again in this weather," Sarah said. "I wouldn't be surprised if Mr. Dennis decides not to come out at all."

"He'll be here," her father said, confident of his power to influence. He seemed pleased to see her. With her father, it wasn't always easy to tell, but he did kiss her forehead and refrained from saying anything remotely critical during the half-hour they sat in the back parlor and chatted before Mr. Dennis arrived. Sarah had visions of her mother lecturing him earlier today on being nice to her so she'd come back to visit more often.

Finally, and against all odds, the maid announced Mr. Dennis. Her father rose to greet him, and as soon as he entered the room, Sarah understood exactly why her parents had been so cooperative in arranging for her to meet him. Unfortunately, it had nothing at all to do with helping Nelson Ellsworth.

9

"RICHARD, MY BOY, HOW ARE YOU?" HER FATHER ASKED, shaking his hand.

Sarah didn't like the sound of that "my boy," especially when she saw that Dennis was just as surprised by the familiarity as she. Felix Decker was never effusive.

"We were afraid you might not make it because of the storm," her father continued.

"I couldn't allow you to think I was afraid of a little rain, could I?" Dennis replied. He did look amazingly dry, considering how the wind was howling outside. Sarah couldn't help wondering how his driver had fared and if he'd agree on the assessment that they were having "a little rain."

"How are your parents?" her father asked, escorting him into the room.

"Very well, thank you," Mr. Dennis replied, recovering quickly. "They asked to be remembered to you both."

While Dennis greeted her mother, Sarah studied him, taking in the details of his appearance with a growing sense of dread. When her father had referred to him as "young" Dennis, she had pictured someone barely old enough to shave. Richard Dennis, however, was at least thirty. While he couldn't be called conventionally handsome, he was certainly appealing in a well-kept, well-bred sort of way. He carried his rather tallish figure easily beneath his tailor-made suit, and he effortlessly exchanged pleasantries with Elizabeth Decker. Sarah knew beyond the slightest doubt that Richard Dennis would prove to be what her mother considered a very eligible bachelor, which explained her parents' willingness to help her in this matter. They had eagerly arranged this meeting in hopes of making a suitable match for Sarah.

"And this is my daughter, Mrs. Sarah Brandt," her father was saying, turning Dennis's attention to her.

"I'm delighted to meet you, Mrs. Brandt," he said with a genuine, if slightly bemused, smile, as he took her offered hand in his. "You misled me, sir," he said, turning back to her father when he'd released Sarah's hand. "I thought this would be a dry business discussion, and here you have provided the company of two very lovely ladies instead."

"Oh, we will be discussing business," Mr. Decker assured him, "but it's Sarah who wished to consult with you, not I."

"And my father was gracious enough to arrange for us to meet," Sarah supplied, trying to keep any hint of annoyance out of her voice. It wasn't Mr. Dennis's fault that her parents wanted to find her a socially acceptable husband. "I hope you will forgive him for misleading you and indulging me."

Now Dennis looked intrigued. "I'm rarely called upon to discuss business with charming females, Mrs. Brandt. For that alone, I would forgive him."

Sarah would have quickly made her case for Nelson Ellsworth, but her parents weren't accustomed to doing things hastily. Getting right down to the issue would be considered bad taste and worse manners. They'd set out to entertain Mr. Dennis, and they would. Her father offered him a drink to ward off the harrowing effects of the storm, and her mother made small talk while Sarah tried to be pleasant. Pouting wouldn't endear her to Richard Dennis, and she needed his help desperately.

Fortunately, Sarah had spent her youth learning just how to conduct herself in social situations, and she called upon all of those skills now. After a few awkward moments, she found herself slipping naturally into the conversation. She hadn't seen most of the people about whom they spoke for many years, but she did remember most of them.

"Surely, we must have encountered one another at dancing classes at some time or another, Mrs. Brandt," Dennis said after a few minutes.

"Sarah is several years younger than you, Richard," her mother explained. "She wasn't even out yet when you married Hazel."

Richard Dennis was *married*. For one second, Sarah thought she'd been horribly mistaken and that her parents hadn't arranged this little party to introduce her to a potential husband. But then she saw the shadow pass across Richard Dennis's finely boned face. She recognized that flash of pain, the same one she felt whenever someone mentioned Tom, and she understood why her parents had considered Richard Dennis so perfect for her.

The shadow passed quickly, however. He was accustomed to dealing with his pain, which mean he'd lost his wife some time ago. "So that explains why I don't recall ever stepping on your toes while trying to master the waltz, Mrs. Brandt," he said with a smile.

"I'm sure you never could have done such a thing, even in your youth, Mr. Dennis," she replied as expected, returning his smile and pleasing her mother enormously.

The maid summoned them to supper, and Mr. Dennis offered his arm. Sarah took it and continued to smile, reminding herself that he was just as much an innocent victim here as she. She only hoped she could lead him to understand that she'd had no part in the planning of this, either. On the other hand, he might be flattered if he thought she was attracted to him or had asked to meet him.

If she decided that was the best course of action, she was more than willing to flatter him to gain his cooperation.

She tried not to think how similar that would be to what Anna Blake had done to Nelson Ellsworth and Mr. Giddings.

Supper was a simple affair with fried oysters, cold chicken, Welsh rarebit, preserved fruit, stewed tomatoes, roasted potatoes, Charlotte Russe, ice cream, and cake.

As they made their way through the various courses, Mr. Dennis eventually had to express some interest in Sarah.

"I'm surprised our paths haven't crossed as adults, Mrs. Brandt," he said.

"We don't keep the same society," Sarah said with a smile. "I live down in Greenwich Village."

He obviously found that odd but was too polite to say so. "It's a very picturesque part of the city," he said diplomatically.

"My husband's work was there, and we enjoyed living in the neighborhood."

"Sarah's husband was a physician," her mother hastily—and somewhat apologetically—explained. "He passed away several years ago."

"I'm sorry to hear it," Mr. Dennis said. "I lost my wife, too. I hope you'll forgive me if I don't have a high opinion of the medical profession as a result." His smile was infinitely sad.

"I understand," she said. "I also wish that medical science could do more to save lives, but even after centuries of study, we still know very little about the causes of death and disease. It's very difficult for me in my own work that I simply can't save everyone."

Sarah ignored the warning look her mother was giving her. She wanted to disenchant Mr. Dennis as quickly as she could and confessing her profession seemed the simplest way to do it.

"Are you a physician as well?" he asked in disbelief.

"A midwife," she said.

"Sarah was always independent," her father explained, with only a hint of disapproval.

"An admirable quality," Dennis said, skillfully concealing whatever his true feelings on the matter might be. "Your life must be very interesting."

Sarah could have shocked him right out of his chair, but she said, "I'd be bored without my work. I need to feel I'm being useful."

Mr. Dennis had most certainly never imagined that a woman might be bored with the life of a society matron. To give him credit, however, he seemed at least willing to consider the possibility. "But surely, you must attend only women of your own class."

"I attend whoever needs my services," Sarah replied. "I don't work to amuse myself, Mr. Dennis. I work to make my own living."

He looked at her as if she were an entirely new kind of creature, but amazingly, she saw no disgust, or even disapproval, in his light eyes. "Hazel, my wife, she sometimes visited a Settlement House on the Lower East Side. I thought she did it because it was fashionable among her friends to play Lady Bountiful to the poor."

"The Settlement Houses provide valuable services to the women and children in that part of the city," Sarah said. "Your wife was also helping save lives, in her own way," she added generously, without any real knowledge of what actual services Mrs. Dennis might have performed.

Sarah's parents were listening to this conversation with growing discomfort. They knew such things weren't suitable topics for discussion at table or between members of the opposite sex at any time. On the other hand, Mr. Dennis didn't seem shocked or even put off by Sarah's unorthodox vocation or her outspoken opinions. They hardly knew what to think.

But Sarah's mother couldn't abide any more of this. "How did your parents enjoy their trip to Europe this summer?" she asked Mr. Dennis, effectively changing the subject for the remainder of the meal.

When the ladies withdrew so the men could smoke their cigars, Sarah steeled herself for her mother's indignation.

"Really, Sarah, must you inform everyone you meet that you are employed as a midwife? Some people might find that distasteful," she said when they were alone.

"I'm not ashamed of my life, Mother, and I hope you aren't ashamed of me."

Her mother frowned, not pleased by Sarah's attempt to make her feel guilty. "It's not a matter of shame. It's a matter of good taste. I thought you wanted Richard's help for your friend. He's much more likely to help you if you excite his chivalrous feelings."

"Instead of putting him off with my *independence*?" she asked with just a trace of irony.

Somehow her mother managed to resist the temptation to argue with her. "I'm simply reminding you that men like to feel superior to women. If we let them believe we are helpless, they will gladly do whatever we require of them and consider themselves honored to have been of service."

"Are you saying that men must be tricked into behaving well?" Sarah asked in amazement.

"Of course they do," her mother said impatiently. "I thought you most certainly must have learned that by now. Men rely on women's gentler natures to help them overcome their baser instincts. A businessman wouldn't hesitate for a moment to dismiss your friend after the scandal he's caused the bank, whether he actually killed that woman or not. I'm not convinced your friend even deserves your help, but since you've chosen to offer it, you must ingratiate yourself to Mr. Dennis to compel him to betray his natural impulse and do something kind instead."

"And it won't hurt if Mr. Dennis is so impressed with my gentle nature that he falls in love with me, either, will it?" Sarah asked with a sly grin.

Her mother shook her head. "I despair of ever seeing you wed again, Sarah. Dr. Brandt must have been a very tolerant man indeed to have endured your willfulness."

Tom Brandt had *reveled* in her willfulness, but Sarah knew her mother wouldn't believe her if she said so. "I'm perfectly happy as I am, Mother, and I have no intention of pretending to be something I'm not just to catch a husband."

"If that's your attitude, then I'm afraid you never will," her mother said sadly.

The two of them sat in uncomfortable silence until the men joined them a few minutes later. Sarah had seated herself on a sofa so Mr. Dennis could sit beside her to facilitate their discussion of what Sarah wanted of him. Fortunately, he took the hint and seated himself just where she'd wanted him.

"Perhaps you'd play for us, my dear," Mr. Decker said to his wife, surprising Sarah. She'd assumed the two of them would want to be included in her conversation with Dennis, but her mother rose obediently—too obediently, which meant they'd arranged this ahead of time—and went to the opposite end of the room where a small piano sat. Her father went with her and turned the pages as she played some simple pieces that were neither loud nor lively enough to interfere with Sarah's purpose but which provided just the right amount of privacy for the younger couple.

"You must imagine I'm going to ask for a very great favor," Sarah said with a small smile when Dennis looked at her expectantly.

"For your sake, I hope you are. I could hardly refuse you anything after your parents have gone to such lengths to ensure my cooperation," he replied with a smile of his own.

"Don't worry, Mr. Dennis. I hope you'll believe that I don't have any designs on your person," she said.

"Why would I be worried by that?" he bantered back. "In fact, I shall be very disappointed if you don't."

Sarah had to stifle a laugh at that. "You must understand that my parents believe I married beneath my station," she explained, "and ever since my husband died, they've been trying to rectify the situation. I had no idea you were a widower when I asked my father to introduce us."

"But your parents did," he said, his eyes twinkling with

amusement. "And they were doing what parents do. Mine do the same thing, Mrs. Brandt, and with amazing regularity. I can't tell you how many women they've thrust into my path in the past five years. It's actually refreshing to discover that others are being imposed upon in the same way."

Sarah shook her head. "We must stop smiling at each other, Mr. Dennis, or my mother will be sending out our engagement announcement in the morning mail."

"And she knows I'm too much of a gentleman to renounce it, so you must help me avoid this very cleverly set trap. Quickly, tell me why you needed to meet me. That should certainly stop us both from smiling."

At the thought of her mission, Sarah did indeed grow solemn. "It's about Nelson Ellsworth."

His smile vanished as well. "Ellsworth? What do you know of him?"

"He's my neighbor, Mr. Dennis, and his mother is a dear friend of mine. I owe her a debt I can never repay, and I can't stand by while her son is ruined through no fault of his own."

Dennis had instantly become the cold-hearted businessman her mother had described. "I don't believe he can be considered free of fault in this matter, Mrs. Brandt. He did seduce that young woman, and it appears that he—"

"Actually, it appears that *she* seduced *him*, Mr. Dennis."

"What?"

"Anna Blake was not what she appeared to be. She took great pains to appear young and innocent, but we now believe she made a career out of seducing and blackmailing vulnerable men."

At least he was still listening. "What do you mean by blackmailing?"

"She would convince a man that she was alone in the world and penniless, then begin an illicit relationship with him. She would pretend to be with child and then demand money from the man. She did the same thing with another man, a married man who couldn't afford a scandal. He actually stole money from his employer to satisfy her demands."

"And she did this to Ellsworth, too?"

"Yes. And she wasn't even with child. She lied about everything, to both men."

Dennis frowned. "All the more reason why a man would be furious enough to murder her, Mrs. Brandt."

"But Mr. Ellsworth didn't kill her. You know him. He couldn't possibly do violence to anyone, certainly not a female."

Dennis smiled condescendingly. "Ellsworth is fortunate to have you as his champion, Mrs. Brandt, but you are hardly in a position to know that for a fact. Men will do strange things when their passions are aroused."

Sarah forced herself not to take offense. "Actually, I *do* know for a fact that Nelson didn't kill her, and the police are going to arrest the real killer very soon."

"How could you know such a thing?" he asked skeptically.

"Because I have been working closely with one of the detectives on the case."

Now she'd shocked him. "You associate with the police?" he asked incredulously.

Once again, she forced herself not to take offense. "Not all of them are corrupt, Mr. Dennis," she chided. "Don't you read the newspapers? Teddy Roosevelt has made significant changes in the department. Officers are promoted on the basis of merit now, and corruption is punished."

Dennis was unconvinced. "You are a courageous woman, Mrs. Brandt, but you're naive if you believe the police are any better than the criminals they purport to control. Not even our friend Teddy can change that."

Sarah wanted to be outraged. She wanted to defend Malloy and convince Dennis of the foolishness of his prejudices, except that she knew he was right. No matter what Teddy Roosevelt told the press or how righteous he tried to be, the corruption in the police department went too deep and had endured too long for a few months of reform to change things. Rumors about Teddy campaigning for

McKinley for president so he could get a more important job in the national government were already rampant. The instant he resigned as police commissioner, the department would return to being just what it was before.

"Mr. Dennis," Sarah said, "all I'm asking is that you give Nelson Ellsworth the benefit of the doubt for the time being. If he really is innocent, as I believe, you will have ruined his life for no reason if you dismiss him from his position. He's the sole support of his widowed mother. Could you live with that on your conscience?"

Richard Dennis sighed in defeat. "I'm sure you wouldn't allow me to, Mrs. Brandt. All right, I'll at least wait to see what transpires. But if he's charged with murder, I will have no choice but to dismiss him. I'm afraid that's the most I can promise."

"Oh, Mr. Dennis, I can't thank you enough!"

"But," he said, stopping her effusive gratitude with an upraised palm, "I can't permit him to return to work until this is settled, one way or the other. Those hounds from the press have been an unbearable nuisance all week, and if he were there . . . Well, I'm sure I don't have to explain. People expect their bank to be quiet and dignified and trustworthy. If it isn't, they move their money elsewhere."

"I'll make sure Nelson understands. He is as concerned about the bank's reputation as you are, and he certainly doesn't want to encounter the press, either."

"But if the killer isn't identified quickly," he warned, "I can't promise how long I'll be able to keep him on."

"Of course, but it won't be much longer," she assured him, without the slightest compunction about lying. She had no idea how long it would take to catch the killer, or if he'd ever be caught at all. But at least she'd accomplished her purpose, and Nelson's career wouldn't be ruined just yet.

"Now tell me, Mrs. Brandt, how on earth did you ever decide to become a midwife?" Dennis asked, changing the subject completely.

Since he seemed to be genuinely interested, she gave him the slightly edited version of the story, simply mentioning that it was a relative's death in childbirth that had inspired her choice of careers. They chatted about inconsequential things for a few more minutes, until her parents judged it was safe to join them again. Then her father engaged Dennis in small talk until their guest deemed he had fulfilled his social obligations. In view of how violent the storm outside had become, this was rather sooner than he might have left, but the Deckers had no choice but to allow him to go.

Sarah gave him her hand, and he bowed over it. "It's been a delight meeting you, Mrs. Brandt. I hope it won't be long until we encounter each other again."

"I hope so, too," she replied sincerely, "and I promise not to ask you any favors next time."

"Even if you did, I could only be flattered by your attention," he replied.

Sarah smiled at the compliment, and he returned her smile. She didn't dare look at her parents. They must surely believe their matchmaking had been a success, and oddly enough, Sarah was no longer annoyed with them for tricking her. Meeting Mr. Dennis had been a pleasure, especially because he'd proven himself a reasonable man by doing what she asked him. Nothing could have made him more attractive to her. No, she wouldn't mind a bit if their paths crossed again.

"Did Richard agree to help your friend?" her mother asked when her husband had walked Dennis out and they were alone.

"Yes, he did," Sarah said. "And thank you for arranging for me to meet him."

Her mother's eyebrows rose. "I thought you were angry with me for that."

"I was merely annoyed, and not because you arranged for us to meet. You should have warned me, however, that he's a widower. I'm not the only widow he's ever been thrown together with, Mother. He had a right to feel he'd been deceived after Father invited him here to discuss business."

"But you *did* want to see him because of a business matter, didn't you, dear?" her mother asked without a trace of regret. "And if he suspected we were bringing him here to meet our daughter, he might not have come at all, especially with the weather being so bad."

"So I'm in your debt," Sarah said with a trace of amusement.

"Of course not," her mother insisted. "We would do anything in our power for you, Sarah, without ever expecting something in return. Surely, you know that."

"Especially if it involves meeting eligible men," she said, not believing her mother's protests for an instant.

"I hope someday you will thank us for that. You and Richard seemed to get on very well."

"Once he agreed to help Nelson, we got along famously," Sarah agreed. "Mr. Dennis is charming. How did his wife die?"

"Brain fever, they said. She fell ill, and the doctors could do nothing for her. They hadn't been married very long. He was devastated, naturally, and he went to Europe for a while to recover."

"And when he returned, his father put him to work at the bank," Sarah guessed.

"Something like that," her mother said. "I don't know all the details."

Her father came back into the room. "Dennis thanked me for introducing you," he said to Sarah. "He seemed quite taken with you."

"Don't sound so surprised, Father," Sarah chided. "I can be very charming when I make up my mind to it."

"Apparently," he replied, "but I felt certain you were trying to put him off with all that talk at supper about being a midwife."

"Not every man would consider that off-putting," Sarah said, wishing she didn't sound so defensive.

"Then we're fortunate Dennis isn't one of them," her father said, annoying her all over again.

"Now, dear," her mother chided, "we mustn't argue. Sarah has made a new friend, and she has also helped her neighbor. It has been a very successful evening."

Her father took a seat opposite her. "So it appears. You would do well to cultivate your acquaintance with young

Dennis," he advised. "He has a promising future, and he
stands to inherit a fortune."

"What other recommendation could I need?" Sarah
replied sarcastically.

"Sarah," her mother cautioned, "there's no reason to
take offense. Your father and I only want to see you comfortably settled. Is that so wrong of us?"

"I'd prefer you wanted to see me happy," Sarah said
with a sigh.

Her mother's smile was sad. "Why can't they be the
same thing?"

Frank decided his chances of finding Gilbert Giddings
at home were better early in the day. Even the worst
drunks went home eventually to sleep it off, and the storm
last night had probably driven Giddings there earlier than
usual. So he set off early Monday morning for the Giddings home. Strong winds had driven the storm out to sea,
but they continued to endanger every man's hat. Frank saw
more than a few scudding along in the gutters before he
reached Giddings' house.

As before, he had to knock several times before Mrs.
Giddings finally—and grudgingly—opened the door to
him. She looked paler than she had the last time he saw
her, and the strain of her circumstances had tightened the
skin across her cheeks so that she looked as if she were
held together with only the sheerest of willpower.

"Is your husband at home?" he asked. He felt sorry for
her, but he couldn't let sympathy stand in the way of doing
his job.

"He's here, but he's asleep," she said. "If you could
come back later—"

"I can't. Wake him up," Frank said, pushing the door
open wide enough to allow him to enter and making her
take a step back. "I'll wait."

She drew a breath, not out of fear but rather to steal herself against even more unpleasantness. "He won't be of
much use to you until later in the morning," she admitted,
although Frank could see it cost her a bit of the tiny scrap

of dignity she had left to do so. "The storm frightened him. He was quite . . . indisposed when he came home."

"I've dealt with drunks before. They usually cooperate pretty easily when they're feeling their worst. Just wake him up and tell him he can either talk to me here or I'll drag him down to Headquarters for a little chat."

He could see the hatred in her eyes, but he figured she didn't hate him for what he was doing to Gilbert. She simply resented him for causing her one more indignity when she wasn't sure she had the strength to bear even that one.

She didn't offer him a seat. There was, after all, no furniture in their front rooms. She simply turned and walked up the stairs, her back ramrod straight, her step slow and deliberate. She knew Frank would wait for as long as it took, so she took her time. It was the one thing over which she had control.

Frank was good at waiting, though, and he got some extra practice now. The silence of the house was oppressive, and except for a loud thump from upstairs that startled him—probably Gilbert falling out of bed or his wife hitting him with the chamber pot—he heard nothing until Mrs. Giddings appeared at the head of the stairs again.

She descended slowly and gracefully, her hand resting on the railing mostly for effect since she didn't appear to need the support. He noticed she had some color in her cheeks now, but she'd blotted every other trace of whatever emotion had caused it from her expression.

"My husband will be down shortly," she said when she reached the bottom of the stairs.

Frank gave her a moment, but she offered nothing else. "Do you mind if I wait in the back parlor? I'd like some privacy when I talk to him."

She'd been purposely rude to him so far, but she simply couldn't deny this request. Good manners had been too thoroughly bred into her. "Come," she said with an air of resignation, and led him to the back parlor, where he'd spoken with her and her son before.

She was going to leave him there, but he stopped her.

"Can you tell me where your husband was the night Anna Blake was killed?"

She looked at him for a long moment. She didn't appear to be thinking or even trying to decide whether to answer or not. She simply stared, a woman who had been pushed to the very edges of her strength and wasn't certain she had any reserves left. "He was at home that night, with me. And our son, Harold," she added.

"Why didn't he go out drinking as he usually does?" Frank asked, knowing he was hurting her but also knowing he needed the answer.

Again the silence before she replied. "Harold got paid that day. He brought a bottle home for his father so he'd stay with us for a change."

That sounded very thoughtful of the boy—and also very hard to believe. Families of drunkards usually did like them to stay at home but not if they were going to be drinking. Frank made a mental note of the niggling doubt and went on. "That means all of you were here, all night. No one went out for any reason?"

"No, we did not."

"Not even your son?"

She stared at him for another long moment, trying to read something into the question. "No, not even my son," she replied finally.

"He didn't even go out to buy his father another bottle?" Frank pressed, remembering what Mrs. Walcott had said about a young man coming to see Anna Blake the night she was killed.

Was that fear in her eyes? If so, she wasn't going to let it break her. "I told you, my son was home all night."

"And what night was this?"

Mrs. Giddings blinked in confusion. "What?"

"What night did your son get paid and your husband stay at home?"

"The night that woman was killed," she said with a trace of impatience.

"And which night of the week was that?" he pressed, testing her since her answers had come too easily.

She took a moment to consider. "Tuesday," she said finally.

"Your son gets paid on Tuesday?"

If he'd thought to catch her in a lie, he was disappointed. She was either a good liar or was telling the truth. "Harold does day labor. Sometimes he gets paid at the end of the day and must get another job the next morning."

Frank nodded. He could check on what the son had been doing that day, but it might not be easy. The people he was working for could be hard to find, since they probably would have moved on to new jobs by now. He might not even know their names, and even if he did and Frank could find them, they might not remember him. In any case, they'd have no idea whether Harold or his father had been at home that night or not.

"Now if you'll excuse me, I'll go see if I can hurry my husband along," she said. "I don't want to keep you any longer than necessary," she added with more than a trace of malice.

Frank didn't take offense, however. He'd been insulted by far more talented people than Mrs. Giddings. He took a seat on the worn sofa to wait, and finally, he was rewarded by the sound of shuffling footsteps in the hallway.

Frank literally winced at the sight of Gilbert Giddings. The man looked as if he'd be better off dead. His eyes were red-rimmed and bloodshot, his face ashen. He held himself closely, as if he were extremely old and feeble—or were afraid of jarring his aching head. He wore a collarless shirt, wrinkled trousers, and carpet slippers. His hair was uncombed and his face unshaven.

"Good morning," Frank said more loudly than necessary.

Giddings grabbed his head with both hands and groaned. This was going to be even easier than he'd hoped.

"Better have a seat, Giddings," Frank suggested in a more moderate tone. "I've got a few questions to ask you."

"I've already told you all I know," Giddings said in a hoarse whisper as he shuffled to a chair and carefully lowered himself into it.

"Where were you the night Anna Blake was killed?" Frank asked, getting up from his seat and walking over to where Giddings sat. Standing over someone, even if they were in fine fettle, was always a good tactic when interrogating them.

"What did my wife say?" Giddings asked, looking up through squinted eyes.

"Don't *you* know where you were?" Frank asked in amazement. "Or are you two trying to get your stories straight?"

"No, I—" Giddings started to say, but he'd forgotten to moderate his tone, and he had to grab his head again. "She told me I was home but . . ."

"But what?" Frank asked, making as if to grab Giddings by the shirt front.

He cringed away, as terrified of being manhandled as he was of loud noises. "Please, don't hurt me," he begged. "I'll tell you whatever you want to know!"

"Where were you the night Anna Blake was killed?" he repeated with far less patience.

"I don't know," Giddings whined. "I don't remember!"

"What do you mean, you don't remember? It was only a week ago."

"I know, but I . . . sometimes, I forget things."

"What kind of things?" Frank asked skeptically.

"Things that happen when I'm drunk," Giddings admitted as tears filled his eyes. "She drove me to this. I can't help myself!"

"Your wife?" Frank guessed.

"No," Giddings said, starting to shake his head vehemently but stopping abruptly when he realized how much pain that would cause him. "No," he repeated more softly, hands bracing his head again. "Anna did it. She was never satisfied. She said she'd go to my wife and my employer and ruin me! I had no choice! So I borrowed the money from a couple of the estates our firm handles. I was going to pay it back, just as soon as I . . ."

"As soon as you what?" Frank asked curiously when he hesitated. "As soon as you killed Anna?"

"No!" Giddings said too loudly and winced at the pain. "I didn't kill her," he added softly.

"I thought you couldn't remember what happened that night," Frank reminded him.

"I don't. I mean, I don't know." Giddings blubbered, awash in self-pity. "I don't know anything anymore."

"I guess that means you also don't know if your wife and son were home that night, either," Frank said.

Even through his haze of pain, Giddings heard the implication. "My wife and son had nothing to do with this. How can you even suggest such a thing?"

"They had a very good reason to want Anna Blake out of the way," Frank pointed out. "She'd taken everything they had and ruined you. They both must have hated her."

"That doesn't mean they killed her!" Giddings protested in a horrified whisper. "Harold is only a boy and my wife could never harm another human being!"

Frank figured his wife was very close to harming Gilbert very seriously if he didn't sober up and start taking responsibility for his family again. That was only an opinion, however, and try as he might, he had a difficult time imagining a lady like Mrs. Giddings stealing through the darkened city streets with a knife concealed in the folds of her cloak so she could murder her husband's mistress. Women hardly ever killed with knives except in the heat of passion or self-defense. They didn't like making a mess. And Anna Blake wasn't killed in the heat of passion or self-defense, as far as Frank could determine, certainly not if her killer had arranged to meet her for just the purpose of killing her.

"Would your wife lie to protect you, Giddings?" Frank asked.

He looked up with his rheumy eyes and frowned. "I have no idea."

"Would she lie to protect your son?" Frank asked.

Giddings face drained of what little color was left. "No," he said, his eyes filled with horror.

Frank didn't think he was answering the question.

10

Sarah made her way quickly down Bank Street, clutching her umbrella against the rains that had returned and trying not to look at the Ellsworths' front porch. Not seeing Mrs. Ellsworth there, waiting to speak a cheery word and commiserate with her, was too depressing after the day she'd had. At least the baby she had delivered today had been born healthy. This morning, upon returning home from her parents' home where she'd spent the night, she'd been trying to decide what she could do that would help exonerate Nelson Ellsworth when an elderly gentleman had come to her door. He'd begged her to come immediately.

His granddaughter was giving birth, he told her, and indeed she was, even though she was only thirteen and hardly more than a baby herself. The girl was, in fact, his great-granddaughter, the illegitimate child of his granddaughter who'd died giving birth to her. He and his wife had taken the child to raise, since their daughter had long since deserted the family. They'd hoped to be able to keep this girl-child from the fates of her mother and grandmother, but she'd been seduced—or raped, the difference was slight for a girl so young—by some older boys in the neighborhood. Even the girl herself had no idea which of them had fathered the child. In spite of all odds, the baby and the mother appeared to be doing well, however, and the baby was a boy. If nothing else, he'd never give birth to a child before even reaching maturity. Of course, he might die of disease or neglect before reaching maturity, too. Sarah couldn't allow herself to think of such things, though. If she did, she'd give up completely.

She'd purchased a copy of the *Evening World* from a newsboy on Fifth Avenue, but she hadn't looked at it yet. If Webster Prescott had written another story about Anna and Nelson, she didn't want to discover it until she was sitting down in the privacy of her own home.

To her relief, no reporters loitered in front of the Ellsworth house this evening. She wondered if they had just taken shelter from the weather or if they were following other threads of the story. She could even go knock on the Ellsworths' front door today without risking making a public spectacle, but she decided to wait until she'd had time to get a bite of supper first. She hadn't eaten since breakfast, having refused the offer of a meal at the flat where she'd delivered the baby today. They hadn't looked as if they could spare any food, and only the fear of wounding their pride had induced her to accept a payment for her services. Fortunately, they hadn't suspected that the amount she'd charged them was only a fraction of her usual fee.

From habit, she glanced over at the Ellsworths' porch as she unlocked her own door and stepped inside. She would never complain again about her neighbor being nosy, she vowed.

She found some bread and cheese and made herself a sandwich. As she sat to eat it, she spread the newspaper on the table in front of her. The headline she was looking for was prominently displayed: ACTRESS PLAYS A DEADLY ROLE.

"Malloy," Sarah muttered, "I hope you know what you're doing."

Although the newspapers did not identify the reporter who had written each particular story, Sarah easily recognized Webster Prescott's handiwork by the content. The article revealed that prior to her death, Anna Blake had made her living "on the boards," playing a succession of minor roles in minor productions produced by minor production companies in obscure theaters. The titles of the plays were suggestive, such as *Molly, Girl of the Streets* and *The Rape of the Sabine Women*. If Anna Blake had appeared in anything like a serious drama, Prescott hadn't seen fit to mention it. He was more interested in sensationalizing her past and making her sound like a scarlet woman who had seduced innocent gentlemen and deserved her awful fate.

Sarah knew perfectly well that Anna Blake *was* a scarlet woman, of course, but she hated seeing the newspaper say so. Too many people already judged females too harshly. Girls like the one whose baby she'd delivered today were branded as harlots and worse, as if they'd chosen their fates instead of being victimized, since men seemed to delight in blaming females for their own debauchery. Heaven knew, the boy who had fathered that girl's baby would never suffer any stigma because of it.

How curious, then, that Mr. Giddings and Nelson Ellsworth had truly fallen prey to a seductress. Women who fell from grace were always branded as evil, but few really were the kind of schemer that Anna Blake was. And oddly enough, such women could only dupe unworldly, middle-class men. Wealthy men would either pay them off or laugh at their threats—if you were rich enough, you need fear nothing. Poor men would also laugh—the poor could not afford niceties like honor and responsibility. Only men who had something worth protecting but little means of protecting it were susceptible to the Anna Blakes of the world.

She had, Sarah reflected, chosen her victims well, however. While Giddings wasn't personally wealthy, he was comfortable enough and so positioned in life that he couldn't afford a scandal. He also had access to ample funds, and if pushed far enough, as he was, he would steal them to protect his good name.

But what still didn't make sense, at least to Sarah, was

why Anna had chosen Nelson Ellsworth. Like Giddings, he did have access to vast amounts of money, even though he wasn't wealthy himself. But as a bachelor, he needn't fear scandal, and if his better nature demanded that he provide for his child, he could marry the mother, which he had offered to do. No matter how many times Sarah thought about it, she couldn't make sense of it. Why choose Nelson?

She'd finished up her sandwich and washed it down with some cider that was beginning to turn. She'd have to offer it to Malloy when he came next. He wouldn't mind hard cider, she thought with a smile.

Briefly, she considered taking the newspaper over to her neighbors, but then she decided against it. She could tell them the information. They didn't have to know Nelson was still being mentioned prominently on the front page of every scandal sheet in town.

Frank cursed under his breath as he made his way through the crowded hospital ward at Bellevue the next morning. Rows of beds lined the walls, most of them filled with men in various stages of dying. No one came to the hospital unless they were dying. The odors of rotting limbs and diseased bowels and God knew what nearly gagged him, but he set his teeth and refused to display any weakness. The smell wasn't really any worse than an ordinary flophouse, he told himself, and he'd certainly seen his share of them, looking for suspects. At least the floors were reasonably clean and the beds had laundered linen and no lice.

But it wasn't really the odors. It was the dying. Frank knew that smell, and it brought back far too many memories.

Finally, he saw the face he'd been looking for. It was paler than it had been the last time he saw it, but he recognized it easily.

"Prescott!" Frank called, hoping the eyes would open. To his great relief, they did.

Webster Prescott smiled wanly at the sight of him.

"How'd you find me?" he asked, his voice faint and breathy.

"You asked for me, remember? The cop who found you in that alley said you just kept begging him to send for me. Said you wouldn't get in the ambulance until he promised. So what in the hell happened to you?"

Prescott's young face wrinkled in pain. "Somebody stabbed me." He gestured toward his left side, and Frank managed not to wince at the thought of how close his attacker had come to his heart.

"I knew that much," Frank said. "You wouldn't say who did it, though. Or why. At least to the cop who found you. He's pretty mad about it, too."

"I didn't want to tell anybody," he said, his voice so faint Frank had to lean closer to hear. "Somebody else might get the story."

Frank shook his head in disgust. "You reporters. All you think about is getting the story. I guess you thought you were safe telling *me*, though. You know how I hate you lot, so I wouldn't go telling your competitors."

"Something like that," Prescott said, smiling a crooked, pained grin.

"All right then, who stabbed you?"

"A woman."

Frank grinned back and shook his head. "They get real upset if you don't pay them," he teased.

Prescott might have been blushing, but he tried not to let on. "No, it wasn't *that*. She . . . she sent a message. Said . . . she knew something . . . about Anna Blake."

Frank raised his eyebrows in surprise. "This was about Anna Blake's murder?"

"Why do you think . . . I was worried about . . . the story?" he asked.

"Let me get this straight. Some woman sent you a message claiming she had information about Anna Blake's death?"

Prescott nodded weakly.

"And she wanted to meet you in an alley?"

"No, in the Square."

"Washington Square?"

He nodded again. "By the fountain."

"Then how did you end up stabbed in an alley?"

"She wanted . . . privacy . . . in the mews."

"You followed her into the stables? The ones behind the houses on Washington Square?"

Prescott nodded.

"And what did she tell you?"

"Nothing . . . she just . . . stabbed me."

This was making no sense. "What did she look like?"

"Didn't see . . . her face. Dark . . . wore a cloak . . . with a hood . . ."

"But you're sure it was a woman?"

"Sounded like . . . Strong, though."

"She was strong? How do you know?"

"Pushed me . . . against the wall. Held my arm . . ." He lifted his right arm and pulled back the sleeve of his nightshirt. Frank saw the faint shading of forming bruises.

If a woman had done this, she was strong indeed. But Frank had another theory that made more sense. "Could it have been a man dressed as a woman? How tall was she?"

Prescott frowned as he considered Frank's suggestion and held up a hand even with his mouth. Prescott was tall, so the height he indicated could have described Frank. Or Gilbert Giddings and his son. But why would either of the Giddings want to kill Webster Prescott? And were they likely to dress up like a woman to do it?

Frank found a chair and brought it over to Prescott's bedside. When he was seated, he pulled out his notebook and a pencil. "You have to tell me everything you've found out about Anna Blake. Don't worry," he added at Prescott's scowl. "I won't sell the story to the *Herald*."

"Or the *Sun*," Prescott added.

"Or anybody else," Frank said. "Now start talking."

Sarah had just returned from the Gansevoort Market, having shopped both for herself and for the Ellsworths, when she found a message from Malloy stuck in her front door. She struggled inside, trying to simultaneously unlock the door, open it, read the note, and not drop her purchases.

He was, he explained, sending this message with a beat cop in hopes that she would receive it as soon as possible. He told her Webster Prescott had been stabbed, possibly by the same person who had killed Anna Blake! He was asking her to go over to Bellevue and make sure the boy was receiving proper care. Malloy, it seemed, had a sentimental streak. Or else he thought Prescott was too valuable a witness to lose.

When she'd made her way into the kitchen and set her market basket down, she reread the note again, looking for some sort of indication that Malloy knew who the killer was and was going to arrest him. But she found not a single clue. Wasn't that just like a man, not to tell her the most important thing?

She hastily put away her own purchases and dropped off the things she'd bought for the Ellsworths. Mrs. Ellsworth obviously wanted her to stay and visit for a while, but when Sarah told her where she was going in such a hurry, the old woman sent her off with a blessing. And a rabbit's foot for good luck. Sarah decided she'd give it to Webster Prescott, since he'd need it far more than she.

Many of the people in the hospital knew Sarah and remembered her husband, Tom, so it took her a while to make her way to the ward where Prescott lay. Fortunately, her status also gave her the ability to inquire about his condition and receive an honest answer.

The news wasn't very good. The knife had missed his heart but had damaged his lung. He'd lost a lot of blood and was very weak. If he got a bad infection, he probably wouldn't make it, and he could hardly avoid getting an infection with a wound like that. And of course, pneumonia was always a possibility, too. On the other hand, he was young and healthy, which meant he stood a small chance.

Sarah found him sleeping, and when she touched his forehead, she detected a slight fever.

"Could I have some water?" he asked hoarsely, without opening his eyes.

Sarah got him a glass of water and held it to his lips while he drank. Then he fell back on the pillow, exhausted. But he did open his eyes to thank her, and his puzzled frown told her he couldn't quite remember who she was. "You're not a nurse," he said.

She didn't like how weak his voice was. "No, I'm Sarah Brandt. I live next door to Nelson Ellsworth."

A healthy reporter would have a dozen questions to ask her—who'd told her he was here, why had she come, what did she want?—but he could only manage a weak, "Why?"

"Mr. Malloy asked me to check on you. I also happen to be a nurse. He wants to make sure you're getting good care," she explained, picking up his wrist and checking his pulse. It seemed very fast. "Are you having a lot of pain?"

His young face twisted. "They gave me morphine, but . . ."

"Do you mind if I check your bandage?"

She didn't wait for a reply. With skilled hands, she adjusted the blanket and raised his nightshirt while still preserving his modesty. The bandage was clean and dry except for a small, fresh bloodstain. Every instinct demanded that she offer to take him home where he wouldn't be exposed to the contagion of the other patients and where she could give him constant care. She didn't, though, because she knew the trip across town would be too much for him in his weakened condition.

"Can you take a deep breath?" she asked, and he merely gazed at her incredulously. "I'll make sure the nurses take special care of you," she told him, "but you must do everything they tell you, even if it hurts. Otherwise, you'll die."

What little color he had left leached away at that. "I don't want to die."

"That's good," Sarah said briskly. "Then be as determined to live as you were to get the story on Nelson Ellsworth. Do you have any family in the city? Someone who can visit you and bring you food?"

"They feed me here," he said, confused.

"You'll need better food than you can get here, and someone to watch over you all the time. You should have beef broth to build your blood. Is there someone who would bring it for you?"

"I have an aunt in Brooklyn," he said doubtfully.

Brooklyn had once been practically another country, accessible only by water, but now that they'd opened that amazing bridge, people traveled from there to the city and back every day. "If you give me her address, I'll send her a message and tell her what you'll need."

Sarah didn't stop to wonder why she was being so considerate of a man who had tried to ruin Nelson Ellsworth's life. From his point of view, of course, he'd done Nelson a good turn by vilifying Anna Blake. And he was just doing his job, after all. Never mind that doing his job meant making other people's lives miserable. None of that really mattered, however, because Malloy had asked her to help him. If Malloy thought he was worth saving, she had no reason to question his judgment. The only thing she questioned was his sudden concern for a man whose profession he despised, but he'd tell her why the next time she saw him. She'd see to that.

Overriding Prescott's feeble protests, Sarah gave him a cool sponge bath in an effort to help his body fight the fever that was building. Then she discussed his care with the nurses on the ward. They were overworked as it was and had no time to give special care to any of their patients, but Sarah extracted promises to keep a close watch on him and to let her know if he got worse.

Only when she'd done all she could for the moment did she suddenly realize that Malloy's concern for the boy might not be so generous after all. "Mr. Malloy said that your stabbing might have something to do with Anna Blake's death," she tried.

When he struggled to reply, she had a pang of guilt over bothering him again, but then she remembered the Ellsworths and how their lives had been practically destroyed by all of this.

"A woman . . ." he said very faintly, "Said she knew something . . . she stabbed me. I think . . ."

Sarah gaped at him, trying to make sense of it. "A

woman who claimed to know something about Anna's death stabbed you?"

He nodded.

This didn't make any sense. Why would someone want to stab a newspaper reporter? She'd been very angry with a lot of them the past few days, but to actually lure one to his death and shove a knife into his side was something else entirely. And a woman, too. How very unusual. This person had wanted Webster Prescott in particular to die. But why? And why him of all the reporters working on the case?

"Did you get some new information recently? Something that hasn't been in the newspaper yet?" she asked.

"Anna's friend . . . at the theater . . ."

"What theater?"

"Tivoli," he said.

"What's her name?"

"Irene."

"What did she tell you?" Sarah asked, leaning over, willing him to answer her. But he was slipping away. The latest dose of morphine was finally doing its job.

"Actress," he muttered before the drug overcame him.

Sarah sighed in frustration. At least she knew he'd been talking to an actress named Irene at the Tivoli Theater. Did Malloy know? Had he gotten all the information from Prescott, and was he even now questioning this Irene? She'd have to track down Malloy immediately and find out. Or else find Irene herself, just in case he wasn't.

Finding Malloy was never easy, and going to Police Headquarters on Mulberry Street in search of him was far from pleasant. On the other hand, she could be fairly certain that an actress would be at the theater where she worked this evening. The hospital would probably let her use a telephone to call Headquarters and leave a message for Malloy. He wouldn't appreciate all the teasing he'd get over it, but that couldn't be helped. He'd also get teased if she went down there in person. She might yet hear from Malloy this afternoon. If not, and if no one decided to deliver today, she could go find this Irene tonight.

First, however, she'd have to get home and post a letter to Prescott's aunt. She'd receive it tomorrow, and if she was any kind of a female, she'd be across the bridge with a basketful of nutritious food for Prescott the same day. Sarah would check on him first thing in the morning, too, and do whatever she could to make him more comfortable.

Meanwhile, she'd wait to hear from Malloy and go visit Irene at the Tivoli Theater.

The theater hadn't opened yet when Sarah arrived that evening, and the front doors were locked. The signs outside urged people to come and see the current product and featured a drawing of a scantily clad female fleeing from an evil-looking man with a handlebar mustache and wearing a black top hat. The names of the actors listed on the sign did not include anyone named Irene.

Sarah knew little about the theater, but she assumed the actors would enter through a rear door, since they had to be at the theater earlier than the patrons in order to prepare for the performance. She had also, in her years of attending the theater, never seen an actor entering or leaving, which meant they came and went at different times and through different doors than the audience. In fact, now that she thought about it, she'd heard about the men who waited outside the theater after a performance to meet the actresses. Weren't they called Stage Door Billys? No, Jimmies or Johnnies or something like that. She couldn't remember exactly. Which meant there must be a stage door that the actors used someplace off the main street, a place where would-be Lotharios could wait.

Pleased at her deduction, Sarah walked to the side of the building until she found the alley that ran beside the theater. Just as she'd suspected, she located an unmarked and inconspicuous door on the side of the building, near the rear. It, too, was locked, but when she knocked, an elderly gentleman opened it and peered out at her suspiciously.

"Yeah?" he asked gruffly.

She tried a friendly smile. "I'm looking for Irene. Is she here yet?"

The smile didn't seem to affect him at all. In fact, he didn't bat an eye. "Who're you?"

Sarah surprised herself with her cleverness. "I'm Irene's cousin, Sarah. I live in Brooklyn, and she told me if I came to see her, she'd show me the stage and everything and let me watch her get ready for the play and—"

The old man interrupted her with a grunt and pulled the door open wide enough for her to enter. "I expect you wanna be an actress, too," he grumbled. "Well, don't get your hopes up, girlie. You're a little long in the tooth to be starting out. Unless you've got nice ankles. They might give you a try if you've got nice ankles. I could check and give you my opinion," he offered, glancing down hopefully.

Sarah glared at him, but he didn't notice because he was looking at the floor, waiting for her to lift her skirt. "I don't want to be an actress," she said. "I just want to see Irene."

He grunted again, this time in disappointment. "She's down there," he said, pointing vaguely toward a hallway and turning away. He'd lost interest since she wasn't going to show him her ankles.

Not wishing to press her luck by asking for more explicit instructions, Sarah set off, figuring if she couldn't find Irene, she'd most certainly find someone who could.

As it turned out, she needed no further assistance. The dingy corridor she entered led past several doors, but only one was ajar. Through it, Sarah could hear the sound of women's voices. Deciding this was very promising, she called into the opened doorway, "Irene?"

The voices ceased, and a long moment of suspicious silence followed.

"Irene, are you there?" Sarah called again, feigning confidence. If Irene wasn't there, she'd have to bluff her way past others the way she'd bluffed past the doorman.

But a voice said, "Who is it?" and Sarah knew she need look no further. She pushed the door open all the way and stepped in to find a narrow room lined on both sides with crudely built shelves that apparently served as dressing tables with mirrors above them. The shelves were littered with the same kinds of grease paints Sarah had found in Anna Blake's room, along with wigs and brushes, combs and hand mirrors, and scraps of ribbon and hairpins and feathers and all sorts of grooming items. At the far end of the room stood racks of what appeared to be costumes, judging by their garish colors and fabrics.

Three young women in various stages of undress stood in the center of the room. The one who wore a wrapper carelessly draped over her underclothes was staring at her most intently, while the other two seemed merely curious. "Hello, Irene," Sarah said to the one who was staring. "I'm Sarah Brandt."

"Do I know you?" she asked warily. She wasn't old, not in years. Her body still retained its youthful curves and her face showed no signs of dissipation. Her eyes, however, revealed a wealth of experience, and they'd taken Sarah's measure in one glance. She didn't seem impressed by what she'd seen.

"I'm a friend of Anna Blake's," Sarah tried.

Instantly, the two curious women moved away and busied themselves with the costumes at the far end of the room. Irene looked even warier now, as if she might bolt. Murder had a way of making people cautious, Sarah had learned.

"A newspaper reporter, Webster Prescott, said you knew Anna," Sarah tried quickly, in an attempt to break through Irene's understandable reluctance to speak of Anna Blake to a stranger. "I'm trying to find out who killed her, and if you could—"

"*You?*" she scoffed. "How could you find a killer? And why would somebody like you care who killed Anna anyway?"

Sarah doubted Irene would understand her concern for Nelson Ellsworth even if she'd felt like explaining it, which she didn't, so she said, "I want to see justice done. The police . . ." Sarah made a helpless motion with her hand. "I don't think they care very much about finding the killer."

"I thought that fellow did it, the one in the newspaper

who was her lover," Irene said. "That's what the reporter said, anyway."

Sarah only needed a second to come up with a new lie. "That's what the police are trying to make everyone believe so they don't have to exert themselves to find the real killer. But he didn't do it, and Mr. Prescott is helping me find out who did."

Irene didn't care about any of this. "I gotta get ready for the performance," she said impatiently.

"I don't want to bother you," Sarah said. "But I only have a few questions, and I'd be willing to pay you for your time. It'll only take a few minutes."

The two women who had been so interested in the costumes suddenly turned their attention back to Sarah. "I knew Anna," one of them offered.

"You did not," Irene snapped. "Shut your lying mouth." Then to Sarah, "Come out here where we can talk."

She led Sarah back into the corridor. Some more women had arrived and were making their way toward the dressing room. Irene took Sarah's arm and drew her down to the far end of the corridor, into the shadows where the gaslights on the walls didn't quite reach.

"I can't talk long," she warned. "What do you wanna know?"

"How long did you know Anna?"

"A couple years. Ever since I joined the troupe."

"She was here when you came?"

"That's right. Been with them a long time, she said."

"Why did she stop acting?"

Irene smiled strangely. "You mean why did she stop working here?"

"Yes."

"She was getting old, you know? Too old for any of the good parts. She could still sing, but they put her in the back row. She didn't like it, but there wasn't nothing she could do about it. Then she met this fellow."

"What fellow?"

"I don't know his name. He'd wait at the stage door for

her. Hadn't nobody waited for her for a long time. We was all pretty surprised."

"What did he look like?"

She shrugged. "Skinny. Short beard. Nice clothes. Good manners. A real dandy. He owned the house where she went to live."

"Mr. Walcott?" Sarah asked in surprise.

"That's him," Irene said. "You know him?"

"Yes. Are you saying he was a Stage Door Jimmy?"

Irene smiled condescendingly. "That's Stage Door *Johnny*, and yeah, he was one. He'd wait out there after the show and give her flowers or something. Some of the swells, they give you jewelry or really nice things. Flowers ain't good for nothing, but they're nice. And Anna, she liked the attention, 'cause she hadn't had any in a while, her being so old."

"How old was she?" Sarah asked in amazement.

"Twenty-five, I think. At least, that's what she'd admit to."

Sarah didn't think that was very old, but since the doorman had deemed her too "long in the tooth" to begin an acting career, she had to assume different standards prevailed in the theater. "I'm sorry I interrupted you. Go on. Mr. Walcott was giving her presents."

Irene shrugged again. "Then next thing you know, she says she's going to live with this Walcott. Says he's got a rooming house where she can live for free, and she won't have to work no more."

That sounded suspicious. The Walcotts definitely gave the impression the girls were paying customers. Unless Anna was a special case. "How would she support herself if she didn't work? Even with a free room?" Sarah asked.

Irene made a face. "We had our ideas. Only one kind of place gives you a free room, but we figured she'd be too old to attract much in that trade either. She said it wasn't that kind of a house, though. Just laughed when I warned her to be careful."

"Why were you worried about her?"

Irene gave her a pitying look. "A girl has to be careful.

Nobody takes care of you for nothing. I figured this fellow wanted something from her, even if I couldn't figure out what it was. But she wasn't worried. She told me she was just gonna do what Francine did and end up rich and living in the country."

"Who's Francine?"

"She worked here, too. She found a rich fellow to take care of her, or that's what she said when she left here. Anna said Mr. Walcott introduced Francine to her gentleman friend and he was gonna do the same for her."

"What does Francine look like?" Sarah asked, thinking of Catherine Porter.

"Short with red hair. Lots of freckles."

Not the same person. "Do you know a Catherine Porter?" she asked.

Irene shook her head. "Never heard of her . . . Oh, wait, could that be Katie Porter?"

"I'm sure it could. She's an actress, too. She has dark hair, very Irish looking."

"That's probably her. I haven't seen her for a while. I thought she'd gone on tour or something. She hasn't been around."

"She lives at Mr. Walcott's house, too," Sarah offered.

Irene registered surprise. "Does she now? Ain't that interesting? I guess it really is a brothel, then. Wasn't Anna surprised?"

"What makes you think it was a brothel?"

"Because of Katie. She never liked being poor. If she couldn't get work on the stage, she'd find some on her back, if you know what I mean. She never would admit to being a whore, because she only did it now and then, but if you say she was working in that house . . ." She shrugged again, her meaning clear.

Sarah was certain the Walcotts didn't operate a brothel, but a woman who'd had experience in both acting and prostitution would certainly be an asset if all the women there were doing what Anna Blake was doing. "Has Mr. Walcott taken an interest in any of the other actresses in the theater?"

"Not that I know of. Listen, that's all I know, and I gotta get back. You said you'd pay me . . ."

Sarah reached into her purse and pulled out five dollars, which was probably what Irene earned here in a week. "Thank you for your help," she said, slipping the money into Irene's outstretched hand.

She counted the money and smiled. "Any time." She stuffed the money down into the bodice of her corset and hurried back to the dressing room without bothering to say good-bye.

Sarah stared after her for a long moment, wondering what, if anything, she had really learned. With a sigh, she made her way back down the corridor to the exit. Maybe, she thought, Malloy had had better luck.

The gaslights were lit by the time Sarah reached Bank Street, and she was wishing she'd worn a heavier coat. Her spirits rose instantly when she saw a man sitting on her front step, waiting for her. She needed to see Malloy and find out what he'd learned. But as she got closer, and the man rose to his feet to meet her, she realized it wasn't Malloy after all.

"Mrs. Brandt," he said with a pleasant smile, pulling off his hat.

"Mr. Dennis," Sarah said, making no attempt to hide her amazement, although she did manage not to sound disappointed. She couldn't help glancing at the Ellsworth house, but no faces stared out of the front windows. Had Mrs. Ellsworth or Nelson seen him sitting here? They would surely wonder about that. Sarah was wondering herself. "What brings you here?"

His smile vanished. "I wish I could tell you I'd come on a social visit, but I'm afraid I have some bad news for you. I wanted to break it to you myself first."

"What do you mean, *first*?" she asked apprehensively.

"I mean, before you read it in the newspaper." He glanced up and down the street, as if trying to judge whether or not he would be overheard.

"Why don't you come inside?" she suggested, instinctively knowing she didn't want anyone else to overhear his news either.

He followed her up the front steps and waited while she unlocked the front door. When they were inside, she removed her jacket and took his hat. He was looking curiously around her office. "This is very impressive. You have quite a bit of equipment here," he remarked.

"My husband was a physician," she reminded him. "This was his office originally. I don't use a lot of it."

He looked a little ill at ease. Most people were in the presence of such intimidating furnishings, but Sarah did nothing to reassure him. She didn't want him to feel comfortable if he was bringing her bad news. She bade him be seated in one of the chairs that sat by the front window, and she took the other.

When they were seated, she said, "You came to tell me something."

His smile was apologetic. "I wish I could have forgotten. This gives me no pleasure, Mrs. Brandt. I know you are a friend to the Ellsworths, and—"

"What is it?" she snapped, her patience stretched to the breaking point after her long and frustrating day.

He blinked in surprise at her tone, but he said, "I had an auditor check our books."

"What books?"

"Our bank records," he explained. "Ordinarily, the bank's records are checked for accuracy only once a year, but in light of what you told me . . ."

"What did I tell you?" Sarah asked with growing alarm when he hesitated.

"That Nelson Ellsworth was being blackmailed by a woman of ill repute."

"I didn't tell you any such thing!" she protested.

He gave her the kind of patronizing look that set her teeth on edge. "You told me that she had demanded money from another man and that he had stolen it from his employer. You also told me this woman had seduced Nelson as well. Mrs. Brandt, I would be foolish indeed—and remiss in my duties—if I didn't reassure myself that Mr. Ellsworth hadn't done the same thing that other man did."

"But Nelson is innocent!"

"Are you saying he didn't give her money?"

"Well, he did, but—"

"I felt certain he had, and I had to make certain that money didn't come from the bank," he said so reasonably she wanted to slap him.

"Nelson would never take anything that didn't belong to him," Sarah insisted.

"Your confidence in him is commendable, I'm sure, but the fact is, Mrs. Brandt, that the auditors found money missing."

"That's impossible!" Sarah insisted.

"I assure you, it's very possible. He stole nearly ten thousand dollars."

II

WHEN MALLOY KNOCKED ON HER DOOR, SARAH WAS still sitting in the chair where she'd been when Richard Dennis had left almost an hour earlier. She forced herself to get up and let him in.

As soon as Malloy saw her face, he frowned. "What happened?"

"I did a very stupid thing," she said, waiting until he'd hung his hat, then leading him back into the kitchen. She didn't even bother to ask herself why she took him into the kitchen. It just seemed the right place to go.

"Does this have anything to do with Anna Blake's murder?" he asked as he seated himself at the table. "Or is this stupid thing something in your regular life?"

"Both," she said, filling the coffeepot with water. "I can't believe I did this." The worst part was that she hadn't mentioned to Malloy that she was going to meet Richard Dennis and ask for his help because she'd been afraid he wouldn't approve. If only she'd given him a chance to talk her out of it!

She put some kindling into the stove and lit it, then fed in some wood until the fire was going. Only when she felt the heat did she realize how cold she'd become, sitting alone with her guilt as night settled over the city. When she had put the coffee on to boil and had nothing left to do, she forced herself to take the seat opposite Malloy and look him straight in the eye.

But when she saw his worried frown, she had to cover her face with both hands and groan. She didn't deserve his concern. At least it would vanish the instant she told him what she'd done. She could deal with his anger. She deserved that, after all.

"I asked Nelson's employer not to dismiss him," she said.

"That doesn't sound so stupid," Malloy said. "Unless he turned you down."

Sarah rubbed her temples where a headache was throbbing. "He didn't turn me down. He promised to help for as long as he could or until Nelson was arrested, which I assured him wouldn't happen."

He didn't say anything, and she hazarded a glance at him. He still looked worried. About her. She wanted to groan again.

"He didn't dismiss Nelson, but he did have some auditors come in to check the bank's books. He was just being careful, he said. Because Anna Blake had blackmailed another man who stole money from his employer to pay her."

"You told him *that*?" Malloy asked incredulously.

"I warned you this was stupid!" she cried. "I was trying to convince him that Nelson was an innocent victim of a evil woman. I wanted him to know just how evil she really was!"

"So he was afraid Nelson was stealing from the bank to pay her off, too," Malloy said. "And was he?"

Sarah buried her face in her hands again. "Oh, Malloy, he couldn't have been! I know Nelson would never steal from anyone!"

"But . . . ?" Malloy said.

She swallowed the bile that rose up in her throat. "But there's ten thousand dollars missing from the bank."

"Good God."

"My reaction exactly."

"Have you told Nelson all this?"

"I haven't had the courage to face them yet," she admitted. "I know he didn't do it, but . . ."

"He'll deny it even if he did," Malloy pointed out. "Is this bank fellow going to press charges against Nelson?"

"He said he wasn't. He said the scandal would be bad for the bank. In situations like this, they handle things very quietly. They'll simply dismiss Nelson."

Malloy's frown deepened. "Ten thousand dollars is a lot of money. I'd think they'd try to get at least some of it back from him. Giddings's law partners made him repay them."

"I got the impression that Mr. Dennis was going to cover the loss himself. He doesn't hold out much hope of getting anything from Nelson, I guess. Mr. Dennis's father put him in charge of the bank so he could prove himself, and he'd rather lose the money than his father's respect."

"How do you know so much about this Mr. Dennis and his personal life?" Malloy asked suspiciously.

This is the part she'd been dreading. "My parents arranged for us to meet last Sunday so I could plead Nelson's case to him. I couldn't just walk into his office, a total stranger, and ask him to do something like that!" she protested at his disapproving scowl. "He'd think I was insane."

"But when Felix Decker's daughter asked him, he couldn't refuse," Malloy guessed.

Sarah didn't like the way that sounded "I'd like to think I also impressed him with my personal charm."

"I'm sure you did."

"What does that mean?" Sarah demanded.

"That means . . . Never mind what it means. How did you find out about the missing money?"

"Mr. Dennis came by this evening to tell me."

"How considerate of him," Malloy said acidly. "Did he go next door and tell Nelson, too?"

"No, I . . ." Sarah hesitated when she realized she hadn't even inquired about this.

Malloy raised his eyebrows. "Was he going to leave that to you?"

"We really didn't discuss it," Sarah snapped. "I'm sure he's going to officially notify Nelson that he's dismissed or something."

"So this visit he made to you, was that considered *un*-official?"

"It was a courtesy, so I wouldn't think he'd betrayed my trust when he dismissed Nelson."

"He's a real gentleman. Except, of course, that he's covering up a crime and letting a thief get away. Wasn't he even interested in finding out if Nelson really was the one who stole the money? Because if he wasn't, then he's still got a thief working for him."

"He . . . I didn't think to ask him that," Sarah admitted. Her headache was pounding even harder now. "I'll go see him first thing in the morning and point that out."

"No, you won't," Malloy said. "I'll go see him."

"He doesn't want the police involved," she reminded him. "If he knows I sent you—"

"He won't know anything. I'll tell him Nelson sent me. Nelson didn't do it, and he wants the real thief caught. He also wants his name cleared, so he asked me to investigate."

That sounded fairly reasonable, she supposed, although Dennis wouldn't like it. "Oh, Malloy, how could this have happened? How could money be missing from the bank at the same time Nelson was being blackmailed?"

Malloy stared at her for a long moment, his broad face expressionless, his eyes dark and unfathomable. "It might be because Nelson really did take the money."

But Sarah had spent the past hour considering that very possibility. "No, I'm sure he didn't take it."

"You *can't* be sure," he reminded her.

"Yes, I can. It's too much money."

"What do you mean?"

"Ten thousand dollars! Anna had only asked for *one* thousand. Before that, Nelson had been paying her rent, but he's a frugal man. He could easily afford an expense like that out of his own pocket, at least for a while. You know Nelson. Even if he could bring himself to steal, he'd never steal ten times more than he needed! He's too methodical and practical."

Malloy didn't argue. She could almost see him considering her theory and coming to the same conclusion she had. "Maybe there isn't any money missing at all," he said after a moment.

"What?"

"Maybe this banker just told you that so he'd have an excuse to get rid of Nelson without losing your good opinion."

Sarah gaped at him. "I'm sure my good opinion doesn't mean *that* much to him."

"Are you?" Malloy asked. "Is this Dennis a married man?"

"He's . . . a widower," she admitted reluctantly, not liking where this conversation was going.

"How old is he?"

"About your age," she allowed.

Malloy nodded as if she'd proven his point.

"What difference could that possibly make?" she asked impatiently.

"Believe me, it makes a lot of difference."

"In what way?"

"In every way." A flush had crawled up his neck. "When a man wants a beautiful woman, he'll do just about anything to keep her good opinion."

Sarah's jaw dropped in surprise, but before she could even frame a response, he said, "The coffee's boiling over."

Instinctively, she jumped up to rescue it. By the time she'd gotten the pot off the heat, burned her finger, found some butter to put on it, and poured them both some coffee, the shock of his remark had passed.

When she turned back to face him, his expression was once again bland, and the flush had faded from his face.

Before she could say a word, he said, "Did you go see Prescott at the hospital?"

"Yes," she said, grateful for the change of subject. She

set the coffee cups on the table and took her seat again. "He's not doing very well."

"Is there any chance he'll survive?"

"He might. He's got an aunt. I'm going to . . . Oh, dear, I was going to write her a letter this evening to ask her to visit him and bring him some nourishing food. Then Mr. Dennis came and . . . I guess I'll have to take him some food myself tomorrow. I was going to go see him anyway. I'd really like to move him here, where I could take care of him, but he'd never be able to stand the trip."

"That's what I figured. If it's any consolation, I think I know who stabbed him."

"You know who the killer is?" Sarah exclaimed.

"It had to be Giddings's son."

"Giddings's *son*? Why would he try to kill Prescott?"

"Because he killed Anna Blake."

"How do you know that?"

"Remember the landlady said a young man came to see Anna right before she was killed? The first time I visited Mrs. Giddings, her son came in and told her she didn't have to worry about 'that woman' anymore. That made me think maybe he knew more about Anna's death than he let on. I didn't know then that he'd visited her the night she died, though. Then Prescott starts snooping around. Sooner or later he was going to find out about Giddings and put his name in the paper, too. The boy wants to protect his mother from any more scandal, so he sends Prescott a note, asking him to meet him. He shows up dressed like a woman and lures him into the alley off of Washington Square and stabs him."

Sarah frowned. "I know we once encountered a woman who dressed up like a man to walk the streets safely at night, but for a man to dress up like a woman . . . isn't that a little far-fetched?"

"What better way to lure Prescott away so he could kill him?" he pointed out reasonably.

Something about the theory bothered Sarah, but she couldn't say quite what. It did make sense, far-fetched as it was. "Why haven't you arrested him yet?"

"I was busy all day on a warehouse robbery, and when I went to their house just now, no one answered the door. I know Mrs. Giddings doesn't want to talk to me again, so she probably just pretended she wasn't home. I'm going to try again tomorrow, and this time if she doesn't open the door, I'll be a little more forceful."

Sarah winced at the thought of him breaking down the door or something equally violent. "My evening was much more interesting, although not much more fruitful. I talked to Irene."

"Who's Irene?"

She stared at him in amazement. "Didn't Prescott tell you about her? She's the actress he found, the one who knew Anna Blake."

"Oh, yeah." He was unimpressed, so Sarah set out to impress him.

"Did you know that Mr. Walcott was an admirer of Anna's, when she was on the stage?"

"What do you mean by 'admirer'?"

"I mean he waited outside the stage door for her and gave her flowers. Then he convinced her to come and live at his house, free of charge, so she could meet rich men like her friend Francine had done."

"Who's Francine?"

"Another actress Anna knew. Irene knew her, too. She went to live at the Walcotts' house a few months earlier. I thought it might have been Catherine Porter by another name, but Francine had red hair and freckles, so it couldn't be the same person. At any rate, Francine supposedly met some rich man and went off with him."

"She must've been the one Miss Stone told me about."

"Who's Miss Stone?"

"The Walcotts' next-door neighbor. She doesn't miss much that goes on in the neighborhood—like another old woman I could name. She said she didn't think this girl's hair was naturally red, though." Sarah smiled in spite of herself. Miss Stone did indeed sound like her own neighbor. "This Francine must've been the woman Prescott was trying to find," Malloy mused. "He said he went back to the Walcott house to find out where she went when she left, but Catherine Porter either didn't know or wouldn't tell him. He'll be glad to know she did so well for herself."

"Irene also knows Catherine Porter, and she doesn't have much good to say about her. It seems that when Catherine couldn't find work in the theater, she sold the one thing of value that she had on the streets."

Malloy raised his eyebrows. "Which would make her very good at doing the same thing Anna Blake was doing, seducing men and blackmailing them."

"That's exactly what I thought, too. And the Walcotts must have known. They may even have encouraged it. But that doesn't make any sense. The Walcotts claimed they take in boarders because they need the money, but according to Irene, Anna didn't even pay any rent."

"She didn't have to. Nelson and Giddings paid it for her," Malloy reminded her.

"Oh, yes, I'd forgotten! That's why she could live there for free, because someone else paid her way."

"And if she was an actress, that explains why she was so good at tricking men into doing what she wanted," Malloy pointed out.

"I remember when I met Anna, I had the feeling something wasn't right. Nelson was trying to reassure her, but she kept insisting on misinterpreting everything he said. It was like she was *trying* to make the situation worse than it really was."

"More melodramatic?" Malloy offered.

"Yes, that's it exactly!" Sarah exclaimed. "She was acting in her own private play."

"I guess the last act didn't end the way she'd planned, though."

Sarah remembered Anna the way she'd looked that evening Nelson had introduced them. The woman had pretended to be fragile and helpless, but even then Sarah had sensed a confidence and strength behind the facade. Anna Blake was a woman who knew what she wanted and was willing to do whatever she had to in order to get it. Only one thing still bothered her.

"I just don't understand why she went out that night. No woman who valued her safety would go into the Square alone at that hour of the night."

"Harold Giddings must have arranged to meet her later," Malloy suggested. "Maybe he threatened her in some way or maybe she thought she could charm him into something if she got him alone. I'll find out everything when I question him."

Sarah frowned. "You're going to give him the third degree, aren't you?"

Malloy's mouth tightened into a thin line. "I do what I have to do, Mrs. Brandt, but *only* what I have to do."

"I didn't mean—"

"I know what you meant. Beating people doesn't give me any pleasure."

"I didn't think it did," Sarah tried, sorry she had offended him. She was never sure exactly what would do it, either, which made it difficult for her to avoid.

"Besides," he said with what might have been a small grin, "it's hard work. Fortunately, Harold Giddings doesn't look like he'll need much convincing to tell everything he knows."

"For his sake, I hope he doesn't."

Malloy drained his cup and set it back on the table decisively. "Now we've got to go next door and tell Nelson about the missing money."

A sick feeling of dread settled into her stomach. "Can't it wait until morning?" she tried.

"I want to go to the bank first thing in the morning and catch this Mr. Dennis before he has a chance to change his mind about pressing charges against Nelson."

"What are you going to say to him?"

Malloy gave her a disapproving look. "Stop trying to change the subject, Mrs. Brandt. Get your jacket. We're going next door."

Frank stuck his hands in his pockets, grumbling about the cold, as he made his way through the brisk morning air to the bank where Nelson Ellsworth had worked. Summer was well and truly over.

He supposed he should have humored Sarah Brandt last night and delayed their visit to the Ellsworths. Neither of them had taken the news of the missing money well, and Frank would have been happy to have waited until morning to witness that scene.

Nelson had been stunned, just the way you'd expect an innocent man to act. Then he'd started ranting about procedures at the bank not being followed when he wasn't there to watch over things. Frank hadn't understood half of it, but he had no trouble at all understanding that Nelson hadn't been involved in the missing money. He was too outraged to be guilty.

Mrs. Ellsworth had been horrified and terribly frightened by the news. While she hadn't for a moment believed her son had taken anything from the bank, she also knew how bad things would look for him. He would make an easy scapegoat, and he had no way to defend himself. A man under suspicion of murder would have difficulty claiming the high moral ground when it came to mere embezzlement.

Frank was glad he'd insisted Sarah Brandt go along with him. He'd been thinking more of her needing to do some penance for her interference, but when Mrs. Ellsworth started weeping, he'd been pathetically grateful to have her step in to offer comfort. Nothing unnerved him more than a woman's tears.

One good thing had come out of the debacle, however. He would now have no trouble at all keeping Sarah Brandt out of the investigation. She'd learned her lesson. From now on she'd be content to look after Webster Prescott and trying to save his miserable life while Frank closed out the case and cleared Nelson's name.

This trip to the bank was just one more aspect of the quest. He only hoped it wouldn't take too much time. He still had to track down Harold Giddings, and he also had to at least pretend he was working on his own cases now and then.

The bank was like so many others in the city. Gleaming pillars supported the granite facade outside. Inside, the gilded ceiling rose up like a cathedral over marble counters topped by teller cages, mediocre statuary, and more pillars. People moved quietly, speaking in hushed tones, as if this were really a house of worship. Maybe it was, Frank, reflected, considering how some people felt about money.

The guard approached Frank almost the instant he entered. "May I help you?" he asked in a voice that was less than friendly. Apparently, he didn't think Frank met the standards of their usual clientele. Or else he recognized him as a policeman and wanted to get him out as quickly as possible.

"I want to see Mr. Dennis," he informed the guard. "I'm from the police."

The guard's eyes narrowed. He was taking his job very seriously. "Is this about Ellsworth?" he asked in a whisper.

Frank gave him a glare that told him he had no intention of discussing his business with anyone less than the boss. The guard's attitude changed instantly.

"I'll . . . Wait here just a minute," he advised and hurried off to whisper something urgent to one of the men sitting behind desks at the rear of the lobby.

This fellow came forward, and a few more minutes of negotiation were required to convince him he'd be well advised to announce Frank to Mr. Dennis without further delay if he wanted to avoid trouble. In a few short moments, he was ushered into a lavish office and presented to Richard Dennis.

Dennis was exactly what Frank had imagined. A man in his prime, Dennis wore his tailored clothes with ease and confidence. Generations of wealth and privilege had produced in him the polish those with newly earned fortunes tried in vain to emulate. Just as it had in Sarah Brandt. Dennis was, in short, everything Frank could never hope to be: the perfect match for her. He didn't bother to analyze the emotions this knowledge stirred in him. He didn't even have a right to experience them.

Dennis's expression told Frank he didn't appreciate

being interrupted but that he would tolerate it because he chose to. For his part, Frank would do well to show his respect and appreciation for the favor. All this communication, and Dennis had yet to utter a word.

Frank broke the silence between them as soon as the door was closed behind him. "I need to talk to you about Nelson Ellsworth."

Dennis sighed with long-suffering. "As I explained to the other detective who called, the bank isn't responsible for Mr. Ellsworth's conduct outside of the bank, and we have no knowledge of his acquaintance with this murdered woman. We have forbidden him to return to work until the matter is settled. I'm not sure what else you can expect me to contribute."

He hadn't asked Frank to sit down, but he did anyway, settling into one of the comfortable chairs in front of Dennis's desk. Dennis favored him with a disapproving frown, which Frank ignored. "I expect you to tell me why you haven't filed charges of embezzlement against Ellsworth," he said.

Dennis's haughty manner faltered a bit, but he regained his composure quickly. "I don't know what you're talking about."

"I think you do. Ellsworth learned last night that he is under suspicion of having embezzled ten thousand dollars from the bank. He claims that he's innocent, and he believes he is only being accused of this crime because the dead woman was attempting to blackmail him."

"No one has accused him of anything," Dennis hastily assured Frank. "Where on earth did he . . . ? Oh, Sarah," he said, answering his own question.

The casual use of her given name sent a surge of anger through Frank, but he said, "Who's Sarah?" with credible calmness.

Dennis was nothing if not a gentleman. "She's a lady of my acquaintance," he said, belatedly discreet. "She also happens to be a friend of Ellsworth's. I suppose I should have asked her not to inform Ellsworth until . . . Well, it doesn't matter. I have no intention of exposing the bank's private business to public scrutiny, which means I have nothing further to say to you. So if you'll excuse me . . ." He began shuffling some papers on his desk, silently dismissing Frank.

But Frank wasn't ready to be dismissed. "Let me understand this, Mr. Dennis," he said, managing to sound somewhat respectful. "You told this lady that Ellsworth stole ten thousand dollars from the bank, but you aren't going to take any legal action against him? How are you going to explain the missing money if you don't?"

Dennis didn't like being questioned, especially when he didn't have a ready answer. "That's really none of your business," he tried.

"You're wrong there," Frank said. "If Ellsworth stole money to pay off Anna Blake, then that gives him a good reason to kill her, doesn't it?"

"I'm sure I have no idea," Dennis said, his patience growing strained.

"But on the other hand," Frank said, as if he were just considering possibilities, "if he'd paid her off with that much money, he really wouldn't *have* to kill her, would he?"

"I'm glad to say I know very little about blackmail and murder." Dennis was angry now and not bothering to hide it.

"Well, I do, and I'll tell you something, Mr. Dennis. If Ellsworth stole your money, then he's probably not a killer, because Anna Blake would've been very happy with ten thousand dollars. And if he didn't steal the money, he might've killed Anna Blake because he couldn't pay her blackmail. Either way, I need to investigate your problems here at the bank so I can be sure. Maybe I should talk to this Sarah, too."

"No!" Dennis was horrified at the thought of someone like Frank speaking to Sarah Brandt. "She knows nothing about what happened here at the bank. I refuse to involve her in this."

"I guess Ellsworth will know how to get in touch with her," Frank said, issuing the one threat he knew would win Dennis's cooperation. He made as if to rise from his chair.

"Wait!" Dennis cried, his dignity forgotten. He'd do

whatever he must to keep Frank from bothering Mrs. Brandt. "The private business of the bank is confidential, but I'll try to answer your questions if I can. No one else needs to be involved. Please, sit down."

Frank settled back into his chair again, managing not to look smug. "I have to find out if Ellsworth killed that woman, Mr. Dennis. If he did, I can arrest him and move on to a new case. If he didn't, though, I need to figure out who did. The question I have is, why aren't you trying to find out if he stole that money?"

"Because I'm certain that Ellsworth did," Dennis insisted.

"Then why not try to get it back? Anna Blake is dead. If he gave it to her, she's not going to put up much of a fight about keeping it, is she?"

"I . . . I hadn't thought of that," Dennis claimed. His face was mottled from the stress of trying to stay one step ahead of Frank.

"And if Ellsworth didn't steal it, that means the thief still works for you. Are you going to give him a chance to do it again?"

Dennis rubbed the bridge of his nose, trying to ward off a headache. Frank knew he should feel guilty for causing the man so many problems, but he didn't. He told himself he was just trying to save Nelson Ellsworth's reputation and position, but he knew that was only a small part of it. The larger part of it was proving to himself that Dennis wasn't worthy of Sarah Brandt. He didn't ask himself why that was necessary. Or how he would convey that information to Mrs. Brandt if he did manage to prove it. He only knew he was compelled to do it and that he enjoyed doing so.

Finally, Dennis looked up, his expression determinedly reasonable. "See here, Mr. . . . I'm sorry, I don't believe I caught your name."

That's because he hadn't been interested in learning it, but Frank simply said, "Malloy."

"Mr. Malloy, no one wants to put their money in a bank if they know funds have been embezzled. While ten thousand dollars is a lot of money, it is nothing compared to what we will lose if our depositors choose to withdraw all their funds."

Frank nodded sagely, encouraging Dennis to continue.

"I have independent means. I will cover the losses myself and make certain this doesn't happen again."

"By making sure Ellsworth never works here again?" Frank guessed. "Even if he's not the thief?"

Dennis gave him a pitying look. "After the scandal he's caused, I could never take him back in any case."

Frank felt another surge of anger and almost reminded Dennis that he'd promised Sarah Brandt to give Nelson his job back if he wasn't arrested for the murder. He caught himself just in time. "So you'll blame him for the embezzlement, even if he's innocent of it?"

"What difference could it make?" Dennis asked, growing more confident. "He'll probably be executed for murder in any case."

"And what if I told you that isn't going to happen?"

Dennis stared at him in confusion. "But he's guilty. The newspapers all agree."

"He hasn't even been arrested yet," Frank reminded him. "If there was any reason to think he's guilty, he'd be in The Tombs by now," he added, referring to the city jail.

Dennis started at him for a long moment while he considered the situation. Frank could almost see him examining and discarding each of his options, one by one. Finally, left with no good choices, he managed a thin smile. "We each of us have a job to do, Mr. Malloy. I know I can count on your discretion, now that you know how important it is to me that the bank not suffer any more from Mr. Ellsworth's indiscretions. I will be extremely grateful if you will keep the information about the missing funds confidential. If you are able to do that, I assure you I will express my gratitude in tangible form. In *very* tangible form."

Frank felt a shock of surprise. He hadn't seen this coming, but he should have. His opinion of Dennis had been very low even before setting eyes on him. Why he should be shocked that the man had offered him a bribe, he had no idea. "And when can I feel free to return and collect your . . . gratitude?" Frank asked.

"When the matter of Mr. Ellsworth's guilt or innocence of murder has been determined," he replied, his confidence restored now that he'd obtained Frank's complicity. Or thought he had.

"Then I suppose I'll be seeing you again, Mr. Dennis," Frank said, rising to his feet. He didn't have to feign a feeling of satisfaction. He was truly pleased with the results of this interview.

"Indeed," Dennis replied. "I shall look forward to it."

Frank saw himself out, and he was smiling grimly as he walked through the front door of the bank into the morning sunlight. He wouldn't have to say very much at all about Dennis to Sarah Brandt except that he'd offered Frank a bribe to keep quiet about the missing money and not interfere with him dismissing Nelson. He might make time to stop by her house this morning just to mention it. He'd only gone a few steps, however, when he heard someone calling his name. He turned to see Nelson Ellsworth hurrying across the street to intercept him.

"Mr. Malloy, I'm so glad I caught you!" he exclaimed breathlessly. He looked much better than he had last night, or any night since Anna Blake had died, in fact. He'd shaved and dressed, as if for work, and his eyes were alive in a way they hadn't been in over a week.

"What are you doing out here?" Frank exclaimed, looking around in case some enterprising reporter was hanging around. "I told you not to leave the house."

"There weren't any reporters, so no one saw me," he said. "I had to see you, and I knew you'd be at the bank this morning. I thought of something last night, after you left."

"Then let's find a less public place to discuss it," Frank suggested, still looking around to make sure they hadn't been seen. He didn't want anyone from the bank to spot them, either, and report to Dennis that Ellsworth had been waiting for Frank outside. He'd think they'd set the whole thing up just to extort a bribe out of him.

Frank led him away, and they walked two blocks until he saw a hansom cab and flagged it down. When the two men had stuffed themselves inside, Frank gave the driver the Ellsworths' address. As the cab started off with a lurch, he finally turned to Nelson.

"All right, what is it?" he asked.

"Last night, after you left, I couldn't sleep," Nelson said. "At first I was just upset. I never stole a penny from the bank. You must believe me!"

"It doesn't matter what I believe," Frank reminded him. "But if it makes you feel any better, I don't think you took the money."

This seemed to be a relief to Nelson, and he sighed audibly. "Well," he said somewhat hoarsely, "that means a great deal to me, Mr. Malloy."

"No, it doesn't mean anything at all unless I can find out who really killed Anna Blake, so if you've got any information—"

"That's just it, I remembered something important last night."

"You know who killed Anna?"

Nelson's face fell. "I wish to God I did. No, it's not that. It was about the bank and the missing money. You said Mr. Dennis discovered it when he asked the auditors to check our accounts."

"That's what he told Mrs. Brandt."

"But that's just it, Mr. Malloy. She only spoke with him on Sunday, and he told her on Tuesday night that they'd discovered the missing money. Even if he'd been able to get auditors into the bank first thing on Monday morning—which would have been very difficult—they would have only had two days to work. Two days at the most! Mr. Malloy, there is no way they could have made a determination like that so quickly!"

I2

Sarah went to her parents' house early, hoping to catch her father before he left for the day. She didn't question why she needed to see him so badly. She only knew she did. She'd spent a restless night after the unpleasant scene at the Ellsworths. Lying awake, she'd remembered every word they'd said, how Mrs. Ellsworth had wept, and how devastated Nelson had looked when he realized that even if he was cleared of murder, he would most certainly lose his position. Most likely, he'd also never get another, no matter how discreet Richard Dennis was.

Only in the wee hours of the morning, when she was exhausted and half-sick with worry, did she remember what was probably the most remarkable part of a very remarkable day. How could she have forgotten? As distracted as she was by everything else, surely having Frank Malloy call her beautiful was the most memorable event she could recall in her recent history.

How extraordinary that he should say such a thing! Especially so because Sarah wasn't beautiful at all. She'd long ago come to terms with that. In her youth she'd been pretty enough, she supposed, because health and youth and good nature combined to make one attractive. But then her sister had died so horribly, and Sarah had grown solemn. Determined not to waste her life, she'd put aside vanities that had no place in her new world.

Tom, of course, had thought her beautiful, but he had been blinded by love. What could have possessed Malloy, however, was a mystery. A delightful mystery, though. When Sarah remembered Malloy's outrage over Richard Dennis's behavior, she felt the strangest heat building inside of her. She needed a moment to recognize it for what it was—pure pleasure! And to her dismay, she realized she was actually blushing just at the memory of it!

She glanced around the crowded railroad car to see if anyone had noticed the color rising in her face, but fortunately, no one was paying her the slightest attention. Quickly, she put her gloved hands on her cheeks to cool them and glanced out the window at the houses passing so quickly and so closely by. To distract herself from disturbing thoughts, she watched for a glimpse of the occupants of the third-floor apartments passing by at eye level and tried to imagine a history for each of them.

By the time she reached her parents' town house on the Upper West Side, she had almost succeeded in forgetting Malloy's strange behavior.

As she had expected, her mother hadn't roused herself yet, but her father was still at breakfast, reading the morning newspapers in solitary splendor in the dining room.

"Sarah," he said, rising to his feet when the maid announced her. He seemed pleased to see her, although his natural reserve made it hard to tell. "What brings you out so early?"

"I was hoping to have a word with you," she said, taking a seat in the chair he pulled out for her at the table.

"You'll join me for breakfast, I hope."

"I've already eaten, thank you."

He instructed the maid to bring her some tea anyway and resumed his own seat. "This sounds serious," he said with a frown. "I don't believe you've ever made a special effort to have a word with me about anything."

"It's nothing you need to worry about," she assured

him. "I just have some questions to ask you about . . . about embezzlement."

"Embezzlement?" he echoed in surprise. "Why? Are you thinking of trying your hand at it?"

Sarah couldn't help smiling at the thought, in spite of the seriousness of the situation. "Of course not, Father. It's just that . . . well, my friend Mr. Ellsworth has now been accused of it, in addition to everything else."

He absorbed this information. "The accusation, did it come from Richard Dennis?"

"I'm afraid so. He called in auditors to check the books on Monday morning, just to be certain everything was in order since . . . You see, the murdered woman was trying to blackmail Mr. Ellsworth."

"I see. Then that would be a sensible precaution for the bank to take. And the auditors did find some discrepancies, I presume."

"According to Mr. Dennis, they found ten thousand dollars missing."

Her father frowned. "That's a lot of blackmail."

"Exactly my reaction. The woman had only asked for one thousand. I can't believe Nelson would have been so foolish. He's honest to a fault, Father. He'd never take money that didn't belong to him, but even if he did, he certainly would have more sense than to take so much, particularly when he didn't need it. He would know that someone would eventually discover the theft, and he'd be caught."

"But if he was desperate . . ."

"He wasn't desperate. Father, the woman claimed to be carrying his child, and he was willing and able to marry her. Why would he steal money from his employer to pay blackmail when he wanted to marry the woman?"

"You're right, that doesn't make any sense."

"But Nelson Ellsworth isn't in a position to prove his innocence of anything at the moment. Mr. Dennis isn't planning to press charges against him, but he'll still dismiss him from the bank because of the missing money.

Nelson will be ruined, and he'll never be able to find a decent job again."

Her father took a sip of his coffee and studied her. "I suppose there's something you want me to do about all this."

Sarah sighed. "I'm not even sure there's anything you *can* do. I guess I was just hoping you might have some advice to offer."

Her father stared at her for a long moment. When he finally spoke, his voice was quiet in a way she'd never heard it before. "I'm gratified that you have come to me, Sarah. A father wants his children to have confidence in his abilities to handle difficult situations."

She hadn't realized it, but that's exactly what she'd done. Once her father had seemed the most powerful person on earth to her. She'd lost respect for that power when she'd seen him misuse it with her sister, but still, deep down where her childhood memories were buried, she believed he could do anything. "I do have confidence in you, Father," she admitted. "But it isn't fair of me to ask you to help with this."

"Quite truthfully, I'm not certain I can. Young Dennis isn't likely to take advice from me about how to run his business. He'd see it as interference, and he'd be right. Going to his father about this would be even worse. I'm not sure I could even make discreet inquiries without offending them."

"I guess I knew that," she said. "I just didn't want to believe it. Please forgive me for putting you in an awkward position."

"Nonsense," he said, brushing away her apology. "I'll give the matter some thought and see what I can do. I can't make any promises, mind you, but—"

"Oh, Father, I'm not asking for any promises. But I don't even know anything about embezzlement. If I did, perhaps I could . . . I don't know, do *something*," she said in exasperation.

"I'm glad to say I know very little about it myself, but I can at least obtain that information with relative ease. I'll take lunch at my club today. Someone there will be only too happy to enlighten me on the subject, I'm sure."

"Thank you, Father. I'd be so grateful."

He peered at her over his coffee cup. "No reason to be grateful, my dear. Now go upstairs and see your mother. I'll send you word when I've learned something useful."

Frank wasn't sure what he was going to do with the information Nelson Ellsworth had given him about the missing money. But first he had to clear the man of murder, or stolen money would be the least of his problems.

Frank had gotten out of the cab, leaving Nelson to make his way home alone, and headed for Police Headquarters on Mulberry Street. He wanted to find Harold Giddings, but he knew he'd have to wait until the end of the workday. His mother would never tell him where he was working today, even if she knew, which was unlikely. In the meantime, he might as well do the job he was being paid to do.

A black Maria was pulling up at the door of Police Headquarters when Frank arrived at Mulberry Street. The closed carriage held the last of the drunks that had been collected off the city streets from the night before. The boys from the press shacks across the street leaned out their windows to see if they recognized any of the faces as someone who might make a good story. Frank pulled his hat lower in an attempt to escape notice as he made his way quickly inside, just in case someone recognized him as being a good source for a story about Anna Blake's murder.

The desk sergeant looked up when he entered, nodding his greeting with a bored expression. Frank wished him good morning.

"About time you showed up, Malloy," the sergeant said. "Some drunk's been asking for you all night."

"A drunk? What's his name?"

"How should I know? Just some drunk. Said you'd vouch for him and we should let him go."

"I'm guessing you didn't," Frank said with a grin.

"Hell, I figured we should send him to the Tombs for life just for knowing you," the sergeant said, grinning back.

Frank was going to head upstairs to the detectives' office, but then he remembered one drunk in particular who might have had him uppermost in his mind this week. He wasn't sure why Gilbert Giddings would think he could trade on his acquaintance with Frank for a favor, but if he was the drunk downstairs, it wouldn't hurt to find out. He might be grateful enough to tell him where his son could be found, if he even knew. Or he might have remembered something new about Anna Blake. "Is this fellow still downstairs?"

"Locked up tight," the sergeant said, turning his attention to the parade of drunks and derelicts being herded in the front door.

Frank made his way down to the cellar of the large, square building, two floors below the street, where the dark, stinking cells held those unfortunate enough to have come to the attention of the police. Strong men had been known to break down and confess to the most heinous crimes to avoid being locked in these cells—or to escape from them to the relative pleasantness of the dismal City Jail.

A quick inquiry of the jailer on duty led him to a cell filled with slowly sobering inmates where he did, indeed, find Gilbert Giddings sleeping off his night's revelries.

"You know him?" the officer asked.

Frank nodded. "Has he ever been here before?"

"Him?" the jailer scoffed. "He's here once a week or more. When he runs out of money, he starts bothering other patrons at whatever bar he's at. They get annoyed, and the next thing you know, the paddy wagon takes them all away."

A new thought occurred to Frank. "Was he here last Tuesday night?"

"I could check."

"Thanks. Meanwhile, open the door. I want to have a word with the gentleman."

The jailer unlocked the cell and went off to check on Giddings's records. Frank stepped into the cell, which was crammed with men curled and huddled in varying degrees of misery on nearly every square foot. Snores alternated with snivels and groans, and the smell of unwashed bodies and vomit rose up like a miasma. Frank stepped over a mass of rags that served as clothing for the man beneath it, and kicked Gilbert Giddings sharply on the hip.

He awoke with a start and looked around in alarm. His red-rimmed eyes quickly found Frank, looming over him, but he needed another moment to recognize him. "Mr. Malloy," he said, his voice hoarse from sleep and excess. He tried to scramble to his feet, but quickly gave up the effort as his head protested painfully. Holding it in both hands, he looked up at Frank again.

"Can you get me out of here? I can't . . . this is so humiliating. A man in my position . . ."

"You don't have a position, remember?" Frank reminded him. "You gave it up for Anna Blake."

To Frank's disgust, the bloodshot eyes filled with tears. "I loved her, Malloy. I would've done anything for her."

"Even leave your wife and son?"

Giddings winced at that. "I wanted to, but she wouldn't let me," he confessed. "She was too honorable."

Frank didn't bother to argue the point. Let Giddings believe what he wanted. "I guess your family was grateful for her sacrifice," he said instead.

"They . . . they didn't understand. I can't blame them, I suppose. They lost so much."

"You son seems more angry than your wife," Frank observed. "He doesn't think much of your Miss Blake."

"He's young," Giddings excused him. "He doesn't know much about life."

"He knows about his life, and his mother's. He knows how you and Anna Blake ruined both of them. He must hate her."

"He doesn't even know her."

Frank wondered if Giddings really didn't know. "Yes, he does. He met her at least once."

Giddings stared blearily at Frank, not certain he'd understood correctly. "Harold couldn't have met her."

"But he did. Went to her house on the night she died. What do you suppose he wanted?" Frank asked.

One of the drunks nearby started coughing. The sound was raw and painful to hear, and Frank couldn't help wondering what disease he might be carrying.

Giddings was looking at the coughing drunk with distaste, probably unaware that he himself looked no better than the filthy, unshaven wretch. At last the coughing stopped, and Giddings looked up at Frank again. "Harold didn't know her," he insisted.

"Then why did he kill her?"

This time Giddings reacted in a normal way. His eyes grew large, first with surprise, then with fury. He even made a valiant effort to rise, ready to confront Frank, but Frank hooked his foot behind Giddings's heel and sent him sprawling back to the floor again.

Gasping with pain from his aching head and his bruised ego, Giddings glared at Frank. "Harold couldn't kill anyone. He's just a boy."

"You better take a good look at him next time you're home," Frank advised. "He's not a boy anymore. He's taken your place as the man of the family."

Giddings winced at the accusation, but he didn't back down. "He didn't kill Anna!" he insisted.

"How do you know? Is it because you killed her yourself?"

Giddings's jaw dropped, but before he could speak, the jailer called to Frank.

"He was here Tuesday night. Came in around nine o'-clock."

"That's pretty early," Frank said, a little disappointed. Of course, that still would have given him time to kill Anna, since the landlady had said she'd left the house before dark.

"He got into a bar fight. He'd been hanging around all evening, cadging drinks, but he didn't have any money of his own, so the crowd got tired of him. Threw him out into the street, but he kept coming back in. The beat cop took him in."

Frank looked down at Giddings. "That was the night Anna died. You told me you couldn't remember what happened that night. What were you doing in the bar?"

He looked up, his eyes resentful. "I didn't remember everything. I went to visit Anna that day, but she wouldn't see me. They wouldn't even let me in. That woman, Mrs. Walcott, told me not to come back again, that Anna was going away."

"So you went to the bar?"

"I couldn't go home. My wife . . . she doesn't understand. So I went out."

"How did you get into a fight?"

"I told you, I don't remember anything after I left her house until I woke up here the next morning."

"Did you try to see Anna that day?"

"I wanted to, but I was too sick. I had to wait until the next morning."

"That's when we met," Frank guessed, remembering how frantic Giddings had been to find her.

Giddings nodded and rubbed his head again, unable to meet Frank's penetrating gaze.

"So that means even if you could remember, you wouldn't know if your son went out to see Anna Blake that night or not," Frank said.

This brought Giddings's head up, his eyes wild with fury. "My son didn't even know where she lived! If you try to blame him for this, just because you can't find her real killer, I'll have your job!"

Frank didn't bother to point out that he was no longer in a position to be any danger to Frank's job. He had more important things to think about. Frank had been hoping that Giddings would turn out to be the one who'd killed Anna. It was still possible, since Giddings claimed not to remember what he'd done that evening. He'd had time to find her and kill her before going to the bar. And if he couldn't remember killing Anna, he could have been truly surprised to learn later that she was dead. That would explain why he'd acted like an innocent man the morning Frank had first seen him. But the boy was still a good suspect, too, and Frank knew for certain he'd seen Anna that night. "Your wife said you were home with her and your son the night Anna died, Giddings," Frank said. "Now why would she say that?"

Giddings rubbed his temples. "She's a good woman. She doesn't deserve this."

Frank gave him another light kick to get his attention. "Where is your son working today?"

Giddings started up stupidly. "How should I know?"

That's what he'd expected, but he still didn't like it. He stepped back over the ragged bundle of a man sleeping between him and the door. The fellow hadn't stirred during the entire conversation, which meant he was either dead drunk or just dead. Frank walked out of the cell, and the jailer closed the door behind him.

"Keep that one until I tell you to let him go," Frank said, indicating Giddings.

Giddings blinked, still rubbing his head. "I thought you were going to let me go," he said.

"Didn't anybody ever warn you that liquor makes you stupid?" Frank asked, then turned away. He needed some fresh air.

From her parents' house on Fifty-Seventh Street, Sarah took the Sixth Avenue Elevated Train down to Twenty-Sixth Street and walked over to Bellevue Hospital to visit Webster Prescott. As she'd feared, he was in a fever and didn't seem to know who she was. She forced some soup down his throat and bathed him with cool water. Then she put some hot compresses on his wound, to draw out the inflammation that was poisoning him. When she left, he seemed to be sleeping more comfortably. She told the nurses she'd be back to check on him later, hoping that would motivate them to give him better than average care in the meantime.

She'd posted the letter to Prescott's aunt that morning. With any luck, the woman would receive it in the afternoon mail and be over to visit him tomorrow. Until then, Sarah would keep a close watch on him. Breathing a silent prayer for his recovery, she left the hospital and stopped in the middle of the sidewalk when she realized she had no idea what to do next.

Malloy, she knew, was going to find Mr. Giddings's son and try to get him to confess to Anna's murder. Sarah should have been relieved. Once the murder was solved, they could concentrate on solving up the embezzlement at the bank and clearing Nelson's name once and for all.

But she didn't feel relieved. She'd never met this boy, but for some reason she couldn't believe he'd killed Anna Blake. And she also couldn't shake off the feeling that she'd left something undone. She thought she knew what it was, too. She'd never gone back to the Walcott house to question Catherine Porter or the maid again. They must know more than they'd told her that first time. The maid hadn't been there, of course, but Catherine had. And she'd been Anna's friend, or the closest thing she'd had to one, at any rate. Maybe, if pressed, Catherine could provide a possible reason why Anna might have gone out to the Square that night. Sarah couldn't shake off the feeling that once she knew that reason, she would understand what had happened to Anna Blake. Or at least she'd have a clue as to who might have killed her. And why.

Pulling her cape more tightly around her, Sarah set off toward the Second Avenue Elevated for a quick trip down-town to the Walcott house.

All the way down on the train, she tried to decide what she should ask the women if she was fortunate enough to get in to ask them anything at all. Catherine might not be home, or the maid might not admit her. If the Walcotts were home, they might throw her bodily into the street. Without Malloy, she had no official reason to question them, and they would surely know it. In fact, she was prob-ably foolish to even consider this. On the other hand, she couldn't just go back to her house and wait. She had to do *something*.

With some trepidation, Sarah climbed the steps to the

Walcotts' front door and knocked. After what seemed a very long time, the door opened, and the maid looked out to see who was there.

"Good morning," Sarah said, not really sure it was still morning but willing to take the chance. "Is Miss Porter in?"

The maid was frowning, trying to place her. Sarah smiled benignly, praying she wouldn't be able to. Finally, the girl said, "You're that lady what was here before about Miss Blake. You come with that policeman."

Sarah managed not to flinch. "That's right. Miss Porter asked me to call when I was by this way again," she lied.

The girl looked doubtful, but she said. "Come in, please, and I'll see if Miss Porter's at home."

Sarah stepped inside, as bidden, but the maid left her standing in the hallway instead of inviting her to have a seat in the parlor, silently telling her she might not really be welcome. Of course, the maid knew perfectly well whether or not Catherine Porter was at home. What she'd meant was that she would check to see if Miss Porter was at home to Mrs. Brandt. If Miss Porter didn't wish to see her, she would simply instruct the maid to say she wasn't at home. It was a convenient fiction that saved people from having to be overtly rude but still allowed them some control over their social lives.

Sarah wasn't quite sure what she would do if Miss Porter refused to see her. She could always force her way past the maid and go upstairs and find the poor woman, cowering in her room. Such an approach was hardly likely to result in Sarah being able to elicit information from Miss Porter, however. She was smiling at the thought when she heard the maid coming down the stairs again. To Sarah's relief, Catherine Porter was right behind her.

She did look wary, Sarah noted, so Sarah smiled in what she hoped was a reassuring manner. "Good morning, Miss Porter. I hope I'm not disturbing you."

"What do you want?" Catherine Porter asked when she was halfway down the stairs, not bothering with the usual social niceties.

A very good question, and one Sarah didn't dare answer truthfully. "I was hoping you would have a few minutes to visit with me. We're still trying to find out who killed poor Miss Blake, and I thought perhaps you might be able to help."

"I already told everyone, I was asleep when she went out that night," she said defensively. She came down a few more steps, though. Sarah could see now that she wore a housedress and her hair wasn't done, so she hadn't been planning on going out or receiving visitors.

Sarah knew Catherine was probably lying about having been asleep, since Anna had left the house in the early evening, but she decided to work up to that question. "I thought perhaps you'd overheard Anna's argument with the young man who came to see her that evening," she tried. She glanced at the maid, who was still hovering, unwilling to miss this conversation, although she should have discreetly withdrawn by now.

For some reason, Catherine glanced at the maid, too, as if looking for reassurance. "Is Mrs. Walcott at home?" she asked the girl.

"No, ma'am. She went out early. Said she wouldn't be back for a while," the girl replied.

Catherine came down the rest of the stairs. "I guess I could spare a few minutes," she allowed. "Although it won't do you any good. I don't know anything that will help." She glanced at the maid again. "Go back to work. It's all right."

The maid nodded reluctantly, then slipped away down the hall. Catherine Porter led Sarah into the parlor and closed the doors behind them. When she turned, Sarah instantly saw the change in her. The last time they had met, Catherine had been worried, but now she looked almost frightened. Her face was pale and lines of strain had formed around her mouth. Her youth and health had been her most appealing features, but those seemed to have faded, leaving her worn and lifeless.

"I don't know anything about Anna's death," she said

before Sarah could even think of which question she wanted to ask first.

"You said you were asleep when Anna left the house that night. What time do you usually retire?"

"I don't know. Nine o'clock. Or ten, maybe. I don't pay attention. I go to bed when I'm tired." She walked over to the sofa and sank down wearily.

"You go to bed after dark, though," Sarah guessed, taking a seat opposite her.

"Sure. I'm not a farmer," she said derisively. She was lying, then, about having been asleep when Anna left the house, which meant she'd also been lying about not knowing why Anna had left.

"I guess you got in the habit of staying up late when you worked in the theater," Sarah tried.

"You have to," she said. "The plays are at night, and by the time you get changed and out of the . . . Wait, how did you know I worked in the theater?" Her eyes widened, and she looked wary.

"You told me," Sarah reminded her, smiling with what she hoped was reassurance. "Your friend Irene said you and Anna and Francine were all actresses."

"Irene," Catherine scoffed. "She's no friend of mine."

"Was Francine a friend of yours?"

"I knew her, if that's what you mean."

"Did you live here when she did?"

"She left before I came."

"Where did she go?" Sarah asked, wondering if this Francine might be able to tell her anything.

"I don't know. Some place in the country. She got a rich man to take care of her, so she left."

Sarah could just imagine. Most likely, the "rich" man was no longer rich, nor was he spending time with Francine anymore. "Is that what you were planning to do? Find some rich man to take care of you?"

"There's nothing wrong with that," Catherine pointed out. "Lots of women do it!"

Lots of women in every class did it, Sarah would have to admit. Becoming a rich man's mistress, or his wife, was one of the few opportunities women had of escaping poverty. Sarah didn't feel like discussing this with Catherine, however. "Did Mr. Walcott court you the way he courted Anna?" she asked to change the subject.

"I don't know what you mean." This time the fear in her eyes was too real to mistake. "Mr. Walcott is . . . he's a married man."

"Married or not, he used to hang around the theater, waiting for Anna and bringing her flowers. Did he do that for you, too?"

Catherine glanced at the parlor doors. Was she worried that someone might be eavesdropping? Or was she worried about something else? "He just . . . he offered me a place to live. That's all. He said he ran a respectable boarding house and I'd like it here."

"Because you could entertain your gentleman callers upstairs with his approval?" Sarah asked mildly.

Catherine didn't like these questions. "I told you, this is a respectable house."

"Not according to the men who used to call on Anna Blake," Sarah said. "They were both permitted above stairs with the full knowledge of the landlords. I can't say for certain what went on in Anna's room, but I do know that both gentlemen in question believed they had gotten Anna with child. This would indicate to me they were intimate with her."

"That was Anna, not me," she insisted.

Sarah decided not to press the issue. "Did you see the young man who visited Anna the night she died?"

"Yeah, but I never saw him before. He wasn't a regular . . ." She caught herself and quickly added, "I mean, he'd never been here that I ever saw."

"What did he look like?"

"I don't know. Young, maybe sixteen or seventeen. Looked like a common laborer, if you ask me. Mary didn't want to let him in, but he pushed his way past her and started shouting for Anna."

"Didn't you ask her who he was?"

Catherine glared at Sarah. At any moment she might realize she didn't really have to sit here and answer these questions. Sarah had no authority at all, but she didn't betray any hint of that. She glared right back at Catherine determinedly. Finally, she said, "Anna said he was Mr. Giddings's son."

"Who was Mr. Giddings?" Sarah asked, managing to conceal her feeling of triumph and hoping Catherine wouldn't remember that Sarah had been here the morning Giddings had come looking for Anna.

"One of her . . . a friend of hers. He helped her with some . . . some business matters."

"I see," Sarah said, seeing more than that. "And what did the boy want with her?"

"I don't know. It wasn't my business."

"Did he go upstairs with her?" Sarah asked, remembering that the coroner had said she'd been with a man shortly before her death.

"Not likely! Not the way they was fighting!"

"They were arguing? What about?"

"I wasn't listening on purpose," she said, defensive again, "but he was shouting. It was hard not to hear what he was saying."

"And what was he saying?"

"He wanted her to leave his father alone. He said there was no more money. I think . . . he said something about her giving the money back, I think. And he . . ."

"He what?"

"He said . . ." Catherine took a deep breath. "He'd kill her if she didn't."

13

Sarah gaped at her. This was even more information than she'd wanted to get. "Are you sure that's what he said?" she asked, still not wanting the Giddings boy to be guilty of the crime.

"Yeah, because Anna started laughing, and he said something like she'd better believe him or she'd be sorry."

Sarah hadn't been trained as a detective, but that sounded like pretty good evidence to her. "And then he left?"

"Yeah, Mr. Walcott told him to leave, and he did."

"Did you say *Mr.* Walcott? I thought he wasn't home that night."

Catherine looked confused and then frightened again. "Did I say that? No, I meant to say *Mrs.* You're right, he wasn't home that night. *Mrs.* Walcott asked him to leave."

"And what time was this when he left?"

"I don't know," Catherine complained. "Early in the evening, I guess. Right after supper."

"And you went to bed immediately?"

"No, I told you, it was still early."

"So Anna didn't leave the house right after that?"

"No, we played checkers for a while, the two of us."

Sarah managed to conceal her surprise. This wasn't what Mrs. Walcott had said. "Did she seem upset by the argument she'd had with the boy?"

"Not a bit. Nothing much upset her, even though . . ."

"Even though what?" Sarah prodded.

"Well, Mrs. Walcott . . . She was mad about the boy coming to the house. She didn't like disturbances. Yelling and carrying on, she says that's low class."

"Did she say anything to Anna about it?"

"Not that I heard. She isn't one to air dirty linen, you know? That's how she always says it. No use airing our dirty linen in public. She'd wait 'til I was gone to say something, if she did."

"And you think she did that night?"

Catherine shrugged. "Like I said, I was asleep. I didn't hear anything." She wouldn't meet Sarah's eye.

Sarah was starting to get a little impatient with Catherine, but she tried not to let it show. "Did Anna get a message that evening?"

"Not that I know of."

Sarah was confused now. "So Anna was still here when you went to bed?"

"That's right. Anna never would go to bed until real late. Then she'd sleep late in the morning, just like when we worked in the theater. I told her it's hard on the complexion to stay up half the night, but she wouldn't listen. Anna wouldn't listen to nobody."

"Was Anna in the habit of going out alone at night?"

Catherine looked at her like she was crazy. "Only whores go out on the street at night. Anna didn't want to be taken for no whore."

"Then why did she go out that particular night?"

"I don't know, I tell you! I wish I did. Then people would stop bothering me. All I can tell you is that she did, and she got herself killed."

"And what's going to happen to you now?" Sarah asked.

Fear flickered in Catherine's eyes again. "What do you mean?"

"I mean, are you going to keep entertaining your gentlemen friends the way Anna did?"

"That ain't none of your business," she said. At last she jumped up from her seat on the sofa. "I've told you everything I know. Now you'd better leave here before Mrs. Walcott gets back."

"Why? Don't you think she'd like to see me?"

"She don't like talking about Anna, especially since that reporter came here snooping around the other day."

Sarah felt a warning prickle on the back of her neck. "Was it Mr. Prescott? From the *World*?"

"I didn't hear his name."

"A tall fellow? Young? All arms and legs?"

"I guess," she said with a shrug. "He was asking about Anna being in the theater and all. Mrs. Walcott sent him packing, and she told me and Mary not to let any more reporters in. There've been a lot of them come by, wanting to know all about Anna, but we never tell them nothing."

"If a lot of reporters have been here, why did that particular one annoy Mrs. Walcott?"

"This one barged right in past poor Mary, without so much as a by-your-leave. Mrs. Walcott threatened to call the police on him," Catherine said. "In fact, now that I think on it, I shouldn't be talking to you at all. How do I know *you're* not working for some newspaper? This could be a trick."

"I assure you, I don't work for a newspaper. I'm a midwife. That's why Nelson Ellsworth brought me to meet Anna Blake in the first place," Sarah reminded her.

Catherine waved this away. "I don't know about any of that. All I know is, you better go now."

Sarah rose to her feet, but she wasn't quite finished. "Do you remember what Anna was wearing that night?"

"What do you mean?"

"I'd like to find out how she was dressed when she went out the night she died. That could tell me who she was going to meet."

"How could what she was wearing tell you anything?" Catherine asked.

"If she was dressed carefully, she was probably going to meet a lover," Sarah said. "If she dressed hastily, she might have been in a hurry. Can you remember?"

"I only know what she was wearing last time I saw her."

"Could you tell from looking at the clothes in her room what she wore to go out that night?"

Catherine cast one anxious glance at the door again. Could she actually be frightened at the prospect of having Mrs. Walcott catch her talking to Sarah? What kind of a relationship did she have with the landlady? Before she could pursue that thought, Catherine said, "I can look at her things. They're all there in her room. Mrs. Walcott won't let anybody touch them. It's not like Anna's going to need them or anything, is it?" she grumbled, opening the parlor doors and leading Sarah up the stairs.

Sarah followed her into Anna's room. The shades had been drawn, and everything was just as she'd seen it last. The place was starting to have that closed-up, dusty smell to it.

"I could wear her things," Catherine was saying. "We were the same size. I don't know why she won't let me have them."

"Maybe she will when this is all settled," Sarah suggested.

Catherine took a quick inventory. "That's funny."

"What?"

"Looks like she didn't change her clothes before she went out. She was wearing her house dress that night. After the boy left, she changed into it. She didn't like to sit around in her good clothes if nobody was coming to call. Clothes cost the earth, you know."

Sarah knew it well. "What color was it?"

"Brown," she said, confirming what Mrs. Walcott had said, although the landlady hadn't mentioned what kind of a dress it had been. Women usually had a dress, usually one past its prime, they kept for doing housework and such. Although Anna wouldn't have done much work, she would have had a shabby dress she wore to be comfortable.

"So she was wearing a house dress. What coat would she have been wearing?"

Catherine looked at everything again. "She only had this cape, and it's still here. Her winter coat is in the trunk. It hasn't been cold enough to get it out. Or at least it wasn't before she died. It's a nice coat, too. Hardly worn at all," she added enviously.

"Did she have a shawl or something?"

Catherine looked at each garment again. "The one she wore around the house. She had it on that night when we was playing checkers. Mrs. Walcott wouldn't light a fire. She said it wasn't cold enough yet, but Anna was always cold."

They could hear the front door opening, and a voice calling for Mary. Catherine's eyes widened in alarm. "Oh, miss, could you . . . I don't want Mrs. Walcott to know I was talking to you. Could you leave by the back stairs so she don't see you?"

Sarah considered refusing. She wouldn't mind seeing Mrs. Walcott again, but not if her presence would make the woman angry. She might need to come back again, and there was no use in antagonizing the landlady unnecessarily. "I'd be glad to," Sarah assured her.

Placing her finger to her lips to signal Sarah to be silent, Catherine led her quickly down the hallway to the back staircase. Sarah stole down the steps and out through the empty kitchen to the back porch.

She wasn't too surprised to find a couple of stray dogs in the back yard, a large brown one and a small black one. Such animals roamed the entire city, scavenging garbage and the carcasses of dead animals when they were lucky enough to find them. These were like most, mangy and scrawny and sniffing around for whatever they could find. They were sniffing at the Walcotts' cellar door, scratching fruitlessly in an effort to get inside. Sarah remembered the maid complaining about how something had died down there. The scent must have attracted these poor creatures.

"Shoo!" she tried, shaking her skirts at them, but they barely spared her a glance before returning to their quest.

Leaving them to it, Sarah made her way out of the tiny yard and into the alley, where she made her escape unde-tected.

Sarah decided to go home before returning to the hos-pital. She wanted to get her medical bag and take it with her this time so she could check Webster Prescott's condi-tion more closely. She also wanted to check on the Ellsworths. They must be nearly insane after being held prisoner in their home for so long. She couldn't do much but try to reassure them that their ordeal would soon be over, but she couldn't just leave them with no news at all.

But when Sarah reached Bank Street, she saw to her dismay that the reporters were back in force. A clump of young men stood gathered on the sidewalk in front of the Ellsworth house, and Sarah muttered a curse when they began to descend on her.

"Who are you?"

"Do you know Nelson Ellsworth?"

"Do you know he murdered a woman?"

The questions came faster than she could even register them. Since she had no intention of answering any of them, she didn't even bother to try. "What are you doing here?" she demanded instead. "Haven't you done enough?"

"None of *us* killed anybody, lady," one of the reporters said.

"Neither did Nelson Ellsworth," Sarah said, pushing her way through them toward her front steps.

"You know him then!" one of them shouted in triumph.

"Are you in love with him?"

"Are you lovers?"

"Are you engaged?"

Sarah rolled her eyes and kept moving.

"Maybe she's the one who stabbed Prescott!" another called.

This stopped her in her tracks. "What did you say?"

"Did you stab Webster Prescott to protect your lover?" a young man with a very bad complexion asked hopefully.

"How did you find out Mr. Prescott had been stabbed?" she demanded.

"How did *you*?" another one countered provocatively.

Sarah sighed in exasperation. "The *police* told me," she said. "Now how did *you* find out?"

"It was in the *World* this morning," one of them said. "A woman tried to kill him because he was getting too close to the truth! Was it you, trying to protect Ellsworth?"

Sarah fought her way through the rest of them and quickly climbed her steps, ignoring their shouted questions and innuendoes. Now she was very glad she'd come home when she did. She had to see Mrs. Ellsworth and make sure she and Nelson were all right after this recent onslaught.

Once safely inside, she didn't even remove her cloak. Making a hasty foraging trip through the kitchen for anything edible she could find, she threw the things into her market basket and slipped it over her arm. Then she snatched up her medical bag and launched herself back into the street again. There was no need to sneak around the back way. She'd simply go in the front door and the devil take them all.

They were like jackals on the scent when they saw where she was going. She didn't allow herself to hear the shouts or the questions as she made her way through them to the Ellsworths' front door. She pounded on it, calling, "It's Sarah Brandt!" so they wouldn't be afraid to let her in.

After a few moments, the door opened a crack. She glimpsed Mrs. Ellsworth's frightened face in the instant before she squeezed through the narrow opening and threw her weight against the door to help the old woman close it behind her. By then the reporters were pounding on it, too, demanding admittance. After making sure it was locked securely, Sarah led Mrs. Ellsworth away to the relative quiet of the kitchen.

"Oh, Mrs. Brandt, I don't know what we're going to do," the old woman wailed. "I thought they'd gotten tired of us, and now . . ."

"They found out someone tried to kill Webster Prescott. It was in the newspapers this morning."

"That doesn't explain why they're here, though. Do they think Nelson did that, too?"

"I'm sure I don't know," Sarah said.

Mrs. Ellsworth looked pale and dangerously frail as she sat down abruptly in one of the kitchen chairs. "How is poor Mr. Prescott doing?"

"He's still alive, or he was the last time I visited him, but he's not doing very well, I'm afraid. In fact, when I went by the hospital to see him this morning—"

"Hospital!" Mrs. Ellsworth cried in horror. "The poor boy is in the hospital? He caused us a lot of pain, but I certainly wouldn't wish that on anybody. Doesn't he have someone to take care of him at home?"

"He has an aunt who lives in Brooklyn, but I just sent her word this morning, so she hasn't had time to get here yet. He's too weak to be moved, in any case."

"Oh dear, oh dear, I knew something terrible was going to happen. My left eye has been itching since yesterday! That's a bad omen, you know. Now if your right eye itches—"

"Mrs. Ellsworth, how are you doing?" Sarah interrupted, having no patience for a lecture on superstitions. "Do you have enough food in the house? I brought some things just in case."

"Oh, my, yes, we haven't eaten half of what you already brought. Neither of us has much of an appetite, as you can imagine."

"Mother, what's going on?" Nelson called from the hallway. The din from the reporters outside had drawn Nelson from his room. He came into the kitchen, a worried frown on his face. He hadn't shaved, and he was in his undershirt and trousers. "Oh, Mrs. Brandt, forgive my appearance!" he exclaimed, humiliated. "I had no idea—"

"Don't be silly," Sarah said. "Of course you didn't. I had to fight my way in here through a mob of newspapermen."

"Good God!" Nelson fumbled for one of the kitchen chairs and sank down into it, just as his mother had. "When will this nightmare ever end?"

"Does Mr. Prescott know who stabbed him?" Mrs. Ellsworth asked hopefully.

"He thinks it was a woman," Sarah said, "although he didn't see her face. It was dark, and she was wearing a cloak with a hood."

"A woman? That's impossible," Nelson declared.

"It does sound unlikely, I know," Sarah admitted, "and of course, Mr. Malloy and I were hoping that whoever stabbed him was the same person who killed Anna Blake. Now we're not so sure, though."

"So that's why the reporters are back," Nelson said. "Do they think my mother stabbed this fellow?" he added bitterly.

"If they don't stop their nonsense pretty soon, I might stab the lot of them," Mrs. Ellsworth said with more spirit than she'd shown in a week.

Sarah smiled in spite of herself. "It wouldn't help," she said. "More would just come to take their places."

"She's right, Mother," Nelson said. "Our only hope is to find out who really killed Anna."

"And how are we supposed to do that when we can't even leave the house?" Mrs. Ellsworth asked in exasperation.

"Mr. Malloy and I are doing everything we can," Sarah assured them both. "In fact, Mr. Malloy believes he's very close to finding the real killer."

"Is it the same person who stabbed the reporter?" Mrs. Ellsworth asked.

"We won't know that until Mr. Malloy questions him."

"I thought you said a woman stabbed him," Nelson said.

"Mr. Malloy thinks it was a man dressed up."

Mrs. Ellsworth frowned. She thought that sounded as preposterous as Sarah did. Then her expression grew calculating. "Are you visiting this reporter at the hospital in case he remembers anything else about his attacker?"

Sarah shrugged. "If he happens to remember something important, I wouldn't want to miss it," she admitted, "but I don't think there's much chance of it. Really, I just feel sorry for him. He was a likable fellow, for a reporter, and I can't stand the thought of anyone suffering alone like that."

"You're right," Mrs. Ellsworth said decisively, rising to her feet. "That poor boy shouldn't be left alone for an instant. Give me a moment to change, and I'll be ready to go with you back to the hospital."

"Mother, what are you doing?" Nelson asked, horrified.

"I'm going to do my Christian duty," she replied.

"Mrs. Ellsworth," Sarah began to protest, but the old woman cut her off.

"You're right, Mrs. Brandt. No one should be left alone in a hospital, especially not someone who might hold a clue to clearing my son's name. I'm not doing Nelson any good here, but I can at least do some good for that poor boy. And if he happens to say something useful, so much the better."

"Mother, you won't even get out the front door with all those reporters standing on the curb!"

"He's right, Mrs. Ellsworth," Sarah said.

Mrs. Ellsworth gave them both a pitying look. "I have no intention of going out the front door. But Mrs. Brandt will. She'll take her time and keep them busy until I can get safely out the back door. I'll wear a veil so I won't be recognized once I'm clear of the house. Then I'll meet you under the Sixth Avenue El at Twelfth," she said to Sarah. "When we get to the hospital, you can show me what to do, and I'll stay with him until . . . Well, as long as I need to."

"You can't do this," Nelson declared. "It isn't safe. I'll go instead."

"Nelson, my dear,'" his mother said kindly. "You couldn't show your face without someone recognizing you. Or were you planning to dress like a woman?" she added wickedly.

Nelson started sputtering a protest, but his mother cut him off.

"I'm going to do this, Nelson. It's not a bit dangerous, and it might even help. Besides, if I don't get out of here soon, I shall go mad."

"Are you sure you're up to this?" Sarah asked in concern.

This time Mrs. Ellsworth's expression was contemptuous. "Are you serious? I haven't felt this alive since I found out about that poor girl's death. I'm going whether you help me or not, so unless you want a parade of reporters following us to the hospital, I suggest you go along with my plan to distract them."

Sarah didn't even need to think it over. "What do you want me to do?"

As they entered Bellevue Hospital, Sarah glanced down at her companion with admiration. Mrs. Ellsworth had swathed herself in a heavy veil that concealed every trace of her identity. She didn't look particularly out of place, either, since women in mourning often went veiled, and her plan to escape the reporters' notice had worked beautifully.

Sarah had endured another round of shouted questions when she left the Ellsworths' house, and had successfully ignored them until the reporters got tired of following her and returned to their vigil. By the time she reached the appointed meeting place, Mrs. Ellsworth was waiting for her, the market basket hanging over her arm, filled with nutritious foods for Webster Prescott.

The two had taken the Sixth Avenue El up to Twenty-Sixth Street instead of walking over to Second Avenue in order to get off the street as quickly as possible. No one had even looked at them twice, though. They had arrived at their destination without incident.

When they reached the ward where Prescott lay, Sarah could see down the length of the room that a woman was sitting next to him, on the far side of his bed.

"It looks as if his aunt is already here," Sarah said with some surprise.

"I thought you only sent her word this morning. How could she have gotten here so quickly?"

"I don't . . . Oh, yes, it was in the newspaper this morning that he was attacked. Maybe she saw it and came over without being summoned. At any rate, we can certainly ask her," Sarah pointed out, leading the way to where the woman sat beside Prescott's bed.

Sarah noticed Prescott's aunt was also veiled, although hers was shorter and much lighter than Mrs. Ellsworth's. She was, Sarah knew, a widow, and she probably wore the veil all the time. Such elaborate mourning was a little excessive, but some women enjoyed flaunting their grief.

As they approached, she saw that the woman was trying to feed Prescott something, but he kept turning his head away.

He said something that sounded like, "Tastes bad," and she could hear his aunt coaxing him softly, the way one did with ill-tempered sick people.

"Mrs. Beasley," Sarah called when they were near enough.

Mrs. Beasley didn't turn. She just kept coaxing Prescott to eat. She must, Sarah thought, be hard of hearing.

"Mrs. Beasley!" she called more loudly as they reached Prescott's bed. "I'm Sarah Brandt, a friend of your nephew's."

Mrs. Beasley's head came up in surprise, and she jumped to her feet, dropping the bowl from which she had been feeding her nephew. It spilled on the bed, all over Prescott, and Sarah and Mrs. Ellsworth instinctively reached to salvage what they could of the porridge.

"I'm so sorry," Sarah said. "I didn't mean to startle you." But when she looked up to reassure Mrs. Beasley, she saw only the woman's back as she hurried away, nearly running in her fright.

"Oh, dear," Mrs. Ellsworth said, watching her disappear out the door. "She's quite shy, isn't she?"

"I certainly didn't mean to frighten her. I should go after her and apologize," Sarah said.

"No!" Prescott said, surprising both women.

"Mr. Prescott?" Sarah tried, wondering if he was talking to her. "How are you feeling?"

"No," he said again, obviously not hearing her at all. "Too sweet . . . Tastes . . . bad."

That's what he'd been saying to his aunt. Sarah wondered what the woman had been feeding him that had caused such a reaction. She lifted the nearly empty bowl to her nose and took a sniff.

How odd, she thought, certain she must be mistaken. But when she dipped her finger in and took a taste, she cried out in alarm.

"Good heavens!" Mrs. Ellsworth exclaimed, but Sarah was calling for the nurse.

One of the nurses came rushing over. "Whatever is the matter?"

"That woman was trying to poison Mr. Prescott!" Sarah cried.

"Poison!" Mrs. Ellsworth was saying, over and over, but the nurse wasn't as impressed.

"Who are you to know such a thing?" the nurse demanded skeptically.

"I'm a trained nurse, and if you don't believe me, taste this for yourself." She offered the bowl to the woman, who reared back in alarm.

"You want me to taste poison?" she asked, horrified.

"It's opium," Sarah said. "A very strong mixture."

Instantly, the woman paled. "What on earth would she have been giving him that for?" she asked.

"Probably to kill him," Sarah said impatiently. "Now hurry and find a doctor."

"Is there a chance to save him?" Mrs. Ellsworth asked.

"He may have saved himself if he refused to eat very much of it," Sarah said, rolling up her sleeves and getting ready to work on Prescott.

"Will he be all right, do you think?" Mrs. Ellsworth asked her later, after the doctor had finished examining Prescott. He lay peacefully on his pillow, but he looked awfully pale from being poked and prodded as the doctor checked to see if he showed any evidence of opium poisoning. He'd been very weak and ill to begin with, and now . . . Sarah simply didn't know. At least the doctor had felt sure he hadn't ingested very much of the opium. If the strain of being saved didn't kill him, he'd probably recover.

The two women were keeping a vigil by his bed. They'd found the basket the woman had used to bring the poisoned porridge into the hospital. Unfortunately, the basket was the kind that was available at every market in the city, and it contained no clue as to who the woman might have been.

"Well," Mrs. Ellsworth said, "I think we can be fairly certain that woman wasn't his aunt."

"She may have been the one who tried to kill him the first time, though," Sarah said. "She could have seen the newspaper story, figured out where he would be, and decided to finish him off."

"Did you see what she looked like?"

"No," Sarah said with a rueful smile. "You were right, a veil is the perfect disguise."

Mrs. Ellsworth had removed hers, and she smiled back at Sarah. "You probably thought I was a worthless old woman."

"I haven't thought that for a long time, not since I saw how you can handle an iron skillet," Sarah said, recalling the time Mrs. Ellsworth had rescued her.

"Oh, yes," Mrs. Ellsworth remembered. "One never knows what one is capable of until the time comes, does one?" She leaned back in her chair with a satisfied grin.

Sarah grinned back. "Now all you have to do is worry about keeping Mr. Prescott alive."

"After what we've already been through, it will probably be very dull work indeed, but I'll do my best. Now I'm sure you have some investigating of your own to do. I'll be fine, and if any veiled women show up and try to give Mr. Prescott something to eat, you can rest assured I will raise the alarm . . . or the skillet, if necessary."

"I know I can count on you. Meanwhile, I've got to find Mr. Malloy and let him know what's happened here."

Frank stood on Giddings's front porch and waited for someone to answer his knock. He'd seen the front curtain twitch, so he knew his presence had been noted. He'd give them another moment before he started pounding and shouting and generally causing a disturbance.

Fortunately, Mrs. Giddings wasn't willing to risk a scene. She opened the door and admitted Frank without a word, closing the door quickly behind him. Her expression told him how much she loathed the sight of him, but she was too much of a lady to actually say so.

"Is Harold here?" he asked.

She seemed surprised. "I thought you were here for Gilbert. What do you want with Harold?"

"I want to ask him some questions," Frank replied.

Her anger evaporated into fear. "About what?"

"That's something I'll discuss with Harold. Now is he here or not?"

"I don't think—" she began, but her son cut her off.

"Who was it, Mother?" he called from the back of the house.

Now she looked frantic. "He's just a boy!" she cried.

Unmoved, Frank headed for the back of the house.

"Wait, I'll get him!" she tried, hurrying after him, but Frank didn't want to take a chance that she'd send him out the back door.

He found Harold seated at the kitchen table, eating his supper. He half rose from his chair at the sight of Frank, but Frank pushed him back down again, none too gently.

The boy's eyes filled with fear, too, and he looked to his mother for an explanation.

"Please," was all she said, and she said it to Frank.

"I hate interrupting your supper," Frank said sarcastically, "but there's a few questions I need to ask you, Harold."

"Is it about my father?" he asked, glancing at his mother again.

"No, it's about you."

"Me?" What color was left in his young face drained away. "What do you need to know about me?"

"I need to know why you went to see Anna Blake the

night she died," Frank said, pulling out another of the kitchen chairs and seating himself.

"He was here that night, with me," his mother said quickly. "I already told you that!"

Frank turned to her with mild interest. "With you and your husband?" he asked.

"Yes, yes, we were all here," she insisted. "Just like I said!"

"Except I found out your husband was in jail that night," he said. "So if you were trying to give him an alibi, you were wasting your time. He's already got a good one." Frank turned back to the boy. "Don't *you* bother lying. You were there at Anna Blake's house. The other women saw you, and they can identify you. Now tell me why you went there and what happened."

Harold looked at his mother again, but not for help. This time his expression betrayed guilt. "I wanted to . . . I thought if I talked to her, told her what we were going through . . ." His gaze kept straying toward his mother. He didn't want her to hear this.

"What?" Frank prodded sharply, drawing his attention back.

The boy swallowed. "I thought I could get her to give the money back," he said. His mother made a strangled sound in her throat, and Harold winced. "I know now that was stupid, but . . ."

"What did she say?" Frank asked.

Humiliation mottled the boy's face. "She laughed at me. She said she'd earned that money, and she was going to keep it. She said"—another glance at his mother—"she said some ugly things about my father. That's when I got mad."

"Did you hit her?" Frank asked.

"Harold!" his mother cried in anguish.

But the boy half rose from his chair again, outraged. "I didn't lay a hand on that little tart!"

"But you did threaten to kill her if she didn't give the money back," Frank said mildly.

"*No!*" Mrs. Giddings screamed.

At the same moment, Harold shouted, "No, I didn't! I never!" He was completely out of his chair now, on his feet and ready to fight.

"Then what *did* you say?" Frank asked softly, not rising to the bait.

He drew a calming breath and forced himself to sit down again. "I said . . ." He took a moment to remember, his young face screwing up with the effort. "I think I said something like, she'd be sorry if she didn't."

"What did you mean that she'd be sorry? That you'd kill her?" Frank prodded.

"No!" He was horrified. "I mean . . . I don't know what I meant. I couldn't *make* her give the money back, could I? And she was laughing at me. I wanted to scare her, that's all. I wanted her to be afraid of me so she'd give back the money."

"And was she afraid of you when you met her later at the Square?" Frank asked.

Harold's eyes grew wide. "I didn't meet her at the Square. I never saw her again. I swear it!"

"She left the house right after you did," Frank said. "And you were still outside, trying to decide what to do next. You followed her, didn't you? You wanted to scare her, so you threatened her with a knife, and when she wasn't afraid, you got mad and you—"

"No!" Both mother and son cried out together.

Mrs. Giddings rushed at Frank, nearly hysterical in her need to protect her child. She raised her fists as if to strike him, but he grabbed them and easily wrestled her down onto a chair. He held her there until her resistance collapsed, and she covered her face with both hands and began to sob.

Harold rushed to her, overturning his own chair in his haste. "Mother, please, don't cry. It's all right. I didn't do anything to that woman. Don't cry, please don't!"

Mrs. Giddings's sobs were raw, as if they'd been torn from her soul. She wasn't a woman who cried easily, but she'd reached the end of her strength. She'd been holding herself together for the boy's sake for a long time, but see-

ing him threatened had pushed her too far. She had no reserves left.

The boy was crying, too, tears streaming unheeded
down his face as he helplessly tried to comfort her. He also
kept swearing to her that he'd never touched Anna Blake,
so she had nothing to fear. Frank had questioned enough
people in his long career that he knew innocence when it
was right in front of him.

He'd misjudged. He'd been so sure the boy had done it
in an insane effort to avenge his family's honor or some
other misplaced loyalty. Harold had certainly had a good
reason to want Anna Blake dead, and he'd been nearby
when she'd been killed. He was also young and foolish
enough to have done something incredibly stupid like ac-
cidentally stabbing a woman to death when he'd only
meant to frighten her. But he hadn't. Frank would have bet
a year's pay on the boy's innocence.

"Hush, now," Mrs. Giddings said brokenly after a few
minutes. She swiped at her ravaged face with the hem of
her apron and patted Harold's arm reassuringly. "I'm all
right. Don't make such a fuss." Then she lifted her gaze to
Frank. Her eyes were red and filled with pain. "He didn't
kill that woman," she said. "I did."

14

"Mother!" the boy cried in horror.

If Frank had entertained any lingering doubts about the boy's innocence, they died in that moment. Obviously, Harold would have done anything to protect his mother from more unpleasantness. In a while, he'd probably realize he could confess to the crime to save her, and then he might even try it, but his first instinct had been to believe her. This meant he had no reason to doubt her word.

"Harold," Frank said kindly, "Leave me alone with your mother."

"No!" the boy said, putting his arm around her defiantly. "I won't let you bully her!"

"I don't need to bully her," he pointed out. "She's already confessed. I just need to ask her a few more questions, and I don't think she wants you to hear the answers."

"It's all right, Harold," his mother said softly, stroking his cheek. "I'm not afraid."

Harold was, though. Frank could see it in his eyes. She was all he had left in the world, and Frank was going to take her away from him. He took her hand in both of his, his grip desperate. "Don't tell him anything!" he urged her. "Don't say another word!"

"I can't live with this any longer," she said, speaking gently to him, as if he were a small child. "I have to clear my conscience. Please, Harold, leave us alone. He's right, I don't want you to hear what I did."

The boy's face crumpled in despair. "Mother, how could you?"

"You wouldn't understand," she told him.

Instantly, his despair twisted into anger. "You did it for *him*, didn't you? Because you wanted him to come back to us!"

"No, my darling," she said lovingly, stroking his hair. "I did it for you."

Sarah walked home early that evening after a fruitless search for Malloy. No one at Police Headquarters knew where he was, or if they did, they weren't going to tell a mere woman, even if they did think she was his mistress.

Such an assumption should have infuriated her, but for some reason, she simply found it amusing. Why couldn't people ever accept that a man and a woman could just be friends? Or even business associates? They always had to believe the worst instead. Or maybe the police always saw the worst, so they naturally assumed it in every situation. Or maybe they enjoyed teasing Malloy too much to even care about the truth. Whatever the explanation, Sarah had to admit she enjoyed her unique status at Mulberry Street. They didn't exactly treat her with respect, but the obvious contempt which had greeted her on her first visit there was gone now. In its place was a strange sort of acceptance. She was the red-headed stepchild who wasn't exactly part of the family but who must be acknowledged, however grudgingly.

What Sarah hadn't considered doing in her quest to find Malloy was going to his flat to leave a message with his mother. She would love to see Brian and check on his progress, but she didn't feel up to dealing with Mrs. Malloy after all she'd been through today. She'd just have to wait until Malloy got her other message and made his way to her. Meanwhile, she would change her clothes and return to Bellevue to relieve Mrs. Ellsworth from her vigil.

But when Sarah turned onto Bank Street, she saw a familiar carriage parked at the curb in front of her house. The matched horses were dozing in the twilight chill, and the coachman seemed to be doing likewise. He'd wrapped a blanket around his shoulders and sat slumped in his seat, his hat pulled down over his eyes. She hoped he hadn't been waiting for her for very long.

She stepped up to the carriage and thumped on the side to get the driver's attention. He started awake and looked around in alarm until he saw her standing below him.

"I'm sorry I frightened you, Patrick," she said. "Why are you here?"

He lifted his hat in respect. "Your father sent me to fetch you, missus. He wants to see you right away."

"Is something wrong? Is someone ill?" she asked with a worried frown.

"Oh, no, ma'am. He just wanted to talk to you, he said. He has some news you've been waiting for."

Sarah remembered his promise this morning to find out what he could about embezzlement and wondered if that could be his news. If so, he hadn't wasted any time. She really should get to the hospital as quickly as possible, but hearing what her father had to say was important, too. The coach would carry her to her parents' home, and then she could have it take her to Bellevue and bring Mrs. Ellsworth home. This would be much safer than allowing the old woman to make her own way home alone, and if any reporters were still about that time of night, the driver could see her safely into her house. As the hour grew later, the traffic would ease, as well, so the carriage would be able to travel relatively quickly through the streets.

"Please wait just a few more minutes while I freshen up," she said to the driver and hurried inside.

When she had made herself more presentable, she also made a stop at the Ellsworth house to tell Nelson his mother was fine. Only then did she allow the carriage to take her up to Fifty-Seventh Street. When she sat down in

the dark comfort of the carriage, she suddenly realized
how very weary she was. She'd begun the day at her parents' home, certain she would soon discover Anna Blake's
real killer. But the more she'd learned from her various
stops, the more confused she had become. Instead of being
clearer, the situation was getting more confusing. Nothing
about Anna Blake made any sense, or so it seemed. Sarah
knew from experience, however, that once she had all the
pieces to the puzzle, it would all make sense. A twisted sort
of sense, perhaps, but a sense she could understand. Probably, she and Malloy just needed to share what they had
learned. Between the two of them, they may already have
the solution and simply not know it yet.

Sarah sincerely hoped that was true. She wanted Anna
Blake's murder to be solved so she could concentrate on
clearing Nelson's name and bringing Mrs. Ellsworth's life
back to normal.

The rumble of the carriage wheels over the rough
streets lulled Sarah into a light doze. The lurch of the carriage when it stopped in front of her parents' house woke
her, and she was surprised to discover she felt somewhat
refreshed from her brief nap

Her parents' home seemed warm and welcoming to her
now, not forbidding as she had seen it just a few short
months ago when she'd ended her long estrangement from
them. Her mother greeted her with a kiss and a worried
frown when the maid ushered her into the family parlor.

"Where have you been, my dear? We were concerned
when Patrick didn't return with you right away."

"I was out running errands," Sarah said with a smile,
not bothering to offer details. Her mother would only be
upset if she knew Sarah had foiled a murder plot, questioned several suspects, and paid a visit to Police Headquarters since she'd seen them earlier today. "I might have
been delivering a baby, you know. In that case, I could
have been gone all night. I hope Patrick would have gone
on home in that case."

"I'm sure he wouldn't keep the horses out all night," her

father said, sharing her amusement as he also kissed her cheek.

Her mother insisted that she eat when she learned Sarah hadn't yet had supper. Since she'd skipped lunch as well, Sarah was happy to accept. She'd have the cook wrap up something for Mrs. Ellsworth and Mr. Prescott before she left, too. Although she was starved, she was also impatient to hear her father's news. Good breeding prevailed, however, and she managed to wait until they were settled back in the family parlor before broaching the subject.

"Your message was that you had some information for me," she said as her father lit his pipe. The sweet aroma brought back childhood memories of happier times, when she and Maggie were children and still believed in fairy tales and happy endings. Now she knew better, but she still enjoyed the fragrance of the smoke.

"I was extremely fortunate," her father said, settling himself in his favorite chair. "Hendrick Van Scoyoc was at the club. He always knows everything that happens in the city."

"He's a gossip, you mean," her mother said.

"I mean he's well informed," her father said. "I won't criticize a man who served my purposes so well and in so timely a manner."

"As you say, my dear," her mother said. "I stand corrected."

"And what did Mr. Van Scoyoc tell you?" Sarah asked, hoping to move things along a little faster.

"I asked him to explain to me how one might embezzle money from a bank. Since he owns several, I thought it a harmless enough question, but he took immediate offense."

"Why on earth would he take offense?" her mother asked before Sarah could.

"Because his good friend . . . Well, let's be discreet and just say a friend of his had recently been a victim of this crime," her father explained. "Or I should say, one of his banks was. Hendrick thought I was being . . . unkind," he said, carefully choosing his words, "in making reference to it. It seems the man has suffered some ridicule from his peers over the incident."

"How interesting," her mother said, obviously entertained by the idea.

"I thought so," her father agreed. "I was apparently among the last to have heard about it. I had to explain my purpose in making the inquiry, so he wouldn't refuse to ever speak to me again. I did not reveal the identity of the individuals involved," he hastened to add. "Even though Van Scoyoc was very interested to learn who else had been victimized. You see, the situations were eerily similar."

"In what way?" Sarah asked, even more interested than her mother.

"The bank employee who stole the money had been, until then, very trustworthy and conscientious. A responsible family man, too. The kind you would never expect to be so foolish."

"What happened, then?" her mother asked, actually leaning forward in her chair in her eagerness to hear the entire story.

"It seems he fell into the thrall of a young woman."

Sarah could hardly believe she'd heard him correctly. "Who was she?"

Her father shrugged, puffing on his pipe. "If Van Scoyoc knows her name, he didn't mention it. But I can't believe he would care to know it. Some Irish girl, I think he said."

Sarah felt her hackles rise over the tone with which he said "Irish," as if the Irish didn't need names, being something less than human. But to Van Scoyoc and her father and others like them, they didn't. It was a hideous injustice, but she must choose her battles. She would fight that one another day. She had more pressing matters with which to deal at the moment. "Why did he think she was Irish?" she asked, recalling she'd noticed Catherine Porter looked Irish the first time she'd seen her.

"I don't . . . Oh, yes, now I remember. Van Scoyoc said something about a red-haired vixen. That must be why I assumed she was Irish." He dismissed the topic with a wave of his hand, although Sarah made careful note that the woman he described might have been the elusive Francine. "In any case, this fellow stole several thousand dollars from the bank before anyone discovered it. He'd given the money to this girl, of course, and once his crime was discovered, she disappeared."

"What happened to the embezzler?" Sarah asked, fairly certain the mystery of Francine's departure was now solved and the identity of her "rich gentleman" discovered. Surely there weren't many other red-haired women in the city doing the same thing. "Was he arrested or did he escape?"

"Neither. He was dismissed from his position, of course, but the bank didn't press charges. The scandal would have ruined them, so they didn't dare."

"Could you find out who this man was?" Sarah asked urgently, certain now he must be another victim of the Walcotts and their tenants.

"I probably could, but I don't believe that would help you," her father said. "According to Van Scoyoc, the fellow hanged himself from shame after it all came out."

"How cowardly of him," her mother said. "And selfish. You said he had a family. What would become of them with him dead?"

"It wouldn't be much different than if he were alive, my dear," her father explained. "He'd never be able to find another position. People talk, you know, and his crime would follow him wherever he went, even if no one spoke of it publicly. At least with him dead, his family could be free of that."

"Yes," Sarah said, unable to keep the bitterness from her voice. "With him gone, they could starve in respectability."

Her father frowned at her tone. "Life is frequently unfair, Sarah. When it is, the innocent often suffer. That's the way of the world, and we cannot hope to change it."

He believed that, of course. They'd had this argument many times. This argument had driven her sister Maggie to her death. Unfortunately, Sarah didn't have the energy to answer it tonight. She had more important things to do, in any case. She, for one, was going to change at least one of the ways of the world and make things better for the Ellsworths and Webster Prescott.

Before she left, however, she still needed a bit more information. "Did Mr. Van Scoyoc explain how one might embezzle from the bank without being caught?"

"Not without being caught. Eventually, the discrepancies would be found, no matter how careful the thief was. Blame might be diverted onto another, but the crime could not be concealed forever. He was also surprised that the discrepancy was found so quickly. He did not believe that such a thing couldn't be discovered in a day, even if the auditors knew what they were looking for."

"Then how does he explain it?" Sarah asked.

"He doesn't. In fact, he doesn't believe they found it at all."

The hour was late by the time Sarah finally arrived at Bellevue. She found Mrs. Ellsworth dozing in her chair, her chin resting on her bony chest, her breath coming in unladylike snores. Webster Prescott was sleeping, too. He seemed to have recovered a bit from his earlier ordeal, and the nurse confirmed he'd been resting comfortably for several hours. Even his fever was a little lower.

Mrs. Ellsworth awoke with a start and a snort when Sarah touched her shoulder. "What . . . ? Oh, Mrs. Brandt," she said in relief. Then she instinctively looked at Prescott. "How is he?"

"He seems to be doing fairly well."

"Oh, heavens, don't say that! It's bad luck to say a sick person is doing well!" she informed Sarah, aghast at her ignorance.

"Oh, I'm sorry," she said, however insincerely. "I mean to say he's not doing as poorly as he was."

"I'm glad to hear it," the old woman replied with some relief.

Sarah bit back a smile. "You've done a good job guarding him, but it's time for you to go home to your own bed now."

"Nonsense! Someone must stay with him all the time. What if that woman comes back to kill him again?"

"Then I'll be here," Sarah told her.

"But you shouldn't waste your time *here*. You have things you could be doing, while I don't have anything to look forward to except more waiting."

"Yes, you do," Sarah assured her. "I need for you to go home and tell Mr. Malloy where I am when he comes looking for me tomorrow. I have some important things to tell him, especially about the woman who tried to kill Mr. Prescott, and I need to see him as soon as possible."

"Then I should stay here while you go find Mr. Malloy," she argued.

"I've spent a good part of the afternoon trying to do just that without success. I left a message for him at Police Headquarters, so I think the best plan is for me to stay in one place and let him find me. But he'll go to my house, and he won't know where else to look unless you tell him."

She started sputtering additional objections, but Sarah cut her off.

"You're going home, and I'm staying here, and I won't hear any more on the subject. Now, I've got a carriage waiting for you downstairs, and you're keeping the poor driver from his bed."

"A carriage?" she echoed suspiciously.

"It's my parents'. They sent me home in it, so I thought I should make good use of it. Now don't make that poor man wait any longer. There's food, too, for your and Nelson's supper, courtesy of my mother's cook. Enjoy it."

Mrs. Ellsworth offered a few more feeble arguments, but finally she surrendered. She really was starting to feel the strain of the day. Before she left, however, she pressed a rabbit's foot into Sarah's hand.

"It can't hurt," she said when Sarah looked skeptical.

"How many of these do you have?" Sarah asked, remembering she'd given one to Malloy as well.

"As many as I need," she replied.

When she was gone, Sarah made herself as comfortable as possible and settled in for a long night.

Frank wondered how Sarah Brandt could give him a headache when he wasn't even with her. He'd been feeling pretty good this morning, having arrested Anna Blake's confessed killer the night before. Although he'd had no reason to be concerned about her comfort, he'd managed to get Mrs. Giddings locked up in The Tombs instead of at Police Headquarters. The Tombs were grim, but they were still far more tolerable than the cellar at Mulberry Street.

Getting Gilbert Giddings released from jail had been the work of a few moments, and he hadn't even had to deal with the man himself. Let his son tell him the awful news about what his wife had done. He never wanted to see that sorry drunk again. Frank's sense of accomplishment had dimmed somewhat when he'd gotten Mrs. Brandt's message, though. He was used to being teased about her, or as used to it as he was ever going to get, but that didn't mean he was used to having her involved in his cases. He'd never get accustomed to that, especially when being involved meant confronting would-be killers in the act, as he'd learned from Mrs. Ellsworth when he'd gone looking for Sarah Brandt at her home.

"I'm sure Mrs. Brandt is perfectly fine," Mrs. Ellsworth said from where she was sitting beside him on the El as they sped uptown toward Bellevue. "We scared that woman off. She won't be back."

Frank gritted his teeth. "If it *was* a woman," he said. "You said yourself you didn't see her face."

"Well, whoever it was who tried to poison poor Mr. Prescott, they won't be back," Mrs. Ellsworth insisted.

Frank only hoped she was right. The thought of Sarah Brandt facing down a killer in the middle of the night on a deserted hospital ward was unsettling, to say the least. It unsettled Frank so much he wanted to strangle somebody. "You shouldn't have come," he said, not for the first time. "I told you I'd get somebody to stand guard over Prescott.

His newspaper will probably hire a guard when they find out what happened. It would make for a good story."

"A guard can prevent the killer from striking again, but he won't be able to give Mr. Prescott the special care he needs," she pointed out. "Besides, I'm tired of being locked in my house day and night."

When Frank had gone to Sarah Brandt's house this morning—and he'd gone the instant he'd gotten her message—the last thing he'd expected was to find Mrs. Ellsworth watching for him.

Well, that wasn't exactly true. Mrs. Ellsworth was *always* watching for something to happen on her street. If she'd been unable to do anything about what had been happening lately, that only made her more anxious to get active again. Frank would've had to tie her hand and foot to keep her from accompanying him to the hospital to find Mrs. Brandt. When she told him about the attempt on Prescott's life, he hadn't wanted to waste time trying to deter her, either.

"If it's any comfort to you, I arrested Anna Blake's killer last night," he told her.

Her eyes widened, almost erasing the wrinkles around them. "Oh, Mr. Malloy! That's wonderful! Who was it?"

"The wife of another man Anna Blake was blackmailing. This man was ruined. He stole from his employer to pay her. When he got caught, he impoverished himself to pay back what he'd stolen. His wife was very angry, so she took it out on the person she held responsible for her troubles."

"That poor woman! The wife, I mean. Anna Blake asked for her trouble, but this poor woman didn't. I guess I can't blame her for wanting vengeance. I probably would've felt the same, in her place."

"You women," Malloy snorted. "You're so cold-blooded."

"I didn't say killing Miss Blake was right," she defended herself. "I just said I could understand why she wanted that woman dead. If my Nelson had been ruined, I might have considered the same thing."

Frank didn't point out that Nelson was as good as ruined unless they could find out who had really stolen money from his bank. Even if they could, it was possible the sensational stories about him that had appeared in the various newspapers would have destroyed his reputation and he would be unable to make a respectable living again. In Frank's experience, innocent people often had to suffer for others' crimes. Nelson Ellsworth would probably be one of them, and there might be nothing Frank could do to save him. He wasn't going to be the one to explain all this to the man's mother, however. His job was hard enough as it was.

To Frank's chagrin, he had to quicken his usual pace to keep up with Mrs. Ellsworth as they walked from the train station to the hospital. The old woman was a caution.

They found Sarah Brandt sitting beside Prescott's bed, feeding him something from a bowl. She glanced up and smiled when she saw them. Frank felt a strange flutter in his chest at the sight of that smile. Or maybe it was from the sight of her. She looked like she hadn't slept in a week, and Frank didn't like that one bit. Why did she feel responsible for sitting up all night and guarding a newspaper reporter she hardly knew, especially one who'd caused her friends so much trouble?

"Good morning, Malloy," she said, her eyes shining, as if she were enjoying a secret joke at his expense. "You're a difficult man to find."

"Finding you isn't so hard," he replied in kind. "I just need to look where you have no business being, and there you are."

"I'm a nurse," she reminded him. "Why shouldn't I be at a hospital?"

"Because . . ." he began, but stopped when he realized he didn't really want to explain. If he did, he'd have to reveal how worried he was about her safety, and then she might start to wonder why he cared so much. This was a topic he didn't even want to consider himself, much less discuss with her. "Have you seen any sign of that woman who tried to kill Prescott?" he asked instead.

"No, but I'm sure she's the same one who stabbed him in the first place," she said. "Nothing else makes sense. And she's also probably the person who killed Anna Blake, although I never would've guessed her killer would be a female."

"Mr. Malloy arrested Miss Blake's killer last night," Mrs. Ellsworth reported helpfully.

Frank shot her a disapproving look, but she wasn't paying any attention.

"Who was it?" Mrs. Brandt asked, brightening at the thought.

"Who . . . was . . . it?" Prescott echoed feebly.

Frank looked at him in surprise, having forgotten he was even there and certainly that he was listening to every word. "You're in no condition to write a story about it, Prescott, so I'll tell you. It was Mrs. Gilbert Giddings."

"*Mrs.* Giddings!" Mrs. Brandt exclaimed in surprise. "I thought you were going to arrest the son!"

"She confessed when I went to question the boy," Frank said. "She was afraid I was going to arrest him for the crime."

"You were," Mrs. Brandt reminded him with a small smile.

"Only if he was guilty," Frank said, not liking the defensive tone in his voice. He didn't need to make excuses to her, he reminded himself. "But he wasn't."

"Did she tell you why she tried to kill Mr. Prescott?" she asked.

Frank shook his head. "She didn't try to kill him."

"But—" she began to protest.

He cut her off. "Not in front of Prescott," he cautioned.

The patient was growing restless, his eyes intent. Frank could almost imagine him mentally composing his story for the *World.*

"How's he doing?" he asked Mrs. Brandt.

She glanced at Mrs. Ellsworth before replying, and he thought she was holding back a grin. "He's not doing as poorly as he was before," she said.

"What does *that* mean?" Frank asked.

"That means it's bad luck to say someone is doing well," she explained, with another glance at the old woman.

Frank managed not to snort in disgust. "So the opium didn't hurt him?"

"He must not have taken very much," she said. "The mixture was very strong, so it was also very sweet. Apparently, that didn't appeal to Mr. Prescott, to his great good fortune."

"Don't like . . . sweets," Prescott explained. He looked as if he were trying with difficulty to keep his eyes open.

"What's going on here?" a woman demanded. "Are you the doctor? Webster, my dear boy! What's happened?"

A small woman inserted herself into the group beside Prescott's bed, forcing her way to him. Malloy was just about to grab her when Prescott said, "Aunt Orpah!"

"Webby, dear, what have they done to you?" she asked, smoothing his hair back from his forehead as she checked for fever. Then she turned accusing eyes to the rest of them. "Who are you people?"

"I'm Sarah Brandt," she said. "I sent you the message about your nephew, Mrs. Beasley."

The woman softened immediately. "Oh, thank you, Mrs. Brandt. It was such a shock! I got here as soon as I could. Webby is my sister's boy, and I promised I'd look after him for her. How on earth you can look after a grown man, I'm not sure, though. He seems determined to get himself in trouble!"

"Indeed he does," Mrs. Ellsworth said. "He's been set upon twice by females intent on murdering him."

Mrs. Beasley looked shocked, but Mrs. Brandt distracted her by introducing the two older women. "And this is Detective Sergeant Frank Malloy," she added. "He's going to find the person who attacked Mr. Prescott."

Actually, Frank wasn't particularly interested in finding out who had attacked Prescott. His concern had been finding Anna Blake's killer and clearing Nelson Ellsworth. Since the person who had attacked Prescott was someone else entirely, he felt no further obligation, especially to someone who had made the Ellsworths' lives miserable. He wasn't going to mention all this to Aunt Orpah, though. He needed her to take over caring for Prescott so he could get Sarah Brandt away from here. Let Aunt Orpah worry about fending off would-be murderesses.

"Mr. Malloy is going to order the *World* to hire a guard to protect Mr. Prescott in the meantime, too," Mrs. Ellsworth added.

Now Frank knew he should have tied her hand and foot to keep her from coming with him today. "I can't *order* them to do it," he quickly clarified, "but I was going to strongly suggest it."

"What a good idea," Mrs. Brandt said, smiling her approval. Frank wished her approval didn't matter so much to him.

"And if *you* can't order them to, *I* can," Mrs. Beasley said tartly, sounding very much like Mrs. Ellsworth. "If they don't, I'll contact another newspaper and give *them* the story in exchange for a guard!"

"Aunt Orpah!" Prescott protested feebly, but his aunt paid him no attention.

Fortunately, the editor at the *World* immediately saw the news story potential in Prescott's situation. Arrangements were quickly made by telephone to dispatch someone from the newspaper both to protect Prescott and to get the full story.

"You mustn't allow them to tire Mr. Prescott," Mrs. Brandt instructed his aunt when the arrangements had been made. "He's still in danger and needs lots of rest."

"I can talk," Prescott protested feebly, but no one seemed interested in hearing him do so.

The three women consulted on what the best course of treatment would be for the reporter. By the time the representatives from *The World* arrived—three of them and all very excited at the prospect of reporting the second attempt on Prescott's life—Mrs. Brandt was finally satisfied that she could safely leave Prescott in his aunt's care.

Frank's goal was to get Sarah Brandt home as quickly as possible since he was afraid she might keel over from exhaustion at any moment. Taking her on the train seemed the most difficult means of travel, but a Hansom cab could barely hold two passengers, and he had to return Mrs. Ellsworth to her home as well. Besides, the train was faster, even if it meant walking some distance both to and from the stations. They managed to make the trip without any mishaps.

Just in case the reporters were still keeping their vigil on Bank Street, however, Frank led the women down the alley behind their houses. A stray dog was rooting through a pile of garbage, and he looked up and growled as they approached. The animal was mangy and scrawny, and Frank hoped it wasn't also rabid. He shouted and clapped his hands, advancing threateningly, and to his relief, the dog tucked his tail and ran.

"You're much better at that than I am," Mrs. Brandt remarked.

"I'm louder," he said.

"And bigger," Mrs. Ellsworth added.

They reached the rear of their houses without further incident. "We'll wait here until you're safely inside," he told the old woman.

Mrs. Ellsworth wasn't eager to be dismissed, however.

"Mrs. Brandt, you need to get some rest immediately," she said. "I'll be happy to come in and fix you something to eat so you don't have to exert yourself."

Frank opened his mouth to protest, but Sarah Brandt beat him to it.

"Thank you so much for the offer, but I'm afraid I must consult with Mr. Malloy before I can even think of resting. I have a lot of things to tell him . . . and to ask him, too," she added with a meaningful look he didn't even try to interpret.

"But you must eat," Mrs. Ellsworth insisted. "You probably haven't even had any breakfast."

"I'll fix her something," Frank said, earning an amazed look from both women. "And if anyone comes looking for Mrs. Brandt to deliver a baby, tell them she's already out on a call," he added to Mrs. Ellsworth.

"Malloy!" Mrs. Brandt protested, but Frank wasn't going to argue that point.

"Don't you want to hear all about Mrs. Giddings's confession?" he asked provocatively, taking her by the elbow and steering her toward her back gate.

"Thank you for your help," she called over her shoulder to the old woman. "I'll check on you this afternoon." Then she said, "Ouch!" because Frank was squeezing her elbow pretty tightly.

But he didn't let her go until he was sure she was safely in her yard with the gate closed behind them, away from Mrs. Ellsworth.

As soon as they were inside her house and the back door was shut, she said, "You better not have used the third degree on Mrs. Giddings."

Frank pulled off his bowler hat and hung it on a hook by the back door before trusting himself to respond to that. "I didn't lay a hand on the woman, or on her son either, for that matter. I figured out from what he told me that he didn't kill Anna Blake. I wasn't even going to arrest him, but I guess his mother didn't know that, which is why she decided to confess."

She pulled off her gloves and then her hat, jabbing the lethal-looking hat pin back into it with far more force than necessary. "Something's not right about this, Malloy," she insisted, making her way into the kitchen without bothering to invite him to follow. He did anyway.

"I don't know why you can't just accept that the woman killed Anna Blake," he tried. "She had every reason to, and she admitted it."

"How did she even know where Anna lived?"

"She followed her son there that night. The boy had followed his father before, so he knew where the house was. Harold wanted to confront her. He wanted her to give back the money she'd taken from his father."

She was stuffing kindling into the stove. "I'm sure Anna found that amusing."

"The boy said she laughed at him, if that's what you mean. Then he left, but his mother waited for a while, so the boy wouldn't see her, and when she saw Anna leave the house, she realized this was her chance. She followed her to the park and stabbed her."

Mrs. Brandt had lit the kindling and looked up while she waited for it to catch. "She stabbed her in broad daylight?" she asked.

"They were standing off by themselves. No one paid them any attention."

"And Anna just lay there until morning?" She was feeding small sticks into the growing flames. "No one noticed her?"

"She must've walked a bit, trying to find some help. But if anyone saw her, they probably just thought she was drunk."

"Wouldn't they have seen the blood?"

"The coroner said she covered the wound with her shawl, probably trying to stop the bleeding."

"And what about the man?"

"What man?"

"The man the coroner said Anna had been with before she died. The sponge, remember?"

He'd been trying not to think about it. "She probably had a liaison with somebody we don't know anything about," Frank suggested.

"Malloy, this doesn't make any sense."

"Murder doesn't *have* to make sense," he reminded her in exasperation. "In fact, it hardly ever does!"

"I'm not talking about the *why*. I'm talking about the *how*. Mrs. Giddings *couldn't* have killed Anna Blake."

"She confessed!" Frank reminded her angrily. "Why would she do that if she didn't kill her?"

"You said it yourself, she thought you were going to arrest her son. She might have done it to protect him. But whatever her reason, she was lying. Mrs. Giddings did not kill Anna Blake."

15

Sarah stuck a log into the stove and slammed the door shut more loudly than necessary. Malloy was glaring at her, but she didn't care. She was right, and she knew it.

"All right," he said, pretending to be reasonable, "if Mrs. Giddings didn't do it, then who did?"

"The same person who tried to kill Mr. Prescott."

"You don't know that!"

"Yes, I do! The person who stabbed him promised him information about Anna Blake's killer. And why would anyone else want to kill him?"

"A hundred reasons! He's a newspaper reporter!" Malloy was shouting now.

"Keep your voice down," she cautioned. "You don't want Mrs. Ellsworth to hear you. She'd be over here in a second to find out what's wrong."

He looked like he might explode, but he drew a deep breath, let it out on a long sigh, and forced himself to sit down at the kitchen table.

Sarah started making coffee while Malloy got his temper under control.

As she set the pot on the warming stove, he said, "Just because the person—and I'm glad you're willing to admit

it might not have been a female—who stabbed Prescott
lured him with a promise of information about Anna
Blake, that doesn't mean he—or she—had any or even
knew anything about the murder at all. It just means that
person knew this was a sure way to get Prescott to a private meeting."

Sarah didn't like this. He was starting to make sense.
"Maybe you're right, but maybe I'm right, too. What if the
person who killed Anna was afraid Prescott was getting
too close to the truth?"

"How would he—or she—know that?"

"Because of Prescott's stories in the paper," she reminded him impatiently. "He was the one who discovered
that Anna was an actress and—"

"*You* were the one who discovered that. Prescott just
happened to be the only reporter we told."

"Fair enough, but still, he was the first one to write
about it. If someone was afraid of what he was finding out,
they could have decided the safest thing to do was kill
him."

"Wait a minute," Malloy said, holding up his hand.
"How would they know it was Prescott writing the stories?"

Sarah had been rummaging around in her cupboard,
looking for something to eat, but this brought her head up
sharply. She opened her mouth to reply, but no words came
for a moment while she thought this through. "You're
right!" she said finally. "*We* knew Prescott was writing the
stories, but no one else would."

"No, they wouldn't," Malloy said. "It's not like they put
the reporter's name on his stories or anything. So it had to
be someone who knew Prescott was the one writing them,
or who at least had heard of him."

"The Walcotts knew Prescott," she remembered. "He'd
been to the house that day we told him Anna was an actress. Then he went back later, right before he was attacked, after he'd talked to her friends at the theater. He
was asking a lot of questions, and Mrs. Walcott got very
upset."

"Did Prescott tell you this?"

"No, Catherine Porter did."

He frowned, surprised and not happy about it. "When did you talk to Catherine Porter?"

"Yesterday. She told me a lot of things, and that's why I was looking for you. I thought you needed to know them, too."

"You went to the boarding house?"

"Yes. I just couldn't make sense of what had happened that night, and I thought Catherine might be able to answer a few of my questions."

Malloy rubbed a hand over his face wearily, although what he had to be weary about, she had no idea. "Why don't you sit down and tell me everything Catherine Porter told you?" he suggested tightly.

"I want to get something to eat first," she said. "You promised Mrs. Ellsworth you'd take care of me, but I can see you have no intention of it." Turning her full attention to the cupboard for a few seconds, she finally found a tin of peaches and started prying it open with the can opener.

Malloy sighed again, this time in martyrdom, and rose to his feet. "Sit down," he commanded her.

"But—"

"*Sit down!* Or I'll get Mrs. Ellsworth over here to make you."

That was an effective threat. Sarah sat, mystified as to what might happen next. To her surprise, Malloy finished opening the can of peaches, poured them out into a bowl, and set it in front of her.

Sarah looked up at him, still not quite certain what to make of this. "I'll need something . . . a fork," she ventured.

To her amazement, he located one without fumbling and put it on the table beside her. "Eat," was all he said.

So she did. And while she did, he found some eggs in her icebox, which was still fairly cool even though she hadn't replenished the ice in several days. Then he located a piece of cheese that was too hard to eat and a dried-up onion. In a few minutes, he'd chopped the onion and put it in a pan to sizzle in some bacon grease he'd spooned from the container by the stove. Then he broke up the cheese and threw it into the pan with the eggs, and before Sarah could quite comprehend what was happening, Malloy set the finished concoction down in front of her.

While he was pouring them each a cup of coffee, she looked up at him in awe and asked, "When did you learn to cook?"

"This isn't cooking," he said. "This is basic survival. How do you think men keep from starving when they don't have a woman to do for them? Now eat."

Sarah had forgotten to finish eating the peaches while she'd watched him, and the aroma of the frying onions had set her mouth to watering. She tucked into the omelet with shameless enthusiasm, not pausing until every bite of it was gone.

"That was delicious," she said, a little chagrined at her gluttony.

"You were hungry," he demurred.

She looked at the bowl of peaches. "Do you want some of these? I don't think I can eat them all after that."

"Try. Then tell me what you found out from Catherine Porter."

Sarah had been so sure she'd be able to recall every detail, but now it seemed days had passed since she'd been at the Walcotts' house. Fatigue made her memory even more sluggish. Maybe she should just try to put things in order. "The night Anna died, the Giddings boy came to see her."

"We knew that."

"They had an argument. He threatened to kill her if she didn't give back the money Giddings had paid her."

"I know, I know," he said impatiently. "Then he left, and she got a message and went out and—"

"No, she didn't!"

"What?"

"She didn't get a message, not that Catherine knew of, and they were together all evening. Also, Anna didn't go out, not right away, at least. The two of them played checkers or something until Catherine went to bed much later."

"But the landlady said she went out right after Harold Giddings left," Malloy protested.

"Then one of them is wrong. I think Catherine was telling the truth, though. Remember she said she was asleep when Anna left the house. She said that long before we knew anything different. She also thought Mrs. Walcott was angry about the boy coming to the house. She doesn't like unpleasantness, Catherine said. Maybe Mrs. Walcott and Anna argued about it after Catherine went bed. Maybe Anna left the house in a huff and got herself killed and now Mrs. Walcott feels guilty, so she made up the story about her getting a message."

"It would've had to be a pretty nasty fight for her to go out alone after dark," Malloy observed. "Would Mrs. Walcott have been that upset about the Giddings boy's visit?"

"I don't know. Maybe we should ask her," Sarah suggested, earning a frown from Malloy. "Or maybe they argued about something else," she tried. "Remember what that actress Irene said about Mr. Walcott courting the girls to get them to move into his house? Maybe his wife was jealous of Anna."

"I guess you want me to ask Mrs. Walcott about that, too," Malloy asked sarcastically.

"Oh, and I almost forgot. Anna was only wearing her housedress when she left that night. No woman would go out in her housedress under ordinary circumstances. She didn't wear a jacket or a cape, either, and it was cold enough that she would've needed one."

"She had a shawl," Malloy said. "I told you the coroner said she'd tried holding it against her wound to keep it from bleeding too much."

"Catherine said she had a shawl on when they were playing their game," she remembered, "because it was chilly in the house. Mrs. Walcott wouldn't light a fire. That means she didn't change anything she was wearing before she went out. Probably, she didn't even go up to her room. She just ran out without any preparation at all. A woman as vain about her appearance as Anna Blake wouldn't do that unless she was very upset. Or desperate. Whatever she was feeling, she certainly wouldn't go out like that if she were meeting someone."

Malloy sipped his coffee, considering all she'd told him. "You've been wondering why she was out alone so late. All right, maybe she had an argument with Mrs. Walcott, but that still doesn't explain why she'd leave the house so suddenly."

"Maybe Mrs. Walcott threw her out," Sarah suggested.

"Even so, wouldn't she have at least packed her things and gotten properly dressed?"

He was right, of course.

"She might have just been going to stay with a friend for the night," Sarah said, still thinking out loud, "until she and the landlady had time for their tempers to cool. Or maybe she was planning to return for her things later, when Mrs. Walcott wasn't home."

"Then that means a stranger killed her while she was walking the streets by herself. Actually, that's more likely, considering what the coroner said."

"Malloy, I'm getting very annoyed with you," Sarah said, frowning because today was the first time he'd bothered to mention that the coroner had told him a lot more about Anna's death than he'd bothered to share with her. "What else did the coroner say?"

Malloy obviously felt no guilt over his omissions. "He said she walked for a distance that night after she was stabbed."

"A *distance*?" she echoed incredulously. "How far?"

"Maybe a few blocks," he said with a shrug. "She must've been trying to get back home after she was attacked."

"If only she'd made it," Sarah sighed. "Maybe she could have at least told someone who stabbed her."

"If she even knew," he pointed out. "If a stranger killed her, then that still means Prescott's attack didn't have anything to do with Anna's murder, and my chances of catching the real killer aren't very good. And don't forget, I still have Mrs. Giddings locked up. No matter what you think, she claims she killed Anna."

"She couldn't have," Sarah pointed out. "Even if she'd followed her son to Anna's house, she wouldn't have stood around on the street waiting for hours in case Anna came out so she could follow and murder her. Why would she expect Anna to come out at all? And she especially wouldn't have stayed there on the street until after dark, for the same reasons it's so strange that Anna went out herself. That's just impossible to believe."

Malloy didn't look happy, and Sarah couldn't blame him. He'd thought he'd solved the case, and now she was proving he hadn't. "Impossible or not, Mrs. Giddings still confessed. And you also haven't convinced me that the same person who killed Anna also stabbed Prescott."

"That's probably because I'm not sure myself anymore. If Anna was killed by a stranger who was trying to rob her or attack her, then there's no reason for there to have been a connection."

"Even if Mrs. Giddings killed Anna, she didn't have any reason to kill Prescott either. In fact, who among the people who knew Anna did? Were her friends at the theater angry about him snooping around?"

"Not at all," Sarah said. "Theater people probably love publicity. Catherine said Mrs. Walcott was angry, though."

"Rightly so. She didn't want bad publicity for herself or her boarding house. But murder is a pretty drastic solution to that problem. You might as well say the Ellsworths stabbed him because he was writing all those stories about Nelson."

Sarah rubbed her temple where a headache was forming. "I'm afraid I'm too tired to figure any of this out right now."

"Then get some sleep. I've got to go back to work myself before somebody notices I'm spending all my time on someone else's case."

He got up and carried her dishes to the sink.

"For heaven's sake, don't wash them," she cried in mock horror. "I don't think my heart could take the shock!"

"Don't worry," he assured her with one of his rare grins.

"I had no intention of it." The grin transformed him, banishing the pain and the years that had hardened him and giving her a glimpse of the boy he once had been. For an instant, she even saw a trace of Brian in him.

Something inside of her warmed and began to melt, a part of her that had been frozen for a very long time. She rose, responding to an instinctive need to be closer to him. Closer to his warmth.

"Thank you for taking such good care of me," she said and impulsively gave him her hand.

His fingers closed over hers, strong and sure, and his grin faded. For a long moment, their gazes locked and held, and Sarah saw something in his dark eyes she'd never seen before. A longing. A need. An emptiness she instantly understood because it matched her own. An emptiness he could fill if only . . .

Suddenly, the place where his hand touched hers began to burn, as if his flesh were searing her, and she snatched her hand back in alarm. And when she looked into his eyes again, she saw only the Malloy she knew, the one who allowed nothing and no one past his barriers. Had she only imagined that moment?

She covered her embarrassment with a forced laugh. "I'll be sure to tell Mrs. Ellsworth you were as good as your word about feeding me."

"She probably won't believe you," he said gruffly, turning toward the back door. He was leaving, and Sarah didn't know whether to be relieved or disappointed.

"What are you going to do about Mrs. Giddings?" she asked for something to say.

He gave her one of his looks over his shoulder as he reached for his hat. "You're like a dog with a bone, aren't you?"

"Yes," she said, glad they were back to their normal bantering again. Perhaps she really had only imagined that awkward moment. She *was* awfully tired. "And you won't scare me off by shouting and clapping your hands, either."

"In that case, I'll just tell you the truth. I'm not going to do anything with Mrs. Giddings."

"You can't mean that!"

"She confessed to a murder," he reminded her, "and now that she's locked up, they aren't going to let her go even if I tell them I don't think she did it after all, which I'm not going to do, because I still think she probably did. Now get some rest. When you wake up, you'll probably realize I'm right, and you'll have to apologize for disagreeing with me."

"Ha!" she replied, making him grin again, but this one was merely cocksure and not the least bit vulnerable or boyish.

"Good day, Mrs. Brandt," he said and then he was gone, setting his hat on his head as he strode quickly out of her backyard.

She closed the door behind him and locked it, suddenly feeling the extent of her exhaustion. No wonder she was having romantic notions about Malloy. She was probably delirious with fatigue.

A few minutes later, she had stripped off most of her clothes, washed, and collapsed onto her bed. The next thing she knew, she was face to face with a vicious dog that was growling and barking, and no matter how loudly she shouted or how many times she clapped her hands, he wouldn't run away. He just kept pawing at the cellar door, trying to get inside. Sarah knew he shouldn't get in, but she didn't know how to stop him. She needed a bone. If she just had a bone to throw to him, he'd go away. But she couldn't find one, not anywhere. And then it didn't matter because the cellar door was opening. Someone was pushing it up from the inside, and the dog was howling and barking and prancing all around, but Sarah was afraid. She didn't want whoever was down there to come out. She wanted to push the door shut again, but she couldn't move. She couldn't move one muscle. All she could do was watch helplessly as the door fell open and Anna Blake stepped out.

She was dead, of course. Sarah could see the bloodstains on her dress, and her face was white, her eyes blank and staring. She was dead and coming out of the cellar, and the dog was going to get her. Sarah opened her mouth to cry out a warning, and the sound of her own voice woke her with a start.

She looked around, surprised to find herself in her own bed, in her own bedroom, gasping for breath and drenched in cold sweat, but completely alone. No dog. No dead Anna Blake. From the angle of the sunlight creeping in around the window shades, she guessed it was afternoon. Except for the aftereffects of her nightmare, she did feel much better. So much better, in fact, that she was positive the murder of Anna Blake had not yet been solved, no matter what Malloy thought.

The only problem was that she had to convince Malloy of it, too, because if she didn't, an innocent woman was going to be electrocuted and a killer would go free.

The City Jail had earned its nickname of "The Tombs" by being the purest example of Neo-Egyptian architecture in the country. Its massive granite structure took up an entire block on Leonard Street between Franklin and Centre, and it housed both male and female adult prisoners, as well as boys who had run afoul of the law. Sarah had certainly never expected to find herself in such a place, but then, since meeting Frank Malloy, she'd done many unusual things.

Inside, the building was immaculate, far different from the interrogation rooms she'd seen at Police Headquarters. In spite of its spotless appearance, however, the place was redolent of the stench of the sewer, having been built on the marshy ground of the old Collection Pond. Its dampness permeated the entire building.

Sarah had to endure a cursory search of her purse and her person before being admitted to the women's section of the jail. Once in the cell block, she was surprised to find the prisoners sitting not in their cells but out in the open hallway that ran between them. The women were engaged in various pursuits, some sewing or knitting or doing other handwork, others just gossiping, and one was even reading what appeared to be a Bible. Except for the surroundings, they might have been women gathered in a public place in any city or town. They all looked up with interest when Sarah came in, perhaps hoping she was a friend or relation who had come to visit them.

Even when they'd satisfied their curiosity and realized she was a stranger to them, they still continued to stare. Probably any visitor at all was a novelty.

"Who're you here to see, miss?" the matron asked her. She was a large, coarse-looking woman, but her eyes were kind. Or at least courteous.

"I'm here to see Mrs. Giddings," Sarah said, hoping she wouldn't have to confess she'd never even set eyes on the woman before, which was why she needed assistance.

"Oh, she's still in her cell, miss. Won't come out with the others. Just lays on her bunk. She hasn't eat nothing, either. Most of 'em are like that at first, not eating and hiding in their cells, but she's worse than usual. It'll be good for her to see a familiar face. Maybe you can cheer her up some."

Sarah certainly wasn't a familiar face, and she didn't know if she could cheer the woman up or not, but she was certainly willing to try. "Which cell is hers?"

The cells were little more than small caves carved out of the granite walls. Only five by nine feet, the room was illuminated by what little sunlight stole in through a small slit cut high in the wall. The barred door was forbidding, but it hung open, as did the doors to all the cells. Unsure of the etiquette of jail visits and seeing no place to knock, Sarah stepped just inside the doorway and said, "Mrs. Giddings?"

The figure huddled on the narrow bed stirred a bit, and a pale face appeared from beneath the folds of the blanket. "Who are you?" she asked dully. Fortunately, the matron had stepped away and didn't hear this question.

"I'm Sarah Brandt. You don't know me. I'm a friend of Nelson Ellsworth's."

"Who's Nelson Ellsworth?" she asked without much interest.

"He's the man who was originally suspected of killing Anna Blake. She was blackmailing him, too."

"Oh. That banker. In the newspapers."

"Yes, that's right. I've been trying to help find the real killer so he could clear his name."

Sarah couldn't make out Mrs. Giddings's expression in the dim light, but she didn't seem very impressed. "Did you come here just to look at me then?" she asked bitterly.

"No," Sarah said. "I came here to find out if you really killed Anna Blake."

This finally got her full attention. She pushed herself up on one elbow. Her hair was disheveled and falling out of its pins, and her eyes were bloodshot and sunken. "Who sent you here?"

"No one sent me," Sarah said. "I came to see you because I want to make sure you're really guilty."

Her eyes narrowed in suspicion. "Why would I say so if I didn't do it?" she asked.

Sarah didn't want to answer that question herself. Instead, she said, "Did you know that Mr. Malloy did not believe your son killed her?"

"What?" She pushed herself up to a sitting position and brushed the strands of hair out of her eyes. "What are you talking about?"

"I'm also a friend of Mr. Malloy, the police detective who arrested you. He told me he realized after questioning the boy that he hadn't killed her. And then you confessed."

Mrs. Giddings rubbed her eyes as if trying to clear her vision. "He was going to arrest Harold. I could see that."

"No, he wasn't. He knew the boy was innocent."

"Since when does that stop the police from arresting someone?" she asked angrily. "I know what they do to people. They beat them until they confess, guilty or not."

"Mr. Malloy doesn't arrest innocent people," Sarah said. "And he wasn't going to arrest your son, even if you hadn't confessed."

"But he was asking him all those questions!" she argued.

"To find out if he could have done it. Mr. Malloy also suspected that you confessed to protect your son."

"Of course I did! I couldn't let him put Harold in a place like this, could I? He's just a boy!"

Plainly, Mrs. Giddings was on the verge of a nervous collapse, and Sarah didn't want to push her too far, but she had to learn the truth. "I know you confessed, but did you really kill Anna Blake?"

"What kind of a question is that? Are you trying to trick me?"

"Not at all," Sarah assured her. "I just want to make sure we have the right person in jail. Because if you didn't kill her, the real killer is still walking free."

"Where's Harold?" she asked, suspicious again.

"I don't know."

"Is he in jail, too?"

"Of course not. I told you, Mr. Malloy doesn't arrest innocent people." She wasn't going to find out what she needed to know this way. She decided to try a different tactic. "Mrs. Giddings, how long did you wait outside of Anna Blake's house before she came out that night?"

Mrs. Giddings stared at her for a long moment, either formulating her answer or trying to decide whether to reply or not. At last she said, "Not very long. I was just waiting for Harold to get well away. I didn't want him to see me and know I'd followed him there. Then I saw her come out."

"How did you know it was she?"

"What do you mean?"

"I mean, had you met Miss Blake before?"

"Certainly not!"

"Then how did you know the woman who came out of the house was Anna Blake?" Sarah pressed.

"I . . . Who else could it have been?" she countered defensively.

Sarah decided not to answer that question. "Why had you carried a knife with you?"

"I . . . I thought I might need it."

"Then you'd *planned* to stab Anna Blake?"

"Yes, yes, that's it," she said almost eagerly. "I was planning to kill her, so I took the knife with me."

"What kind of a knife was it?"

"What do you mean?"

"I mean what kind of a knife was it? Where did you get it? How big was it? Where did you carry it? When did you pull it out? Did you stop Anna Blake and try to talk to her first? Did you tell her who you were? Did you ask her to leave your husband alone? Did you beg her to give back the money she'd taken from him?"

"Stop it! Stop!" she cried, covering her ears.

"What's the matter, Mrs. Giddings? Don't you know the answers to those questions? The real killer would!"

"I do! I do! I just can't think!"

"Then take some time to think. Where were you when you stabbed Anna Blake?"

She looked up, suddenly confident. "Under the hanging tree in Washington Square, just where they found her."

"Why didn't anyone notice you stabbing another woman to death in broad daylight?"

"I . . . No one was around. We were alone there, under the tree. She laughed and said she'd never give my husband up. I couldn't help myself. I stabbed her."

"And she fell down dead?" Sarah asked.

"Yes, that's right. Right where they found her."

"What did you do with the knife?"

"I don't know, I . . . I dropped it, I think. Yes, that's right. I dropped it somewhere. I don't remember where."

Sarah was aware that some of the women had begun to gather outside Mrs. Giddings's cell to listen to this curious exchange. She only hoped the matron wouldn't come over and order her out for upsetting a prisoner or something. She took a step closer to where the woman sat on the bunk.

"Mrs. Giddings," she said, keeping her voice calm and sure, "I don't believe you killed Anna Blake."

"Yes, I did! I swear it! I told that policeman. He believed me!"

"No, he didn't, not really," she lied. "And now I know you didn't. Anna didn't die the way you described, but you

didn't know that because you weren't there. All you knew
was what you read in the newspapers, but they didn't know
what really happened either. Only the real killer knows."

"I know! I do! Just give me a chance to remember!" she
tried, desperate to make Sarah believe her.

"Mrs. Giddings, you don't have to protect your son. We
know he didn't kill Anna Blake. And your husband was in
jail that night, so he couldn't have killed her either. There's
no reason for you to pretend you did it anymore, and if you
insist on doing so, you'll only be protecting the real murderer."

"I wanted her to die," the woman said hysterically. "I
wanted her to suffer the way I suffered!"

A murmur of approval went through the crowd of
women gathered outside the cell, but Sarah didn't ac-
knowledge them. "Of course you did. But your son needs
you, Mrs. Giddings. You won't help him by letting yourself be executed for a murder you didn't commit."

"I couldn't let them take him to jail!" she said, her voice
breaking. "It doesn't matter what happens to me."

"Yes, it does!" Sarah said, going to her. She sat down on
the edge of the bunk and took the sobbing woman in her
arms. "Harold needs you. That's why you must tell the
truth and save yourself."

The matron had finally taken notice of the gathering
crowd and come to see what the disturbance was. Afraid
the woman would order her out, Sarah looked her straight
in the eye with all the authority her parents had trained her
to use on unruly servants and said, "Mrs. Giddings is going
to be just fine now. Do you think she could have a cup of
tea and something light to eat?"

It worked. The matron broke up the gawking crowd and
sent someone for the tea. Sarah kept comforting Mrs. Giddings until the woman was finally able to talk again. Then
she poured out her story of anger and humiliation at having her life ruined by a cheap, lying strumpet. Then, just
when she'd thought nothing could be worse, Malloy had
come to her house and accused her son of killing that

woman! She'd only done what any mother would have to protect her child.

"You were right. I didn't kill her," she said when she'd unburdened herself. "Does this mean I can go home now?"

"I'm afraid not," Sarah said. "At least not right away. You did confess to a murder, and even a guilty person could be expected to have second thoughts and insist she was innocent after spending a day in The Tombs."

"What you mean is that no one will believe me now if I tell the truth," she said miserably. "What have I done?"

"I'm sure they'll believe you when we find the real killer," Sarah said. "I just had to be sure you really hadn't done it before I went any further."

"How can you find the real killer, though?"

That was a very good question, and Sarah was saved from having to answer it when a young woman came to the door of the cell carrying a tray.

"I have tea, for the lady," the girl said in a musical accent. She was small and very neatly dressed, and her large hazel eyes were full of pity.

"I couldn't," Mrs. Giddings protested, but Sarah said, "Thank you," and went to take the tray. They had put some crackers and a bowl of soup on the tray, too.

"The lady is very sad," the girl said. "But she will get used to it here. We will take care of her. She does not have to be afraid."

"That's very kind of you," Sarah said, and suddenly she realized to whom she was speaking. "Are you Maria Barberi?"

"My name is Barbella," the girl corrected, and Sarah remembered Malloy telling her the newspapers had gotten it wrong. This was the woman who had cut her lover's throat out of despair when he refused to marry her. She had been tried for murder and sentenced to death, but she'd recently been granted a new trial.

"I thought your trial was supposed to start last week," Sarah remembered, realizing she hadn't seen any mention of it in the newspapers.

"It was, but now they say next month. So I wait." She

looked at Mrs. Giddings. "Do not cry. You will get used to it."

As Sarah watched Maria go, she was conscious of the irony. Maria Barbella's first trial had sold millions of newspapers for months. If her new trial, which had been scheduled to begin two days before Anna Blake was killed, had begun then, it's possible that Anna's death wouldn't have gotten any notice at all. Instead, it had served to replace this postponed scandal and sell newspapers in the meantime.

"I suppose you can get used to anything," Mrs. Giddings murmured.

"Let's hope you don't have to," Sarah said briskly, setting the tray down on the bunk. "Now you must eat something to keep up your strength. You need to stay strong for your son."

By the time she left The Tombs, Sarah's own stomach was growling. She'd been in such a hurry to get to the jail and see Mrs. Giddings, she had neglected to eat herself. She bought a sausage sandwich from a street vendor and wolfed it down in a very unladylike manner. Then she headed back uptown to keep the promise she'd made to Mrs. Giddings to make sure Harold Giddings was all right.

Keeping that promise gave her an excuse to ask the boy some questions of her own. She wanted to clarify in her mind exactly what had happened the night Anna Blake died and who had been at the boarding house with her. Then, she was sure, she would know who the killer was.

16

Sarah found the Giddings house easily enough from the directions Mrs. Giddings had given her. When she saw the neighborhood and how the family had once lived, she realized just how much damage Anna Blake had done to them. Mrs. Giddings had told her they'd sold nearly everything they owned to repay her husband's law partners. Her husband's career was ruined, he could no longer work in his profession, and her son had found what work he could just to keep food on the table. In the same situation, Sarah thought she might well have considered murdering Anna Blake herself.

No one answered her knock at the Giddings house for so long that Sarah was afraid she wasn't going to have her opportunity to question Harold Giddings. But the door opened at last, and the boy himself stood there. She knew it must be he from his bloodshot eyes and his tormented expression.

"Who are you?" he asked, unknowingly echoing his mother's suspicion.

"I'm Sarah Brandt," she said, smiling reassuringly. "Your mother asked me to check on you and make sure you were all right."

"My mother?" he cried almost desperately. "How is she? She told me not to visit her, but I can't stand not knowing what's happening to her!"

Sarah had been worried he wouldn't believe her, but he must be even more trusting than she'd hoped. "If you'll invite me in, I'll be glad to tell you everything I know," Sarah said gently.

Instantly flustered, the boy stepped back to admit her. "I'm sorry I was rude," he said. "I didn't know who you were."

"That's all right." Sarah said, stepping into the foyer. She looked around. Every room she could see stood empty of furniture. "Is there someplace we could sit down?" she asked.

"Oh, yes," the boy said, eager to please now. "We've still got . . . I mean, the back parlor. Just . . . follow me."

He led her down the hallway and into a room that still held some of its original furnishings. Sarah could imagine the family gathered here in the evening during happier times, before Gilbert Giddings had betrayed them and destroyed their lives.

"Is your father here?" she asked.

"No," the boy said, his anger at his father painfully obvious. "He hasn't been here in a couple days. I hope he never comes back. I hope he's dead in some gutter."

Sarah didn't chasten the boy. He had a right to his feelings, and she could certainly sympathize with them. "Your mother is concerned that you're remembering to eat and get enough sleep," she began.

"I'm not very hungry," he said. "All I can think about is . . ."

"I know, but your mother is doing fine. The jail isn't so very bad, and the women aren't locked up all day. They can socialize and sew if they wish."

"I don't want her to socialize with criminals," the boy objected.

Sarah didn't point out that his mother was herself a confessed murderer. "And I would like to see her released, since she really didn't kill Anna Blake."

"She didn't?" the boy asked incredulously. "She swore she did it! I couldn't believe it, but she kept saying it, over and over. That policeman believed her, too. I begged him not to take her away, but she told me not to argue with him, that he didn't have any choice."

"She lied because she thought the detective was going to arrest you for the crime," Sarah explained.

"Me? Why would he arrest me?" he asked in genuine bewilderment.

Now Sarah could understand how Malloy had known he was innocent. "Some policemen don't particularly care if they arrest the right person, so long as they arrest someone."

The boy frowned. "How could they do that? They'd never be able to prove an innocent person did it."

"They have methods of persuasion," Sarah said. "They usually manage to obtain confessions, even from innocent people."

Harold paled. "Is that what they did to my mother?"

"Oh, no. She'd already confessed willingly," Sarah reminded him. "She's being well treated, and you don't have to be afraid for her. But I'm sure you don't want your mother in jail, especially if she didn't kill anyone, and neither do I. I'd much rather have the real killer locked up."

"Who is the real killer?" he asked anxiously.

"I don't know yet, but I was hoping you'd be able to help me find him."

"How could I do that?"

"By telling me everything that happened the night you went to see Anna Blake."

"I already told that policeman everything, and he arrested my mother," he reminded her.

"I know, but I'm hoping there was some detail that you'd forgotten or didn't think to mention to him."

The boy frowned. "How can that help?"

"I won't know until I hear what happened. Now tell me everything. Start at the beginning."

His young face screwed up with concentration. "My father didn't come home that night. My mother pretended it didn't matter, but she hated the thought that he was with that woman. I'd followed him once, to see where he went. We knew about her after . . . Well, after he had to pay back the money he stole from his law firm. He had to tell my mother everything then. I just wanted to see her. I wanted to know why he did this to us."

"Of course you did," Sarah said to encourage him. "So you knew where she lived."

"I thought he might be with her that night, so when I got to the house, I made them let me inside. I don't know what I would've done if he was there, but he wasn't. I didn't ask about him, of course. I just told them I wanted to see *her*. The man didn't want to let me in, but—"

"Man?" Sarah echoed in surprise. "What man?"

Her vehemence startled him. "There was a man there. He was pretty mad, but that woman, Miss Blake, she told him not to worry, she could handle me."

"Do you know who he was?"

The boy shook his head.

"What did he look like?"

He tried to remember. "A little shorter than me. Dark hair. A beard."

"Was the beard long or short?"

"Short."

"Was he fat or thin?"

"Thin. I think he didn't want to fight me, even though he pretended he was going to if I didn't leave. He wasn't very big."

"How was he dressed?"

The boy shrugged. "I don't know."

Sarah fought her urge to snap at him impatiently. "Was he wearing a suit? Did he look like he was visiting or did he live there?"

"Oh, he lived there."

"How do you know?"

"The way he acted. How he treated me, too, I guess. Oh, now I remember. He was in his shirtsleeves. No collar either. He looked like he'd been sitting around reading the paper or something. I think he had slippers on, too."

This was very interesting. The man must have been Mr. Walcott, but Mrs. Walcott had claimed he wasn't home that night. Why had she lied? And now Sarah remembered that Catherine Porter had slipped and mentioned that Mr. Walcott had ordered the boy out. She'd corrected herself when Sarah had called her on it, but now Sarah realized it hadn't been a mistake. Could they both have been trying to give Walcott an alibi?

"Who else did you see when you were there?"

"Just those two. And the maid, of course."

"Are you sure? No other women?"

He thought for a moment. "I think . . . maybe there was another woman upstairs. I think she was watching."

"What did she look like?"

"I didn't really see her face. I just sort of noticed that someone was there."

A woman watching from upstairs would have been Catherine Porter, Sarah guessed. "And did you see anyone else?"

"No, that's all. I'm sure."

Sarah couldn't imagine a scene like that happening in the house without Mrs. Walcott coming to investigate. Of course, she might have been out. On the other hand, she'd told Malloy she was there, and that *she'd* been the one who had ordered the boy out.

"Did I tell you anything that helped?" he asked.

"Maybe," was all Sarah could say.

"What are you going to do now?"

"I'm going to ask Anna Blake's landlady a few more questions," she said.

"Can I go with you?" he asked eagerly.

"I know you want to help, but I don't think the Walcotts would be very happy to see you again."

"Who are the Walcotts?"

"They own the house where Anna Blake lived."

"Oh."

"I'm just going to ask a few questions," she explained. "Then I'll take this new information to Mr. Malloy. And then, I hope, he will arrest the real killer, and your mother will be free."

"What questions are you going to ask?"

Sarah wasn't sure herself. "I'll figure that out when I get there."

To Sarah's relief, the El wasn't very crowded. The hour was later than she'd realized, and most of the workers had already made their way home. Sarah sat, staring blindly out the window at the buildings whizzing by, and tried to piece together everything she'd learned about that night. Anna had been home with Catherine and Mr. Walcott and maybe Mrs. Walcott, too. Mr. Walcott was sitting around in his shirtsleeves. Harold had come barging in. Mr. Walcott hadn't wanted him there, but Anna Blake had enjoyed tormenting the boy. Harold had threatened her, and then he'd left. Anna had played checkers with Catherine until Catherine went to bed, well after dark. According to Catherine, Mrs. Walcott was probably angry with Anna, but she hadn't said anything to Anna in Catherine's presence. This meant she was either there when Harold came or returned home later.

After Catherine went to bed, something had happened, and Anna had gone out. Either she got a message from someone or she'd had a quarrel with Mrs. Walcott or maybe Mr. Walcott or both of them, and she'd left the house. Then she'd been stabbed at some unknown location. She'd been trying to get back home, but she'd fallen in Washington Square and died there before she could.

Sarah remembered what the coroner had said about Anna having been with a man shortly before she died. Could that man have been Mr. Walcott? Was that what she and Mrs. Walcott had quarreled about? Was that why Mrs. Walcott had lied about what time Anna left the house? And why had everyone lied about Mr. Walcott being home that night? The answer was obvious, and Sarah had a pretty good idea she now knew who the killer was. She should probably go straight to Malloy with the news, but she was afraid he wouldn't act on it unless she had more than just a suspicion. She only needed one more piece of information, and she could get it from either of the Walcotts. *If* she could get them to cooperate without arousing their suspicions.

Night was falling as Sarah reached the house on Thompson Street. She'd miscalculated the time, forgetting how short the days were getting as October advanced. A light was burning in one of the front rooms at the Walcott house, however, so Sarah knew someone was home.

No one answered her knock at first, but she wasn't going to give up, not when she was so close, so she kept on knocking. Finally, the door opened a crack, and half of a face peered out cautiously.

"Is Mrs. Walcott home?" Sarah asked when the person didn't speak.

The door opened a bit wider, revealing that the person behind it *was* Mrs. Walcott. She was a far different Mrs. Walcott than Sarah had seen before, however. Instead of her extravagant wig, she wore a dust cap on her head, as women did to protect their hair from dirt when housecleaning. Or when women who wore wigs wanted to relax from the weight of them and still not reveal the condition of their real hair. The cap fit closely, which meant there wasn't much hair underneath. Probably, Mrs. Walcott was going bald for some reason, so she did not even go bareheaded in the privacy of her own home. And instead of one of her stylish gowns, she wore a simple housedress that was faded from many washings. Her face looked faded, too, as if strain had leached the color from it. The only thing that hadn't changed about her appearance was her expression. She still looked cool and calm and more than a little condescending.

"What are you doing here at this time of night, Mrs. Brandt?" she asked. Her voice hadn't changed, either. She was still cultured and precise.

"I happened to be in this part of the city, and I thought I would stop by and see how you're faring. I also wanted to let you know how the investigation is going," Sarah lied. "We have some new information."

Mrs. Walcott looked past Sarah, as if expecting to see Frank Malloy. "Are you alone?" she asked in some surprise.

"Yes. As I said, I was in the neighborhood, delivering a baby," she added, embellishing her lie to sound more plausible. "I thought it was still early enough to stop by on my way home. May I come in?"

"Certainly," she said, stepping aside to allow her to enter. The house was as chilly as the street outside, and Sarah remembered Catherine Porter mentioning that Mrs. Walcott didn't like to build a fire.

"Is Miss Porter in?" Sarah asked, pulling off her gloves.

Mrs. Walcott stiffened at the question and proceeded to close the door very carefully, not looking at Sarah. "No. No, she isn't."

Her reaction had been so odd that Sarah felt a frisson of alarm. "Is she all right?" she asked.

Mrs. Walcott managed a strained smile. "I'm sure I have no idea. Please, come in." She led Sarah into the front parlor, the room where a lamp burned.

Mystified, Sarah followed her into the parlor and took the seat Mrs. Walcott indicated. The landlady sat down across from her, in front of the cold fireplace, and folded her hands demurely in her lap. She wasn't wearing the mitts she usually wore, and she folded her hands tightly, as if she were ashamed of them or something. Perhaps she was. Perhaps that was why she wore the mitts in the first place.

"You said you had some news," Mrs. Walcott said. "About Anna's death."

"Yes, I . . . Mrs. Walcott, I don't know how to say this without sounding rude, but I'm afraid I have to ask you again if your husband was at home that night."

Mrs. Walcott stared at Sarah for a long moment, as if trying to read her thoughts. "I am assuming that you believe he was, in spite of what I told you."

"Yes," Sarah said. "In fact, I now have very good reason to believe he was."

Mrs. Walcott sighed and dropped her gaze. "I don't suppose I need to lie anymore. Yes, he was here that night."

"Why did you lie about it before?" Sarah asked.

Mrs. Walcott's expression hardened, and her eyes were full of hatred when she looked up again. "I love my husband, Mrs. Brandt. I wanted to protect him. Anna Blake's death was no great loss to anyone, and he didn't really mean to kill her—"

"Your *husband* killed Anna?" Sarah cried, trying not to sound exultant at having proved her theory so easily.

Mrs. Walcott nodded, her entire body rigid with emotion. "I couldn't bear the thought of losing him," she said, pulling a handkerchief from her sleeve and dabbing at her eyes. "I knew he wasn't always faithful to me, but . . . He could be so loving. I would have done anything to protect him."

Sarah couldn't help feeling compassion for this woman, even though she would never understand the kind of devotion that led a woman to lie for a man like that. "Has something happened to change your mind?" she asked gently.

"Oh, yes," she said bitterly, her eyes bright with unshed tears. "You asked me if Catherine Porter was here. The answer is no, she's gone. She and my husband left together."

Sarah gaped at her. "You mean they ran away together?"

"So it appears. My husband had decided he could no longer stay in the city, you see. He was afraid that sooner or later your Mr. Malloy would figure out that he had killed poor Anna. He led me to believe he and I would go together, so I helped him with the arrangements. It was wrong, I know, but I couldn't help myself. I would have followed him anywhere, you understand, but when I woke up this morning, he and Catherine were both gone. He left me a note . . . He was very unkind." Her voice broke, and Sarah's heart ached for her.

How many women had she met in the city who had been victimized in just this way by men too selfish to consider anything except their own desires? Sarah might despise the weakness that made women prey to such deception, but even more, she hated the cruelty that took advantage of it.

"We'll find him, Mrs. Walcott," Sarah promised. "I'll get word to Mr. Malloy, and he'll start the search."

"They could be anywhere by now," Mrs. Walcott pointed out. "I'm afraid you'll never be able to locate them."

She was right, of course. With a day's head start and no idea even in which direction they had gone, there was little chance they'd ever be found. They could have even stayed right here in the city and disappeared into the teeming tenements without a trace.

"Won't someone be worried about you, Mrs. Brandt?" Mrs. Walcott asked as she dabbed at her eyes again. "It's quite dark outside now. I feel guilty keeping you here, listening to my troubles."

"I'm used to being out at all hours," Sarah reassured her. "And there's no one to wait up for me. I'm a widow."

"I'm so sorry to hear that. You're such a young woman."

Sarah waved away her sympathy. "You're very upset. Can I get you something?"

Mrs. Walcott dabbed at her eyes again. "I'd love some tea, but let me get it. It will give me something to do. I'm so tired of sitting around feeling sorry for myself. Please, just wait right here. I won't be a minute."

When the landlady had gone, Sarah realized that the mention of tea had started her stomach growling. Except for the sausage sandwich she'd gobbled earlier today, she hadn't eaten since . . . since Malloy had fixed breakfast for her. The memory sent a wave of heat washing over her, and she was very glad to be alone, because she had the terrible feeling she might actually be blushing.

To distract herself from such unsettling thoughts, she got up and began to walk around the room, carefully examining every detail. For the first time, she realized that the room contained not one personal item. People usually had framed photographs of loved ones or a sampler or other mementos. Sarah remembered that the Walcotts had bought the house from an old man, and most of the furniture had been his. But surely they would have brought some of their own things with them. If they had, however, none of them were displayed here.

Mrs. Walcott reappeared a few minutes later, carrying a tea tray. Sarah had been hoping she would include something edible, but the tray bore no cookies or other delicacies. She set the tray down on a side table, and proceeded to pour two cups.

"Do you take milk?" she asked Sarah.

"No, thank you."

"I hope you don't mind. I sweetened the tea in the pot. I always do when I'm making it for myself, and I just forgot this time."

"That's fine," Sarah said. "I like it sweet."

Mrs. Walcott stirred Sarah's cup, then handed it to her before filling her own.

Sarah took a sip. The tea was extremely sweet, making her empty stomach clench with happiness. She wanted to gulp the whole cup at once, but good manners prevailed. Waiting until Mrs. Walcott was seated again, she asked, "Would you mind telling me what really happened the night Anna died?"

Mrs. Walcott took a fortifying sip of her tea. "I wouldn't mind at all, since I no longer have any reason not to. I was very upset with Anna that night."

"Because the Giddings boy came to the house?" Sarah guessed.

"No, that was merely an annoyance. I was upset because I'd found Anna and my husband together that night," she said bitterly. "I was furious, of course, and jealous and humiliated. I ordered Anna to leave. I know you're thinking I should have been angry at Oliver, and I was, but I'm afraid I wanted to blame Anna for everything. She ran out into the night, and Oliver went after her. He wouldn't tell me what happened between them, but when he returned, he had blood on his clothes, and he said Anna wouldn't be coming back. He begged me to forgive him, and he promised he would never be unfaithful to me again."

"And you believed him?" Sarah asked incredulously.

Mrs. Walcott's pride was all that held her together. "I wanted to believe him, Mrs. Brandt. I know that makes me a fool, but he swore he'd never cared for her, not the way he cared for me. Of course, I didn't know Anna was dead until the next morning, when the police came. I thought . . . Well, I don't know what I thought. Oliver had left by then and asked me to say he hadn't been home at all that evening. He didn't come back for several days. I was afraid he'd never come back at all."

Sarah took another sip of the tea, and this time the sweetness was cloying, making her feel slightly nauseated. That would teach her not to eat. "I suppose all of this happened later in the evening," Sarah guessed. "After Miss Porter went to bed."

"Yes, I'd retired myself, but something awakened me. When I saw Oliver wasn't in bed, I went looking for him, and . . . that's when I found him with Anna," the other woman explained, her eyes clouded with the painful memories. "I was grateful Catherine slept through the whole thing. There was certainly no reason to air our dirty linen in front of her. Now, of course . . ." Her voice trailed off.

"Now you probably wish you had," Sarah guessed.

"Perhaps if she'd known Oliver's true character, she wouldn't have run away with him," Mrs. Walcott said sadly. "Of course, I realize he was probably dallying with her all along, too."

"Did your husband admit to killing Anna?" Sarah asked, hating to cause the woman more pain, but knowing it was necessary. "Did he tell you how it happened?"

"Is your tea too hot?" she asked suddenly, her tone oddly insistent. "Or did I make it too sweet?"

Too sweet. A memory stirred, the faintest of warnings. Sarah looked down at the cup, trying to remember, but a sudden disturbance distracted her. Someone was yelling outside, and several dogs began barking furiously. "What on earth?" she asked, quickly setting her cup and saucer down. She almost missed the table, and the cup teetered dangerously before Mrs. Walcott caught it.

"It's nothing to be alarmed about, just those stray dogs," Mrs. Walcott said reassuringly. "We can't seem to get rid of them."

But someone was calling Sarah's name, the person who was shouting over the barking dogs. She was sure of it. She stood up, but she must have risen too quickly, because she felt dizzy. *Something is wrong with the tea!* her mind cried, but she couldn't seem to focus on what it might be.

"Mrs. Brandt! Get out of there! Come quick!" the voice was calling, and Sarah responded instinctively, moving toward the door.

Mrs. Walcott grabbed her arm to stop her, but she shook her off. "Someone needs help," she said, her words sounding oddly slow to her own ears.

"Mrs. Brandt! Get out of there!" the voice was screaming, desperate now. It was vaguely familiar, the panic unmistakable.

Mrs. Walcott grabbed her again, her hands amazingly strong, like a man's. Sarah shoved her away, panic making her stronger, too. The woman hit a table, lost her balance, and fell, but Sarah couldn't stop to help her. She had to get to the voice.

She was running now, through the house, toward the kitchen, even though her feet felt as if they weren't even touching the ground. The dogs, she knew, were in the backyard. They wanted to get in the cellar. Wasn't that what had happened in her dream? She was so confused. She only knew she had to get to the backyard.

The gaslights were on in the kitchen. She saw the back door and made for it. Mrs. Walcott was behind her, shoes scuffling on the bare floor as she ran to catch up. Sarah threw open the door and launched herself out onto the porch. She caught one of the posts to keep from falling headlong down the steps.

Vaguely aware that Mrs. Walcott had followed her onto the porch, Sarah concentrated on trying to make sense of what she saw in the backyard. Harold Giddings was waving a stick, trying to chase away a pack of stray dogs who were, in turn, trying to get past him into the open cellar doors. He was alternately screaming at the dogs and screaming for Sarah.

An elderly woman, in her nightclothes and carrying a lamp, stood peering at the curious scene from the next porch. Other lights were coming on, and people were starting to shout complaints about the disturbance.

"Harold!" Sarah shouted over the din, and the boy looked up.

"Mrs. Brandt! There's somebody dead down there!" he cried, pointing toward the open cellar doors.

She leaned forward so she could see into the opening. Someone had lit a lamp in the cellar, and there she saw a large brown dog, the one she herself had tried to shoo away the other day. He was digging furiously, and down in the hole he had dug was what appeared to be a mass of red hair.

Red hair. Irish girl. Francine. Moved to the country.

Sarah wanted to scream, but the sound lodged somewhere in her chest. Behind her, someone gasped, and she turned to see Mrs. Walcott. Except her cap had come off in the struggle, and now Sarah could see what it was about her hair she'd been trying to hide. It was cut like a man's. Now she was Mr. Walcott without the beard!

And whoever she was, she was running away. No, *Mr.* Walcott was running away, and he was the killer!

Something in Sarah seemed to explode, flooding her with fury. Somehow she forced her sluggish body to move, and then she was running down the hallway after Walcott. "Help me, Harold!" she screamed, praying he heard her. Remembering the hands that had tried to hold her from answering Harold's call, she wasn't sure she'd be able to restrain Walcott by herself, but she'd do it as long as she could.

The woman's skirts impeded Walcott's progress enough that Sarah caught him as he was opening the front door. Not knowing what else to do, she threw both arms around his waist and fell to her knees. She wasn't sure if she'd intended to do that or if her knees had simply given out, but her dead weight had stopped him, so she hung on for dear life, still screaming for Harold to help her.

Walcott struggled fiercely, and something struck her in the temple, sending stars streaking across her vision, but she didn't let go. She wouldn't let go, not until someone came to help. She wasn't going to let Walcott get away with murder. Then Walcott was falling, and someone else was there. Arms and legs, thrashing around, and a stick rising and crashing down. Then everything was still.

17

SARAH PRETENDED SHE DIDN'T HEAR MALLOY SWEARING when he was out in the backyard, looking in the cellar. She held the cool cloth to her bruised forehead and closed her eyes, wondering if the dizziness was from the blow she had taken or from the opium in the tea.

"Are you all right, Mrs. Brandt?" Harold Giddings asked solicitously.

"Yes, thanks to you," Sarah said, opening her eyes to smile up at him. She was sitting at the table in the Walcotts' kitchen. "Have I told you how glad I am you followed me here?"

"At least three times," Harold said, taking a seat opposite her. He rubbed his eyes as if trying to erase a vision. "I don't guess I'll ever get that picture out of my mind. The dog digging down in the cellar and all that hair. That poor woman didn't hardly have any skin left on her face."

"The memory will fade in time," Sarah said, recalling some of the terrible things she'd managed to push to the back of her memory. "Why did you go in the backyard anyway?"

"After I followed you here, I thought somebody might see me if I was on the street, so I went around back. The cellar doors were open and there was a bunch of dogs in there, digging at something. I could smell something dead, so I figured it was an animal. I scared most of them off, but that one wouldn't pay me any mind at all. I couldn't see much, but then the kitchen lights came on. Then I could make out a lantern sitting on the cellar steps. I had to wait until the person left the kitchen. Then I lit the lamp and saw what they'd been digging up . . . Well, that's when I started yelling for you to get out of there."

"Thank heaven you did. She was trying to poison me. I guess I would've ended up down in the cellar, too." Sarah shuddered at the horrible thought. Another terrible thing she would have to make herself forget.

"That's exactly where you would've ended up," Malloy said, coming in from outside. He was angry, and she couldn't blame him. She'd almost gotten herself killed. "It would've been crowded though. Walcott's already got two people down there, and we found Catherine Porter's body in her bedroom. She was wrapped up, ready to go down as soon as it got dark. Walcott already had the hole dug."

Sarah felt the gorge rising in her throat, but she swallowed it down, determined not to be sick in front of Malloy. She was already humiliated enough. "Poor Catherine."

Malloy made a rude noise. "Poor *Catherine*? She was probably blackmailing some unfortunate man just like Anna Blake was."

He was right, of course, but she certainly hadn't deserved to die for it. And nobody deserved to be buried in a cellar. "Wait, did you say *two* bodies were already buried in the cellar?" she asked.

"Yeah. The one Harold found was the red-haired girl who used to live here."

"That must be Francine. Walcott told the other girls that Francine had found a rich husband and moved to the country," Sarah remembered. "Were there other girls before her?"

"One that I know of. The lady next door told me her name was Cummings or something."

"Is she the other body?"

"No, it's a man. Probably the old man who owned this house. Walcott told people he'd sold out and moved away, but apparently, they'd killed him and put him in the cellar."

Sarah groaned.

"Does your head hurt?" Harold asked. "He hit you before I could get to him."

"Let's hope he knocked some sense into her," Malloy said without the slightest trace of sympathy.

Harold glared at him, but he didn't notice. He was heading down the hall.

"Where are you going?" Sarah demanded.

"To see if Walcott has recovered enough from Harold's strong right arm to answer a few questions."

"I'm going, too!" Sarah said, jumping to her feet. She was instantly sorry. She hadn't drunk very much of the tea, thank heaven, but enough to dull her senses. That, combined with the elbow she'd taken to her temple, was enough to make her wish she'd risen more slowly from her chair.

"Suit yourself," Malloy said, but he didn't wait for her.

"I'll help you," Harold said, taking her arm. "I want to hear what happened, too!"

Walcott was sitting in the parlor, hands tied in front of him and looking foolish wearing the housedress with his masculine haircut. A uniformed policeman stood guard over him. Someone had tied a bandage around his forehead, where Harold had struck him with the stick he'd been using to frighten the dogs away. He looked a little woozy and very angry.

"It's late," Malloy was saying, "and I'm tired, so please don't make me exert myself, Walcott. Just tell me the whole story, and that cut on the head will be the worst thing that happens to you tonight."

Walcott was trying to look bored, but when he saw Harold and Sarah come into the room, his expression hardened. *"You,"* he said. "This is all your fault!"

At first Sarah thought he was addressing her, but then she realized he was glaring at Harold. "Because he came here to the house?" she guessed.

"Anna was a fool!" Walcott said. "She was never satisfied. I told her over and over again not to be too greedy, but she wouldn't listen."

"Is that why you killed her, Walcott?" Malloy asked. "Because she was greedy?"

"No," Walcott said, turning his anger on Malloy. "Because she was stupid."

"How was she stupid?"

"First she wouldn't be satisfied with what Giddings could afford to pay her. She made him steal from his company, which drew attention. If they'd pressed charges against him, we would have had the police here in an instant, asking all kinds of questions. And then she picked Nelson Ellsworth. That was the stupidest thing of all."

"He was a mistake, wasn't he?" Sarah guessed. "Because he wasn't married."

"She was supposed to check!" Walcott shouted. "She just asked some kid on the street who lived in the house. She didn't bother to find out that the Mrs. Ellsworth who lived there was his *mother*!"

"So that's why you were so angry with Anna," she said, earning a black look from Malloy, which she ignored. "Because she'd chosen a man who couldn't be blackmailed and because she'd drawn attention with Mr. Giddings."

"She was causing too much trouble, and she wouldn't stop," Walcott said coldly. "I had to get rid of her before she ruined us all."

"Is that why you killed Francine, too?" Sarah asked. "Because she was causing trouble?"

"No, because she got sentimental." Walcott gave her a condescending glare. "One of her gentlemen friends killed himself, and she started feeling guilty. She even started talking about doing penance for her sins and maybe even going to the police, so I had to silence her."

"The way you silenced the old man who owned this house?" Malloy said.

"It wasn't like that," Walcott said. "The old man wasn't supposed to die. I'd thought of this foolproof way to make money, and I needed a house. Ellie knew about this old man who had one."

"Who's Ellie?" Malloy asked. "Is she buried in the cellar, too?"

Walcott gave him an irritated glance. "Ellie Cunningham, and no, she's not buried in the cellar or anywhere else. I met Ellie when we were in a play together and—"

"You're an actor?" Sarah cried, earning another black look from Malloy.

"Yes, an excellent actor," Walcott said smugly. "I fooled *you*, didn't I? I fooled everyone."

He was right, of course. "I'm sorry I interrupted you," she said. "Please continue."

"Ellie and I started this thing together. She charmed the old man into renting us a room. Told him I was her husband. We gave him a little opium to keep him happy so he wouldn't notice the gentlemen callers Ellie had. We might've given him too much, or maybe his time was just up, but one day he just died. We decided no one would miss him, and why should we leave and let the house go to some stranger? So we buried him in the cellar and told people we'd bought the house from him and he'd moved away."

"What did you do with this Ellie?" Malloy asked.

"Nothing. She got bored and wanted to go back on the stage. She went on tour, and I never saw her again. By then I had Francine, though, so we didn't miss her."

"And after Francine ended up in the cellar, you got Catherine and Anna," Malloy guessed. "What I want to know is why Anna didn't end up in the cellar like the others."

Walcott gave him an impatient look. "She was supposed to, but . . . I gave Francine opium and she died real quick, like the old man," he said, apparently forgetting his fiction that the old man's death had been an accident. "But with Anna . . . she was the one who got the knife. She was going to stab *me*, so I was just defending myself. I was going to put her in the cellar with the others, except she wasn't dead. She was just pretending. While I was outside, opening the door to put her body in before Catherine saw it, she got away. I tried to follow her, but I lost her in the dark."

Sarah looked at Malloy, and she knew they were thinking the same thing. Now it all made sense! The reason Anna had left the house so late at night, alone, was that she was running for her life. They'd assumed she'd been trying to get home after being stabbed, but she'd really been trying to get away. She'd managed to reach the Square before collapsing. No one there would have helped her or even taken particular notice. They would just have assumed she was drunk and let her lie there and die.

"Why did you try to kill Webster Prescott?" Malloy asked.

Walcott managed a sneer. "Who says I did?"

Before anyone could blink, Malloy gave him a backhanded slap, surprising a gasp from Sarah and a cry of outrage from Harold.

Malloy turned to them in disgust. "If you don't have the stomach for this, you better leave now."

Harold looked pale, and Sarah felt very light-headed again. She'd known Malloy's tactics could be rough, but seeing them was much worse than simply knowing about them. Still, he was dealing with a man who had killed four people. She took a deep breath and said, "You can go if you want to," to the boy.

Harold shook his head determinedly.

Sarah looked up at Malloy. "We'll stay."

He narrowed his eyes, but he didn't challenge her decision. "Don't make me ask you again, Walcott," he said.

"Prescott was too smart," Walcott said quickly, obviously anxious to avoid another blow. "He'd found out about Anna, that she was an actress, and then he came here, asking more questions. He frightened Catherine, and I was afraid she might say something to him if he got her alone. I had to take care of him."

"You must be losing your touch," Malloy said. "First Anna gets away, then Prescott. You botched it *twice* with the reporter."

Walcott gave Sarah a black look. "You turn up like a bad penny."

"Don't expect me to apologize," she said.

"Why did you have to kill Catherine Porter?" Malloy asked.

Walcott sighed. "I'll always regret that. I was very fond of Catherine, but she'd figured out what happened to Anna. I had to get away before you figured it out, too, and I couldn't leave her behind to tell what she knew."

"So you decided to pretend that you'd run away with Catherine and left your poor innocent wife behind," Sarah guessed.

Walcott just gave her a derisive stare.

"Are we going to find your wife buried in the cellar, too?" Malloy asked him.

Walcott gave him a pitying look. "Haven't you figured it out yet? There is no Mrs. Walcott. I'm the entire Walcott family." He smiled at his own joke.

"I found the wigs and the fake beard in your bedroom," Malloy said. "What gave you the idea to dress up like a woman in the first place?"

"After the old man died, I needed a wife," Walcott said, obviously proud of his ingenuity. "Ellie couldn't be living with a single man. That wouldn't be respectable. So we invented Mrs. Walcott."

"What do you mean, invented her?"

"I created the character," Walcott bragged. "I became Mrs. Walcott whenever we felt that we needed her."

"You've needed her a lot lately," Sarah observed.

Walcott didn't seem the least bit chagrined. "I found I enjoyed being Mrs. Walcott. And the gentlemen callers were much more comfortable dealing with a female landlady. It was my greatest role, and I believe I handled it admirably. I fooled all of you," he reminded them again.

Plainly, Malloy found the whole idea distasteful. "Didn't Anna and Catherine and the others think it was strange having you dressed up like a woman all the time?"

"They didn't seem to. Actually, I think it excited them. The very afternoon Anna died, she came to me and—"

"That's enough," Malloy said, glancing meaningfully at Sarah and Harold.

They stared back blankly, shocked into silence by the strangeness of the tale.

Someone started knocking on the front door, and one of the policemen opened it. Sarah looked out into the foyer to see an elderly woman come in with a covered plate in her hands. "I'm Miss Stone from next door," she was explaining to the policeman. "I brought some food, in case anyone is hungry."

Sarah's stomach growled. She was on her feet in an instant. "I'm very pleased to meet you, Miss Stone," she said, grateful for a chance to escape this bizarre conversation, and hurried out to accept her gracious gift.

"You did that on purpose," Sarah said.

She and Malloy were finally alone, riding uptown from The Tombs in a Hansom cab. Oliver/Olivia Walcott was locked up at Police Headquarters, and Harold Giddings had gone to be with his mother at the city jail. He'd vowed to stay there until morning, when she would be officially released. Malloy had managed to find a cab. He even knew the driver, which meant they would probably make it safely home.

"What did I do on purpose?" Malloy asked. It was very dark in the cab, and she couldn't see his expression.

"Hit Walcott," she said. The opium was wearing off, or at least she thought it was. She just felt very relaxed, but that could be simple fatigue. She didn't even want to know how late it was. Or rather how early. "You hit him on purpose so I would see you do it."

"How much opium did you swallow?" he asked.

"Not very much. I'm right, aren't I? You wanted me to despise you."

"Mrs. Brandt," he began in that reasonable tone she hated.

"Don't waste your breath, Malloy," she chided. "I know I'm right. What I don't know is why. Why don't you want me to like you, Malloy?"

"I thought opium made people sleepy," he said. "Why don't you fall asleep? I'll wake you up when we get to your house."

"I don't want to go to sleep. I want to know why you don't like me, Malloy. I like you, even if you do hit people."

He sighed. "I never said I didn't like you, Mrs. Brandt."

Reasonable again. She wanted to smack him. "And why don't you ever call me Sarah? You think I'm beautiful, but you never call me Sarah."

He muttered something she didn't understand.

"You *do* think I'm beautiful," she insisted. "You said so!"

"Yes, I do," he said grudgingly. "And I do like you, *Sarah*. Now let's talk about something else, because you're going to be very embarrassed if you remember any of this conversation tomorrow."

"No, I won't," she informed him. She didn't feel the least bit embarrassed! "And I still want to know why you hit that man in front of me. You wanted me to see it, didn't you?"

"Why would I want you to see it?"

Sarah was getting very annoyed with him. He usually wasn't this dense. "Because you wanted me to think badly of you, and I demand to know why!"

"You do, do you?" he said in a very odd tone.

"Yes, I do, and I'm not getting out of this cab until you tell me!"

"I don't want to tell you."

"Then what *do* you want?"

She knew he was looking at her, although she doubted he could see very much in the darkness. "I want to *show* you," he said.

The next thing she knew, his hand was on the back of her head and his mouth was on hers. She felt a thousand sensations at once, the scratch of his beard, the taste of his lips, the scent of him engulfing her. The night exploded into shooting stars, and Sarah wanted to catch each one and hold them to her heart.

But before she could even react, he was pulling away and reaching up to bang on the roof of the cab.

"Pull over here, Henry!" he called out to the driver.

"What are you doing?" Sarah asked in confusion. Her world was still swirling, but the cab lurched to a stop.

Malloy said, "That can be part of your opium dream, Sarah," and jumped out. "Take the lady home and make sure she gets inside safe and sound, Henry," he called up to the driver.

"Malloy!" she called, but he was already disappearing into the darkness. She thought about going after him but couldn't think of a good reason to. Because she wanted him to kiss her again? Of course she did, but a lady didn't chase a man down for that! Besides, she mused with a smile as the cab rattled into motion again, she didn't have to. He would be back. She was perfectly sure of that.

Malloy didn't like a case with loose ends, and this one seemed to have a hundred of them. He'd spent the morning getting Mrs. Giddings released from jail and dealing with her and her son's gratitude. Having escaped that, he had to go uptown to the bank where Nelson Ellsworth had worked to convince Mr. Richard Dennis to hire him back or risk having Frank raise a scandal about the supposed missing funds in his bank.

Frank had a hunch that Dennis had reasons of his own why he didn't want anyone to know about the missing money that had nothing at all to do with avoiding a scandal. His first theory was that Dennis himself had taken the money, maybe even after he found out about Nelson being blackmailed, figuring he could accuse Nelson of it and escape detection. His other theory was, in some ways, even worse. That version had Dennis making up the story about the missing money so he could dismiss Nelson and still keep Mrs. Brandt's good opinion.

Either way, Frank had him. And since Frank enjoyed having wealthy men bend to his will, he was glad to see how quickly the guard at the bank ushered him back to the vice president, who ushered him to Mr. Dennis's office. He was instructed to wait outside the closed door, however, because Mr. Dennis was already meeting with someone. The vice president assured him that Mr. Dennis would be more than happy to assist him the moment he was free.

Frank settled in to wait, but after only a few minutes, the door to Dennis's office opened. Frank started to rise from his chair, but he stopped when he saw who came out with Dennis.

"I know you won't regret this, Richard," Sarah Brandt said. She was looking back at the man over her shoulder as he escorted her out, but Frank didn't have to see her face to know she was smiling.

"How could I ever regret doing you a favor, Sarah?" Dennis said in an unctuous tone that set Frank's teeth on edge. How dare he talk to her in that tone of voice? How dare he call her Sarah?

"I'll see you tomorrow evening then," she said, giving him her hand.

He took it in both of his, and Frank found himself on his feet. Only in the nick of time did he stop himself from striding over there and ripping them apart.

"I'll call for you at eight," Dennis said.

"I'll look forward to it," she said, sounding like she really meant it, and then she turned and saw him standing there. "Malloy," she said in surprise. "What brings you here? I hope the bank hasn't been robbed."

She smiled at her own joke, giving Frank a moment to recover. He'd imagined how she would react the next time they met. He'd been hoping she wouldn't remember that he'd taken advantage of her, or at least most of him had been hoping that. The other part had hoped she would and that she'd . . . Well, he hadn't gotten past that in his imagining, because he wasn't sure how she should feel about it if she did remember. It seemed, however, that she didn't remember a thing, if he could judge by her expression.

"I came to see Mr. Dennis," he said, glancing past her.

Dennis was frowning. He didn't remember who Frank was, the bastard.

"I've already told him that you caught the killer," she

said, saving Dennis from having to admit his memory lapse. And saving Frank from the humiliation of having to reintroduce himself. "He also agrees that since Mr. Ellsworth was innocent, he should have his old job back as if nothing had happened."

"What about the missing money?" Frank asked, addressing the question to Dennis, who didn't like it one bit.

"It seems that was just an accounting error," Dennis said quickly. "As I explained to Sarah . . . Mrs. Brandt, I couldn't believe such a sum could have gone missing, so I had the auditors check again. I never believed Mr. Ellsworth was responsible, in any case."

Frank could have argued with him, but he knew when to be gracious in victory. Nelson had his job back, and no one was going to be prosecuted for embezzlement. Frank would make sure Mrs. Brandt understood exactly what Dennis had tried to do. All was right with the world once again. Or it would be in a second.

"You'll let me know if there's any more trouble here, won't you?" Frank said. "I've taken a personal interest in your establishment now, and I wouldn't want to see you have more bad luck."

He'd hoped Dennis would be smart enough to understand his unspoken message—that if he tried to pin some later crime on Nelson just to get rid of him, Frank would be watching. To his credit, Dennis gave him the phony smile that rich men gave when they knew a less worthy opponent had the advantage over them. "I appreciate your concern, Mr. Malloy, and I'm sure you won't have to trouble yourself anymore."

He didn't offer to shake hands, so Frank stepped back to make room for Sarah to precede him out.

"Good day, Richard," she said, giving him another of her smiles. "Mr. Malloy." Her smile for him was smaller. And sly. Frank was sure it was sly.

He was going to follow her when Dennis said, "Let me give you something for your trouble, Malloy."

Frank would never forgive him for saying that where she could hear. He gave the man a look that drained the blood from his face. "It wasn't any trouble," he replied very distinctly and turned on his heel.

Mrs. Brandt was waiting for him out on the sidewalk, pretending to be ransacking her purse for something. She looked up and smiled at him the way she usually did when he came out the door. "Good morning, Malloy. Did you get Mrs. Giddings out of jail?"

"She and Harold should be home by now," he replied, searching her face for any sign that she remembered what he'd done last night. He saw none. "How are you feeling this morning?"

"You mean after the opium?" she guessed, her eyes glittering knowingly. "Just fine. Except everything that happened last night seems like a dream. A very bad dream. Please tell me I didn't imagine that Mr. Walcott is safely locked up."

"You didn't, and he's the talk of the city. They aren't quite sure whether to lock him in the men's or the women's section of the Tombs. The women at the house might not have thought he was strange for dressing up like a female, but everyone else in the city does."

"Not many men could have carried it off," she said. "I think he was right, it was his greatest role."

The morning light had turned her hair the color of gold, and he didn't remember ever seeing her look so beautiful. The knowledge was like a piece of jagged glass in his chest. "What kind of a deal did you make with Dennis to save Nelson's job?" he asked, unable to keep the anger from his voice.

She smiled the way she did when she knew something he didn't. "I didn't make a deal. I simply told him that my father couldn't understand how the auditors had discovered the missing funds so quickly, and we were sure there must be some mistake. A mistake like that could ruin the bank's reputation, along with his. Then I reminded him of how faithful an employee Nelson had always been, and how tragic it would be if he were to suffer for crimes he hadn't committed. A female can make her point just as effectively as a man, if she knows how, Malloy. Richard understood exactly what I was saying and the consequences he would face if he insisted on dismissing Nelson."

Which would have included never seeing Sarah Brandt again. Frank could understand the man's decision to do her bidding. "And now you're going to see *Richard* tomorrow night." He sounded childish, even to himself.

"He invited me to the opera. I haven't been to the opera in years, so I accepted. Don't look so disapproving, Malloy. I'll start to imagine you're jealous." She smiled and shook her head in mock disgust. "Now tell me, when does Brian get his cast off?"

Frank blinked at the sudden change of subject. "Next Wednesday morning."

"Could I come?" she asked. "I'd like to be there."

She was only being kind, he told himself for the thousandth time and ignored the small spark of happiness she'd caused him. She was asking because she adored his son, and who could blame her? "I know the boy would like it," was all he trusted himself to say.

That seemed to please her very much. "I'll see you at the doctor's office, then. And Malloy, thank you for working so hard on this case." She gave him her hand, just the way she had to Dennis. "I know the Ellsworths will want to thank you, too, but I wanted you to know how much I appreciate it."

Her gloved hand felt small and fragile in his, and once again he experienced the rage he'd known last night when he'd realized how close Walcott had come to murdering her. "Just don't think you're going to be investigating any more murders, Mrs. Brandt," he told her gruffly. "This is the last time I'm going to see you almost get killed."

"I'm afraid I have to agree with you, Malloy," she said with a wan smile, "and you know how much I hate agreeing with you on anything."

It took a moment for him to realize the emotion he was feeling was regret. As much as he wanted to protect her from danger, he also didn't like the thought of never having her involved with his life again. Not that he had any right to be involved with her under any circumstances.

This was really for the best. After what he'd done in the cab, he knew he could no longer be trusted to keep his feelings for her in check. At least she didn't remember his indiscretion. He was sure now, because if she did, she wouldn't still be so friendly to him.

He realized he was still holding her hand, and he released it. "Uh, I guess I should get back to work."

"And I should go to the hospital to check on Mr. Prescott."

"How is he?"

"He's still alive. That's always good."

They'd run out of things to say, but Frank didn't want to say good-bye. He was also acutely aware that he had no other choice. "I'll see you on Wednesday, then. Unless something comes up, and you can't make it," he added quickly, giving her permission to cut him completely out of her life, if that's what she wanted to do.

"Good day, Malloy," she said and turned away.

She'd gone a few steps before he thought of something else. "Mrs. Brandt?"

She turned, an expectant look on her face.

"Tell Prescott I hope he's feeling better."

"I will," she said. She started to turn away again, but stopped and looked back at him with a small grin. "And Malloy, after all we've been through, I think you should call me Sarah."

Had she winked? Malloy was sure she'd winked just before she turned away again, but it was probably just a trick of the bright sunlight. Women like Sarah Brandt didn't wink. But if she *did* wink, that meant . . . No, she couldn't possibly remember. She wouldn't even be speaking to him if she remembered.

Would she?

Frank had to admit he didn't know. He wasn't even sure he wanted to. Just leave well enough alone, he told himself. And keep on pretending nothing untoward had happened. Unless she brought it up, of course, which she'd never do because she didn't even remember.

By the time he'd settled all that in his mind, Sarah

Brandt had rounded the corner and disappeared from sight. Frank made his way back to Mulberry Street.

The desk sergeant greeted him with the usual lack of enthusiasm and informed him that someone they'd locked up overnight wanted to see him.

"Says he has information you want," the sergeant said.

"I don't need any information," Frank replied wearily. "I locked up the killer last night."

"We told him, but he said it wasn't about that case. Said it was something else, something real important, and you'd want to hear what he had to say."

Since most of Frank's cases were solved by some bum who wanted a bribe for turning in a friend, he figured he should at least hear what this fellow had to say. There was still that warehouse robbery he was working on. The owner had offered a big reward, but so far he hadn't had any luck finding the missing merchandise. In cases like that, a lot of crooks didn't even bother trying to fence the stolen goods. They'd just wait for the police detective to track them down, turn the merchandise over, and split the reward with him. Just another cost of doing business for the merchant, and everybody benefited.

Frank found the right cell, and at the sight of him, one of the prisoners inside hurried over to the bars. "Malloy, do you remember me?"

He was shabbily dressed, his hair long and greasy, his face small and sharp, like a weasel's. "Finn, is it?" Frank asked.

"Finnegan," he corrected with a grin that showed blackened teeth. "I heard you was asking around about a murder."

"You're too late, Finnegan. I already arrested the killer."

"The one what killed the doctor?" he asked in dismay.

"What doctor?" Malloy asked.

"Young fellow. Doc Brandt, his name was. It's been a couple years now, but—"

"What do you know about it?" Frank snapped, reaching through the bars and grabbing the man by his lapel. He hauled him up against the bars until his face was squished between them.

"Easy there, boss," Finnegan said, his voice high with apprehension. "You don't have to get rough. I'll tell you without that!"

"Tell me, then," Frank said, not letting him go.

"Well, I . . . I don't know much myself, you understand, but I can give you a name, somebody what does know."

"You're right, that's not much," Frank said, releasing him slightly, then banging him against the bars again. He figured Finnegan was just angling to get out of whatever fix he'd gotten into and knew somehow that Frank had been asking around about Dr. Brandt's death.

"You can trust Ol' Finnegan," he said desperately. "I wouldn't lead you wrong. This fellow, he knows all about what happened to the young doctor. There's some swell involved in it, too. I don't know his name, but Danny does."

"Danny who?" Frank asked skeptically.

Finnegan grabbed on to the bars so Frank couldn't slam him again. "I don't know his last name, but if you get me out of here, I'll take you to him."

"And this Danny will just tell me everything out of the goodness of his heart?"

"I didn't say he'd tell it willing, did I? All I said was he knows. Getting him to tell, I guess that's your job, ain't it?"

Frank stared at the little weasel of a man. Chances were he was lying through his teeth. Chances were there was no man named Danny, and if there was, he didn't know a thing about Tom Brandt's death.

Frank had already warned Sarah Brandt that she wasn't going to be involved in any more murder investigations. This meant she wasn't going to be involved with Frank, either. She'd soon lose interest in Brian, too, and then he'd never see her again. That was exactly what should happen, too. Hadn't he just told himself he didn't even have a right to know her? If he started investigating her husband's death in earnest, though, sooner or later he'd have to involve her again. That would be wrong. And cruel. Selfish, too.

"Guard," he called, releasing Finnegan. "Open the cell. I want to question this prisoner privately."

Author's Note

WHEN I WAS DOING RESEARCH FOR THIS BOOK, I CAME across an account of the trials of Maria Barbella, the Italian woman I mentioned in the story who had slashed her lover's throat because he refused to marry her. Her story was a classic case of justice denied because the defendant was a poor immigrant. Maria was fortunate to attract the attention of a wealthy patroness who championed her cause and won her a new trial. The second time, she was found not guilty because she was temporarily insane, one of the first individuals to be acquitted on those grounds.

As I read Maria's story, I was struck by how contemporary it sounded. Maria's case was first tried in the media of her era, the dozens of scandal sheets that passed for newspapers at the time. They judged her guilty and made a case against her before she ever came to trial. As reporters vied to make the story more sensational so they could sell more papers, the truth was mangled beyond recognition. Maria spent a long year on death row before she was granted a new trial.

Maria became a media celebrity in particular because she was the killer. In most cases where a lover was killed, the victim was the woman, and the man went on trial. In such cases, the woman's reputation was often destroyed in the press until the public came to believe she'd only gotten what she deserved. Today we call this putting the victim on trial, and the tactic continues to work, convincing juries to free even the most heinous of murderers.

I continue to be amazed at how little has changed in the hundred years since Frank and Sarah walked the streets of New York City. I hope you find reading about it as fascinating as I find writing about it. Please let me know what you thought of this book. You may contact me at:

Victoria Thompson
PO Box 638
Duncansville, PA 16635
http://members.aol.com/vestinpa/index.html

And now a preview of

Savage Run

a Joe Pickett novel
by acclaimed mystery writer
C. J. Box

I

Targhee National Forest, Idaho
June 10

ON THE THIRD DAY OF THEIR HONEYMOON, INFAMOUS
environmental activist Stewie Woods and his new bride
Annabel Bellotti were spiking trees in the Bighorn National Forest when a cow exploded and blew them up.
Until then, their marriage had been happy.

They met by chance. Stewie Woods had been busy
pouring bag after bag of sugar and sand into the gasoline
tanks of a fleet of pickups that belonged to a natural gas
exploration crew in a newly graded parking lot. The crew
had left for the afternoon for the bars and hotel rooms of
nearby Henry's Fork. One of the crew had returned unex-
pectedly and caught Stewie as Stewie was ripping off the
top of a bag of sugar with his teeth. The crewmember
pulled a 9MM semi-automatic from beneath the dashboard
and fired several wild pistol shots in Stewie's direction.
Stewie had dropped the bag and run away, crashing
through the timber like a bull elk.

Stewie had outrun and out-juked the man with the pistol and he met Annabel when he literally tripped over her
as she sunbathed nude in the grass in an orange pool of late

afternoon sun, unaware of his approach because she was listening to Melissa Etheridge on her Walkman's head-phones. She looked good, he thought, strawberry blonde hair with a two-day Rocky Mountain fire-engine tan (two hours in the sun at 8,000 feet created a sunburn like a whole day at the beach), small ripe breasts, and a trimmed vector of pubic hair.

He had gathered her up and pulled her along through the timber, where they hid together in a dry spring wash until the man with the pistol gave up and went home. She had giggled while he held her—*this was real adventure,* she'd said—and he had used the opportunity to run his hands tentatively over her naked shoulders and hips and had found out, happily, that she did not object. They made their way back to where she had been sunbathing and while she dressed, they introduced themselves.

She told him she liked the idea of meeting a famous en-vironmental outlaw in the woods while she was naked, and he appreciated that. She said she had seen his picture be-fore, maybe in *Outside Magazine*?, and admired his looks—tall and raw-boned, with round rimless glasses, a short-cropped full beard, and his famous red bandanna on his head.

Her story was that she had been camping alone in a dome tent, taking a few days off from her free-wheeling cross-continent trip that had begun with her divorce from an anal-retentive investment banker named Nathan in her home town of Pawtucket, Rhode Island. She was bound, eventually, for Seattle.

"I'm falling in love with your mind," he lied.

"Already?" she asked.

He encouraged her to travel with him, and they took her vehicle since the lone crewmember had disabled Stewie's Subaru with three bullets into the engine block. Stewie was astonished by his good fortune. Every time he looked over at her and she smiled back, he was pole-axed with exuber-ance.

Keeping to dirt roads, they crossed into Montana. The next afternoon, in the backseat of her SUV during a thunderstorm that rocked the car and blew shroud-like sheets of rain through the mountain passes, he asked her to marry him. Given the circumstances and the super-charged atmosphere, she accepted. When the rain stopped, they drove to Ennis, Montana and asked around about who could marry them, fast. Stewie did not want to take the chance of letting her get away. She kept saying she couldn't believe she was doing this. He couldn't believe she was doing this either, and he loved her even more for it.

At the Sportsman Inn in Ennis, Montana, which was bustling with fly fishermen bound for the trout-rich waters of the Madison River, the desk clerk gave them a name and they looked up Judge Ace Cooper (Ret.) in the telephone book.

Judge Cooper was a tired and rotund man who wore a stained white cowboy shirt and an elk horn bolo tie with his shirt collar open. He performed the ceremony in a room adjacent to his living room that was bare except for a single filing cabinet, a desk and three chairs, and two framed photographs—one of the Judge and President George H. W. Bush, who had once been up there fishing, and the other of the Judge on a horse before the Cooper family lost their ranch in the 1980s.

The wedding ceremony had taken eleven minutes, which was just about average for Judge Cooper, although he had once performed it in eight minutes for two Indians.

"Do you, Allan Stewart Woods, take thee Annabeth to be your lawful wedded wife?" Judge Cooper had asked, reading from the marriage application form.

"Anna*bel*," Annabel had corrected in her biting Rhode Island accent."

"I do," Stewie had said. He was beside himself with pure joy.

Stewie twisted the ring off his finger and placed it on hers. It was unique; hand-made gold mounted with sterling silver monkey wrenches. It was also three sizes too large. The Judge studied the ring.

"Monkey wrenches?" the Judge had asked.

"It's symbolic," Stewie had said.

"I'm aware of the symbolism," the Judge said darkly, before finishing the passage.

Annabel and Stewie had beamed at each other. Annabel said that this was, like, the *wildest* vacation ever. They were Mr. and Mrs. Outlaw Couple. He was now *her* famous outlaw, although as yet untamed. She said her father would be scandalized, and her mother would have to wear dark glasses at Newport. Only her Aunt Tildie, the one with the wild streak who had corresponded with, but never met, a Texas serial killer until he died of lethal injection, would understand.

Stewie had to borrow a hundred dollars from her to pay the Judge, and she signed over a traveler's check.

After the couple had left in the SUV with Rhode Island plates, Judge Ace Cooper had gone to his lone filing cabinet and found the file. He pulled a single piece of paper out and read it as he dialed the telephone. While he waited for the right man to come to the telephone, he stared at the framed photo on the wall of himself on the horse at his former ranch. The ranch, north of Yellowstone Park, had been subdivided by a Bozeman real estate company into over thirty 50-acre "ranchettes." Famous Hollywood celebrities, including the one who's early-career photos he had recently seen in *Penthouse,* now lived there. Movies had been filmed there. There was even a crackhouse, but it was rumored that the owner wintered in LA. The only cattle that existed were purely for visual effect, like landscaping that moved and crapped and looked good when the sun threatened to drop below the mountains.

The man he was waiting for came to the telephone.

"It was Stewie Woods, all right." He said. "The man himself. I recognized him right off, and his ID proved it." There was a pause as the man on the other end of the telephone asked Cooper something. "Yeah, I heard him say that to her just before they left. They're headed for the Bighorns in Wyoming. Somewhere near Saddlestring."

● ● ●

Annabel told Stewie that their honeymoon was quite unlike what she had ever imagined a honeymoon to be, and she contrasted it with her first one with Nathan. Nathan was about sailing boats, champagne, and Barbados. Stewie was about spiking trees in stifling heat in a national forest in Wyoming. He had even asked her to carry his pack.

Neither of them had noticed the late-model black Ford pickup that had trailed them up the mountain road and continued on when Stewie pulled over to park.

Deep into the forest, Stewie now removed his shirt and tied the sleeves around his waist. A heavy bag of nails hung from his belt and tinkled while he strode through the undergrowth. There was a sheen of sweat on his bare chest as he straddled a three-foot thick Douglas fir and drove in spikes. He was obviously well practiced, and he got into a rhythm where he could bury the 6-inch spikes into the soft wood with three heavy blows from his sledgehammer; one tap to set the spike and two blows to bury it beyond the nail head in the bark.

He moved from tree to tree, but didn't spike all of them. He attacked each tree in the same method. The first of the spikes went in at eye level. A quarter-turn around the trunk, he pounded in another a foot lower than the first. He continued pounding in spikes until he had placed them in a spiral on the trunk nearly to the grass.

"Won't it hurt the trees?" Annabel asked as she unloaded his pack and leaned it against a tree.

"Of course not," he said, moving across the pine needle floor to another target. "I wouldn't be doing this if it hurt the trees. You've got a lot to learn about me, Annabel."

"Why do you put so many in?" she asked.

"Good question," he said, burying a spike in three blows. "It used to be we could put in four right at knee level, at the compass points, where the trees are usually cut. But the lumber companies got wise to that and told their loggers to go higher or lower. So now we fill up a four-foot radius."

"And what will happen if they try to cut it down?"

Stewie smiled, resting for a moment. "When a chainsaw

blade hits a steel spike, the blade can snap and whip back. Busts the saw-teeth. That can take an eye or a nose right off."

"That's horrible," she said, wincing, wondering what she was getting into.

"I've never been responsible for any injuries," Stewie said quickly, looking hard at her. "The purpose isn't to hurt anyone. The purpose is to save trees. After we're done here, I'll call the local ranger station and tell them what we've done. I won't say exactly where we spiked the trees or how many trees we spiked. It should be enough to keep them out of here for decades, and that's the point."

"Have you ever been caught?" she asked.

"Once," Stewie said, and his face clouded. "A forest ranger caught me by Jackson Hole. He marched me into downtown Jackson on foot during tourist season at gunpoint. Half of the tourists in town cheered and the other half started chanting, 'Hang him high! Hang him high!' I was sent to the Wyoming State Penitentiary in Rawlins for seven months."

"Now that you mention it, I think I read about that," she mused.

"You probably did. The wire services picked it up. I was interviewed on *Nightline* and *60 Minutes. Outside Magazine* put me on the cover. My boyhood friend Hayden Powell wrote the cover story for them, and he coined the word 'eco-terrorist.'" This memory made him feel bold. "There were reporters from all over the country at that trial." Stewie said. "Even the *New York Times*. It was the first time most people had ever heard of One Globe, or knew I was the founder of it. Memberships started pouring in from all over the world."

One Globe. The ecological action group that used the logo of crossed monkey wrenches, in deference to late author Edward Abbey's *The Monkey Wrench Gang*. One Globe had once dropped a shroud over Mt. Rushmore for the President's speech, she recalled. It had been on the nightly news.

"Stewie," she said happily, "You are the real thing." He

could feel her eyes on him as he drove in the spiral of spikes and moved to the next tree.

"When you are done with that tree I want you," she said, her voice husky. "Right here and right now, my sweet, sweaty . . . *husband*."

He turned and smiled. His face glistened and his muscles were swelled from swinging the sledgehammer. She slid her T-shirt over her head and stood waiting for him, her lips parted and her legs tense.

Stewie slung his own pack now and, for the time being, had stopped spiking trees. Fat black thunderheads, pregnant with rain, nosed across the late-afternoon sky. They were hiking at a fast pace toward the peak, holding hands, with the hope of getting there and pitching camp before the rain started. Stewie said they would hike out of the forest tomorrow and he would call the ranger station. Then they would get in the SUV and head southeast, toward the Bridger-Teton Forest.

When they walked into the herd of cattle, Stewie felt a dark cloud of anger envelop him.

"Range maggots!" Stewie said, spitting. "If they're not letting the logging companies in to cut all the trees at taxpayer's expense, they're letting the local ranchers run their cows in here so they can eat all the grass and shit in all the streams."

"Can't we just go around them?" Annabel asked.

"It's not that, Annabel," he said patiently. "Of course we can go around them. It's just the principle of the thing. We have cattle fouling what is left of the natural ecosystem. Cows don't belong in the trees in the Bighorn Mountains. You have so much to learn, darling."

"I know," she said, determined.

"These ranchers out here run their cows on public land—our land—at the expense of not only us but the wildlife. They pay something like four dollars an acre when they should be paying ten times that, even though it would be best if they were completely gone."

"But we need meat, don't we?" she asked. "You're not a vegetarian, are you?"

"Did you forget that cheeseburger I had for lunch in Cameron?" he said. "No, I'm not a vegetarian, although sometimes I wish I had the will to be one."

"I tried it once and it made me lethargic," Annabel confessed.

"All these western cows produce about five percent of the beef we eat in this whole country," Stewie said. "All the rest comes from down South, in Texas, Florida, and Louisiana, where there's plenty of grass and plenty of private land to graze them on."

Stewie picked up a pinecone, threw it accurately through the trees, and struck a black baldy heifer on the snout. The cow bolted, turned, and lumbered away. The small herd moved loudly, clumsily cracking branches and throwing up fist-sized pieces of black earth from their hooves.

"I wish I could chase them right back to the ranch they belong on," Stewie said, watching. "Right up the ass of the rancher who has lease rights for this part of the Bighorns."

One cow had not moved. It stood broadside and looked at them.

"What's wrong with that cow?" Stewie asked.

"Shoo!" Annabel shouted. "Shoo!"

Stewie stifled a smile at his new wife's shooing and slid out of his pack. The temperature had dropped twenty degrees in the last ten minutes and rain was inevitable. The sky had darkened and black coils of clouds enveloped the peak. The sudden low pressure had made the forest quieter, the sounds muffled and the smell of cows stronger.

Stewie Woods walked straight toward the heifer, with Annabel several steps behind.

"Something's wrong with that cow," Stewie said, trying to figure out what about it seemed out of place.

When Stewie was close enough he saw everything at once: the cow trying to run with the others but straining at the end of a tight nylon line; the heifer's wild white eyes; the misshapen profile of something strapped on its back that was large and square and didn't belong; the thin reed of antenna that quivered from the package on the heifer's back.

."Annabel!" Stewie yelled, turning to reach out to her—but she had walked around him and was now squarely between him and the cow.

She absorbed the full, frontal blast when the heifer detonated, the explosion shattering the mountain stillness with the subtlety of a sledgehammer bludgeoning bone.

Four miles away, a fire lookout heard the guttural boom and ran to the railing with binoculars. Over a red-rimmed plume of smoke and dirt, he could see a Douglas fir launch like a rocket into the air, where it turned, hung suspended for a moment, then crashed into the forest below.

Shaking, he reached for his radio.

2

EIGHT MILES OUT OF SADDLESTRING, WYOMING, GAME
Warden Joe Pickett was watching his wife Marybeth work
their new Tobiano paint horse, Toby, in the round pen
when the call came from the Twelve Sleep County Sheriff's office.

It was early evening, the time of night when the setting
sun ballooned and softened and defined the deep velvet
folds and piercing tree greens of Wolf Mountain. The normally dull pastel colors of the weathered barn and the red
rock canyon behind the house suddenly looked as if they
had been repainted in acrylics. Toby, a big dark bay gelding swirled with brilliant white that ran up over his
haunches like thick spilled paint upside down, shone deep
red in the evening light and looked especially striking. So
did Marybeth, in Joe's opinion, in her worn Wranglers,
sleeveless cotton shirt, and her blonde hair in a ponytail.
There was no wind, and the only sound was the rhythmic
thumping of Toby's hooves in the round pen as Marybeth
waved the whip and encouraged the gelding to shift from
a trot into a slow lope.

The Saddlestring District was considered a "two-horse
district" by the Game and Fish Department, meaning that

the department would provide feed and tack for two
mounts to be used for patrolling. Toby was their second
horse.

Joe stood with his boot on the bottom rail and his arms
folded over the top, his chin nestled between his forearms.
He was still wearing his red cotton Game and Fish uniform
shirt with the pronghorn antelope patch on the sleeve and
his sweat-stained gray Stetson. He could feel the pounding
of the earth as Toby passed in front of him in a circle. He
watched Marybeth stay in position in the center of the pen,
shuffling her feet so she stayed on Toby's back flank. She
talked to her horse in a soothing voice, urging him to gal-
lop—something he clearly didn't want to do.

Persistent, Marybeth stepped closer to Toby and commanded him to run. Marybeth still had a slight limp from
when she had been shot nearly two years before, but she
was nimble and quick. Toby pinned his ears back and
twitched his tail but finally broke into a full-fledged gal-
lop, raising the dust in the pen, his mane and tail snapping
behind him like a flag in a stiff wind. After several rota-
tions, Marybeth called "Whoa!" and Toby hit the brakes,
skidding to a quick stop where he stood breathing hard, his
muscles swelled, his back shiny with sweat, smacking and
licking his lips as if he was eating peanut butter. Marybeth
approached him and patted him down, telling him what a
good boy he was, and blowing gently into his nostrils to
soothe him.

"He's a stubborn guy—and lazy," she told Joe. "He did
not want to lope fast. Did you notice how he pinned his
ears back and threw his head around?"

Joe said *yup*.

"That's how he was telling me he was mad about it.
When he's doing that he's either going to break out of the
circle and do whatever he wants to, or stop, or do what I'm
asking him to do. In this case he did what I asked and went
into the fast lope. He's finally learning that things will go
a lot easier on him when he does what I ask him."

"I know it works for me," Joe said and smiled.

Marybeth crinkled her nose at Joe, then turned back to

Toby. "See how he licks his lips? That's a sign of obedience. He's conceding that I am the boss. That's a good sign."

Joe fought the urge to theatrically lick his lips when she looked over at him.

"Why did you blow in his nose like that?"

"Horses in the herd do that to each other to show affection. It's another way they bond with each other." Marybeth paused. "I know it sounds hokey, but blowing in his nose is kind of like giving him a hug. A horse hug."

"You seem to know what you're doing."

Joe had been around horses most of his life. He had now taken his buckskin mare Lizzie over most of the mountains in the Twelve Sleep Range of the Bighorns in his District. But what Marybeth was doing with her new horse Toby, what she was getting out of him, was a different kind of thing. Joe was duly impressed.

A shout behind him shook Joe from his thoughts. He turned toward the sound, and saw ten-year-old Sheridan, five-year-old Lucy, and their eight-year-old foster daughter April stream through the backyard gate and across the field. Sheridan held the cordless phone out in front of her like an Olympic torch, and the other two girls followed.

"Dad, it's for you," Sheridan called. "A man says it's very important."

Joe and Marybeth exchanged looks and Joe took the telephone. It was County Sheriff O. R. "Bud" Barnum.

There had been a big explosion in the Bighorn National Forest, Barnum told Joe. A fire lookout had called it in, and had reported that through his binoculars he could see fat dark forms littered throughout the trees. It looked like a "shitload" of animals were dead, which is why he was calling Joe. Dead game animals were Joe's concern. They assumed at this point that they were game animals, Barnum said, but they might be cows. A couple of local ranchers had grazing leases up there. Barnum asked if Joe could meet him at the Winchester exit off of the interstate in twenty minutes. That way, they could get to the scene before it was completely dark.

Joe handed the telephone back to Sheridan and looked over his shoulder at Marybeth.

"When will you be back?" she asked.

"Late," Joe told her. "There was an explosion in the mountains."

"You mean like a plane crash?"

"He didn't say that. The explosion was a few miles off of the Hazelton Road in the mountains, in elk country. Barnum thinks there may be some game animals down."

She looked at Joe for further explanation. He shrugged to indicate that was all he knew.

"I'll save you some dinner."

Joe met the Sheriff and Deputy McLanahan at the exit to Winchester and followed them through the small town. The three-vehicle fleet—two County GMC Blazers and Joe's dark green Game and Fish pickup—entered and exited the tiny town within minutes. Even though it was an hour and a half away from darkness, the only establishments open were the two bars with identical red neon Coors signs in their windows and a convenience store. Winchester's lone public artwork, located on the front lawn of the branch bank, was an outsized and gruesome metal sculpture of a wounded grizzly bear straining at the end of a thick chain, its metal leg encased in a massive saw-toothed bear trap. Joe did not find the sculpture lovely but it captured the mood, style, and inbred frontier culture of the area as well as anything else could have.

Deputy McLanahan led the way through the timber in the direction where the explosion had been reported and Joe walked behind him alongside Sheriff Barnum. Joe and McLanahan had acknowledged each other with curt nods and said nothing. Their relationship had been rocky ever since McLanahan had sprayed the outfitter's camp with shotgun blasts two years before and Joe had received a wayward pellet under his eye. He still had a scar to show for it.

Barnum's hangdog face grimaced as he limped aside

Joe through the underbrush. He complained about his hip.
He complained about the distance from the road to the
crime scene. He complained about McLanahan, and said to
Joe *sotto voce* that he should have fired the deputy years
before and would have if he weren't his nephew. Joe suspected, however, that Barnum also kept McLanahan
around because McLanahan's quick-draw reputation had
added—however untrue and unlikely—an air of toughness
to the Sheriff's Department that didn't hurt at election
time.

The sun had dropped below the top of the mountains
and instantly turned them into craggy black silhouettes.
The light dimmed in the forest, fusing the treetops and
branches that were discernible just a moment before into a
shadowy muddle. Joe reached back on his belt to make
sure he had his flashlight. He let his arm brush his .357
Smith & Wesson revolver to confirm it was there. He
didn't want Barnum to notice the movement since Barnum
still chided him about the time he lost his gun to a poacher
Joe was arresting.

There was an unnatural silence in the woods, with the
exception of Barnum's grumbling. The absence of normal
sounds—the chattering of squirrels sending a warning up
the line, the panicked scrambling of deer, the airy winged
drumbeat of flushed Spruce grouse—confirmed that something big had happened here. Something so big it had either cleared the wildlife out of the area or frightened them
mute. Joe could feel that they were getting closer before he
could see anything to confirm it. Whatever it was, it was
just ahead.

McLanahan quickly stopped and there was a sharp in-
take of breath.

"Holy shit," McLanahan whispered in awe. *"Holy
shit."*

The still-smoking crater was fifteen yards across. It was
three feet deep at its center. A half dozen trees had been
blown out of the ground and their shallow rootpans were
exposed like black outstretched hands. Eight or nine black
baldy cattle were dead and still, strewn among the trunks

of trees. The earth below the thick turf rim of the crater was dark and wet. Several large white roots, the size of leg bones, were pulled up from the ground by the explosion and now pointed at the sky. Cordite from the explosives, pine from broken branches, and upturned mulch had combined in the air to produce a sickeningly sweet and heavy smell.

Darkness enveloped them as they slowly circled the crater. Pools of light from their flashlights lit up twisted roots and lacy pale yellow undergrowth.

Joe checked the cattle, moving among them away from the crater. Most had visible injuries as a result of fist-sized rocks being blown into them from the explosion. One heifer was impaled on the fallen tip of a dead pine tree. The rest of the herd, apparently unhurt, stood as silent shadows just beyond his flashlight. He could see dark heavy shapes and hear the sound of chewing, and a pair of eyes reflected back blue as a cow raised its head to look at him. They all had the same brand—a "v" on top and a "u" on the bottom divided by a single line. Joe recognized it as the Vee Bar U Ranch. These were Ed Finolla's cows.

McLanahan suddenly grunted in alarm and Joe raised his flashlight to see the Deputy in a wild, self-slapping panic, dancing away from the rim of the crater and ripping his jacket off of himself as quickly as he could. He threw it violently to the ground in a heap and stood staring at it.

"What in the hell is wrong with you?" Barnum asked, annoyed.

"Something landed on my shoulder. Something heavy and wet," McLanahan said, his face contorted. "I thought it was somebody's hand grabbing me. It scared me half to death."

McLanahan had dropped his flashlight, so from across the crater Joe lowered his light onto the jacket and focused his Mag Light into a tight beam. McLanahan bent down into the light and gingerly unfolded the jacket; poised to jump back if whatever had fallen on him was still in his clothing. He threw back a fold and cursed. Joe couldn't see for sure what McLanahan was looking at other than that the object was dark and moist.

"What is it?" Barnum demanded.

"It looks like . . . well . . . it looks like a piece of *meat*." McLanahan looked up at Joe vacantly.

Slowly, Joe raised the beam of his flashlight, sweeping upward over McLanahan and following it up the trunk of a lodgepole pine and into the branches. What Joe saw, he would never forget . . .

From national bestselling author

VICTORIA THOMPSON

THE GASLIGHT MYSTERIES

As a midwife in turn-of-the-century New York, Sarah Brandt has seen pain and joy. Now she will work for something more—a search for justice—in cases of murder and mystery that only she can put to rest.

MURDER ON ASTOR PLACE

MURDER ON ST. MARK'S PLACE

MURDER ON GRAMERCY PARK

MURDER ON WASHINGTON SQUARE

MURDER ON MULBERRY BEND

MURDER ON MARBLE ROW

MURDER ON LENOX HILL

MURDER IN LITTLE ITALY

MURDER IN CHINATOWN

"Tantalizing."—Catherine Coulter

penguin.com